MEL BEEBY
AGENT ANGEL

the
divine
collection

THREE AMAZING
MISSIONS
IN ONE BOOK!

MEL BEEBY
AGENT ANGEL

the
divine
collection

making
waves

budding
star

keeping
it real

ANNIE DALTON

HarperCollins *Children's Books*

Making Waves first published in Great Britain by HarperCollins *Children's Books* 2003
Budding Star first published in Great Britain by HarperCollins *Children's Books* 2004
Keeping it Real first published in Great Britain by HarperCollins *Children's Books* 2005

First published in this three-in-one edition by HarperCollins *Children's Books* 2005

HarperCollins *Children's Books* is a division of HarperCollins*Publishers* Ltd
77-85 Fulham Palace Road, Hammersmith, London W6 8JB

The HarperCollins *Children's Books* website address is

www.harpercollinschildrensbooks.co.uk

2

Text copyright © Annie Dalton 2005

ISBN-13 978 0-00-719074-4
ISBN-10 0-00-719074-3

Printed and bound in England by
Clays Ltd, St Ives plc

Mixed Sources
Product group from well-managed
forests and other controlled sources
www.fsc.org Cert no. SW-COC-1806
© 1996 Forest Stewardship Council

making waves

This book is for Michael Cooke, who showed me Cockpit Country and helped me to imagine wicked Port Royal and the Black River Morass. Grateful thanks to Curdella Forbes and Nadi Edwards for recommending books, and a big thank you to Maria for sharing her brilliant ideas!

CHAPTER ONE

I miss heaps of things about my old life. Funny little things, like the smell of the face cream Mum uses last thing at night. Then there's the major stuff, like not being around to see my little sister grow up. Some days I miss Jade so badly, I'd willingly walk over burning coals to be with her for just one hour.

But you know one thing I really don't miss at ALL?

All that *posing* humans feel they have to do! Why do people DO that? Nobody really wants to be a fraud, do they? I know I didn't. Deep down I was desperate for my mates to like me just the way I was: bad habits, impossible dreams and all. Yet I kept up this big act, like I only cared about airhead stuff – style makeovers and shopping – and I wouldn't recognise a deep thought if it bit me on the bum. WHY? Why didn't I give my friends the chance to know the real Melanie Beeby?

I was just too scared basically. After my dad walked out, I didn't have much faith in the real Melanie. (Kids think it's their fault, don't they?) So I invented a new improved personality to hide behind. Like, "I'm so sassy. I'm the princess of cool!"

But kids weren't designed to fake their way through life, and a couple of weeks before my thirteenth birthday, the cracks began to show.

The weather was foul this particular day, absolutely chucking it down, and my step-dad, Des, had offered me a lift to school. Unfortunately we got stuck at some roadworks. We got stuck so long, it would have been quicker to crawl to school on my hands and knees. Suddenly I started stressing. You know, REALLY stressing. Telling myself I was going to be late again and this time it wasn't even my fault. Telling myself I was stupid to stay up half the night, making elaborate birthday invitations for my friends. Friends who didn't really care. Friends who didn't actually know me.

The thought of faking it through my own birthday celebrations just finished me off. I quickly stared out of the window, but little gasping sounds must have given me away.

I felt Des put a clean tissue in my hand. "It's going to be OK," he said quietly. "One of these days you'll find a real soul-mate, and you'll never look back."

And without any warning, I was suddenly in the middle of this HUGE mystical experience! The gridlocked lorries belching toxic fumes, the giant diggers and earth movers, the workmen in their shiny rain slickers, the little plastic bags tumbling about in the wind, all started to shimmer with otherworldly light.

"Omigosh!" I breathed. "I didn't know this world was so beautiful!"

A workman gave me a cheeky smile, and flipped his sign to read GO. The traffic queue started moving. The magical glow slowly faded, and I started feeling just a little bit silly. I decided it must have been a trick of the light. I wasn't actually convinced that deep stuff like immortal souls or Good and Evil really existed.

They do, as I was just about to find out!

The day after my birthday, I'd arranged to go shopping with my mates. My birthday cash was burning a hole in my pocket, and I was desperate to buy — I forget what, exactly. It's irrelevant anyway. Angel HQ, a.k.a. the Agency, had made other plans...

One minute I was crossing the street, humming a carefree tune, then BANG! I was soaring through the air like a swallow, skimming over rooftops, whooshing through clouds, and not only was I not showing signs of slowing down, I risked being singed by passing meteorites!

I was having my first Out of Body Experience. Not to beat about the bush, I was seriously dead. A joyrider had knocked me down in the street. No doubt this was all part of some massive heavenly design which I'll never entirely understand. Celestial personnel would have been watching over me for days. Quite probably they were in the car, when I was having my pre-birthday wobbles. The Agency never lets anyone die alone. They're v. strict on that point.

But like most humans, I had rather fixed ideas about what happens to the recently deceased. Since I didn't meet up with a dead relative, or zoom down a tunnel towards the Light, the D-word never entered my head! I just thought the usual scientific laws had been suspended for some reason. Why else would I be skimming through space as gracefully as I flew in dreams as a little kid?

I could hear strange and lovely sounds, like the throbbing of a huge invisible humming top. When I hear them now, I know I've come home. But to the old Mel Beeby, home meant a two-bedroomed flat on a housing estate. Not a vast glittering void, filled with cosmic sound FX.

Then BAM! I was set down on solid ground. I was in a crowd of chatty teenagers, heading towards a pair of tall, very swanky gates. On the other side was what seemed like a posh high school.

Of course, by this time I'm totally reeling. I'm like, what on EARTH am I doing here! Then I saw the view. And you know what? *It wasn't Earth.*

An exotic cityscape flashed and shimmered in the morning light: soaring glass skyscrapers, sparkling golden domes, curved roofs that looked almost airborne. It was like a city in the most wonderful dream you ever had. But I had the disturbing feeling that I wasn't dreaming.

Everything seemed so alive. Even the light was more super-alive than the kind I was used to. And the air! When I breathed in, I went tingly from head to toe. It smelled *wonderful* – almost, but not quite, like lilacs.

But the sign outside the school gates sent me into a spin of pure confusion.

The Angel Academy

I told myself it was just a wussy name. It didn't mean this was a school for actual angels. And OK, so these kids looked incredibly happy and confident. And OK, so they all had a rather unusual radiant glow. They probably just had excellent skin-care regimes.

Isn't that completely classic! I'm standing like six inches away from the Pearly Gates, furiously trying to convince myself I'm not in Heaven!!

Sometimes I think I'd still be standing there, but just then another glowing girl hurried past with her mates. Everything about this girl was familiar. Her glossy black curly hair, her tough-girl walk, the sparky intelligence in her eyes.

And for the first time in years I did something that was NOT typical Melanie. I actually followed this fabulously cool person through the gates.

The two of us kind of fell into step. Not intentionally. It just seemed to happen. We kept exchanging astonished glances. Like, what IS going on here?

"Do I *know* you?" I blurted out suddenly.

And you know what? She was thinking exactly the same thing!

That's how I met my soul-mate, Lola Sanchez, Lollie to her friends.

Relax! I know what you're thinking, but no, a person does NOT normally have to die to find friends. This is basically a friendly universe, OK? Great mates can turn up anywhere and everywhere; even my old hellhole comprehensive.

But until the shock of being blasted out of my old life opened my eyes, I didn't know this. Plus, and this is pretty crucial, I didn't actually know how to BE a friend. I just knew how to fake it.

Luckily I was so shocked by my own death that for one life-changing moment, I forgot to pretend. This sparky stranger seemed like a long-lost part of me, and I wasn't about to let her vanish!

It probably sounds as if I'm just telling you how Lola and I met up, as some kind of ice-breaker, before zooming on to something more major. I'm not. The fact is I desperately need you to understand why Lola is so special to me.

Listen, that girl has loads of friends. Lola is a friend magnet! Yet from my first day at the Angel Academy, she made it her business to be there for me – yes, ME! Day after day, this hugely popular girl was encouraging me to do my best, letting me cry on her shoulder when I'd made yet another cosmic boo-boo, and booting me back out into the Universe to try again and again. Now that's true friendship, right?

It was Lola who finally taught me I didn't have to fake it to be popular. "Melanie, I have met teeny-weeny *worms* with better opinions of themselves," she sighed. "So your papa left you. That was harsh, girl. But get over it, you're in Heaven now. Time to lose that airhead disguise!"

Lola had only known me a few days when she said that, and already she knew me better than I knew myself! And this girl and I had SO much in common. Which is insane, since Lollie originally comes from the twenty-second century! Yet we had the same mad sense of humour, we loved almost exactly the same styles of music. And we regularly borrowed each other's clothes.

I felt so lucky it almost scared me. And it wasn't too long before I had a totally good reason to feel this way.

Our history group had been doing this huge project on ancient Egypt. Our teacher, Mr Allbright, decided it would be helpful to experience the vibes for ourselves. Omigosh, the hassle we had on that trip!! Not to mention the *dust!* The instant we got back, Lola and I dashed back to our dorms and showered like demons.

Now I was catching up on homey chores: watering my thirsty baby orange tree, checking through my post. Lola was sitting on my bed in her PJs, writing up her report.

Before she died and became an angel, my soul-mate lived in a vibey third-world city. Lollie herself is a mix of a dozen different nationalities: Portuguese, Dutch, African. She even has Mayan ancestry – can you believe that? Her granny told her that's where she got her great cheekbones!

I glanced across at this amazing girl and I thought how we would never even have met if it wasn't for a total miracle. (No, trust me. Mel Beeby winning a cosmic scholarship is a miracle!)

All at once I felt this pang of – I don't know – *foreboding*. "Lollie, we're always going to be friends, aren't we?" I asked anxiously.

She peered at me over her little reading glasses. "What's wrong, girl? Not having a big bad premonition, are you?"

I gulped. "I was just thinking I couldn't bear it if I had to go back to that phoney person I used to be."

Lola leaned over and patted my hand. "That's not going to happen! We're soul-mates, babe. We knew each other back at the Dawn of Creation." She gave me a mysterious smile. "And I'm pretty sure we've been reunited for a reason!"

I felt a prickle of excitement. "Are you serious?"

Her eyes sparkled. "This is still like the apprenticeship stage. But once we've got through our angel warrior training, we'll be incredibly wise and strong—"

"—but in a cute way," I suggested, giggling.

"*Cute?*" Lola sniffed. "We'll be gorgeous!! We'll be such an unstoppable cosmic force, the PODS will go whimpering back to the Hell dimensions like ugly little puppy dogs!"

"You think so?" I said wistfully.

Lola's brows drew together. "Are you doubting the sacred words of La Sanchez?"

I swallowed. "Suppose we'd met on Earth? As humans I mean? Would we have recognised each other then?"

Lola looked surprised. "Sure!"

"But would we though?" I persisted. "There's so much pressure on that little planet, Lollie. Even angels can't hear themselves think."

"Hey girl, I'd know *you* anywhere! I'd feel it – in here." Lola pressed her hand to her heart. "So would you."

I was so touched I didn't know what to say.

Suddenly, Lola was completely distracted. She jumped up and turned up the volume on my radio. "I just can't get enough of this tune!" she sighed happily. "It is totally, totally luminous!"

The radio station was playing a hip-hop remix of *True Colors*. We started to sing along. Lola literally sings like an angel. I sing more like a little squeaky reptile. But it sounded OK when we sang together. It sounded nice.

But I must have been having a big bad premonition after all. Three weeks after our conversation, my soul-mate and I were torn apart, separated by something so dark, it could only have been invented in one of the Hell dimensions. Like all truly terrible things, it happened on Earth.

But it began with Brice.

CHAPTER TWO

Sorry, I've got to interrupt the flow. I'm worried you don't understand about the war. That cosmic war I'm always on about? I'm not sure you realise how big this is.

It's MASSIVE. Battles between the two major cosmic agencies are going on in every single century in human history. This conflict gets more intense every day. Want to know what we're fighting over?

YOU.

The PODS, a.k.a. the Powers of Darkness, a.k.a. the Opposition, want total control of your souls. They want you to live your life in a kind of dreary waking dream where nothing matters because nothing feels real. They want you to forget who you are.

You think that couldn't happen, right?

You think you'd know if someone was interfering with your head?

Look, I don't have time to get into PODS strategies right now, but trust me, OK? Those guys have been around for AEONS. They know a zillion dirty tricks to play on human minds. Our school library has a ton of books devoted to that one subject alone.

My agency, on the other hand, doesn't want to own anybody's soul, thanks. We think your soul is your personal property. We do have an agenda, but it's the total opposite. We want you to wake up and remember who you really are, so you can have a fabulously rewarding time on your gorgeous little planet!

Check this – life on Earth was actually meant to be FUN.

Unfortunately, the Dark Powers have lulled millions of human beings into a state of cosmic amnesia. They've been doing it since Time began. They're *still* doing it today. Now I'm going to let you in on another celestial secret.

You are the reason the Heavenly City never sleeps. Yes – you!

When I look out of the dorm window at night, I can see brilliant star bursts of light over the Agency Tower, *FLASH*, *FLASH*, *FLASH*, about a heartbeat apart. Know what that is? Each star burst is an agent returning from, or departing to, Planet Earth. Plus we have Heaven-based agents beam uplifting vibes at you morning, noon and night. Joy, Peace, Love, whatever. Those aren't just words in Christmas carols, you know, they're powerful energy vibrations. We can actually see them on the Angel Watch computer screens, forming a beautiful web of light around your gorgeous little blue-green planet.

That's how precious humans are. That's why the Agency will never give up on you, EVER. Your family and friends might give up on you. You might even give up on yourself. Hey, your dog might give up on you! But the Heavenly City stays open for business twenty-four-seven.

Which brings me right back to Brice, one-time cosmic dropout, now humiliatingly doing retakes at the Angel Academy.

I'm not sure there is such a thing as an average angel, but if so Brice is definitely not it. The guy wears ripped T-shirts advertising bizarre celestial rock bands. He is basically a total outlaw.

What is a boy like that doing in Heaven? Ooh, good question. I could tell you he's a bad boy who sold his soul and accidentally found his heart. Or I could say he used to be a fallen angel who got homesick for the Light. But the truth is a little more complicated.

I ran into him on my first field trip to Earth, when he was working for the PODS. Technically we were cosmic enemies. Technically, Brice and I were also total strangers. Yet for reasons I won't go into, it felt like he knew me a *leetle* too well for comfort. Lola believes our meeting was some big prearranged karmic thing. She says when we met up that day in foggy 1940s' London, our souls went, "Omigosh, it's you!"

"Brice made a big mistake," Lola explained solemnly. "One day he woke up and found himself on the totally wrong side in the cosmic war. He needed to find a way back home, and you were it, girl."

Maybe, maybe not. But when the heavenly authorities finally agreed to let Brice come back to our school, I was completely disgusted. I couldn't believe I had to share Heaven with this devious dirtbag!

According to our headmaster, you see, Brice's dodgy past was all water under the bridge. Michael's theory was, if you wait long enough, trees evolve into diamonds, and bad boys come good.

At the time I'm like, yeah right, and we're all made of stardust and what's that got to do with the price of cheese?

But now I've started to wonder if there's something in this evolution stuff after all, because gradually my feelings towards Brice began to change.

It was disturbing at first, looking up in the library to see my cosmic enemy feverishly turning pages at the next table. Plus, for a boy who once hobnobbed with demons, he looked kind of vulnerable. I'd seen Brice's dangerous side, however, so I had no intention of being suckered in. But as the months passed, I started to get used to having him around.

After he came with me and Lollie to Victorian times, I began to feel almost, well, *fond* of him.

The day after we got back from ancient Egypt, Brice was slumped at the back of the class wearing shades, and a T-shirt that said ASTRAL GARBAGE.

He wasn't the only one feeling hungover that day. We'd all been humungously affected by some toxic ancient Egyptian vibes. Everyone was suffering, including Mr Allbright.

Halfway through the lesson, our teacher noticed my new Emily Strange top and went up the wall! "A garment decorated with a skull and crossbones is *not* suitable clothing for school, Melanie," he said in a shocked voice.

"I think it's sweet," I objected. "It's a sweet, fun, retro thing."

"Pirates were not sweet, Melanie. They certainly weren't fun. They were calculating, cold-blooded murderers."

Lola and I secretly hid our smiles. You see, on our trip to Elizabethan England, Lollie and I had met the sweetest pirate ever. His daughter, Cat Darcy, was in love with Shakespeare. I'm not name-dropping, it's true! Though actually, the world's most famous writer went under the name of Chance, back then. He was going through a really bad patch and Cat's pirate dad helped to straighten him out. Listen, I'm not saying piracy is cool. And I'm not saying Cat's father was a harmless pussycat. I'm just saying that even a pirate can surprise you by having a heart.

Mind you, I was pretty sure Mr Allbright knew this already. And to be fair, our teacher is not normally the type to stress over an innocent fashion statement.

He was stressing because:

- He'd been zapped by toxic vibes like everyone else, and
- We were rapidly approaching the end of term and NO ONE in our class had shown any interest in entering the HALO awards.

"I've got entry forms here," he said reproachfully at the end of the lesson. "Think about it at least."

Lola and I didn't pay too much attention. We had to dash to the library to catch up on an assignment. We'd been scribbling madly for about ten minutes, when Brice mooched around the stacks.

"Fancy skiving off?" he said in a casual voice.

Lola sighed. "Love to, babe. Unfortunately we have to do this thing."

Brice cleared his throat. "That's a shame. I had

a proposition. I was wondering if you'd both be interested in a joint entry for the HALO awards."

Lola looked puzzled. "Who with?"

He went red. "Well, me, obviously."

I couldn't believe my ears. "You are kidding!"

Brice scowled. "Is there some reason I shouldn't enter?"

"Of course not," said Lola quickly. "The awards are open to every trainee in the school."

"You've got to admit it's a bit out of character," I grinned.

I meant it as a joke, but Brice just muttered something uncomplimentary and stormed out.

Lola and I looked at each other.

"That went well," she said in a small voice.

I felt like a really bad person, but I wasn't ready to admit it. "That boy has such a major chip," I complained.

Our buddy Reuben came over. "You guys look upset."

Lola started to explain but other library users started ssshing.

"Let's go to Guru," Reuben suggested. "You can tell me there."

"Why not," Lola said bleakly. "My concentration's totally shot."

Guru is less than five minutes' walk from our school. We grabbed an outdoor table in the sun and ordered the café's special Aztec hot chocolate, otherwise known as the trainee angel's cure-all.

I think Mo, the guy who runs Guru now, sensed something was up, because when he brought our order he tactfully left extra marshmallows.

Lola was too upset to notice. "It's really hard for Brice to ask people for help," she said miserably. "And we laughed in his face."

"We did NOT laugh in his face," I objected. "We were just – surprised."

"You told him he was a phoney," Reuben pointed out.

"It was a joke, man! The guy used to live in the Hell dimensions! I can't believe he's that sensitive."

"Believe it," said Reuben.

Lola's eyes were huge with worry. "This is a really tough time for Brice, Melanie. He's on probation and everyone at our school knows it."

The extra marshmallows were going to waste so I popped two into my hot chocolate and immediately felt ashamed.

When Brice first got a scholarship to the Angel Academy, I'm sure he secretly dreamed of climbing all the way to the top of that dizzy ladder to the stars. Instead, he tripped over a monster snake and went slipping and sliding all the way back to square one. Now he was having to start his gruelling game of cosmic snakes and ladders all over again. Only this time everyone was watching...

"Winning a HALO would be like saying he was rehabilitated," Lola was saying earnestly. "He wouldn't have to spend his angelic career looking over his shoulder."

"Lollie, if this was me, you'd tell me to get over it."

She patted my hand. "True! But if you asked us to back you, we'd do it like a shot. We wouldn't even think about it."

I felt myself go all emotional. "Really?"

My mates nodded vigorously.

A worry slid into my mind. "You don't think this was a test? Like Brice was checking to see if we're really his friends?"

Reuben winced. "Actually—"

"Omigosh!" I wailed. "I feel *terrible*. Now he's

going to think we've been faking. We've got to go and find him."

"Too obvious," Reuben advised. "He'd hate it if he knew we'd been talking about him. Bring it up casually next time you see him."

"Why do I have to bring it up?" I whinged. "Why can't Lola?"

She went pink. "Because it would be better coming from you."

I got my chance that night at the Babylon Café.

The Babylon is our fave place to go dancing. They have the best live music ever. But if you want to cool off or just chill with your mates, you can go outside into their magical gardens. They're designed so they literally seem suspended in midair. At night they're all lit up with twinkly white lights.

I'd gone out for some air when I spotted Brice in the shadows, watching the dancers. It was a warm night, but he wore his jacket collar turned up, and his hands were jammed into his pockets. Somehow Brice was always on the outside, looking in. The thought gave me a funny pang in my heart, because I remember how that feels.

I took a deep breath and went up to him. "Hi."

"Nice dress." There was absolutely no expression in his voice.

"Thanks. About this morning—"

Brice's jaw muscles tensed. "It was a dumb idea."

"It wasn't. I was tired and crabby. I wasn't thinking."

He shrugged. "Whatever."

I almost stamped with frustration. "Could you just listen?"

"*You* listen, sweetheart," he blazed. "You were right the first time. I am not the HALO type."

"There isn't a HALO type, fool! That's what I'm trying to tell you. I'd love to enter the awards with you."

"Yeah, right," he jeered. "I saw how you both rushed to sign up."

"I mean it! I've never won anything in my entire existence. OK, at my old school, I won a box of cheap chocs in a raffle. But I've never won an actual *award*. It'd be cool to win a HALO, like getting an angel Oscar."

Brice scowled. "Is that the speech? Will you stop bugging me now?"

"No, actually," I said sweetly. "I'm going to keep bugging you until you tell me what we have to do to enter."

There was an interesting silence while Brice chewed at his lip.

"Well for a start, we fill in the forms," he said cautiously. "The HALO judges might not accept us. They don't always."

"They will! I know they will!" I bubbled. "Oh, this is SO great! Let's do it first thing tomorrow."

"If you want," he shrugged. "It's really no biggie."

Liar, I thought. This was obviously HUGE for Brice. I could tell he still felt really bruised.

You know that thing? The bimbo thing that I'm not meant to do any more? I think maybe I do it because I don't know what else TO do.

I looked at him under my lashes. "Brice, how do HALOs work at high-school level exactly? At the angel nursery where I help out, kids are doing really cute projects."

"Maybe you didn't notice, but I don't do 'cute'," he said with distaste. "We'd be in the advanced section, darling."

I knew he was thawing slightly, so I did another

Bambi-eyed flutter. "I still don't quite understand," I said innocently. "What would we have to do?"

"We have to go on a blind date with destiny."

"Omigosh! Tell me more!" I giggled.

I know, I know, I should have more pride. But hey, it worked.

"We volunteer for an unknown mission," Brice explained. "The HALO panel put their heads together to discuss our various strengths and weaknesses. On that basis, they decide what cosmic experiences are likely to stretch us and take us to the next angelic level, yadda yadda."

"Yadda yadda," I echoed, to show I was keeping up.

"They pick a suitable time and place, and off we go."

"Sounds like a huge challenge," I said in my most impressed voice.

"I think that's the general idea," said Brice. "Evolution and all that."

"Well, definitely count me in, babe."

"What about Lola? Is she in too?"

"Oh, I really couldn't say," I said innocently. "You'll have to ask her."

He grinned. "Yeah right! Like you two don't discuss *everything*!"

I blushed. Brice definitely wouldn't want me to know about the night he and Lola got all romantic under the stars last holidays!

"Oh, look! Lollie's over there by the fountains!" I exclaimed with relief. "Ask her yourself."

Brice sauntered over. I saw him and Lola deep in conversation through veils of falling water.

Yess! My ploy had worked!

I know, I know! I'm in Heaven now. I should drop the airhead disguise, but sometimes it comes in SO useful!!

The judges did accept our entry as I somehow knew they would.

But now it's confession time. On the day Mr Allbright was due to announce our time destinations for the HALO, I had genuinely good intentions. No, I really did! I was all set to take notes and ask questions. And believe me, I truly wish I had.

But when our teacher told us we'd be going to seventeenth-century Jamaica, everything else flew out of my head. I practically went into orbit!! I'm like, "Woo! I am SO packing my bikini!"

I literally didn't hear another word anyone said!

I'd always felt a mysterious connection with Jamaica. Some of my friends at my old earth school told me how amazing it was, and I'd dream about going to see it for myself. But this was going to be SO much better! We were going to time-travel to this gorgeous tropical island, *centuries* before the tourist invasion. We'd see the island of Jamaica in its original unspoilt state!

I'd have loved to stay and chat about our mysterious Caribbean mission with my HALO teammates, but all three of us had appointments elsewhere. Lola had a singing lesson. Brice trudged off for his weekly chat with our headmaster, one of the conditions of his probation. And I help out at the angel nursery school most Wednesday afternoons.

I flew back to our dorm to change. I burst into my room, still buzzing with excitement and caught sight of myself in the mirror. I was clutching an official-looking Agency folder.

"I don't believe it!" I wailed. "This is so unfair!"

I'd been so busy daydreaming about tropical sunshine, I hadn't noticed Mr Allbright give out our bios for the mission. An angel only needs a cover story if she's going to be visible.

I could forget the cute bikini. Chances were I'd be going to Jamaica in a corset!! But like Reuben says, "Angels gotta take the yin with the yang." I decided that wearing a corset would be a really small price to pay for a working holiday on a paradise island.

When I got to the nursery school, the children were just finishing their yoga practice. They looked so-o sweet, sitting in the lotus position on their little pink mats! I have learned such a lot from those angel babies. They can be incredibly wise. They can also be incredibly naughty!

Their rehearsal for the preschool HALO show was a riot. Afterwards I helped Miss Dove clear up. "Thank you for helping, Melanie," she said warmly. "I know the children are hoping you'll come and help on the big day. Friday isn't your usual day for coming in, but do you think you could make it?"

Being appreciated makes you feel all warm and fuzzy, doesn't it? When I feel like that, I'd do anything for anyone.

"Wouldn't miss it for the world," I beamed.

Next morning I woke with a bloodcurdling shriek.

I'd only promised to help Miss Dove on the same day we were due to fly out to seventeenth-century Jamaica!

If it was anyone else but those little angel kids, I'd have pulled a Houdini and wiggled out of it. But I owed them big time. I'd had some dark times when I first got here and Miss Dove and her preschoolers saved my sanity. I was desperately disappointed, but I didn't feel like I had a choice.

Someone would have to take my place on the HALO mission.

I just hoped Brice would understand.

CHAPTER THREE

Two hours later I was sitting on a patch of daisies outside the school library, sobbing my heart out. Reuben had tactfully brought me outside before I made a total fool of myself.

"I said there was still time to get someone else," I hiccupped, "and he just went ballistic! He said I had *ruined* his chances of getting a HALO!"

"He's upset," Reuben said calmly. "He's having one of those cosmic wobbles like we all do."

I hunted for a fresh tissue. "Brice has wobbles?" I sniffled. "I don't think so."

"Mel, get real! The guy's only been back in Heaven a few months. When he came back his clothes still reeked of sulphur, remember?"

I blew my nose. "I know. Lola had to take him shopping," I remembered. "He's been through stuff I can't even imagine."

"Ssh, it's going to be OK." Reuben was rubbing my back in soothing circles. Unlike me and Lola, Reubs is pure angel, and though he doesn't look particularly tough, he has this inner strength that comes from having grown up in the angel bizz.

"I don't know what to do, Reubs!" I wept.

Reuben thought for a moment. "What does Helix say?" Helix is my official angel name. It's a really big moment when a trainee gets his or her true angel name. But Helix is also like, my inner angel, and I'm meant to tune into her when things get rough. Unfortunately, when things get rough I find it hard to believe I even HAVE an inner angel.

"You tell me," I choked. "You're the angel. I'm just a – a faker!"

He laughed. "Rubbish. Your inner angel is always online."

"If you say so," I snuffled. "But I'm going to feel really stupid when nothing happens."

I shut my eyes and took slow, deep breaths. The

Angel Handbook said it was hard to connect with your inner angel if you were upset. After a few minutes, the centre of my chest began to feel like I'd swallowed a tiny hot potato and it was still trapped halfway down. It seemed as if Helix was keen to get in touch with me too.

When I opened my eyes some time later I felt stunned. "Helix says Brice needs me. He and Lola both need me on this mission."

"Problem solved," said Reuben cheerfully.

I sighed. "What she didn't say, is how I can be in two places at once!"

My buddy rolled his eyes. "Duh! Remind me what that big A on your jacket stands for again?"

"I know! I'm an angel! Tell me how that helps?"

"You're a celestial being, Melanie! Time is not a problem."

"It isn't?" I said hopefully.

Apparently it wasn't. Reuben suggested a v. sensible alternative scenario. Lola and Brice would go ahead as planned. I'd keep my promise to my baby angels, jump into my seventeenth-century corset, sprint down to the Agency, catch the first available portal and join the others in the sun. Sorted!

"The time technicians will get you there a few hours after Lollie and Brice at most."

I was stunned. "You're a genius!"

"Thanks," Reuben said modestly. "You'd better tell Brice, so Mr Allbright can make arrangements."

"Brice could have told me this," I said suddenly.

Reuben gave me a lopsided smile. "I expect he thought you knew."

I went cold. Brice didn't realise I was being dense. He thought I was fobbing him off with any old excuse. He thought I genuinely didn't want to go!

"Sorry, gotta go!" I said urgently. "Later, Reubs."

I went hunting for him all over the campus, but Brice had totally gone to ground. Just as I'd given up all hope I saw a familiar figure in an outsized hoodie trudging out through the gates.

"Brice – wait!!"

He waited with a bored expression.

Trust me, no one does "bored" like Brice. He's like a porcupine, always putting up sharp prickles. But I told myself I wasn't going to let him get to me. This time I'd get it right.

"I've, erm, just been talking to Reuben," I began.

"And I should care because?"

And BOSH! My good intentions went out the window just like that!

"You should care, you thick bozo, because Reuben reminded me I'm a celestial being. Which means I could be on your HALO team, assuming you still want me. So do you or don't you? I haven't got all day, you know!" I was literally yelling into his face.

Brice looked genuinely shocked. "You're being unusually forceful."

"Yes, I am," I snapped. "I'm sick of tiptoeing round you, like you've got some fatal disease, you moron."

He gave a startled grin. "That's a fine way for a celestial being to address another celestial being!"

I glared at him. "OK, then: jerk, creep, dirtbag. Take your pick."

The grin vanished. "Your point being?"

"My point being that real friends don't tiptoe round each other."

There was an electrifying pause.

"Friends?" Brice repeated.

I smiled down at my shoes. "Obviously there's still a way to go. But if trees can turn into diamonds, anything's possible, right?"

I could feel Brice looking at the top of my head. "OK, Mel Beeby, future friend," he said softly. "What's the game plan?"

Confession time. No, really, BIG confession time.

I TRULY intended to read my bio. The night before our mission, I actually curled up in my uncomfortable school armchair and opened the first page, but then Lola popped her head round the door to see if I fancied a takeaway. She hadn't read her bio either. So we both went into total denial mode and ordered this massive feast from the Silver Lychee! A bit naughty I know, but their food is SO-O delicious!

Over our meal, my friend and I got into this really deep conversation and before we knew it, the evening had flown by.

Eventually, Lola started collecting up takeaway cartons.

"*Hey, carita!* We didn't do our fortune cookies!"

"We can do them now!" I said, stifling my yawns.

Lola's fortune said she was going to risk everything for love. Mine said I would have to learn to tell the real from the unreal.

"How come I never get to fall in love?" I moaned.

I could weep when I remember us innocently reading our cookie fortunes. If we'd shared our bios then, things might have been so different. But I started on about my stupid corset and that led into happy reminiscences about Shakespeare's girlfriend.

"Cat Darcy had it all," Lola sighed. "She was pretty, smart, brave."

"It must have been a nightmare being a black person in England then. The Elizabethans treated her like she was some exotic pet."

"Chance didn't," Lola said softly. "Shakespeare, I mean."

"Those two were true soul-mates, weren't they?"

"I wanted them to get it together, didn't you?"

"Totally. But if Chance had gone to sea like Cat's dad suggested, he'd never have discovered he was a play-writing genius."

Lola did one of those stretches that makes her look just like a cat. "Gotta move my angel booty," she yawned. "Brice is picking me up in two hours."

I gave her a hug. "Watch out for the Caribbean love-interest."

"And you go on keeping it real, girlfriend!"

I heard Lola pattering down the hall in her little beaded slippers, and the soft double clunk as her door opened and closed.

Next morning there was a note pinned to my door: Soul-mates see each other's true colours, no matter what. Big love 2U, Lollie

It was like she knew.

A few minutes before I was due at the nursery school, I finally glanced through my bio. I couldn't see too much to worry about. The character in my cover story even shared my real first name to my relief.

Melanie Woodhouse had grown up in England, but her parents had died and she'd been sent to Jamaica to live with her uncle and aunt. They were called Josiah and Sarah Bexford and owned a sugar plantation with the magic name of Fruitful Vale.

This is going to be SO sublime, I sighed happily. I was OK with being visible now. For one thing, when you're visible you can enjoy the local food. Once my friend Lateesha's mum cooked this massive Jamaican Sunday brunch for us. Ohhh! It made my mouth water to think of it.

When I got to the nursery, everyone was outside in the sun. Chairs were set out in rows for specially invited guests. Our headmaster was in the front row, chatting to Miss Dove. At least he was trying to! Several overexcited preschoolers had decided to use him as a climbing frame.

Michael seems so human and easy-going, it's easy to forget he's an archangel; until you look into his eyes. Omigosh, those scary-beautiful eyes just see right into your soul!

"Melanie!" he said warmly. "I hope you're going to sit next to me! It's been too long."

"Hey, who's fault is that? *I* turn up every day!"

It's a standing school joke that our headmaster is almost never around. As archangel with special responsibility for Earth, Michael is constantly jetting off to historical trouble spots. Yet here he was, keen to see the little nursery school angels do their stuff, looking slightly tired but totally serene.

Preschool angels obviously can't go off on dangerous missions. But they're desperate to do their bit for the Universe. Miss Dove wanted to encourage this positive attitude, so she'd arranged for them to perform their HALO contributions in front of a friendly heavenly audience.

The children had been practising for WEEKS. The Rose group performed last of all, looking totally darling in their miniature school casuals. They'd organised (you're not going to believe this!) a Giggle Marathon!

I'd already seen them in rehearsal, but it got me every time. There's something about preschool angels laughing. They sound SO naughty!

Soon everyone in the audience was laughing helplessly. Michael totally couldn't stop. He even set Miss Dove off and she is the soul of professionalism, believe me.

Finally the children took their bow, still giggling. Some of them could hardly stand by this time!

"Thank you," Michael told them, wiping his eyes. "Who'd like to tell me about this unusual project?"

One of my favourite preschoolers stepped forward. Obi has absolutely no hair, almost invisible eyebrows, and the calmest face you have ever seen. He looks just like a mini Buddha.

"Miss Dove said to think of a project that could make Earth a happier place," Obi said shyly. "So Maudie said we should just giggle and have fun. She said our vibes will beam all the way to Earth and children will catch them and start giggling and feel happy again."

"Is that right, Maudie?" Michael asked gently. "Was this your idea?"

She gave him an awed nod. "Yes, because giggling is catching. When I start I can't ever stop."

There was a kiddies' party afterwards. Unfortunately, I only had time to grab a fairy cake before I had to leave.

I was SO touched when Michael offered to take me down to the Agency and see me off.

"I'm glad you felt able to support Brice's HALO entry," he said as we purred downtown in his awesome Agency car. "This one could be quite a challenge for you all."

"Oh, we're old hands now. We'll be fine!" I said airily.

No matter what time you go, it's always crowded in Departures. I rushed into the ladies' cloakroom and came out feeling self-conscious in my seventeenth-century cap and gown.

One thing I find so comforting, is the way the Agency gets every teensy historical detail just right.

Like the coin purse hanging at my waist had items of real seventeenth-century jewellery in it. Nothing flash. Just the type of sweet simple trinkets my character would have.

Michael and I joined the long queue for angel tags. No one is allowed to leave Heaven without them. They basically tell the Universe that we're on official business, plus they keep us in touch with all the angelic support guys.

I saw a sudden flicker of worry in Michael's eyes. He'd seen my teacher talking to a junior agent. "Excuse me, Melanie, we may have a problem." Michael hurried over to Mr Allbright.

I had a bad feeling in the pit of my stomach. I caught confused snatches of their conversation. Communications between Heaven and Earth had been disrupted in the early hours, only seconds after two trainees left on a HALO mission.

I knew it had to be Brice and Lola.

I heard Michael say, "And there's been no word? Well, page me as soon as you hear anything."

The agent hurried away. Michael and Mr Allbright went into a huddle but this time I couldn't hear what they said.

I'd collected my tags. Now I didn't know what to

do. I glanced up to find Al, my favourite maintenance man, at my side.

"Your portal's ready, doll, but it looks like we've got a bit of a situation," he said sympathetically.

Michael and Mr Allbright came over, looking really grim.

"I'm calling your mission off," Michael said bluntly. "We're fairly sure your friends arrived in the right time slot, but unusual atmospheric conditions are making it impossible to pick up signals. Mr Allbright and I have considered various options and decided to send in a SWAT team."

"To get them back? No way!" The words burst out before I'd even thought. "It's the worst thing you could do!"

Michael looked startled. "Melanie, we're trying to *save* him."

"Yeah, save his hide, but what about Brice's self-respect? He'd think he was a major loser. You've got to let him sort this out on his own."

Mr Allbright had joined us. "This is not about doubting Brice's ability," he said quietly.

"Oh, really! What is it about then?" I was fuming.

He sighed. "It's about the school acting responsibly."

"You're wrong," I said angrily. "You're not seeing the big picture."

Michael took a breath. "Your friends could be at risk. I've decided to bring them home. That's all there is to it."

"NO! Whatever it is, Brice and Lola can deal with it. Why won't you *trust* them?" I was yelling at an archangel, but I knew I was right.

"I'm sorry, Melanie," he said, "this is one for the professionals."

I was getting that burning hot-potato sensation. My inner angel wanted to get in on the discussion. "Tell the truth, babe!" she whispered. "But try not to lose your temper."

I forced myself to calm down. "Listen, everyone knows Brice and I aren't exactly bosom buddies. When he came back I was just waiting for him to screw up. The way I saw it, I was right and good, and he was bad and wrong. If he screwed up, he'd be bad for ever, and I'd be good for ever. That's how I was thinking."

"I fail to see—" Michael began.

"That's what I'm trying to TELL you! If you rush to his rescue, you're as good as telling him he's got no future as an agent!"

"On the contrary, we're showing him how much we value—"

I cut across him. "Can you see Brice doing some heavenly desk job? Omigosh, Michael! It would kill him!"

He looked upset. "Melanie, there will be other opportunities—"

"Not like this. I truly think this could be a cosmic thingummy. A turning point, kind of. Like, if Brice can get through this, he'll know he can make it in the angel bizz."

"What if he doesn't get through it?" Mr Allbright's brow was puckered with worry.

"I can't think that far," I confessed. "I just know you've got to give him a chance."

They exchanged glances.

"Excuse us," Michael murmured.

My headmaster and Mr Allbright went off into a huddle. I was so tense I was literally digging my nails into my palms. Their private conflab lasted for aeons. Mr Allbright kept shaking his head dubiously. Eventually Michael walked back to me. His expression was so grave that I felt sure it was bad news.

"Mr Allbright and I have agreed that you must do what you think is right," he said in a quiet voice.

I went weak with relief. "I promise I won't let you down."

Urgent squawking sounds came over Al's headphones. The time technicians were getting twitchy.

"Hate to hassle you people," Al said apologetically, "but we're cutting this really fine."

"Just let us have a few more seconds." Michael's scary-beautiful eyes searched mine. "I know Lola is your best friend, but I'm not sure you realise how dange—"

I shook my head. "It isn't just Lola."

"You feel responsible for Brice, is that it?"

"I think," I started shyly. "I think when Brice met me in London that time, it reminded him what he'd lost. In a funny kind of way, I'm the reason he came back to our school. He signed up for the HALO mission because I promised I'd be on his team. Now something's gone wrong." My eyes stung with tears. "I should have been there, Michael. I *have* to go."

This time Michael didn't attempt to change my mind. He simply held out his hand for my tags. "Shall I fasten those?"

He did up the clasp, and I found myself engulfed in the fizzy rainbow cloud of Michael's energy field. I literally saw light and colours whooshing everywhere! All at once, my heart was burstingly full of love. It was like the tiniest glimpse of how it might feel to be an archangel.

I tottered into my portal, still fizzing with angelic electricity.

"Take care, Melanie," Michael said softly. "Call the Agency as soon as you can."

"I will!"

"Good luck, doll," called Al.

The glass door slid shut. Al said something into his headpiece, then gave me a thumbs up. I waved to show I was ready.

We must have been cutting it REALLY fine, because next minute my portal lit up like a laser show and I was blasted out of Heaven.

Soon afterwards, I felt the familiar jolt, as the portal burst through the invisible barrier that separates the angelic fields from the human realms of Time and Space. I wasn't actually watching. I was emptying out my flight bag, desperately trying to find my bio. I'd planned to have a quick last-minute read. Omigosh, Melanie,

I scolded myself. You'd better not have left it behind!

But as it turned out, reading was not an option. Seconds later, my portal started pitching about like you would not believe. We'd hit major cosmic turbulence.

Must be those weird atmospheric conditions Michael was talking about, I thought anxiously.

I glanced through the window and was alarmed to see time zones streaming past in a multicoloured blur. We were travelling fast, even by Agency standards. Screechy metallic sounds started up under my feet. The portal began to judder. I could literally feel my back teeth vibrating.

I hit the PANIC button. "Help!" I shouted. "Get me back. We'll have to abort this mission. This thing is shaking itself to pieces!"

Weird staticky sounds came from my radio, making me clutch my ears. My radio link was malfunctioning along with everything else.

"Help!" I called again. "Al? Michael? Can anyone hear me?"

Outside, history was flashing past my eyes like colours in a migraine.

I thought I was going to dissolve with terror. Could angels actually DIE? It was one of those technical details I was always intending to look up. Now it could be too late.

"Michael, if you can hear me, please help!" I moaned. "Please, please..."

Then a jagged hole tore in the portal and I was sucked out into space.

Chapter Four

In my dream I was lost in roaring darkness. Lightning flashes showed lurid glimpses of a terrifying dream world. FLASH! Palm trees bent almost double. FLASH! A wooden chair sailing through the air. FLASH! Water rushing – a river? A lake? And again pitch black.

The roaring, rushing nightmare went on for what seemed hours. Nothing was solid. Nothing made sense. Nothing felt real.

Then I felt gentle hands take hold of me inside my dream, lifting me up as if I weighed no more than air. I was laid on something soft and carried through the lashing wind and rain. My rescuers called to each other in a musical dream language, a language I miraculously understood.

"She is here," they told each other. "She flew here on the wings of the storm. Now the end is coming."

Another flash showed me a brief, electrifying vision: six or seven concerned faces gazing down at me through the falling rain. They wore strange ornaments made of pearls and seashells. The colours shimmered against their half-naked bodies like colours you only see in dreams...

I opened my eyes and found myself lying in a large four-poster bed. Velvet curtains had been looped back at one side. An oil lamp made silky gleams on polished wood. Everything else was in deep shadow.

There was a strange fog inside my head, making it hard to think.

I didn't know where I was. And omigosh, this was really bad. I didn't actually know *who* I was!

I heard stealthy creaks. My heart thumped like a rabbit's. Someone was in my room, and I didn't know if they were friend or foe.

"Is anyone out there?" I whimpered.

I heard more creaks as someone shifted his or her weight in a chair. Then I heard slow shuffling footsteps. An old black woman peered through my curtains. "Lawd a mercy!" she exclaimed. "You come back to us!"

I could have cried with relief. She knows who I am, I thought. Now I'll find out what's going on.

"Have I been away?" I said huskily. My throat was incredibly sore.

"You been sick, bad bad, Miss Melanie."

Miss Melanie. That had to be me. This old woman must be my nurse.

"I'm very thirsty," I croaked.

"Have a sip a dis cordial. Don't sit up too fas'," she warned.

The cool drink was blissful, but the effort of drinking wore me out. I collapsed back on my pillows, trembling.

I felt haunted by my horrible nightmare. I wasn't sure if I was truly awake, or if this was just another episode in the same dream.

Nothing seemed fixed or solid or familiar. The room, the old-fashioned bed, the tired old nurse.

I watched her from under my eyelashes, wondering what it was about her that disturbed me. Her eyes are so sad, I thought. Next minute this thought slipped away and I found myself glancing nervously into the corners of the room.

There was something creepy about those shadows. They might morph into something else when I wasn't looking. Something evil.

You're being pathetic, I told myself. *You're in a big comfy bed in this lovely peaceful room. You're weak from this illness, that's all. There's absolutely nothing to be scared of.*

Except that I'd lost my memory.

The old nurse bustled about, sponging my hot face, bringing clean cool sheets, plumping up pillows.

"This is really sweet of you," I said.

She gave me a startled look, like I'd said something bizarre.

"I seem to have forgotten your name," I said apologetically. "This illness has made me feel a bit confused."

"Dey call mi Quasha," the old woman said. "But mi true name Quashiba. In Africa times, all girls born on a Sunday called dat."

I gasped. "Omigosh, we're in Africa! I had no idea."

She laughed. "Dis not Africa! Dis place Fruitful Vale, your uncle's plantation. You don' remember Massa Bexford and Lovey meet you at di harbour, drive you here to Fruitful Vale?"

I shook my head. "I don't remember a thing. What happened to me?"

"You got sick on the boat, girl-chile," she said. "Missus don' think you gonna live."

Quashiba told me that on my first night, I'd become delirious and wandered out in a hurricane. But my uncle's driver, a man called Lovey, found me before I came to any harm.

This was getting more bewildering every minute. How could I have forgotten who I was?

It made me genuinely panicky. I felt as if I couldn't breathe.

Gotta get some air, I thought urgently. *Deep breaths.*

"Can you open the shutters?" I asked Quashiba. "It's quite stuffy in here."

There was no glass in the window, just slats you opened or closed. Quashiba pulled a lever, letting in shimmery bars of moonlight. The room filled with the high shrill sounds of crickets. Delicious scents floated in out of the darkness. I lay back on my pillows. The night breeze felt blissful on my sweaty skin. I could see the blue-white pulsing of a star between the wooden slats. And suddenly I knew.

"I'm in Jamaica!" I breathed.

Quashiba clapped her hands. "You remember, eh! You in Jamaica in Fruitful Vale. Your uncle, Massa Josiah Bexford, own all di lan' from here to Orange Park."

I had to turn my face to the wall. Relief at getting my memory back was making me weepy and I didn't want Quashiba to see. I didn't belong in this place. I wasn't even human. I was an undercover angel on a mission to help a friend get back his self-respect. My portal had mysteriously autodestructed on the way. By a miracle, I'd survived unscathed. Apart from a touch of cosmic amnesia.

I burrowed into my pillows. Just as soon as I had my strength back, I'd have to track Brice and Lola down. Hopefully it wasn't too late. Hopefully we could keep our joint date with destiny.

First, I thought, I'll have a tiny little snooze...

Angels have fabulous powers of recovery! Next morning I was tucking into a Jamaican-style breakfast on the veranda outside my room.

I'd just started on the yummy fried plantain, when a white lady with a parasol appeared on the steps. My "Aunt Sarah" had heard of my recovery.

"I am relieved to see you are better, niece." My aunt looked flushed and hot in her tightly-laced gown. I heard her corsets creak as she bent to kiss my cheek. She caught sight of my plate. "What was Quasha thinking!" she exclaimed. "Bringing you this revolting native food!"

"I asked her to. I love yam and plantain," I said in surprise.

Aunt Sarah looked faint. "Oh, but my *dear*, wouldn't you prefer something less *foreign*? A cup of beef tea? Or calves' foot jelly?"

Euw! The foods my aunt thought suitable for invalids sounded far, far more weird than yam!

To my relief my aunt totally accepted that I was the human in my Agency cover story. Though to be quite honest with you, I think Aunt Sarah would have talked to anyone. I shouldn't be mean, but she just about talked my ears off. Apologising about a million times for not nursing me herself, and hinting at a v.

mysterious loss that had left her feeling very low.

"I fear that in my depressed condition I would have caught the contagion and become ill myself," she said.

I didn't like to pry into her personal business but I could tell my aunt was hoping for a reaction, so I said sympathetically, "Omigosh, what happened?"

Aunt Sarah dabbed her eyes with a lace hankie. "Little Phoebe died," she said. "I didn't know it was possible to shed so many tears."

Well, I couldn't just leave it hanging.

"Don't tell me if it upsets you," I said in my gentlest voice. "But who was, erm, Phoebe?"

"My love bird," choked Aunt Sarah. "Every time I see that empty cage..." My aunt quickly turned away, her shoulders shaking.

I felt really sorry for her actually. No one should have to be that lonely, should they?

I thought I'd try to distract her by asking if I could see around the house. I was still in my nightie, but Aunt Sarah caught hold of my hand like a little girl who wants to be best friends, and led me eagerly along dimly lit corridors. She explained that the shutters had to be kept closed to protect her furniture from the strong Jamaican sunlight.

"I had everything sent out from England," she said proudly.

I think Aunt Sarah probably had more English furniture than they had in England. Stiff English chairs upholstered in flowery satin. Huge oil paintings of glowering English ancestors. Highly polished cabinets crammed with English china and glassware that looked totally unused. It wasn't a home at all. It was a museum.

As we walked through this totally depressing series of rooms Aunt Sarah confided how difficult she found life in the tropics. The snakes. The heat. The humidity. "And that terrible hurricane, my dear! I thought the roof was going to blow right off!"

I had an alarming thought. "When was the hurricane exactly?"

"A week ago today. You'd just arrived, poor child, when it started to blow."

Eep! I thought. The Agency would be wondering why I hadn't called home. I felt furtively under the collar of my nightdress and went weak with relief. The tags were still there.

"Have you tried sugar cane yet? You really must!" Aunt Sarah smiled properly for the first time and I was horrified to see gruesome black stumps. Sugar cane was obviously one foreign food my aunt enjoyed to the max.

I'd never seen cane growing, so my aunt took me on to a veranda with a view over cane fields. After the permanent twilight inside the house, my eyes were totally dazzled by the acres of lush tropical foliage.

"It's an amazing colour," I breathed. "Almost blue!"

"When cane stalks turn that blue popinjay colour, it means the cane is ripe. My husband starts harvesting when the Christmas breeze begins to blow." She gestured at the palm trees busily clacking their fronds like gossipy grannies.

I was confused. "Is it Christmas then?"

My aunt laughed with a flash of her disturbing teeth. "Everything must seem strange to you, my dear."

"It does seem quite strange," I said truthfully.

Aunt Sarah patted my shoulder. "It will be good to have some female company. The men only come indoors to eat and sleep. And quarrel," she added with a sigh.

"Don't they get on?"

"My nephew, that's your cousin, Beau, and Mr Bexford are constantly at loggerheads. Mr Bexford's brother sent Beau out to Jamaica to learn the plantation business. My husband says he is a foolish young hothead. And Beau says—" My aunt stopped herself abruptly. "Listen to me rattling on! Now you are up and about again, we shall be able to talk every day!"

"Yes, that will be lovely," I said brightly.

I really hope I find the others soon, I thought nervously, as my aunt launched into another long story about her difficult nephew.

You can't afford to let yourself get distracted on a mission, or you'd never get anywhere. I was sorry for my aunt but I hadn't come to Earth to be her full-time companion.

Luckily, Aunt Sarah remembered she had to see the cook about a blancmange or whatever, so I was able to escape. I rushed back to my room, struggled into my seventeenth-century clothes, (with help from Quashiba) and took myself for a walk in the Caribbean sunshine.

Omigosh, how *did* European women survive, wearing that dreadful underwear? I was practically fainting after five minutes. I literally had to rest under a mango tree, like a frail heroine in an old-fashioned book.

It was lovely actually. I could feel calm mango-tree vibes humming inside the tree's knobbly bark. "Hi tree," I whispered. "I'm a visiting angel, but you knew that, didn't you?"

There was no one around, so I took the opportunity to call home. I clasped my angel tags, and tried to tune into my heavenly energy source – and got absolutely *nada*. I couldn't believe it, I'd been here *days* and communications were STILL down!

I could feel myself starting to panic. Don't be a quitter, Melanie, I told myself firmly. The glitch could be just one way. The Agency may still be able to pick up incoming calls.

I beamed a quick progress report to Angel HQ on the off chance that some junior agent would pick up my signal.

Hi, this is Melanie. Erm, I just wanted you to know I'm fine. I had, erm, a little setback but don't worry, I'm back on the case and hopefully I'll run into the others any time now. Erm later!

Not the most polished performance, but I'd got distracted halfway through. Beautiful, spine-tingling harmonies came and went on the Caribbean breeze. The cane-cutters were singing.

I gazed across fields, hazy with heat, at the figures working their way steadily down the rows. The rhythm of the singing perfectly fitted the swing-and-slash motion of the workers, as they hacked down the cane.

Something in their voices brought me out in goosebumps. I suddenly felt this intense emotion welling up inside me. The only word to describe it is suffering. A pain and suffering too deep for tears.

These weren't my feelings. I could feel them seeping out of the earth and rocks, and quivering through the mango tree. They were coming from the island itself.

It doesn't make sense, I thought. Jamaica is the closest thing I've seen to Heaven on Planet Earth. What could be wrong with Paradise?

I saw someone strolling towards me through the heat haze and hastily pulled myself together.

There was something oddly familiar about him.

This person had a stiff way of walking, and he wore strange, stiff, seventeenth-century clothes, yet he totally reminded me of— Omigosh, it WAS! It was Brice!!

I rushed to meet him, almost weeping with relief.

"Thank goodness you're safe! I've been SO worried!"

I babbled on about the hurricane and my illness, "I'm SO sorry! I must have set our mission back by *aeons*, but I'm fine now. We can get started any time you say!"

I finally stopped for breath. Brice looked surprisingly dashing in his baggy shirt and knee breeches. Plus he totally had seventeenth-century manners.

"Calm yourself, cousin," he said. "You are not quite recovered, I fear."

"Oooh!" I teased. "That's no way to greet your heavenly rescuer!"

Brice gave me a strange look. "Do I seem as if I need rescuing?"

"Well duh! Obviously you don't! But we didn't know that, since you never actually bothered to phone home! Angel HQ wanted to call off the whole mission, can you believe! But I said to leave you exactly where you are, because you were a big angel now and you'd handle it."

I was grinning like a loon. Brice was not grinning back.

"You should not be walking out of doors at this time of day," he said in a disapproving tone. "You may have a brain fever."

"OK, drop the act, angel boy!" I sighed. "It's getting tedious now. I want to hear the game plan – I assume you guys *do* have a game plan?"

But Brice seemed determined to kid around. "Didn't Aunt Sarah tell you that you must never walk outdoors without your parasol? Particularly in the middle of the day?"

"Oh ha ha! Like I'd be seen dead with a stupid para—"

I broke off. The chilling truth dawned on me.

Brice wasn't kidding.

Stay calm babe, I told myself. *Better find out how bad this is.*

My heart was banging around in my chest, but I managed to fake a ditzy giggle. "Silly me! I can't seem to remember what they call you! My memory is just all over the place."

Brice gave a curt nod. "It is to be expected after such a severe illness. I am your cousin Beau."

Omigosh, I thought. *Tell me this isn't happening.*

"You've turned pale, little cousin," he said gallantly. "Lean on me if you feel faint."

I felt faint all right. My deluded angel buddy seemed to think he was the human in his Agency story line. What in the world was I going to do?

Beau/Brice had begun to lead me back towards the house.

"*Wait!*" I said desperately. "I absolutely don't have brain fever. I feel fine, truly. And I was just teasing about the angel thing." I faked peals of laughter. "You should have seen your face!"

Brice dropped my arm abruptly. "You have an unusual sense of humour," he said coldly.

I giggled madly. "Everyone says that. But I truly meant no harm. I was just, erm, amusing myself talking nonsense!"

I thought this sounded convincingly seventeenth century, but Brice frowned. "I have no time to talk nonsense to young ladies. My uncle had to stay over at our plantation in

Savannah la Mar. I have to take care of business in his absence. I was on my way to the mill when I saw you."

"Can't I come?" I coaxed. "I've been indoors for days."

"The mill is no place for a young English lady," said Brice stiffly.

I clasped my hands. "Please! I'll just watch. I won't get in the way."

He sighed. "Very well. But fetch your parasol."

"I'll be back in two ticks! Don't move!"

I picked up my skirts and went skipping back to the house, like an innocent little orphan. Inside I was in turmoil.

It absolutely wasn't safe for Brice to be here in this state. An angel with this level of cosmic amnesia was a sitting target for the PODS. I had to get him home. *How do you plan to do that, babe? I asked myself. Communications are down or had you forgotten?*

We'd managed to get Reuben back to Heaven that time in Elizabethan England, I remembered, but Lola had been with me then. Two angels can send much, much stronger angelic signals than one.

There's your answer, Mel, I thought. Now stop making mountains out of molehills. Together Lola and I can definitely generate enough angel power to get an SOS to Heaven. Sorted!

All I had to do was find her.

CHAPTER FIVE

"Those are called trumpet trees." Brice pointed to a grove of immensely tall, very slender trees. I'm not sure why they were called trumpet trees. Their leaves looked more like huge fans.

We were walking along a shady track; walking very slowly actually. I know it was hot, but I have to say Beau/Brice didn't seem that keen to reach our uncle's sugar mill. He kept stopping to show me tropical plants along the way.

I dutifully repeated their names to show I was paying attention. Rose apple, soursop, guango trees. All the time I was trying to think of a way to drop Lola casually into the conversation. Asking if he'd run into any nice angels recently was obviously out. I could try asking if he had any other female cousins living nearby? The Agency had made me and Brice relations, so chances were they'd made Lola some kind of rellie too.

If ONLY I'd read my friend's bio...

Or even your own, babe, my inner angel commented.

I heard scuffling sounds. A little girl came stumbling down the track in her bare feet, struggling to balance a basket on her head. Her dress was so tattered it was virtually hanging off one shoulder. She lowered her eyes, mumbling, "Morning Massa. Morning miss," as she staggered past.

"Morning, Bright Eyes," Brice called.

The little girl made me think of my little sister Jade. "Bright Eyes is a sweet name," I said wistfully. "And she does have lovely eyes."

"She's very light-skinned, did you notice?" Brice sounded edgy.

"Not really," I said. "People come in all colours, don't they?"

He sighed. "I keep forgetting you've just come from England. In a few months you'll be like all the

other white people on this island. It's their curse. They can't escape."

"You're a white person too," I pointed out. "Will you escape?"

He gave a bitter laugh. "I think I was born an outlaw."

Babe, you have no idea, I thought.

A cool whirr of wings fanned my face. A magical little bird appeared in front of us, hovering over a bush of vivid pink blossoms. Its wings were vibrating so fast they were literally a blur. The tiny bird plunged a long, needle-like beak into a blossom, to drink the invisible liquid inside, then whirred away.

"Was that a real humming bird?" I breathed.

"They're as common as blackbirds here. The best time to see them is at sunrise, or just after the rain."

I explained that humming birds were on my personal list of Caribbean "must-sees", along with fireflies.

Brice gave me a sad half-smile. "Do you think you will like Jamaica?"

"It's beautiful," I said. "But I haven't really been here long enough to know if I'll like it."

We were walking past large rhubarb-type plants which Brice said were cocoa plants. They had leaves like heart-shaped umbrellas, easily as big as dinner plates.

"Jamaica is a place you either love or hate!" he said. "I love it, but I hate what we have done to it in a few short years."

"Have you been living here long?" I asked slyly. I was kind of interested to hear what he'd come up with. But it's like he didn't hear.

"Have you heard of the Taino?" Brice asked out of the blue.

"Not really, I don't know much about Jamaica at all." I blushed. "The Taino IS a Jamaican thing, right?"

"Taino means 'good and noble people'. It's what the indigenous Indians of this island called themselves: the people who lived here before the Europeans came."

"I had no idea anyone lived here," I said guiltily.

"There were many such tribes, all with different names, scattered throughout the Caribbean, but white people prefer to forget about them. They like to pretend the New World was empty when Columbus got here. Though they are extremely interested in the cities the original inhabitants are supposed to have left behind."

"These Indians actually built cities?" I'd imagined them living in tepees and whatever.

"They lived simply, in complete harmony with the Earth. But they were also wonderfully skilled craftsmen. For instance, the Taino knew how to use seashells so cleverly that they looked like precious gemstones."

"So what was that you said about a city?"

Brice explained that the first Europeans to arrive in the New World heard tantalising rumours of an ancient city buried deep in a jungle in the Americas. The details varied. Generally the city had been abandoned owing to some horrific natural disaster. In some stories, the city was in Venezuela, sometimes Mexico or Surinam. But the crucial element of the story never changed. There were always fabulous quantities of Indian gold.

Brice gave a painful laugh. "Many white explorers have died attempting to find this city. You could see it as poetic justice."

I sensed that there was something he wasn't telling me. "But what happened to the Taino themselves?"

"Sometimes I think I see their spirits in the woods," he said in a low voice.

The blue sky was cloudless yet I shivered as if a shadow had slipped between us and the sun. "They're *dead*? ALL the Taino?"

"Almost all. A few tribesmen survive in the hills."

"But why would anyone...?"

Brice swallowed. "They got in our way."

After that we just walked on without speaking. But the sound of our shoes rustling through dead and dying leaves suddenly seemed abnormally loud. The idea of ghostly tribesmen watching us from between the trees really disturbed me.

I was becoming aware of an overpowering pong, sickly-sweet and unbelievably foul. Eventually I had to cover my nose.

"You can smell the molasses," Brice explained. "Take my handkerchief."

Shortly afterwards we crossed into the mill yard. This wasn't some picturesque windmill, like mills in picture books. It was powered by six sweating oxen, urged on by drivers with curses and thumps. Instead of mill stones, the sugar mill had three gigantic vertical rollers, as fat as tree trunks and as tall as your average seventeenth-century adult male.

The rollers revolved with hollow rumbling sounds that echoed through the cobbled yard. You could feel it vibrating in your bones and the roots of your teeth. Men were working frantically to keep this monster fed, unloading harvested cane from the carts, stripping away the useless cane trash with knives. The dust and little loose fibres from the trash got everywhere, drifting around our feet, blowing in the workers' eyes.

"The original Taino word for Jamaica was *Xaymaca*," Brice said into my ear. "It means Land of Wood and Water. Wonder what they'd think of it now?"

He was angry. Why wouldn't he be? He was seeing the world through an angel's eyes. As I looked around at this hellish scene, I felt angry too.

The mill workers were all half-naked except for filthy loincloths. Many had ugly scars on their sweating backs and legs. Some had fingers, or parts of fingers, missing. All of them were black.

Brice kept up his grim commentary in my ear, as we made our way through rising clouds of dust.

"Our last mill-feeder, Mingo, got so tired he fell asleep on his feet and lost his hand in the press. He was lucky."

I stared at him. "He was *lucky*?"

"Mingo's brother got dragged in through the rollers last year."

We watched the new mill-feeder deftly handfeeding cane stalks through the rollers, risking his life with every stalk. Treacly brown liquid spurted into a trough at his feet. I tried not to picture Mingo's brother's body being crushed like sugar cane, his red blood mixing with the molasses.

I followed Brice into the boiling house. It was like being inside an oven. I could literally feel the moisture being drawn from my body. The combination of the tremendous heat and molasses fumes, made it next to impossible to breathe.

Five giant copper kettles were suspended over a blazing furnace. Inside the kettles, the boiling molasses blipped and bubbled like an evil magician's brew.

A half-naked boy, of eight or nine years old, was keeping the furnace going with bundles of cane trash. He'd reached the zombie stage of exhaustion, running mechanically from the trash pile to the boiling kettles, from the kettles to the trash pile.

I was fuming by this time. What were the Bexfords *thinking*, making people work in these horrific conditions? Suppose some of that scalding sludge splashed on the little boy's skin? Suppose he stumbled and knocked a kettle flying? The blistering-hot molasses would stick like boiling glue.

Brice had to talk business to the overseer, a sandy-haired Scot and the only white worker in the yard. I grabbed the chance to beam loving vibes to the little boy, then I went outside and beamed heaps more to the mill-feeder. Reuben says it's WAY better to light one tiny candle than to whinge about the dark.

I can't say, obviously, if beaming vibes helped dispel any cosmic darkness for those humans, but it had a huge effect on me.

I found myself taking a hard look at the overseer. When Brice emerged, mopping his perspiring face, my question just burst out.

"Why does that man have a whip?"

An alarmed ripple went round the yard. Brice hurried me out of earshot. "Where have you been hiding, cousin?" he hissed furiously. "Why do you *think* that man has a whip? To show my uncle's slaves who has the power. To stop them rising up and killing their owners in their beds – shall I go on?"

I couldn't speak. At some point I thought I might want to be sick.

"Slaves?" I whispered. "Those people are slaves?"

Brice gave an angry laugh. "Do you imagine plantation owners could live like emperors if we PAID our workers?"

The clues had been there from the start. The pride and pain in Quashiba's voice when she talked about African names. The haunted harmonies floating from the fields, the suffering that came seeping out of the blood-soaked earth of Jamaica itself.

I had no excuse for my ignorance. We had learned all about this particular form of slavery at my old school. Human slavers stole thousands and millions of other humans from Africa, shipping them across the sea to work in the plantations of the Caribbean, and forcing them to work in the conditions I'd just seen.

Yet I'd pushed this information to the back of my mind. I'd wanted to have my own cool little Caribbean experience. Like la la la, hello humming birds, hello mango trees...

STOP IT! I told myself.

Slavery was way too dark to take on by myself. I had to concentrate on my own small cosmic task; getting Brice back home to Heaven before he got into any worse trouble.

To do this, I needed angelic backup, and I didn't want to waste another minute faffing around. I had the definite feeling time was running out.

"I need to find a girl called Lola," I blurted out. "Do you know her? Quashiba says she can sew." I was improvising frantically.

Brice looked totally thunderstruck, then tried to cover his shock. "Erm, yes," he said in a slightly too-casual voice. "I do, indeed, know a Lola."

I was so happy, I almost hugged him!

"*Really!*" I said. I literally felt giddy with relief. This was the best news I'd had since I left Heaven.

You see Mel, I told myself, the simple approach is often the best!

A teeny worm of doubt crept in. "I expect she lives a long way away, doesn't she?"

"If we're talking about the same person, she lives here at Fruitful Vale. But I don't think it can be the same Lola." Brice sounded really cagey but this clue passed me by.

"No, it is. It has to be," I burbled. "Can you take me to her?"

"I don't think I can, no," he said, to my dismay. "Anyway, I don't think Lola would want visitors."

"Why ever not?"

He couldn't meet my eyes. "Before you arrived from England, Lola was accused of stealing from the kitchen. My uncle has strong opinions about stealing. The overseer gave her a beating."

I gave a nervous laugh. "No, no, sorry, we're getting our wires crossed. This Lola's an – a – very proud person." I was so freaked that I'd almost said "angel"! "She doesn't steal from kitchens," I added firmly.

Brice swallowed. "To my uncle she is just another thieving slave."

There was a sudden humming in my ears. The dusty mill yard, with its feverish activity, wobbled like a mirage.

"She *can't* be a slave!" I whispered. "Lola's not even African!"

I immediately wanted to bite my tongue off. What a dumb thing to say. Like, if she'd been pure African it would be OK to beat her like a dog.

Brice gave his painful laugh. "One drop of African blood is enough to condemn someone to a life of slavery. I heard an entertaining debate between my uncle and an English vicar who'd recently arrived in Jamaica. They were trying to decide whether Africans have souls. I suggested it would be more educational to find out whether plantation owners have souls."

"I have to see her," I told him shakily. "It's vitally important!" Horror was pulsing through me in waves. While I'd been lolling around convalescing, my friend had been suffering the worst humiliation Planet Earth had to offer.

Brice sounded despairing. "Lola was sold a few days ago."

My heart almost stopped with fright. "She's GONE! But you said—"

"I meant there's no point you going to see her. Lovey is driving her over to St Mary's first thing tomorrow."

I'd only just got here in time.

I caught hold of his sleeve. "Take me to her. Take me now!" I must have sounded mad.

"I can't. My uncle could come back at any moment. He would be extremely displeased if—"

"I don't CARE!"

Bruce looked suspicious. "Forgive me, but what exactly is so important about this piece of sewing?" Brice asked.

I grabbed at the first excuse that came into my head. "I, erm, lost heaps of weight while I was ill. I've got this gorgeous dress for the Christmas party and now it totally won't fit. I need Lola to alter it before she goes."

Brice looked disgusted and no wonder. He must have thought I was turning into one of those ugly Europeans before his eyes. But he nodded reluctantly. "Very well."

The slave huts had been built as far as possible from the main house, behind a natural screen of coconut palms. The huts were thatched with palm leaves, and looked and smelled completely squalid. Garbage lay rotting everywhere. I suppose no one had the heart to clean up.

There was unexpected beauty though, even in this depressing little village. The garden plots where slaves grew their own fruits and vegetables glowed with life and colour. I could literally feel the love and care that went into them.

An old man crouched outside his hut, tying up a flowering vine that had come away from its stake. "Massa," he mumbled.

His eyes followed us resentfully as we walked past. I could feel other pairs of eyes watching from the dark, strong-smelling interiors of the huts. The hostility in the air made it hard to breathe.

I hoped Brice was wrong. I hoped the ghosts of the Taino weren't watching what Europeans were doing to their peaceful Land of Wood and Water. In just two hundred years, it had been turned into a hellhole.

I was finding Jamaica's dark side way too hard to handle. But I told myself I didn't have to handle it much longer.

Once I'd hooked up with Lola, we'd all be zooming back home.

I tried to make my voice sound casual. "Which hut is Lola's?"

Brice pointed. "Hurry. My uncle could come back any minute."

The path to Lola's hut was edged with rough scented grasses. I tore off a blade as I passed, inhaling its lemony perfume. I was nervous for no reason. *Lola's on your side, fool,* I reminded myself. Pretty soon this will all be over. This time tomorrow lover boy will have his memory back and we'll all be drinking hot chocolate at Guru.

The door to Lola's hut was open. Inside was a woven sleeping mat and an old cast-iron cooking pot. Balanced over the stewpot was a crudely shaped wooden spoon, carved out of some kind of gourd. It seemed that these three pitiful objects were the sum total of her possessions.

I remembered Brice arguing furiously with Mr Allbright about a week after he joined our history class. "Millions of human children are dying of hunger because rich countries couldn't care if they live or die! And the powers that be say we mustn't interfere with their free will! Well, that sucks! If you want humans to change, angels are going to have to make waves!"

I stared at that dented old stewpot and I wanted to make waves, like you would not believe. I wanted a humungous tidal wave to roll in and wash slavery from the face of the Earth for ever.

I was feeling electricky tingles, normally a sure sign that other celestial agents are in the area. The thought of seeing Lola was such a relief, I practically fell over myself to get to the rear of her hut.

A golden-skinned girl in a fraying head-tie was stretching up to peg a tattered cotton blouse on the line. She winced and clutched her side.

I ran forward. "Lola? Are you OK?"

She spun in terror then clutched her chest. "Miss! You frighten mi. Mi tink a bad duppy creep up when mi nah lookin'."

I felt confused. This girl looked like Lola, but she didn't sound or act like her.

Don't be stupid, Mel, who else could she be? I told myself quickly.

Yet something was off. Lollie and I normally hug, even if we've only been apart for like, *a day*. But I got the definite feeling that hugging would not be a wise move. My friend was keeping her eyes fixed stonily on the ground, as if she didn't want me to know what she was thinking.

That was another disturbing thing. Lola and I almost always do know what each other is thinking. Now she was completely shut down. I could just feel incredibly hostile vibes.

She's angry, I thought shakily. She thinks I abandoned her.

I swallowed. "You've had a terrible time," I said. "Did the overseer really beat you?"

"Mi belong Massa," Lola said in a sullen voice. "Massa can do what him like."

The soles of her bare feet were filthy from walking about the plantation without any shoes. She was wearing a shapeless old skirt and blouse in faded blue. The same sun-faded blue cotton I'd seen on Quashiba and Bright Eyes. Slave clothes.

I felt my heart contract. "Lollie, I swear, I've been ill, or I'd have come sooner."

"Mi hear 'bout dat," she said in her new singsong voice. "Lovey find you in di bush. Dey say you like to die."

My best friend sounded like she wouldn't have cared either way.

"Babe, drop the slave-talk, please!" I pleaded. "This isn't you."

Lola made a rude sound, like sucking spit through her teeth. "Nuttin wrong wid me, miss. You di one talkin' foolishness."

"Lola, LOOK at me!" I practically yelled at her.

My friend reluctantly met my eyes, and I felt as if I was falling through space. There was no warmth, no spark of recognition. Just pure hate.

"You really don't know who I am," I whispered.

Beau/Brice came up behind us, looking frazzled.

"I see you're up and about, Lola," he said in a falsely bright voice. "The pain isn't too bad today?"

Lola blushed. "No, Massa," she said. "Pain nah so bad today."

The two of them were being just a bit too careful not to look at each other. Brice and Lola might have lost their memories but they definitely hadn't lost their cosmic chemistry.

Their obvious attraction only made me feel worse.

I felt so alone, I can't tell you. I wanted to wake up in my room at school, and rush next door to Lola. I wanted to tell her about the horrible dream I just had where we were on a nightmare mission to Jamaica, but she'd somehow forgotten we were friends. I wanted to hear her say, "Poor you, babe! Dreams are SO weird!"

But my nightmare still went on. I turned and fled back to the house.

My aunt was sitting on her veranda, chewing furiously on a chunk of sugar cane. Beside her was a dish of mangled spat-out stalks. As I fled past, she called brightly, "Would you like to sample some, my dear! Sugar cane is so soothing to the nerves."

I looked at this woman who wept over dead birds while her husband tortured human slaves, and I wanted to despise her, but I knew she was as lonely and lost as her slaves.

I excused myself, saying I needed to rest. Then I shut myself in my room and threw myself on my bed. I was so upset I couldn't even cry. *What am I going to do?* I thought. *What am I going to DO?*

Somewhere between Heaven and Earth, something had happened to my friends; something which made them forget their true identities. Unlike yours truly, Lola and Brice had clearly read their cover stories. Now they believed they actually were these fictional humans. They were living their parts for real.

This mission was meant to get Brice back on his feet. Instead he and Lola had been ensnared in some dark game of seventeenth-century Consequences. White nephew of rich plantation owner meets fiesty slave-girl in steamy Jamaica. And the consequence was...

I was playing a lonely game of angels all by myself.

I truly don't think I have ever felt so alone. I won't lie to you, I could feel myself being sucked down into this like, total marsh of self-pity.

But then I did something that I think shows I'm starting to mature as a celestial trainee: I asked my inner angel for advice.

I sat down in the lotus position and closed my eyes. After a while I felt the familiar burning hot-potato sensation spreading through my chest. I don't see my inner angel. It's more like I could feel her vibes building up inside me. And this time I heard her voice as clear as a bell.

"Hi babe," Helix said. "Poor you! It must be scary, seeing your friends like this."

My eyes filled with tears. "It's so scary I can't tell you. It's like they've been hypnotised."

"Isn't it?" she agreed warmly. "Lola isn't a slave.

Brice isn't her master's nephew. It's just a story line some Agency scriptwriter thought up for them.

"I'm so confused, Helix. How come this kind of thing can happen to angels?"

"It's a bummer," she said. "The fact is, thoughts are incredibly powerful. On Earth, if you think something's true, it usually becomes true."

"For humans, yeah," I objected. "But we're supposed to know how this stuff works!"

"OK, OK, listen. Angels are immortal beings operating at v. intense energy levels, right?"

"Right," I agreed.

"Plus they have humungous thought power, agreed?"

I remembered how the angel preschoolers grew teeny baby trees in like, ten minutes flat. "Agreed," I said.

"Without their angel memories, Brice and Lola grabbed at what seemed to be reality. They're actually creating this whole scenario minute by minute. If they saw what was happening, they could step out into angelic reality just like that. But to them it feels like this *is* reality."

"Actually it kind of feels like reality to me too," I said miserably.

"I know, hon. So here's a teeny cosmic hint. If something makes you feel small, lost and hopeless, it probably isn't real!!"

Helix went on to tell me some other private angelic stuff, which I'm not supposed to share. After what seemed like blissful aeons of time, I opened my eyes.

It was amazing! I had bags of energy suddenly. All my self-pity had vanished, and I saw the whole thing with total clarity. And I knew now why I'd had to come on Brice's mission.

It was like that gruesome fairy story about the three blind old women, who had to share one eye between them.

I had to see for all of us. And I had to remember for all of us. But I couldn't do that if I got sucked into the illusion along with my friends. It seemed like Brice, Lola and I were trapped in separate movies. It even seemed like my soul-mate hated me. But these were just illusions.

Lola and I had a truly special bond. Even before we met, we were already connected. This connection was still there, even if Lola couldn't see or feel it. I just had to find a way to remind her. I had to find a way to help my best friend see through her fog of cosmic amnesia. I'd creep out after dark and go to her hut. Whatever it took to get through to Lola, I'd do.

Now that I had a plan, it seemed OK to have a little siesta.

When I woke up it was dark. I smoothed down my crumpled gown, put on my seventeenth-century cotton cap and little leather slippers and crept out of the house.

Stars sparkled high above the plantation. Some of the stars were so tiny they were just scatters of glitter dust. Crickets sang their metallic 'sweet-sweet' song from every tree and bush, like a chorus of tiny bicycle bells. And I became aware of another faint, thrilling sound vibrating through the night like a heartbeat. A faraway beating of drums.

As I got nearer to the slave quarters, I saw the flicker of cooking fires through the palms. I could hear voices murmuring, sounding warm and intimate in the dark. I felt all the fine hairs rise on the back of my neck. The Bexfords had a piece of Africa, right here in their back yard; a living, breathing, stolen piece of Africa. A three-year-old child would know how precious this was. Yet the Bexfords and their kind had no idea.

I had to pinch myself. "You're in Jamaica, Melanie..." I whispered. "You're in Jamaica, listening to African slaves talking in the dark."

I can't explain why, exactly, but I felt like I was supposed to be here. I felt, I don't know, *honoured*. I glanced up at the stars, and for a moment I had a dizzy sense of being part of that vast shimmery totally mysterious pattern.

I must have been invisible standing in the shadowy coconut grove, because two figures sped softly past me without even noticing I was there. It was Brice and Lola! "What on earth?" I gasped.

I raced after them, trying not to trip over my stupid gown, and finally caught them up in the stables.

A lighted lantern made a pool of weak yellowish light. A horse was nervously shifting its hooves on the straw. I saw the whites of its eyes gleaming. Brice was murmuring soothing words as he adjusted the saddle.

"What's going on?" I said breathlessly.

My friends froze guiltily. I could see Lola's pulse beating in her throat. I could smell hay and horses, and the strong-smelling coconut oil she used on her hair.

"Mi tell you dat white girl bring trouble!" she hissed to Brice as if I wasn't there. "She tell Ole Massa for sure!"

"Who am I? The secret police?" I said angrily. "Don't be stupid. I'm not going to tell anyone."

It might be an illusion, but Lola's hostility was really hard to take.

Brice fastened the girth on the nervous horse. "We're leaving this place."

"I'd sort of worked that out," I said. "Where are you running to?"

"Don' tell her, Massa!" Lola cried. "Ole Massa set dogs on wi."

I took several deep breaths. "I'm not your enemy. I won't tell. You don't have to be scared of me, OK?"

The sound of drumming was getting louder, as if the wind had suddenly changed. A horse whickered from its stall.

Lola shot me a look, half scared, half triumphant. "Mi nah scared a you!" she said. "Young Massa buy wi freedom. He buy all wi freedom!"

I was stunned. "He's going to free you ALL?"

"Just our slaves at first," Brice explained. "There's a place up in the hills. People call it

Cockpit country. Hundreds of runaway slaves live up there."

Isn't that incredible. Brice couldn't remember his name or heavenly address. He certainly had no memory of the Agency. Yet he had made up his mind to save slaves single-handed. It's like he *knew* he was supposed to be on a mission. He'd just forgotten he didn't have to do it alone.

If this had been the normal Brice I could have reasoned with him. I could have said, "You tried that rescue-trip before and it got you into deep poo." Brice's previous rescue attempt ended in a long and gruesome exile in the Hell dimensions, where he only survived by doing freelance work for a number of Dark agencies.

But the Beau Bexford Brice didn't know about Hell dimensions or warring cosmic agencies. He was saving the world, the only way he knew how. So I stuck to basics. "Where are you going to get that kind of money?"

"You don't need to worry about that," he said cagily.

Please, please say he isn't planning a robbery, I prayed. I didn't think the Agency would be too thrilled if Brice robbed a bank, even if his motives were *really* pristine. For once I didn't have to think about what to do next.

"I want to go with you!" I said in a bright voice. "I think what you're both doing is, erm, amazing and I want to help."

Lola did her rude tooth-sucking sound. "It look like three people can sit on dat poor lickle horse to you?"

"Then steal two horses, girlfriend," I said. "I'm coming and that's final."

Brice shook his head. "I can't let you do that. I couldn't guarantee your safety."

"I don't care," I said stubbornly. "I'm coming."

Lola was scowling horribly. No way did she want me on their romantic trip! "Tie her to a coconut tree! Massa nah find her till mawnin'."

Illusion or not, Lola's attitude was really getting under my skin. I flashed my sweetest smile. "You tie me up, babe, and I'll scream the place down, and you'll have that whole slavering-hunting-dogs scenario you're anxious to avoid."

Well, I wasn't trying to win a popularity contest. I was following the first law of angelic teamwork. Keep your team together at ALL times.

You need me, I told them silently. I'm your seeing-eye angel.

Perhaps my cosmic vibes got through to him, because Brice reluctantly saddled a second horse. Lola was visibly fuming. Instead of riding with the handsome Young Massa, she was stuck with me.

"Where are we going by the way?" I asked her as we spurred our horses into the night.

Lola's answer gave me the chills.

"Port Royal," she snarled. "Di wickedest city on Earth!"

CHAPTER SIX

Early next morning, we were riding single file through a misty river gorge. Ladders of sunlight slanted down through the mist. Now and then I had to push aside lush tangles of vines that hung down like curtains. A bird called the same two-note song over and over. It felt like we were all alone at the green dawn of the world.

Well, if it wasn't for the vibes. I'm serious! It's a miracle I didn't break out in blisters! As the morning went on, I genuinely started to wonder if my best friend was plotting to poison me. Lola kept stopping to pick stinky plants she spotted by the track.

"Dis herb good for mi skin, Massa," she'd tell Brice, stuffing some obscene hairy root in her bag. And she'd shoot him this intimate smile. Sometimes she'd tell him it was a herb that would make her hair shine, or whiten her teeth, the scheming little minx. When Brice wasn't looking, she'd dart spiteful looks at me. Like: "You better not cross me, girl, or I'll put these little babies in your stew!"

I was relieved when Brice said we were breaking our journey in a place called Spanish Town. It was getting hot, plus my angelic backside was SO sore. This wasn't really so surprising. My previous horse-riding experience was basically nil.

In Spanish Town a huge street market was in full swing. Old ladies in vividly-coloured head-ties squatted in the shade beside heaps of yams, bananas and sweet potatoes, pots, pans and bales of cloth, singing out to passers-by.

This was the first real town I'd seen since I'd arrived. A little girl ran alongside trying to sell us some freshly-picked oranges. Brice threw her some coins and we rode along, slurping at the greenish-skinned fruit.

"Why's this called Spanish Town?" I asked in a juicy voice.

"The English captured Jamaica from the Spanish," Brice explained. "It's the perfect base for attacking foreign ships."

I was shocked. "Isn't that piracy?"

He grinned. "Piracy is exactly what it is."

"Sorry, I don't believe you," I said primly. "I can't believe the government would encourage pirates."

He laughed out loud. "Why not? The government gets the loot!"

I could feel Lola fidgeting sulkily behind me. I was always trying to include her, but she totally refused to join any conversation I was a part of. The bottom line was: I wasn't meant to be there.

We stopped at an inn on the outskirts and seated ourselves at an outdoor table in the leafy shade of a passion-fruit vine. A slave-girl brought us our breakfast. She looked genuinely shocked to see two white people sitting at the same table as their slave.

Brice and Lola spent the meal whispering to each other. I didn't want to be a gooseberry, so I concentrated on trying to find something I could eat. It was a somewhat weird breakfast, I have to say. The stewed goat looked really stringy, plus there was this evil Jamaican green vegetable that someone had boiled to a slimy pulp. The coconut cake seemed the safest bet. Dry but quite edible, washed down with a beaker of fresh cane juice.

While we ate, a vulture circled lazily overhead in a cloudless blue sky.

Lola shook her fist. "G'way!" she threatened. "You nah get dinner today, John Crow!"

How did Lola KNOW this stuff? I wondered.

My friend had lived in seventeenth-century Jamaica for less than ten days. But when she hummed to herself, she sang authentic slave tunes! She knew which local plants made your hair shiny. She even knew how to tie a head-tie, African-style. And Brice knew all about sugar mills and pirates and stealing horses. It's like my friends had plugged into some cosmic equivalent of the Discovery Channel!

I was still puzzling over this when Brice went off to get supplies. The minute he was out of sight, Lola let me have it.

My Lola has a real way with words. But this Lola came out with stuff that made your eyes water. Even when she was insulting you she talked sheer poetry. Lola told me that young Massa Bexford might be taken in by my sweet innocent manner but she'd had me totally figured from day one.

According to her, I was a little gold-digger determined to get my hooks into my rich cousin. I know! She was convinced I wanted to marry him for his inheritance! According to Lola, also, I was just pretending to care about slaves. White people were all the same, purely out for themselves.

Let me tell you the really disturbing thing. By the time Lola had finished with me I'd started to think she was right. Being white was starting to seem like a really unpleasant disease. I literally felt like I might be emanating a pale poisonous glow. Purely by walking round inside my skin, I was a living advertisement for Evil.

If I'd been human, I think I'd have crawled into some dark hole and died of shame. Lola was meant to be my best friend but she couldn't even see me. It totally broke my heart that Lola couldn't see the real me hurting inside.

I know! It's embarrassing. She's the slave, yet I want *her* to pity me, the poor misunderstood white girl!

I had to shut my eyes to stop the tears from falling.

My inner angel had just been waiting for the chance to put a stop to all this nonsense. A message flashed up on my mental screen: *A soul-mate's colours shine through no matter what.* Lola's parting words.

I felt all the stress drain out through the soles of my feet. Lola wasn't a slave. I was not an evil white-skinned devil. None of this was real. We're just angels, I thought. Angels passing through.

I was so relieved to be back in angelic reality that I was smiling through my tears.

Lola gave a scornful snort. "You laugh like stupid! But you don' know nuttin! You don' even know why we goin' to Port Royal. But Massa tell me. Massa tell mi everyting!"

Poor girl. She was so desperate to prove that the young Massa loved her best that she blurted out the whole plan.

It was complete madness. The whole enterprise depended on Brice selling a treasure map he'd acquired from a pirate called Bermuda Jack, in return for a bottle of rum. This wasn't your regular treasure map, mind you. It was a map leading to an ancient Indian city. A city made of pure gold. I *know*! You couldn't make it up!!

"Massa get a heap a gold for dis map," Lola said proudly. "A whole heap a gold."

"Why are we talking about gold?" Brice had come up behind her.

Lola almost wet herself with shock. She backed away from him, guiltily. "Mi nah want to tell her, Massa. She drag it outa me!"

It's OK, I didn't take it personally. Now I was back in angel mode, I understood exactly where she was coming from. Reuben and I were slaves once in ancient Rome, but unlike Lola, we knew we were undercover angels. If things had been different, who knows how we'd have behaved?

"I'm not angry," Brice consoled her. "I was planning to tell my cousin everything anyway."

And once we were back on the road to Port Royal, my angel buddy told me the whole crazy story.

Brice hadn't bought a map from a pirate. He'd bought HALF a map. Obviously that made me feel much better.

Bermuda Jack had told Brice that if he reached Port Royal before the Christmas breeze stopped blowing, he'd find the owner of the map's missing half staying at a certain tavern in Port Royal. "Jack said she'd give me hundreds of Spanish doubloons for my half," he said eagerly.

"The other owner is a lady?" I said in surprise.

Brice grinned. "A very beautiful lady, by all accounts."

Lola made a noise that sounded exactly like ripping velcro.

"And is the Christmas breeze still blowing?"

He gestured at the palm trees busily clicking their fronds. "It'll blow for a few days yet."

"I hate to be dense," I said. "But why didn't Jack sell his half of the map and pocket the doubloons."

"Oh, he says it's cursed. But that's just superstition," Brice said casually.

See what I mean about that boy? Just as I'm thinking things can't get much crazier, he throws in a curse!

"Naturally, the Taino wanted to discourage Europeans from plundering their sacred golden city," he explained, "so they spread all these stories to warn them off."

"Wait – slow down! This city is SACRED?"

Brice looked shifty. "Allegedly."

"Personally I'm wondering if this Indian city even existed," I said. "Maybe the Taino were just having a laugh?"

"My map is genuine," Brice said confidently.

"But how can you be sure?"

He pulled a crackly piece of parchment out of his shirt. The map fragment was badly scorched at the edges as if it had been rescued from a fire in the nick of time. And the sinister spattering of faded brownish splodges was almost certainly a trail of human bloodstains.

But at the top in shaky script was a name that set my heart racing.

Coyaba, City of the Gods.

I'd never heard of this city before, yet when I saw the name, about a zillion angel volts went off inside my head and, like Brice, I knew this was the real thing.

But that just made it worse. I had the definite feeling that Heaven's favourite bad boy was getting in way over his head.

Someone had to make him see sense before he did something we'd all regret. Someone like me.

"Erm, hate to be a party pooper, but if this map is for real, it's incredibly precious. What if this lady in Port Royal is just like all those other Europeans, purely out for herself. Don't you think it's a bit dodgy giving her directions to an ancient golden city? Do you really think the Taino would want her to have their gold?"

Lola gave me a poisonous look. "Massa don' business wid dead people gold," she flashed. "Massa just wan' set wi free."

"But it doesn't belong to him, Lola! Hello! The *City of the Gods*?! Trust me, if you let pirates loose on a sacred Taino city, that could have really dark consequences!"

Brice was glaring at me now. "Slavery also has dark consequences. The Taino are dead. I'm more concerned with the sufferings of the living."

Lola gave me a triumphant smile.

I probably should have left it, but something niggled at the edges of my mind.

"I don't totally understand what you need all these doubloons for," I said to Brice. "Why do you need so much cash?"

"Guns and ammunition are expensive," he said coolly.

My jaw dropped. "Guns and—"

"The rebel slaves deserve all the help we can give, don't you think?"

No need to check Agency policy on this one. I opened my mouth twice, then shut it for good. I didn't feel up to explaining to Brice why this was such a bad idea.

We rode on to Port Royal in a rather strained silence. I tried reminding myself that I was an angel on a mission, but I felt more like a tin can that had accidentally got attached to a v. hyperactive dog. I was supposed to be working on a brilliant strategy to get my friends back to Heaven. Instead I was being dragged helplessly from one insanely complicated situation to the next.

We trotted along the bumpy potholed road, under palm trees waving graceful fronds in the tropical breeze. The sun was hot. The sky was blue. But my heart felt as heavy as lead. I don't know how far it was to Port Royal, but it felt like a long way in that atmosphere, believe me. Gradually the lush vegetation of inland Jamaica was replaced with dry-looking scrub and cacti. By late afternoon I smelled salt on the breeze. Minutes later we rode into a little settlement known as Passage Fort, where we were to get the ferry to Port Royal.

We had to leave the horses at the town's one tavern.

"No horses, mules or horse-drawn carriages are allowed in Port Royal," Brice told us. "The city is barely half a mile wide and extremely densely populated. You will notice the buildings are unusually tall. The city folk soon ran out of building land, and since they couldn't build outwards, they built upwards instead!"

We hurried down to the harbour just as the sun was starting to set. Besides us, there were two other passengers, a nervous white merchant and his very handsome young slave. The slave was hopefully checking Lola out, but she only had eyes for the young Massa.

I really enjoyed that boat trip actually. We passed tiny uninhabited islands looking exactly like tropical islands you see in cartoons.

We were halfway to Port Royal when we heard an appalling ruckus floating across the water. Pistols firing, bells ringing, drunken voices singing and squabbling in every language under the sun, drums beating, whistles blowing. I thought some mad carnival was going on, but Brice said this was normal for Port Royal. With a flash of fear I remembered that Lola had called it the "wickedest city on Earth".

The dock was unbelievably crowded. The moment we got off the boat there was this total stampede. Rough humans of both sexes rushed at us, yelling threateningly in our faces, poking and prodding at us, mostly trying to sell us stuff we didn't want.

This was a city where pirates basically ruled. Its lanes and alleyways swarmed with buccaneers of all colours and nationalities. It even *smelled* wicked. The streets literally stank like they'd been marinaded in Jamaican rum! Just about every other building was a pirate tavern, a gambling den, or a "punch-house". Lola looked disturbed when she saw the punch-house girls with their plunging bodices and crudely made-up faces.

In a street behind the Turtle Market, we passed a gun shop, where pistols were laid out on black velvet like a lady's jewels. A drunken pirate suddenly pushed his face into mine, making kissing noises. He was quite old and his leathery face was seamed with scars.

Lola flew between us and gave him a massive thump in the chest.

"G'way, you boldface devil, you!" she said fiercely. "You tink dis nice girl business wid you! Tcha!"

He slunk away mumbling apologies.

"Thanks, Lola," I said gratefully.

Lola just gave me one of her looks. Like, "You think I *want* to be your babysitter?"

"Do try to look as if you know where you're going," Brice sighed.

On the other side of the street, a pirate dressed in silks and velvets, was stopping passers-by at gunpoint, challenging them to a drinking contest from a barrel of Jamaican rum!

I scurried after Lola and Brice. "And do we? Know where we're going?" I asked nervously.

Brice said we were looking for a tavern called Diego's Whiskers. Naturally, I thought he was kidding. But Brice assured me the name was for real; Diego had been a notorious Spanish pirate who finally got blown to pieces by English buccaneers.

"What was so special about Diego's whiskers?" I asked. "Did they glow in the dark or something?"

Brice grinned. "English seamen are always boasting about singeing their enemies' facial hair," he said. "It's the ultimate insult!"

He seemed more like the old Brice now we'd left the plantation. He seemed thrilled with himself, to be honest: setting off to do a nefarious deal with a mysterious lady, a bloodstained treasure map in his pocket, and an adoring slave-girl by his side.

However, I was getting twitchy. I reckoned it would be dark in about five minutes max. We're talking Jamaican darkness, right? Five short minutes before the streets of dilapidated high-rise tenements turned into inky black canyons. This thought seemed to occur to my friends at approximately the same moment. No one actually mentioned lurking robbers or cut-throats but everyone suddenly picked up the pace.

Brice led us down an extremely evil-smelling alley, running parallel to the waterfront. I could hear the hollow sloshing of waves against wooden piers and the rhythmic creaking of ships' timbers.

We hurried along, scattering pigs and chickens in our haste to get under a roof before nightfall. Brice peered at an inn sign in the gathering dusk. It was peppered with bullet holes and totally impossible to read, but he strode through the door of the tavern without a second's hesitation. Amnesia or no amnesia, the bad-boy radar was functioning as well as ever!

Brice glanced around the crowded bar, nodded matily at the landlord and, without breaking stride, ducked through a door marked PRIVATE.

Lola and I beetled after him, not wanting to be left alone with the pervy old sea dogs who formed Diego's select clientele.

We found ourselves in a long, low room with dark wooden beams. The air was thick with rum and tobacco fumes. A dozen ferocious seafaring-types were yelling at each other through the fog. They'd obviously been drinking heavily for hours, if not days. Every person in this room had an opinion and every person was bellowing his opinion at the top of his lungs, backing it up by hammering his fist or the barrel of his pistol on the table.

But the most opinionated person in that room was actually a girl. A booze-swilling, pistol-toting girl, it's true. But still a girl, no more than sixteen years old.

She had her back to me, so I couldn't tell if she was really beautiful, like people said, but it was obvious she had great style. Her rustling skirts of crimson silk were looped up to reveal creamy lace petticoats and boots of gorgeous Spanish leather. Her shiny black hair had been oiled like a flamenco dancer's and swept up with combs. Rubies and sapphires twinkled on the pirate girl's fingers and swung sparkling from her ears.

Brice coughed. "Sirs, madam?" he said politely. "May I enquire – if this is the right place?"

Ten pirates' hands drew ten swords with a thrilling clash of steel. The eleventh pirate snatched up a chair, aiming it menacingly at Brice's head. He was growling, literally growling like a dog.

The girl started to laugh, a wild tipsy laugh. "You've come to the right place, sir – for a fight!"

She swung to face us, still laughing.

My heart almost stopped. I *knew* this girl!

"Cat!" I breathed. "Cat Darcy?"

I knew this was impossible. Shakespeare's girlfriend would have to be over a hundred and twenty years old by now!

"I am Mariah Darcy," the pirate girl said haughtily. "Catherine Darcy was my grandmother. Who are you, miss? And why do you burst in on our private soiree?"

Brice stepped forward. "I have something in my possession that I was told would interest you."

Mariah gave one of her wild laughs. "Oho! You've been speaking to Bermuda Jack!" She gestured imperiously to her men. "Sheathe your swords! Caleb, stop that ridiculous growling, put down the chair and tell the landlord to bring more rum! These people are our guests."

I was still reeling from the bizarre cosmic coincidence. I could NOT believe we'd bumped into Cat's granddaughter!

She could almost be Cat's double, I thought wonderingly.

Angels aren't meant to get involved with their humans, but on our mission to Elizabethan England, Lola and I developed a genuine affection for Cat Darcy. It was a relief to know she'd eventually found love and had a family. No guy could have measured up to Will Shakespeare obviously. But she'd survived their break-up and made a new life for herself and that was really good news.

But as I gazed at Cat's seventeenth-century descendant, I started to wonder if I was seeing things. I was picking up tiny lightning flashes every time Mariah laughed. Lola seemed equally baffled.

Finally I caught on. At one stage in her pirate career Mariah had lost an eyetooth, and a diamond had been wired into the gap.

Coo-er, I thought. The piracy bizz must be paying really well.

I thought Cat's pirate dad would probably be really proud if he could see his stylish great-granddaughter carrying on the family tradition.

These are the kinds of moments I usually share with Lola, and I instinctively turned to smile at her, but she just blanked me and turned away.

I bravely pulled myself together. One day we'll laugh at this, babe, I told my friend silently. And that's a promise.

It was past three in the morning and the candles at Diego's had almost burned down to tiny stumps.

The remains of a huge pirate feast were scattered over the table. Oyster shells, gnawed pork ribs, the heads of giant prawns. But the drinking went on and on. And Beau Bexford and Mariah found more and more in common.

"Each of us is a freedom fighter in our different ways! Freedom is the most important thing in life, don't you agree?" The pirate girl had been licking pork grease from her fingers, but she stopped to give Brice an intimate smile.

Brice threw down a shot of rum and yelled, "To freedom!"

Mariah let out a wild yodel. "Aye! To freedom!"

Those pirates who could still stand, jumped to their feet and knocked back more slugs of fiery white rum. "To freedom!" they roared.

The pirate girl sat back down, showing lacy petticoats. "Only the souls of outlaws are truly free," she announced. "That's why the world hates us! Isn't that true, men?"

And the other pirates cheered and pounded their fists on the table until the wooden planks vibrated like a drum.

I don't know why, but while you were with Mariah Darcy, you forgot to ask really obvious questions. Like, are you sure that's why people hate you? Are you sure it isn't because you hack off their limbs with cutlasses? Plus the robbing and pillaging might put people off!

It sounds ridiculous, I know, but that night not a word of criticism entered my head. To be honest with you, I admired Mariah to the point of total and utter envy. She had it all. Beauty, brains, her own ship. Plus a loyal band of followers to do her bidding. (No, really! Some of them were quite cute in an unwashed Hell's Angels kind of way!)

At a time when a girl's career options often consisted of being locked away in a convent, or dying hideously in childbirth, this girl had the entire Caribbean ocean for her playground.

What I envied most of all was Mariah Darcy's confidence. You just knew she didn't stay awake at nights, beating herself up over some stupid little mistake. Mariah answered to no one but herself.

And as the night went on, the pirate girl revealed a softer side. OK, so she was a bit woozy from the rum, but she seemed genuinely inspired by Brice's desire to help his father's slaves. She fished her half of the map out of her blouse, and she and Brice placed their two halves side by side so you could see how exactly they fitted.

"Let me tell you something," she slurred. "I could retire from piracy tomorrow, if it was gold I craved."

My buddy's eyes glinted. "Isn't it?"

She shook her head. "I have pots of gold," she boasted. "Crates and barrels full of gold. Gold means nothing to me. What I crave, Mr Bexford, is adventure!"

"Oh really," he said politely. "I thought it was freedom."

She wagged her finger. "Now now, sir! Let's not quibble over words! My point is, like you, I detest all forms of slavery. That's why I'm declining your offer! I've decided NOT to buy your half of the map."

Brice looked confused. "I see. Naturally it's yours to do—"

"I haven't finished, Mr Bexford! I propose, sir, that you and I mount a joint expedition to find this city. Any gold we find will be used to resettle your unhappy slaves." Mariah leaned forward. "What do you say?"

Omigosh how thrilling, I thought excitedly. Say yes!

I know! I was totally caught up in the moment. One night with pirates and my angelic scruples go right out the window!

Brice would have made a great poker player. I could NOT have told you what that boy was thinking. We were all holding our breath, except for Lola, who seemed to be struggling to stay awake.

"What is your answer, Mr Bexford?" Mariah's voice had a bit of an edge this time.

Brice pushed back his chair so dramatically that I truly thought he was going to storm out. "I say we drink another toast," he said coolly. "I accept your generous proposal, Miss Darcy."

Mariah let out a piercing yodel of triumph. The pirates whistled and stomped their feet to show their approval. One of the pirates produced a fiddle and started to play a sea shanty. Another pirate picked up some silver spoons and beat out a lively rhythm.

Brice bowed to Mariah. She took his hand, laughing her tipsy laugh, and they swung each other recklessly around the room as the other pirates clapped and whistled.

I was in complete pirate mode by this time as you know, and I really fancied boogieing with a pirate myself. Unfortunately Lola was almost falling asleep in her chair.

"Come on girlfriend," I sighed. "Time for some beauty sleep."

Brice had rented us two rooms for the night. My friend was so out of it that she let me support her as far as the door, then she shrugged me off.

The music had switched into something fiery and Spanish. I glanced back wistfully and saw Brice and

Mariah doing a lot of stamping and sexy peacock-type strutting. Two outlaws closing their deal in true outlaw style.

Who'd have imagined our maverick buddy would end up going into partnership with Cat Darcy's pirate granddaughter! In my wildest fantasies I couldn't come up with something like that.

I felt a flicker of excitement. *Mel, this is WAY too karmic to be a coincidence*, I told myself. OK, the Agency couldn't have known for sure, but they must have allowed for this mind-blowing possibility in their cosmic calculations.

And suddenly I was flooded with relief.

Omigosh, I thought, *this was meant to happen! I'm NOT a failure! We were supposed to come to Port Royal and hook up with Mariah.*

It totally didn't matter that I still hadn't managed to figure out a way to get my friends home. My friends weren't supposed to go home, because – omigosh, omigosh! – despite everything, we were still totally on track for Brice's HALO award!!!

I wanted to yodel like a sexy pirate girl. Instead I stood at the top of the stairs, fanning myself frantically, trying to absorb this amazingly good news.

Finally I'd calmed down enough to go into our room.

When I walked in, Lola muttered something I didn't catch and went on carefully pouring water into a cracked china bowl.

I have to say Diego's Whiskers wasn't exactly four-star accommodation. The bed curtains were visibly mouldy (euw!), and there were tiny lizards glued to the walls, looking like bizarre ornaments.

My friend leaned over the bowl to wash her face. Suddenly I saw something glint in the candlelight. My heart practically flew into my mouth. It was Lola's angel tags!

This was my chance.

Say something, Mel, I told myself. *Say something NOW.*

I cleared my throat. "Lola, this is going to sound like I'm making it up, but please hear me out, OK?"

I tried to explain what had happened in terms a seventeenth-century slave-girl could relate to, deliberately avoiding words like "Heaven" and "angel". If I hit her with the heavenly terminology right off, she'd think I was a nutter. So I just reminded my friend that the three of us came from a place where nobody went hungry and everything was free. In this wonderful country, slavery didn't exist.

"But something happened to you and Brice, erm Beau, on the way here," I explained. "Something that made you forget who you really are."

Lola yawned like a sleepy little cat. "Mi nah forget nuttin. You da one who confuse. You all di time talkin' wild-wild."

"I can prove it," I said eagerly. "When we leave our home to go travelling, we wear these." I showed Lola my tags. "See? They're exactly like yours."

She pulled a face. "Tcha! You can buy dem kinda ting in any slave market in Jamaica."

I was so disappointed. Whatever Lola was seeing, she wasn't seeing the same object. I could see she was completely exhausted so I let it go for the time being.

There was only one double bed in our room. Lola was all set to sleep on the floor, but I managed to persuade her we could share.

Before she went to sleep, my friend wrapped her sheet around her face and upper body. I guess she wanted to protect her face from prying eyes (mine) while she was sleeping. But it left her feet bare and vulnerable. I noticed a woven friendship bracelet around one ankle and felt my eyes fill with tears. I had made that bracelet for Lola one lazy afternoon in Heaven, a few weeks after we met.

I lay awake for a long time, listening to my soul-mate breathing softly inside her private cocoon. I could hear fiddle music and roars of laughter coming from downstairs. Plus some kind of drunken ruckus seemed to be going on in the alley outside.

After a few minutes I got up and wedged a chair under the door handle. Then I went back to bed and slept like a baby.

I must have gone back to Heaven in my dreams, because when I woke next morning, everything seemed clear. A little too clear, actually.

I had to giggle into my pillow so as not to wake my sleeping friend.

I couldn't believe I'd wanted to run off with the pirates! *Some angel you are, Mel Beeby!* I scolded myself.

After my sleep, I felt totally connected to the higher angelic realms. For once in my life, I knew exactly what I was going to do. I pictured myself walking down the corridor and knocking on

Brice's door. I pictured him appearing in the doorway with a wondering expression.

The true Brice was getting closer to the surface. I'd seen it in his eyes yesterday. If I went while I was zinging with angelic energy, I wouldn't have to worry about finding words. He'd look into my face and it would be like a light switching on. This bizarre illusion would vanish like a mirage and Brice would remember who and what he really was.

I knelt on our bed and peeped through the slatted window at the alley below. A drunken pirate sprawled face-down in the dirt. I couldn't see his face but I didn't think he was one of Mariah's. Chickens were carefully pecking around him. They probably saw this kind of thing all the time.

Do it Mel, I told myself.

I tiptoed out of our room in my petticoat and bare feet.

The door to Brice's room was wide open. A slave-girl was sweeping the floor, raising clouds of dust. Sunshine streamed through the window slats making the tiny dust specks dance in the light.

"Where's Mr Bexford?" I asked in dismay.

She shrugged. "Massa gone long time."

Brice had left while we were still sleeping.

He must have run off with Mariah Darcy to find Coyaba, City of the Gods.

CHAPTER SEVEN

Lola sat on the edge of the bed clutching her raggedy bag full of smelly poisonous plants. She was shivering. She just went on sitting there shivering and staring emptily into space. After a while the bag slipped to the floor but she didn't seem to notice.

Two tiny lizards, no bigger than children's hairgrips, unglued themselves from the walls and skittered over to look at her in concern. They looked at me too, as if they were waiting for me to do something. But I just stood in the middle of the room, feeling useless.

What do you say to a runaway slave-girl when

the one white person she trusted abandons her without a word?

I was bitterly disappointed. I had put myself through the wringer to help Brice. Well, that jerk had just thrown away his last chance. And let's face it, he had had the MOST last chances.

No more sympathy for you, mister, I thought grimly. *You have blown it, totally.*

Being mad with Brice was quite therapeutic, but it didn't actually solve anything. In addition to her cosmic amnesia, my soul-mate was now utterly traumatised. To cap it all, we were stranded in Port Royal with absolutely no cash.

Mel Beeby, you are out of your depth with this one, I thought miserably. *Michael offers to send in a SWAT team, but oh no. You have to know best.*

The teeny lizards had skittered up one of the mildewed bed curtains. They clung there side by side, watching me and Lola with their beady bright eyes.

I was so upset, I went a bit mad. I started talking to the lizards in my head.

"Got any ideas?" I asked them miserably. "I'm not proud, you know. All suggestions gratefully received, believe me."

An ugly little bug flew past. Lizard Number One shot out its tongue and – bosh! – the bug was gone. Lizard Number Two went pattering down the curtain and across the floor. I thought it was hunting for an ugly bug of its own, but it kept pattering along until it reached my clothes. I'd dropped them in a heap the night before.

The lizard zoomed up the heap and froze dramatically at the top. You could almost hear it saying, "Ta-da!"

When I saw what it was standing *on*, I almost screamed. Can you believe I'd forgotten that purse?! A purse FULL of jewellery!

Omigosh, Melanie, I thought, *everything's going to be OK!*

Don't get me wrong. Jewels wouldn't mend Lola's broken heart. It wasn't the jewels that were making me so excited.

It was knowing I wasn't alone. I'd forgotten that really crucial heavenly messages always get through – via a lizard if necessary!

Of course, now that I'd remembered I was an angel, I was able to see my situation in a different way.

I felt a rush of shame as I realised I'd been doing exactly what angels are not supposed to do. I had judged our angel buddy without knowing the facts.

The fact is, Melanie, you DON'T know what happened last night, I reminded myself. *OK, it looks like Brice has gone back to his bad old ways. It also looks like Lola and I aren't friends. And that's SO not true.*

At that moment my friend looked up. "What mi do?" she asked in a trembling voice. "Mi cyan go back to Fruitful Vale. Mi cyan stay in dis wicked place. What mi do?"

I couldn't believe it. My friend was talking to me! She had actually asked for my help.

I didn't care that she didn't know who I was. I was much too grateful. *Don't blow this Melanie*, I told myself shakily.

This was the breakthrough I'd been waiting for.

I daringly sat down beside my traumatised friend. "It's going to be all right," I told her softly. "If your master went off without you, there's probably a good reason. Probably he thought it would be too dangerous."

Lola stared at me as if I'd started talking in Martian. "Too dangerous for me? Too dangerous for ME, a slave!" Then she completely exploded.

"Nuttin safe for slaves, NUTTIN!" Her face was quivering with rage and distress.

I was scared I was going to cry. Lola and I were only inches apart, yet there was this howling chasm between us. I wanted to make all her pain and suffering go away, but I didn't know how.

I groped blindly for words. "I know I don't understand what it's like to be a sl—"

Lola covered her face with her hands. I could hear gasping sounds.

The tiny soul-mate lizards were back on the wall, looking like they'd never moved. I got the feeling they were still watching. In a funny way those little lizards gave me courage.

I reached out to touch my friend, lost my nerve and pulled back. Tears spilled down my face.

"I'll never understand, will I?" I wept. "Oh, but Lola, I do *want* to."

My martial arts teacher says sometimes the hardest thing in the Universe is just to stay still. He says when we stop trying to fix everything and just stay still, we leave a space for miracles to happen.

Well that morning at Diego's, when Lola finally decided to trust me, I stayed still. Sometimes I wanted to run out of the room in pure horror at the things she was telling me. But I didn't. I didn't try to comfort her or make her feel better. I didn't try to make it into *my* story by nervously interrupting to explain that all white people weren't monsters. I just sat totally still and listened and it was truly the hardest thing I have ever done.

Lola wasn't really a slave, but I knew the things she was telling me were really true. And so I listened, not just with my ears, but with my whole hurting angel heart.

There was one time, though, when I wasn't able to keep quiet.

In a wistful voice, Lola was telling me how different Young Massa was to his uncle. Young Massa treated her with respect, not like pervy old Josiah, blatantly paying visits to the slave-women's huts at night.

"Ever see dem lickle yella-skin pickney runnin' round di plantation?" my friend asked abruptly. "Bright Eyes and dem?"

I figured "yella-skin pickney" meant "light-skinned children" and quickly nodded.

Lola gave me a meaningful look.

I was horrified. "You're not serious! Bright Eyes is old Master Bexford's little girl?"

"An' Jewel an' Precious." Lola gave a bleak little shrug. "Precious gone now. Ole Massa sell her las' month."

I had to wrap my arms around myself so as not to feel the ache inside. I thought of a slave mother choosing the most beautiful names she knew. I thought of her having to stand by helplessly as her master sold their little daughter like you'd sell a puppy. And I understood why Brice thought he had to buy the guns and ammunition.

When Lola finally stopped talking, it wasn't because she'd run out of stories, it was pure exhaustion.

I poured water into the bowl and washed my face. After checking carefully for lizards, I started struggling into my seventeenth-century clothes.

Lola looked stricken. "You go leave now, miss?"

I gave her a tired grin. "No babe, I'm taking you to breakfast."

It was more peaceful than you'd think in the courtyard at Diego's. The high walls kept out most of the street noise. Only sporadic gunshots in the distance reminded me we were in pirate territory. We were sitting in the shade of an old mango tree. Sunlight filtered through star-shaped leaves sending starry patterns flitting across our faces.

It was more like brunch than breakfast. It was past midday, but we seemed to be the only guests up and about. We didn't talk much. I think we both felt like limp rags. When we'd finished our roast breadfruit and ackee and saltfish, the girl came to see if we wanted anything else.

I had a sudden longing for something sweet. "I don't suppose you have hot chocolate?" I asked impulsively.

The hot chocolate at Diego's was so thick you practically had to eat it with a spoon. It smelled of nutmeg and cinnamon and something I couldn't place.

I kept catching Lola looking at me with a baffled expression. It was the same way she'd looked at me that day we first met in Heaven. Like she was thinking, who IS this girl?

I cleared my throat. "That place I told you about? We drink hot chocolate there all the time."

She gave me a wan smile. "Dey have streets pave wid gold in dat place too? Girl-chile, you always talkin' wild!"

"We're friends there," I insisted. "And no one thinks it's strange."

My friend sighed. "Dat place sound nice. Mi have a dream 'bout a place like dat."

I grabbed her hand. "Lola, I swear to you. It wasn't a dream!"

She shook her head vehemently. "Mi wake in dat stinking lickle hut, all bruise an' mash-up from Massa's beating. An' mi know dat other place not real."

I didn't ask Lola any more about her dream of Heaven. It was too painful for both of us.

And even if I could get a message back to the Agency, going back home was out of the question. We couldn't leave without Brice.

My friend and I sat at our table under the mango tree for a long time. Neither of us spoke, but it wasn't unfriendly.

And as we sat there, a daring plan formed in my mind.

I took a breath. "Last night, when they put the map on the table, I managed to get a look."

Lola sat up straight. "You know where dem go?"

"Not exactly. But that city isn't in the jungle, like people thought. It's in the middle of something called the Black Morass. No, sorry, the Black River Morass. Whatever a 'morass' is," I added sheepishly.

Lola shook her head. "Morass a bad ting. You get suck under di mud. Lungs jus' full up an'—" She made a graphic choking noise, rolling her eyes up into her head. "You dead."

"I thought it might mean that," I sighed. "Well, that's where the city is, so there you go."

Lola gasped. "Miss, bad duppy live in dat city!!"

"This entire island is full of bad duppy. Jamaica is practically built on dead people's bones! But we need to find Bri— erm, Beau Bexford, before something terrible happens."

My friend started to protest.

"Listen, babe," I said firmly, "as I see it, you've got three choices. Go back to Fruitful Vale and be beaten to death. Stay in Port Royal and wind up entertaining pervy pirates for a living. Euw!" I pulled a face at her. "Or, groovy Option Three, to join forces with the weird white girl, set off to find your boy Beau, and see what happens next."

After a while Lola looked up, her eyes dark with worry. "You tink Massa in danger?"

I pressed my hand to my chest. "I can feel it."

Lola nodded. "Mi feel it too." She leaned closer. "Las' night mi hear dat pirate girl tellin' Massa dey sail round di coast to a place where hill country start."

"Ooh, Lola!" I teased her. "I thought you were asleep!"

She gave a sly giggle. "Hear more tings dat way."

"Can you remember what the place was called?"

Lola shook her head ruefully. "It drop outa mi head."

I had a flash of inspiration. Angels have brilliant photographic memories, plus Mr Allbright makes us play angelic observation games all the time. I'd never had to do this exercise under pressure, but if I could remember the name of this place, we'd have a landmark for the starting point of our journey.

I shut my eyes, trying to recreate the blood-stained map fragments in my mind's eye. It worked. I could see the coastline with total clarity. Unfortunately I had no idea which landmark was the crucial one. I was on the verge of panicking when, for absolutely no reason, song lyrics floated up from the bottom of my mind. A song Lola put on tape for me, for when I needed a boost: *Sisters are Doing it for Themselves.* I mentally scanned along the Jamaican coastline, and there it was!

"Three Sisters," I said abruptly. "Three Sisters Cave."

Lola clapped. "Dat di one!"

Lola and I went back to our room. We couldn't exactly tell anyone the real reason we needed to go to Three Sisters Cave, so we cooked up a story about how my childhood sweetheart was waiting for me somewhere on the beach nearby. I know it sounds a bit dodgy, but people married really young in those days.

It took ages to make the wording of my tale of True Love seem convincingly natural, but finally we were ready to check out.

Before we went back out into the real world, I wanted to make something totally clear.

"Everyone out there will assume you're my slave," I said.

Lola quickly lowered her eyes. "Yes, miss."

"Stuff 'yes miss'!" I said fiercely. "'Yes miss', is

banned for ever. My point is, you and I know different. From now on we're partners."

Lola opened her mouth.

"Partners," I repeated firmly. I gave one last glance around our room. "Don't you want your herbs?" I said in surprise.

Lola had left her withered collection of poisonous plants on the bed.

She just shook her head.

I gave a nervous laugh. "Does that mean you've stopped wanting to poison me?"

My friend shook her head again. "Mi nah poison you, girl-chile."

I was genuinely touched. "Really?"

Lola's eyes glinted. "Where we goin', dey got alligators!"

We went down to the docks and asked around for a boat to take us to Three Sisters Cave. Every person we spoke to looked blank and passed us on to someone else. Off we'd trudge to another sleazy waterfront location and I'd tell our story again.

It got really boring hearing myself repeat the same thing over and over. After a while, Lola and I started adding colourful touches.

My sweetheart and I were to be married as soon as he got his inheritance. Meanwhile my evil uncle was in hot pursuit. My wicked uncle had wanted to marry me off to his pervy best friend, but I was determined to marry my true love.

At last someone directed us to a boat called the *Susannah*. When we got there the *Susannah* turned out to be a full-sized sailing ship. Dirty and dilapidated, but way too grand for what we had in mind.

I was going to say we'd try somewhere else, when a sharp-eyed deckhand came dashing down the gangplank. "You the young mistress wants to hire a boat?"

Wow, news travels fast in Port Royal, I thought. The deckhand had actually been told to look out for us! A minute later we were on board, talking to the captain!

I have to say Captain Plum didn't exactly fit my picture of a sea captain. He was quite old and his clothes were greasy and grimy. There were icky bits of food in his beard and his eyes were red-rimmed from drinking too much rum. But as I told my story he made sympathetic noises in all the right places. When I'd finished, he shook his head as if he couldn't believe what this world was coming to.

"I can pay," I said quickly. "My uncle didn't take all my jewellery."

The captain looked thoughtful. "We're bound for Hispaniola on the next tide. We shall be sailing past the very landmark where your young man is waiting."

I felt a prickle of excitement. "That's fantastic! Does that mean you'll take us!"

Captain Plum put his head on one side like a wise old bird. "Did I hear you say you had a little jewellery, young mistress? I'd gladly take you for free, but I'm not getting any younger and times are hard."

I kept back a sweet little bracelet for emergencies, and poured the rest into the captain's hands. This was such a cool way of doing business! Way more romantic than cash or credit cards.

It seemed like we'd only just found the *Susannah* in time. Just minutes later, her rusty old anchor was hauled up dripping on to the deck. Her sails filled with a rush of wind and, with mighty creaks and groans, the battered old sailing vessel eased away from the waterfront.

As we sailed away from Port Royal, I couldn't stop smiling.

You're finally losing it, babe, I told myself. *There is absolutely nothing to smile about. May I just remind you that we don't actually have a map!*

Could two angels find their way through the Black River Morass without a map? I had no idea. Could we track Brice down before he helped to plunder a sacred city and blew his final last chance of having a career as an angel? I didn't know that either. All I knew was that my friend and I were a team again. We had made a plan and we had followed it through. Now we were on a seventeenth-century sailing ship watching pelicans fly home to their nests, or wherever pelicans sleep at nights.

I was SO happy I started humming our *Sisters* theme tune. This is what Mariah means about being free, I thought. Life is so-o much more fun if you just go for it!

Lola and I watched the whole sunset from beginning to end, until the sun vanished into the sea in a final fabulous blaze of colour.

The ship sailed on through a deep blue dusk. I could see glittery trails of phosphorescence on the water. I became vaguely aware that the sweet greenhousey smells of Jamaica were fading. There were just smells of rope and tar and sea salt. Instead of hugging the Jamaican coastline, the *Susannah* was heading out to sea.

Lola looked bewildered. "What happen?"

"It's fine," I told her cheerfully. "The sailors are just trying to avoid rocks or something. They'll correct their course in a few minutes."

I heard stealthy creaking sounds. A man with a knife between his teeth swung himself up on deck, landing as softly as a cat.

Before we could raise the alarm, a dozen or so hard-faced men came swarming over the side. At the same moment, a galleon flying a sinister black flag loomed out of the dusk.

The *Susannah* been captured by pirates!

Chapter Eight

The *Susannah*'s crew stood by sullenly as the pirates swept through the ship, tearing open hatches, taking trunks, crates and boxes.

They jemmied open one of the boxes and I was astonished to see precious metals glittering inside. Apparently Captain Plum was some kind of smuggler. But when they found the guns and barrels of gunpowder, I was genuinely shocked. Was there *anyone* who wasn't a pirate in Jamaica?

A young black buccaneer was supervising the pillaging, setting up a chain gang to pass the loot up from below, making sure his men didn't miss anything crucial. He had his hair tightly braided into hundreds of gleaming plaits and he wore a rich crimson waistcoat over a baggy white shirt. The sleeves glimmered in the Caribbean dusk. I have to say he was really good-looking; well, if you go for gangster types.

I heard him talking angrily to Captain Plum at one point, but I was too confused and scared to take it in. The *Susannah*'s captain wasn't exactly the friendly character I'd thought.

All the pirates carried knives or evil-looking cutlasses, except the pirate chief – he had a sword with a jewel-encrusted hilt. For backup, he had two pairs of pistols hanging at the end of a silk sling over his shoulders.

He only spoke when necessary and I never saw him actually hurt anyone. Yet each time he came close, I instinctively backed away. He gave off this totally electric vibe. The vibe of someone with absolutely nothing to lose.

The pirates brought their ship, the *Santa Rosa* alongside the *Susannah* and two of her crew wedged a plank between the decks.

Lola and I watched in amazement as the pirates performed a reckless trapeze act, ferrying huge trunks and crates across this madly wobbling bridge as if they were just popping next door.

When the last boxes had been taken on to his ship, the pirate chief gestured to me and Lola. "Now make haste, pretty ladies."

I looked helplessly at Captain Plum. Surely he wouldn't allow us to be abducted by dangerous buccaneers?

To my dismay he just exploded. "Do what he says, wench! And take the slave-girl with you!"

Seconds later I was inching across the plank, trying not to look down. I could hear Lola's scared breathing behind me and the swoosh of waves far below. I told myself it was a good thing it was dark. I'd never know if those were actual sharks circling below or purely imaginary ones.

The minute we tottered on to the deck, the *Santa Rosa*'s pirates surrounded us like hungry hyenas.

Of all the times for Mr Allbright's words to come back to me. *Pirates were not sweet, Melanie... They were calculating, cold-blooded murderers...*

I felt as if the whole world had turned upside down. I couldn't imagine why they'd kidnapped us. Did we look like people who have gold and jewels stashed away? A deeply unpleasant thought crept into my mind. I hope it's not because we're girls, I thought nervously, and they want to—

Suddenly I was gabbling at top speed. "I think there's been a mistake. We aren't rich. All I've got left is—"

I groped wildly for my purse. There was just a severed cord hanging from my waist. A tousle-haired pirate cabin boy waved my purse cheekily from a nearby ladder. He pulled out the bracelet and bit it to test the gold.

"We are not common thieves!" The pirate captain yanked the boy off the ladder, cuffed him round the ear and returned my bracelet with a bow.

"Leo hasn't been with us long. He gets carried away," he explained apologetically. "Allow me to introduce myself. I am Rufus Valentine, captain of the *Santa Rosa*." He chuckled. "At least I am now!"

I looked at the rough-looking men in earrings and bandannas, and at the stacked boxes and barrels they'd taken from the *Susannah*. Then I stared up at the ominous black flag flapping in the evening breeze. Even the ship had been stolen by all accounts.

"I'm sorry," I said, "but you look like thieves to me."

Captain Valentine gave another low chuckle. "We're thieves, little mistress! Just not *common* thieves."

"Oh, right, my favourite kind," I said angrily. "I suppose you steal from the rich and give to the poor?"

His smile faded. "I am not so noble as your Robin of the Woods. But villains who prey on helpless females deserve to be taught a lesson."

I felt like I was missing something. "I'm sorry?"

"I am afraid you were too open about your personal affairs. Every water rat in Port Royal has heard that your fiancé is to come into a large inheritance. The captain of the *Susannah* was going to keep you hostage and demand a ransom for your return."

I stared at him. "You're telling me you *rescued* us?"

He gave another deep bow. "I was honoured to be of service."

I don't think I have ever felt so stupid. Our story had rebounded in the worst way.

"But in the future it would be wise to be a little more discreet," Captain Valentine suggested.

I could feel my face burning but I knew I'd better come clean. "Erm, actually, there is no inheritance. We made that up. There is no fiancé either."

The pirate raised an eyebrow. "Then why did you charter the Susannah?"

Great, he doesn't believe me, I thought.

"It's kind of personal," I told him.

"It must be something important," the pirate said softly, "for you to put yourself and your slave in such danger."

"It is important," I said. "And Lola's not my slave. Look, everything isn't always about money, OK? There is NO fiancé. And there is NO inheritance. If you rescued us to do Captain Plum out of the ransom, you're out of luck. That bracelet your little sonny boy pinched just now, is all we have left in the world."

The pirate looked astonished. "Mistress, did you think—"

"You know what," I interrupted angrily, "Columbus should have stayed at home to raise pigs and done everyone a favour!"

"Pigs?" he echoed in a bewildered voice.

"Everything's been galloping downhill since he came to the Caribbean. Everyone wants a piece of whatever is going and no one cares who they hurt to get it. Well I've HAD it with the New World. I've had it up to here!"

A stunned silence descended. The pirate ship was so hushed I could literally hear Lola's teeth chattering. She probably thought we were going to be fed to the sharks. All the pirates were totally riveted. I think they were dying to know what would happen next.

Nothing did for several nerve-wracking moments. I'd just decided to beam some uplifting vibes quick-smart, when Captain Valentine did something I totally didn't expect.

He took off his beautiful waistcoat and draped it respectfully around my shivering friend's shoulders. "The night air is cool, little sister," he told her, "and your dress is thin. I suggest we go below."

He gave me a cool smile. "I do not want your ransom, mistress. You and your friend are my guests. My crew and I are humbly at your service."

I followed the captain in a daze. A pirate who rescued females in distress? Was Captain Valentine for real?

But when I saw the captain's private quarters, my jaw absolutely dropped. It was gorgeous! Everywhere you looked there was something beautiful, an exotic rug, a silk hanging, a painting. Shelves were crammed with leather-bound books, several written in foreign languages. They weren't just for show. He had what looked like a poetry book lying open on his desk.

"Please," he said. "Make yourselves comfortable."

Lola and I seated ourselves self-consciously on a wooden settle.

"You are now under my protection," he said gravely.

"OK," I squeaked.

"I give you my word you will come to no harm," he went on. "I would very much like to help you."

Some people would say a pirate's word wasn't worth much. Obviously I didn't trust Captain Valentine an inch. Though he was incredibly charming. Lots of people are charming, Mel, I reminded myself. Especially if it gets them what they want.

On the other hand, did I have a choice? I asked myself.

I took a major risk. I told Rufus Valentine everything that had happened, carefully leaving out references to angels or amnesia. I'm afraid I totally got on my soapbox when I described the treatment of the slaves on my uncle's plantation. And after that Lola started shyly chipping in. She'd obviously decided to trust the pirate chief too, and this Lola was not the trusting type, as you know. It started feeling just like old times with both of us talking at once and setting each other straight. I could see this really amused him.

We told Captain Valentine about hot-headed Beau Bexford and his outrageous scheme to set the Fruitful Vale slaves free. And we described how Bermuda Jack had sold my cousin part of a map showing the whereabouts of an ancient Taino city. "It's SO bizarre," I said. "Beau is incredibly respectful of Taino culture, yet he seems to think it's cool to rip off their gold just so long as it's in a good cause." I gave Lola a stern look. "And before you say anything, babe, I KNOW it's dead people's gold, OK? But it just doesn't seem right."

We told the captain how the three of us left Fruitful Vale at dead of night and rode off to Port

Royal to find the mysterious owner of the map's other half.

The captain shook his head at me. "You clearly have a relish for danger, little mistress," he said, with a straight face. "I had no idea I was rescuing an adventuress."

"The most dangerous thing on the journey was Lola," I giggled. "She wanted to poison me."

Lola made her eyes wide and innocent. "Mi never poison you. Mi jus' pick mi lickle herbs dem, and look at you, like dis!" She shot me an evil look under her brows, then creased up laughing.

The pirate looked uneasy when I mentioned Mariah Darcy, but he listened attentively until I had finished. Then he got up to pace.

"So Mistress Mariah is mixed up in this," he said.

"You know her!" I was suddenly intrigued.

"I knew her at one time," he said rather grimly. "But I did not like the company she keeps." He sighed. "I am afraid your cousin will not find his gold. This worries me. I have heard of this city and it is precious, but for reasons Mistress Darcy and her kind will never understand."

"Oh she isn't interested in the gold!" I said eagerly. "Mariah said if they found gold, he could keep it to save the..."

The captain and Lola were staring at me as if I was bonkers.

"She was lying, wasn't she?" I said in a small voice.

"When Mariah wants something badly, she can make you believe ashes are stardust." He twiddled one of his braids thoughtfully. "I suppose you didn't get a look at that map?"

"We think the city is hidden in something called the Black River Morass," I said. "And we're fairly sure Mariah was heading for a landing place near Three Sisters Cave."

"I know it. I'll take you there at first light. It will take at least two days to reach the Morass, going through Cockpit Country."

"Isn't that where rebel slaves hide out?" I asked.

Captain Valentine looked evasive. "So they say. But I have heard many strange stories about those hills. People say that when the soldiers come with muskets and hunting dogs, things happen which cannot be explained. Out of nowhere, the mist comes down and the men find themselves walking in circles. They stumble into bogs or fall into ravines. Their dogs mysteriously go missing. Yet a slave can hide in those hills for weeks and months and never be found. So I have heard."

My arms had come out in goosebumps. "You make it sound like the country is alive," I told him. "Like it's deliberately taking the slaves under its protection."

"It feels like that sometimes." The pirate's voice sounded dreamy and far away. Then his mood changed abruptly. "But you young ladies are under *my* protection. Tonight *I* shall draw you a map of the quickest and safest route through the hills."

I suddenly understood something about Captain Valentine, and I was shocked to the core.

"You were there!" I said. "You were hiding, while the soldiers blundered around in the mist. You were a runaway slave."

Lola gave me a look and I saw that she had known all along. I had done that ugly European thing again, talking about things I couldn't begin to understand.

I started to apologise, but the pirate was already speaking.

"Yes," he said quietly. "I was a slave. I belonged to a white man by the name of George Wainwright Valentine. When I was six years old I saw George Valentine beat a young man to death for daring to look him in the eyes. I vowed then that I would run away as soon as I was grown."

"Omigosh, how can you bear to use that man's name?" I said in horror. "You aren't a slave any more. Why ever don't you choose a new name?"

To my amazement he smiled. "I have earned 'Valentine'. I have worn it like a second-hand boot. I have stretched and worked at it over the years, until it stopped pinching and became mine. I never knew my true name or my true parents. I don't even know what language they spoke. The very words I use, I borrow from books written by white men."

When I first saw Rufus Valentine I felt scared of him because I guessed he was a man with nothing to lose. I hadn't realised he'd lost everything before he was even born.

He seemed to know what I was thinking.

"Yes, little mistress," he said softly. "The world can be harsh. Yet still, it is good to be alive!"

We slept in a spare cabin on silk sheets which Captain Valentine insisted had belonged to a Spanish Infanta.

The tousle-haired cabin boy woke us at sunrise. "The captain says to bring you these," he grinned.

He had brought us a bundle of old but perfectly clean clothes. Stripy cotton tops, pirate bandannas to protect our heads from the sun, and breeches drastically faded by salt and sun.

Yay! I can finally ditch that corset, I thought gratefully.

To my surprise, Lola chose the blue top and bandanna, so obviously I took the red. I didn't say anything but I couldn't help being puzzled. Lola's slave clothes were blue. You'd think she'd be desparate for a change. But it was like she felt safer sticking to something she knew.

We creased up laughing when we saw each other in our pirate gear.

But I felt a happy little buzz. In our matching clothes, we finally looked like equals. We looked as if we could actually be friends.

We went to say our goodbyes to Captain Valentine.

He seemed genuinely sorry to see us go. "I advise you to get out of sight as soon as you reach dry land. The militia watch this part of the coast like hawks, and the *Santa Rosa* is a Spanish vessel. If they see you in those clothes they will shoot first and ask questions afterwards."

He raised my fingers to his lips. "Farewell, little mistress."

OK, so it was just a charming gesture, plus he kissed Lola's hand immediately afterwards, but ooh la la! Say what you like about this mission, I thought, but we are certainly seeing life!

We clambered down a rope ladder to a waiting dinghy. As we pulled away from the *Santa Rosa*, I waved shyly to Captain Valentine.

Our pirate boatman spoke practically no English. He rowed us as close as he could get without running aground, then solemnly handed us two small bundles that obviously contained food.

I wondered what Mr Allbright would think if he knew we had met yet another pirate with a heart. Handsome Captain Valentine had been for real after all. He had even drawn us a map to help us reach the Black River Morass.

We splashed ashore and scrambled quickly up the rocks and out of sight, in case the English militia were watching from some secret outpost.

The first part of our journey took us through rocky hills where nothing grew but scrub and cactus. The barren landscape gradually gave way to coconut palms and rippling fields of sugar cane.

At midday we stopped to rest in the shade of a palm tree, and ate some of our pirate provisions. The ship's cook had packed tiny hard-boiled eggs and strips of dried meat and a type of flat bread which Lola said was made from cassava root.

When we'd finished lunch, we wandered around for a while like happy little kids, picking tropical fruit and berries. Lola picked a fruit she called "sweet sop". It didn't look that special but it was gorgeous. You broke open the shell and there was this delicious natural custard inside. I caught Lola watching me as I slurped at this unexpected treat.

"What?" I said.

My friend's eyes were dreamy and unfocused, almost as if she was seeing *through* me to someone or somewhere else.

"Nuttin," she said softly. "Just tinkin' 'bout dat dream city you talk 'bout."

I got a tingly feeling inside. Lola's memory was coming back, I was sure of it. But I didn't want to push her before she was ready, so I just said, "Oh that's all right. I thought maybe I was dribbling down my chin."

That afternoon we kept up a cracking pace, despite the intense heat. By sunset we had reached the foot of some really peculiar hills. They looked like upside-down puddings with hollowed-out depressions in between.

I saw Lola's face light up. "See dem lickle valleys. Dey look jus' like cockfightin' pits! Mus' be why dey call dis Cockpit Country, eh?"

I'd never seen cocks fighting, but it had to be gruesome. I suppressed a shiver. "You could be right."

"Ole Massa Bexford jus' love cockfightin'," Lola remembered. "A whole heap a dem white massas come over and dey make di poor birds fight-fight till one dead. Mi watch one time, but it make mi spit up everyting in mi belly."

But as we stood there, mopping sweat from our faces and gazing at the amazing view, all the cruel goings-on at Fruitful Vale seemed like a bad dream.

"Slaves call dis place nutha name some time," my friend said, almost whispering the words. "Dem call it di Land of Look Behind."

"The Land of Look Behind," I repeated. It sounded like a place in a story.

I felt so proud of us I can't tell you. Lola and I had been abandoned in a violent city without any money, without even a map. We'd been tricked by pirates and captured by a totally different set of pirates. Yet here we were in the foothills of the Land of Look Behind, in hot pursuit of our angel buddy.

It was going to be dark, so we found a guango tree with spreading umbrella-type branches, and made a rough kind of camp. We piled up dry leaves for a mattress (first checking for snakes!). Lola lit a fire and we shared our pirate rations.

In a movie, this would be the scene where the two angel girls end up having a meaningful talk in the firelight, shed some tears and finally iron out their misunderstandings.

In a movie, though, they'd leave out the mosquitoes. I doubt even Albert Einstein could have had a meaningful conversation with vicious bloodsucking insects attacking exposed bits of his anatomy. Actually, I have this theory. I think mosquitoes adore angels! I think we're like this amazing cosmic delicacy, that they totally can't have too much of. Lola and I did *try* to talk, but we had to keep interrupting each other with frantic slapping sounds.

I started to think we'd be swatting mozzies until daybreak. But when you've been walking in the open air from dawn till dusk, pure exhaustion takes over.

Lola and I gradually slid down until we were lying under our guango-tree umbrella. The whine of mosquitoes began to mix itself into an atmospheric soundtrack, along with chirping crickets, tree frogs and soothing rippling sounds from a nearby stream. I could see showers of tiny stars dancing in the dark. *Melanie this is so cool, you're finally seeing fireflies*, I thought drowsily. I wanted to stay awake watching the tiny magic dancing lights, but my eyes kept closing.

I wondered where Brice was and if he was watching fireflies with Mariah Darcy. It was so weird the way he'd left us in Port Royal like that. Weird and deeply worrying. I truly tried not to think the worst, but I had this horrible suspicion that our night with the pirates had brought out our buddy's dark side.

Look at the effect they had on you, Melanie, I told myself. *And you're a complete wuss.*

In the movie of our lives, I would have fallen fast asleep at this point and had a dream that told me exactly what was going on for Brice.

But my dreams seemed every bit as confused as waking life. Brice was standing on some crumbling stone steps in the moonlight, watching Mariah's pirates loading fabulous Taino treasures into canoes.

In my dreams he wore normal clothes and looked just like he did in real life, hands in pockets, collar up round his ears. Same lonely, complicated Brice.

"You should be happy, angel boy," I told him. "You found the city."

Brice looked sick with fear. "There's been a mistake," he told me. He pointed to a huge carving of a Taino god that was towering over us like some ancient tree. The god's carved face wore an expression of deep suffering.

"Omigosh, it's got tears," I said in surprise.

At that moment the carved tears became real. They streamed down the wooden face of the god. By the time they reached the ground they'd become a torrent, thundering through the city, sweeping away temples, pirates, canoes and treasures.

I woke screaming, "I'm sorry! I didn't mean to!"

Lola was staring down at me in concern. "What happen?"

"I just had a bad dream. I'm OK honestly."

Lola lay down again.

After a while I felt her hand grope for mine.

We slept like that, hand in hand, until morning.

Some dreams hover over you all the next day like the wings of a sinister bird. You can still see sunlight and blue sky. You go about your business as normal, yet your dream casts a shadow you totally can't ignore.

I loved Cockpit Country. I absolutely loved the round pudding-shaped hills. I loved how green everything was. The sheer variety of trees and flowers blew me away. Palm trees with silver leaves. Vivid blue morning glories and golden black-eyed susans.

One time, Lola silently pointed out a plantation of yams obviously being cultivated in one of the fertile "cockpits" between the hills. A shiver of happiness went through me to think I'd seen a secret garden tended by runaway slaves.

I especially loved the yams. They looked oddly alive. It was almost spooky. Like green giants that might uproot themselves any minute and go galumphing over the hills.

But most of all I loved that Lola and I were getting reacquainted.

She still wasn't totally my Lola, but she was excellent company all the same. She took everything in her stride. Nothing fazed her, not even when I got confused by Captain Valentine's map. We must have wasted a good hour before we got back on track, but Lola said philosophically, "So it go!"

One time I fell in the stream and soaked myself to the skin. Lola laughed so much she almost fell in herself.

But lurking under these happy moments, like disturbing music in a film, were the dark vibes from my dream. They made things feel not quite real:

like this was just a holiday from the horrors of real life.

And as you know, holidays can't last.

Towards the end of the afternoon, we were making our way through a deep valley, knee-deep in lush green ferns and wild flowers. There was dense thicket on either side. Somewhere a bird was singing for pure joy.

I'm not sure that is a bird actually, I thought.

At the same moment I heard the tiniest twig-crack. Lola froze. By then it was too late.

We were surrounded by half-naked humans brandishing spears.

Lola and I were too shocked to move. Who were these flat-faced dark-skinned people? They weren't slaves. They weren't like any people I'd seen in Jamaica. Yet I felt I had seen them before.

When you're scared, random things jump out at you. I found myself focusing for no reason on their headdresses and jewellery. The elaborate collars and amulets were made from shimmery seashells, cut so cleverly they could have been precious gems. The exotic feathers braided in their hair made them seem magical, almost childlike; the kind of people who might have existed when the world was new and simple.

I hadn't seen these people because they were practically extinct. I was looking at the last survivors of the Taino.

CHAPTER NINE

There were seven canoes altogether, gliding through the water as silently as shadows. We shared a canoe with the chief's grandson, a boy called Marohu, and a wiry little dog with alert pointy ears.

We were going to Coyaba, the City of the Gods, and something huge was going to happen there.

I had asked the chief if it was a good something, or something bad, but he had just shaken his head. "Something hard," he said quietly.

We paddled down silent backwaters, between steep banks lush with ferns and orangey-gold black-eyed susans. After an hour we reached a place where three rivers met and went speeding out into wide open water. I could hear tropical birds calling to each other high in the trees.

Marohu looked rigid with nerves. I couldn't blame him. Who'd want to be in a canoe with the Angel of Death?

That was me, in case you're wondering. The Taino chief had been expecting me. He wasn't called a "chief" by the way. Strictly speaking he was a cacique, (it actually sounded like kaseek). That meant he was like the leader of the tribe and a holy man all rolled into one. He hadn't been expecting me in person. He wasn't looking out specifically for an angel-girl called Mel Beeby. I was more like a sign: She who Flew on the Wings of the Storm. The final sign their world was ending.

You know how it is, you're trying to lighten the atmosphere, so you chat madly about anything that comes into your head. I focused on the dog, the way you do. How sweet it was, how well-behaved, its perky little ears.

Marohu gradually relaxed. He told me his dog was called Beetle. Like all Taino dogs, Beetle was barkless. "Better for hunting," he explained shyly. "Barking dogs scare the animals."

Lola looked baffled when I translated this conversation.

"How you can speak to dese people?" she hissed. "How dey know you?"

"I have no idea, babe," I said truthfully. "But where we come from, we understand all the human languages."

It probably seems like I was taking this really calmly?

I didn't have a choice. To the Taino, I was a messenger from their gods. This wasn't a part I'd have chosen, obviously. That wasn't the point. Mysterious cosmic forces were clearly at work and I felt I had to go with the flow.

Luckily it's hard to take yourself too seriously when your face is being licked by a rapturous Taino hunting dog.

Marohu was mortified. He kept saying he didn't know what had got into her. Normally Beetle was as good as gold. But I knew she couldn't help it. The poor little thing was just overexcited by our angelic vibes.

"Is a dream, dis," Lola murmured to herself. "Soon mi wake. Mi wake an' hear Quashiba singin' in she hut."

It seemed like a dream to me too; travelling in a canoe with a boy from a tribe that was about to vanish for ever.

We sped down the wide river under a green canopy of leaves, until the sun sank low in the sky. At a sign from the old cacique, the Taino lifted their canoes out of the water. The men slung hammocks between palm trees and lit a fire. One of the Taino had been catching fresh-water fish. The men gutted the fish, wrapped them in some kind of aromatic leaves, impaled them on sharp wooden skewers and baked them over the fire. Tricky to eat with fingers, and just a teensy bit too hot, but ooh, so dee-licious! There was cassava cake to fill any empty spaces and coconut water to wash it down.

Afterwards the cacique asked to speak with me. He was really old; in his eighties, maybe even his nineties. His eyesight was bad, and he must have been stiff and tired after hours in a canoe, yet I could feel this amazing vibe coming from him. I got the strangest feeling that he knew who I was. I mean *really* knew. In fact, I started wondering if this wise old man might be some kind of earth angel.

He started by telling me about Coyaba, the City of the Gods. For thousands of years, he said, native people travelled there in canoes from all over the Caribbean to honour their gods.

After Columbus discovered the Caribbean, this all changed. His people were initially willing to live with white people in peace, but there were so many of them; they came like hordes of locusts, and they seemed to want to own Xaymaca in a way the Taino totally didn't understand. How could you own trees or birdsong?

The Europeans forced the Taino to work in their fields. Some actually hunted the tribespeople for sport. Many died of the white man's diseases. Others killed themselves in despair. Soon only a few were left, hiding out in the hills.

"Yet still the location of the sacred city was fiercely protected," the cacique told me. "Each generation of Taino memorised the secret route, passing it down from generation to generation."

I was feeling increasingly uncomfortable.

"It isn't really made of gold, though, is it?"

For the first time the old man seemed irritated, as if I was missing the point. "Ah those mysterious golden cities," he sighed. "Soon my people will vanish like a bird trail in the sky, and all the gold in creation will not bring us back."

"I – I hate to tell you this, but I think someone's betrayed you," I said miserably. "Someone drew a map of the route. I saw it in Port Royal. A friend of mine got hold of one half. Someone called Mariah Darcy has the other."

The cacique sighed. "I have heard of this young woman. And what I hear worries me greatly. So much intelligence and beauty, yet inside she feels empty. Always hungering for something she can't have."

"That's too harsh," I objected. "Mariah is—"

"Your friend on the other hand," the old man continued firmly, "is descended from a long line of rats' arses."

(Sorry, he might not have said "rats' arses" exactly, but it's the closest word I can get to the Taino.)

I stared at him, open-mouthed. "You *know* about Brice?"

"Rats' *arses*," he repeated in a louder voice. "Yet his soul shines like moonbeams on water."

My heart was thumping. "You think Brice is in danger, don't you!"

The cacique's eyes were troubled. "Evil hovers over this boy like the wings of a vulture. I ask myself, 'Why are these dark beings going to so much trouble to destroy him? He must have made them very angry.'"

It was a warm night, but I could feel chills going up and down my back.

"Your friend lived in utter darkness. Yet he found the strength to leave. Such souls have a rare power. They are not afraid of the world's dark places. They shine light on them."

I didn't quite buy the cacique's version of an angel loner who sat around listening to Astral Garbage CDs. I opened my mouth to tell him that at this moment his precious shining light was looting his sacred city to buy guns.

But the old man's next words sent a jolt of fear into my heart.

"That is why the Dark Forces are trying to destroy him. They are playing with him. They have been playing with you all."

When I went back, Lola was fast asleep.

As I lay rigid in my hammock, totally traumatised by what I'd heard, Lola spoke to me. "I wish I could see this place," she whispered. "I should love to speak all the languages like you."

My skin prickled with angel electricity.

Lola had spoken in her normal voice.

We were on our way well before it was light.

We had breakfast on the move, nibbling at flat cassava bread as we went along. I gave most of mine to Beetle. I was too edgy to eat.

I wanted to ask Lola if she remembered talking to me in her sleep, but Marohu was there, plus my friend seemed tired and preoccupied.

For the first two hours the river was fast and deep-flowing. Then it divided off into an absolute maze of channels that wandered off, looping and crisscrossing the boggy flood plains, looking like some nightmarish brainteaser: *Find Your Way to the Sacred City*. Tortured-looking mangrove trees reared up out of the water forcing Marohu to paddle around them. We had now entered the Morass itself. When I saw how skilfully the Taino guided their canoes along the secret waterways, I realised I'd been insane to think we could find Coyaba on our own.

The Morass wasn't black, it was slimy green and

brown. After just an hour in this place, I started to feel like these were the only colours left in the world. Sludgy brown water, greenish-brown reeds, slimy sinister trees.

Since my scary talk with the cacique, I'd had the sense of being watched by something evil. Here, in this unbelievably creepy place, I felt the Dark Powers coming closer.

Everything about the Morass was sinister: the steamy suffocating air, the sinister screechy birds that we never actually saw, but sounded huge. Ominous bubbling, sucking sounds were literally coming from inside the swamp. Worst of all were the writhing mangrove roots that looked like agonised body parts of people who had been buried alive, and who died struggling to get free. And over it was this all-pervading stink of rotting vegetation and marsh gas.

Suddenly there was an explosion of sound. An alligator shot out of the reeds and came speeding towards us like a torpedo. Marohu paddled us frantically out of reach.

After my heartbeat returned to normal, I still found myself seeing those cold yellow eyes. Had it truly been an alligator? Or something worse?

And then, without warning, it was over. Marohu just stopped paddling and our canoe glided silently into a lake.

It was like going from darkness into light. Birds sang. A soft breeze trembled through the fronds of palm trees. And tiny white clouds reflected back in the clear, still waters of the lake.

Marohu paddled the canoe towards a towering cliff where a ledge of rock made a natural landing stage. From here you could see a flight of steps in the rock face. We helped Marohu drag the canoe out of the water, then followed the Taino up the steps.

At the top was the entrance to what looked like a large cave, but was actually the entrance to a tunnel. On either side of the entrance were enormous wooden pillars carved with images of the Taino gods.

A shiver went through me as I recognised the weeping god I had seen in my dream. I wanted to run, but I couldn't. This wasn't about me. I wasn't an individual to the Taino. I was the angel of their Last Days. I was *She who Flew on the Wings of the Storm*. I took a deep breath and followed the others into the tunnel.

The cacique walked ahead of us holding up a burning torch. I saw dim, ancient paintings flickering on the smooth rock face. They looked like birds and animals. But I think they were also gods. There were more steps at the end of this tunnel. We climbed and climbed in the flickering gloom until my legs were on the verge of giving out. Then we emerged in the sunlight and there were no words.

I saw my own wonder and astonishment reflected in Lola's face.

She had seemed in a kind of trance since we'd joined forces with the Taino. But as we finally stood inside the City of the Gods, I felt something change. I felt her start to wake up.

Listen, I can tell you what we saw. I can tell you about the actual physical stuff we saw in the City of the Gods. I could list Taino houses, gardens and fountains. I could describe the huge open space with benches, where the Taino used to play an incomprehensible sacred game that makes absolutely no sense if you're not Taino. I could get all lyrical about the carvings encrusted with shimmering seashells and all that jazz.

That would be missing the point. This stuff – the playing field, the quaint Taino objects, their fabulous flair for working with shells – was not what made the city so magical. You couldn't just carry off their *stuff* and knock up a sacred city of your own.

Can you imagine somewhere, *anywhere*, on Planet Earth where you can just breathe in pure peace? Where you can just, like, mingle with invisible gods? The awesome power of this place made me tingle all over.

We were walking slowly towards a small shimmering Taino temple. It seemed to be constructed entirely out of mother-of-pearl seashells.

I thought of how the first white men who came to Jamaica used to hunt the Taino for sport, as if they were animals!

We've got to save this place, I thought suddenly. *People have to see this. They have to know how incredibly wise the Taino really are.*

I was going to say something, but one of the Taino gestured fiercely for everyone to stay quiet.

When I saw what was happening inside that beautiful little temple, I had to bite my lip to stop myself crying out.

One of Mariah's men was kicking angrily at the base of a shrine, scattering shimmery shell fragments with his boot.

Kneeling on the ground, hands tied behind his back, was Brice, looking sick with fear, just as he had in my dream.

Mariah was watching him with a narrow-eyed expression. She had one beautiful leather boot resting on an overturned statue as she raised her pistol and deliberately aimed it at his head.

Chapter Ten

In that hideous moment, when I saw Mariah getting ready to blow my friend to pieces, I understood what was so evil about the PODS. I understood what they'd done.

The Dark Powers are playing with you.

They'd studied us like a project. The creeps had studied us and taken notes and they'd figured out the things that make us who we are. Brice's compulsion to make waves, Lola's incredible ability to risk everything for love, and my desire for adventure. They'd taken everything that was deepest and best, and used them against us; planting drunken pirates and intriguing map fragments. And, like ants high on honey, we'd followed their sticky trail to Port Royal – where Mariah was waiting.

I'm not completely stupid. I did get that Mariah wasn't like, a *nice* person. But because she was Cat's granddaughter, and because she was beautiful and kind of thrillingly dangerous, I told myself it was OK.

Here in the City of the Gods I saw what she was; a human so empty, she was no longer quite human.

Mariah Darcy had sold her soul to the PODS.

As I stood watching her finger teasingly release the catch, I thought that Brice had never really stood a chance.

When you don't like yourself, when you don't know who you are, when you think you're all alone in an unfriendly universe, it leaves you open to believing all kinds of garbage. For example, that you can create a peaceful world by stealing gold to buy guns. Or that a girl pirate with a diamond tooth is the answer to your prayers.

Let's face it, Melanie, said a despairing voice inside my head, Life is basically a vast, pointless game. Even angels are just helpless pawns...

Then I felt a familiar hot-potato feeling inside my chest. *Who's thinking this stuff?* I thought. *It's certainly not me. I'm not a pawn. The hell I am! Angelic reality is SO much bigger than this.*

It was like I'd been trapped inside a lonely dark bubble all by myself and POUF! it burst and I was in a different movie.

Three Taino marksmen stepped out into the open and started firing darts. Several pirates crumpled to the ground and started snoring like stunned rhinos.

It was one of those moments when Lola and I didn't have to speak. We didn't even glance at each other. We knew Mariah was momentarily shocked so we just ran at her, jumping the pirate girl from behind, and wrestled her to the ground. I grabbed the pistol, but the vibes were so foul I dropped it in absolute revulsion.

Marohu had sliced through the ropes that bound Brice. Our buddy quickly picked up the pistol and jammed it in his belt. All three of us exchanged amazed glances. I saw baffled recognition in my friends' faces.

They're back! I thought deliriously. I rushed forward to hug them, fatally taking my eyes off Mariah.

I guess people become pirates for different reasons. I think Mariah took to piracy because when you feel that empty, not getting what you want is worse than being dead. I think after all her scheming, Maria couldn't stand to leave Coyaba empty-handed.

I saw her lunge at an exquisite Taino carving on the altar.

The statue of the weeping god had been much bigger in my dream, but its grieving expression was just the same.

"Mariah, don't!" I shouted.

The statue wasn't meant to be moved. It was part of the altar in some way. Mariah took a lethal-looking knife out of her belt and levered frantically with the blade. The blade snapped off but the damage had been done.

The ground started vibrating. There were hideous grating and rumbling sounds and a yawning crack appeared in the temple floor. I watched, paralysed, as the two jagged halves began to move apart.

Brice didn't even hesitate. He rushed forward to save her, but Mariah fell flailing into the chasm.

We stared down in horror.

A supernatural wind whipped our hair across our faces. The sky grew dark overhead.

"Quickly! We must leave!" said the old cacique.

We fled back along the tunnel. Sounds of groaning came from deep inside the earth. Blocks of stone crashed down around us.

Outside, trees writhed in this sudden hurricane as if they were trying to uproot themselves. The waters of the lake seethed and churned like a cauldron.

"Come with me," Marohu's grandfather told us. We jumped into his canoe and he paddled us fearlessly into the storm. I was too shocked to be scared. I was too shocked to feel anything at all. I had just watched a human plunge screaming to a hideous death. I thought the sound of Mariah's screams would echo through my head for ever.

There was a sudden thunderous roar. We turned our heads to see the cliff collapsing in agonising slow motion and disappear into the lake.

The old cacique watched as the sacred city of the Taino sank for ever. His eyes were clouded with pain. I saw his lips move. He was talking to someone. Not us. He'd forgotten we were even there. He was talking to one of his gods.

"They did not understand, O Cloudless One," he said softly. "But one day they will feel lost without you. They will be drawn to look for you in places of wood and water. They will remember you, and understand they must change their ways."

There's a feeling you get when you have to leave Planet Earth, no matter what's going on at that moment. Like, say someone's world has just disappeared for ever. It makes no difference. It might seem inhuman, but it's a call angels totally can't ignore.

"It's time," I whispered to my friends. I didn't want to disturb the distressed cacique while he was grieving privately with his god.

Brice and Lola were still shell-shocked, but they reached instinctively for their angel tags. As my hand closed around the platinum disc I felt the unmistakeable buzz of angelic electricity. The broken cosmic connection had been repaired.

"We're ready," I told whoever was on duty.

A whoosh of white light lit up the lakeside.

When I opened my eyes we were surrounded by delighted heavenly personnel; communications guys, maintenance people, time technicians, all talking at once and slapping us on the back.

Our clothes were filthy. Our hair was dusty and matted. Lola and Brice looked traumatised. We'd been duped by the PODS. We'd watched helplessly as the sacred city of Coyaba was destroyed, but I had brought my friends safely home.

CHAPTER ELEVEN

For three days I couldn't even visit her. That's how ill Lola was.

It's not good for an angel to forget who she is for so long. It's not good for us to be cut off from heavenly support systems, and wander round exposed to toxic vibes. What the PODS had done to my soul-mate had burned her deep, deep inside. I didn't know if she'd ever get over it.

The first time I visited her, it was torture. Imagine me and Lola not knowing what to say to each other!

She lay there in her bed in the sanctuary, staring out at the garden, and it was like she was just waiting for me to go away and leave her alone.

I was hurt at first. Then I figured out why she couldn't talk to me.

It hadn't happened to me.

I never had to wake in a dark stinking hut, stiff and bruised all over from a senseless beating because I had the tiniest trace of African ancestry. I hadn't suffered such total cosmic amnesia that I believed this was who I was: a member of a subhuman species, a being regarded with such contempt that white people asked each other, in your presence, if you even had a soul.

Like I said at the beginning, my soul-mate and I were torn apart by an evil force. Who knew it would be so hard for us to find our way back?

Michael took me out to tea at Guru and told me I had to be patient. "Give her time."

"But we've been through so much together!" I said miserably. "Doesn't she realise I'm her friend by now?"

"She doesn't know what she knows," he said. "She isn't sure if she's an angel or just a slave-girl dreaming she's in heaven. Cosmic amnesia strikes to the absolute core of what you think you are."

Michael went really quiet after that and there was this feeling in the air that I just can't describe.

Back in my room, I was totally perplexed. Did he mean it had happened to him? Could a high being like Michael actually forget who and what he was? Did this kind of thing happen all the time then? Immortal beings getting trapped inside a PODS illusion, forgetting why they came to Earth, unable to find a way home?

I wondered if I'd ever met an amnesiac angel while I was alive. But how would I know? I'd have just assumed they were human, when all the time they were lying awake at nights, aching and aching inside, because something huge was missing but they couldn't remember what.

Two weeks after Lola came out of hospital, she appeared in my doorway. "Hi."

She'd been crying. She came in and curled up on a floor cushion and blew her nose. She tried to speak, but she couldn't get any words out.

"Babe, what's wrong?" I said anxiously.

Lola burst into tears. "I miss you. Isn't that stupid? You're right here in this room and I'm really missing you."

My eyes filled with tears. "I miss you too."

I didn't know what else to say. Well, I could think of plenty, but if I blurted the wrong thing, it could set us back *weeks*.

What should I do? I was practically wringing my hands. I heard myself say, "Boy, right now I could really do with a couple of lizards."

Lola stared open-mouthed, not knowing whether to laugh, cry, or give me therapy. I saw her brush away the tears from her face. "Erm, is the lizard problem new, girlfriend?" she asked cautiously, "or is it like, this shameful childhood secret you couldn't bring yourself to share until now?"

"Actually it goes back to that morning in Diego's," I told her.

"Diego's," she repeated. "That mission was something else wasn't it?"

"Just a bit."

"So what's with the lizards?" she asked curiously.

"I was having personal problems. I had to ask some lizards for help."

Lola went quiet again and I guessed she was picturing that shabby room at Diego's. "You know what was so scary?" she said suddenly. "I'd forgotten what it's like being human. I'd forgotten how lonely it feels sometimes. And when you're a slave, omigosh Melanie! I didn't trust anyone at Fruitful Vale, even the other slaves. But I really trusted Brice."

I giggled. "Boy, you were in big trouble."

She gave me a sideways glance. "The weird thing was I kind of recognised you."

I was stunned. "You did?"

"I just didn't trust what I felt. With Brice it was kind of different. You know." Lola went slightly pink.

"You really knew me?" I wanted to make sure.

"Somewhere inside I did. I just couldn't think why you wanted to know me. I'm so sorry, Mel, I just imagined you having all these like, dark motives."

My soul-mate looked tearful again so I quickly changed the subject.

"Talking of Brice. How's he doing these days? He hasn't said two words to me. Just beetles off after class to work in the library or whatever."

"How would you feel if you were him?" Lola asked softly.

"Like poo," I said. "He got Mariah totally wrong."

"He didn't. He got her right away."

I stared at her. "You think?"

"I know," she said firmly. "He knew something wasn't right. But he did that thing Brice does. He took it all on himself."

"Brice has to do it alone," I agreed. "He's the original DIY guy."

"Poor babe. His mission didn't quite work out like he hoped."

While she was talking, Lola was rolling up the cuff of her jeans so I could see she was still wearing my fraying friendship bracelet.

"It got a bit faded in Jamaica," she said in a hinting tone.

"I'll make you a new one," I said. "Just give me time."

The day after our conversation, Lola and I received invitations to attend the Angel Academy HALO awards. I know!

"How come we got invitations?" I asked my friend in amazement. "We've never been invited before."

"Maybe we've won an award?"

I knew she was just joking.

"Yeah right," I said. "That really special award you get for helping to sink a sacred city."

I felt a little pang for Brice. He'd tried so hard. Life can be really unfair.

The HALO ceremony was ridiculously short notice, plus we were revising for exams, so I didn't even have time to buy clothes. I had to wear that glittery grey dress I bought the first time I went shopping with Lola. My soul-mate wore a similar dress in pale gold and we put each other's hair up.

We examined ourselves in her mirror.

"Hey we look hot, girl!" she grinned.

When we arrived, the hall was packed out with agents and trainees, all dressed up to the nines.

All around us kids were spouting advanced angel jargon. You know that type who love talking in initials? DS for Dark Studies and TTs for time technicians.

Lola fished out a pen from her bag and wrote C.W.O.T on her hand. "Complete Waste of TIme," she whispered. We both sniggered like naughty children.

Then I saw something I never thought I'd see in this universe.

I nudged Lola. "Look who's sitting across the aisle."

"How DID they get that boy in a suit?" she said wonderingly.

I giggled. "From the look on his face he's wishing he was back in the Hell dimensions."

The ceremony kicked off with the usual speeches about teamwork, yadda yadda, then people were called up to receive their awards.

It was warm in the hall, and I was tired from staying up revising. I kept almost nodding off. Now and then there'd be a burst of applause and I'd jump awake guiltily and realise where I was.

Suddenly there was a huge outbreak of clapping and cheering.

I practically leapt out of my seat. "What's happening?"

Lola was looking stunned. "We won an award!"

"Don't be stupid," I told her.

"I mean it. We won!"

My voice shot up an octave. "What the sassafras for?"

"I'm not sure. I think it was 'Brilliant teamwork under unusual adversity'," she said.

Everybody was craning round, wondering why we weren't going up to get our trophies.

Mr Allbright stood up. "They're in shock," he told the audience. A ripple of laughter went round the hall.

I followed Lola self-consciously to the front. My knees had totally turned to water.

Brice was waiting for us, looking like some alarming stranger in his suit. We all filed up the steps and there was Michael smiling at us.

Some strange Agency type I had never seen in my life made a speech about how we were the finest example of something or other he'd seen in such young trainees.

Apparently we were supposed to say something. Unfortunately, I'm utterly phobic about public speaking. I completely froze. Brice just stood glowering at the audience. Not the most shining example of angelic teamwork, you have to admit. Lola saved the day luckily. She stepped up to the mike, beaming and looking absolutely divine in her glittery gold dress, thanking everyone for supporting us while we were going through our ordeal.

"But most of all," she said breathlessly, "I want to thank my team-mates, Mel and Br—"

Brice turned white and bolted out of the hall.

"Better go after him," Michael whispered in my ear.

I found him outside the building, practically in tears.

"Hey, you're missing your big moment," I said. "What's up?"

Brice shook his head. "I've been asking myself the same question. I think I got scared."

"Of an *award* ceremony! After the stuff you've seen?"

He wiped his eyes, trying to laugh. "It wasn't stage fright, darling. It was more like that old Taino guy watching his city go under the water. Like my entire life was ending or something."

"WHY? This is just the beginning. You wanted that award, that's—"

"I *know*," he said angrily. "Look, this is humiliatingly cheesy, but maybe I'm not sure I deserve it.

"Why ever not?" I said. "You didn't know who you were but you had all these like, amazing *principles*. You even tried to save Mariah, when I'd have been tempted to—"

"I know, I know, OK? Spare me. So am I like, a really good boy now?" Brice peered down at his suit in a kind of horror. "Because, be honest, sweetheart. Is this really me?"

I felt like slapping him. "This is ridiculous, man! Why are you so hung up about a stupid suit?"

"Because..." Brice struggled for words. "I knew how to do *twisted*, OK? It worked for me. I'm not sure I can hack that other stuff."

"I don't see a tragedy here," I said firmly. "I don't even see a teeny weeny problem."

"You don't?"

I patted his shoulder. "Absolutely not. You can be twisted if that's your style. You can be that twisted angel boy who goes around in a stinky Astral Garbage T-shirt. You can be that dark dangerous stinky teenage angel."

Brice perked up. "Dangerous? Ooh, sounds promising!"

I swatted him with my sparkly clutch bag. "Come on. Let's go and rescue poor Lola from the AWTIIs."

He looked blank.

"Angels Who Talk In Initials!" I grinned.

We started walking back.

But I could see Brice was still terrified, so I did that thing I still occasionally find myself doing, when things get heavy. That airhead thing.

"Incidentally," I giggled. "You owe me BIG time, angel boy! Do you have ANY idea what a nightmare you put me through?"

Brice looked bewildered. "For making you enter the HALO awards?"

"No, dirtbag! For making me wear a corset!"

budding
star

For Maria, who solved several crucial problems with one flash of inspiration; Terry Hong, whose expertise and insights helped to give this story its final shape; and Miryam Sas, for her well-timed words of encouragement.

CHAPTER ONE

One sunny morning, a few hours after my thirteenth birthday, I totally amazed myself by unexpectedly becoming an angel.

This was not a career option I'd seriously considered to be honest. I'd been thinking more along the lines of "TV presenter". OK, strictly speaking, I'd have preferred "girl hip-hop artist", but one of my mates played my voice back when we were messing around with her sound system one time, and I sounded *exactly* like a tiny cartoon animal!

Like most of my mates, I had this idea that the sole purpose of human existence was to get myself on telly. But if I couldn't even *sing*...

After stamping around like a drama queen for a few days, I decided I'd have to break into show biz some other way. Maybe I'd be one of those cute teen celebs who get paid squillions on the basis of their warm bubbly personalities?

This probably sounds v. v. shallow, but like I said, I hadn't realised the teenage angel option was available. Even if I *had* known, the all-important entry qualification (i.e. being completely and utterly dead) would have definitely put me off.

Back then, you see, I believed that when you died, you lost absolutely everything that made you "you". So when the speeding Ford Fiesta knocked me down, that sunny summer morning, and I found myself in the Afterlife, very much in one piece, I went into pure shock!

I'm like, "You mean I get to live for EVER!! Are you SERIOUS!"

At first my new existence felt completely unreal. Everything seemed super-sparkly and *humongously* intense. I don't think there was one single moment when anything was just ordinary.

I'd wake in my tiny dorm room at the Angel Academy and I'd have to rush to the window to see if Heaven was still there!

The view blew me away every time. I'd never even *seen* fifty per cent of these colours back when I was human. I'd never seen strange futuristic skyscrapers, either, soaring up into fluffy white clouds, or a city that shimmered softly with its own mysterious inner light.

What I *totally* couldn't seem to get my head round, was that *I'd* been touched with this same special heavenly shimmer-dust.

I'd catch sight of myself in the mirror and just gaze at my reflection in absolute awe. Was that REALLY me? This was the girl I'd secretly longed to be back on Earth. Now, for reasons I didn't completely comprehend, she'd shown up in Heaven! A cool vibey Mel Beeby to fit my cool vibey environment.

You know those feel-good fantasy series they put out on TV? The kind you just have to drop everything to see. The opening credits flash up and something inside you goes, "Yess! This is how life's *supposed* to be!" Well, the Heavenly City is like that, except it's real.

The school campus I had to cross each morning on my way to class was not just some fake movie set. I could sit down on real grass, mash real daisy stems with my fingernail and make a real live heavenly daisy chain! The teenagers milling around in their cool casuals were not hired extras, but genuine angel trainees. And the dark-haired girl in jeans and cowboy boots racing towards me, waving madly, *definitely* wasn't a made-up character! Lola Sanchez was my real, and totally crazy, best friend.

It's a bizarre thought that if Lollie and I hadn't both died at such a tender age, we probably wouldn't have met. Though we have the same mad sense of humour, and almost identical taste in clothes and music, my soul-mate originally hailed from a vibey Third World city exactly one hundred years in my future! Like our teachers say, the Agency moves in SUCH mysterious ways.

The Agency is what we call the massive angelic operation, which keeps the Universe humming smoothly twenty-four-seven. There's a zillion-plus Light Agencies, if you want to get technical. But since they're all working towards the same aims, (universal peace, blah blah) everyone refers to them as "the Agency". Most kids from my school end up working for them after they graduate.

Lola and I had our sights set on being actual celestial agents, along with Reuben, our other big buddy. We were going to blaze through history side by side, scattering the Powers of Darkness with our angel super powers, bringing hope and harmony to Planet Earth; or something along those lines!

I think it's really touching that Reuben cares so much about making Earth safe for humankind, since he actually grew up in the pure shimmery environment of Heaven. He says when he was little he thought everywhere was like that! He'd never set foot on Earth before he met me and Lollie.

Isn't that mind-bending!! Three teenagers from drastically different cosmic backgrounds, studying in the same school by day, and bopping to the same heavenly hip-hop grooves by night; as if stuff like life, death, time and space had no influence over our individual destinies whatsoever!

I wish I'd known this kind of thing was possible when I was human. Maybe I wouldn't have spent so much of my time fighting Mum and Des for the remote, feeling deeply grumpy because I'd never be as rich, famous or fabulously good-looking as the kids on TV. But I truly *never* imagined the cosmos was this amazing!

What I also never imagined was the pressure. Kids like me, who get into the Academy on cosmic scholarships, are under *unbelievable* pressure. We basically get chucked in at the deep end with all the pure angel kids, and everyone expects us to get on with it.

Our teachers just go, "Yes, dear, I know you got fatally injured in a train crash / hit by a stray bullet / knocked down by a joyrider or whatever your sad story is, and had to leave your heartbroken families behind, but would you mind just packing your flight bag and running down to Terminal Twenty-two? There's a major crisis in ancient Wherever."

But you weren't going to hear me complaining. I'd been enrolled in a fast-track angel-training programme, at the most fabulous school in the Universe. Me! The girl who once sat in the back of the class, flicking through *OK!* magazine and gossiping about the cool characters in *Buffy*.

This was my chance for a fresh start and I knew it. So instead of running around the school in my underwear, tearing out large chunks of my own hair, going, "Aargh! I'm dead. I'm dead!!" I packed a few girly essentials in my bag, threw on my pristine new combats, laced up my funky boots, and bravely set off to ancient Wherever with the rest of the guys.

This way of life began to feel almost normal. I got used to carrying a beeper, so the Agency could reach me any hour of the day or night. I got used to hanging out in historical hot spots, wearing the same filthy clothes for days, and living on angel trail mix. OK, I never quite got used to the trail mix. I ate it though.

It got so I couldn't imagine *not* being in the angel biz. I wanted to do this fabulously rewarding job for always and always...

And then, quite suddenly, I didn't.

OK, so it wasn't entirely sudden. Even by angelic standards, I'd been pushing it. I'd been on seven tough missions in a row, including an absolutely epic assignment to ancient Rome, where among other things, I got my heart well and truly broken. I can say that now. At the time there was so much going on I hardly noticed.

My next mission had to be the most harrowing assignment ever. Brice, this weird boy we know, had come back to school after a long spell as a cosmic dropout. Anyway, he got it into his head that if he won a HALO, people at school would finally get off his case. I should probably explain that Lola has a *leetle* thing for Brice, and I'm becoming strangely fond of him myself, so we let him sweet-talk us into submitting a joint entry.

I arrived in seventeenth-century Jamaica a few hours after my mates, to find a full-scale hurricane blowing. Unfortunately, by the time I finally caught up with my buddies, they were suffering from drastic cosmic amnesia. They didn't remember they were on a mission. They didn't remember they were angels. More disturbingly, my soul-mate Lola didn't know me from – well, she just didn't know me.

Hey, I'm a professional. I coped! We actually won a HALO, for teamwork "under unusually adverse cosmic conditions". Brice is still in shock to this day! Big happy ending all round! And it was, or it would have been. Except for the dreams.

The nightmares started as soon as I got back from the mission, and after that they came every single night without fail. The plot lines were pretty samey. Basically, I was on a mission to rescue my little sister Jade from faceless evil beings who'd overrun my planet since my death. I'd shoot awake in a cold sweat, literally screaming.

Did I run to my school counsellor and tell her about my disturbing experiences? Yeah, right! That would have been admitting I couldn't cope. I just told myself dreams didn't count. Dreams weren't real. Anyway, they're private. Only you, the dreamer, knows about them. It's almost like nothing happened, right?

My panic attack was not private sadly. Short of putting up posters and hiring an actual stadium, it couldn't have been more public if I'd tried.

It took place in front of, ooh, let me see: my entire history class (except for Reuben who was away on a trip), four guys from the maintenance crew, two dishy young time technicians, thirty primary school children who happened to be visiting Angel HQ, plus their teachers obviously.

Oh, and Fern, one of the junior agents. I think Fern was born grown-up. She's still really young, but she wears smart little suits and v. high heels, and you never saw her smile, just as you never saw her without her Agency clipboard. (Lola reckons she sleeps with it under her pillow.) Well, she was there. I think that about covers it.

This might sound strange, but my public freak-out took me completely by surprise. Despite the queasy sensations in my gut area every time I so much as thought about leaving Heaven, I believed I was fine. I believed this up to the moment we had to walk into the time portal and go whizzing off to— It really doesn't matter where, because I never actually got there. My heart started pounding as if it was going to explode. My vision blurred, and my ears felt as if my head was being forcibly held underwater.

I was breathing in huge frantic gasps, yet I couldn't seem to suck in enough oxygen. Then I simply bolted, but backwards, like a panicky baby elephant; reversing blindly past engineers and bewildered school children, leaving my classmates in shock.

Lola came rushing after me. "What's wrong, *carita*? Are you ill?"

"Maybe," I whimpered. "I don't know."

"Are you having one of your big bad premonitions?"

"I don't know." And I burst out crying.

My friend tried to calm me down, saying all trainees had wobbles sometimes, and would it help if she sang our special theme tune, but that just made me completely hysterical.

Lola didn't know what to do with me. "Why isn't Reubs here?" she muttered. "He sure picked his moment to go on a tiger-watching trip."

Mr Allbright came over looking concerned. "Is there a problem?"

"I can't do it," I choked. "I can't go in that portal."

He gave me a searching look. "Been having bad dreams? Cold sweats? Upset stomach?"

I nodded dumbly.

"You're obviously in no condition to go time-travelling. I'm sure Fern won't mind taking you back to school."

Lola wanted to stay behind to make sure I was OK, but Mr Allbright said I probably just needed a rest. So they all went off without me.

Fern drove me back to school in an Agency car. I was sure she was secretly disgusted with me. She was just too professional to let it show.

We pulled up outside my dorm. Before I could get out, she did this nervous cough. "I'm not a medic," she said in her cool grown-up voice, "but I'm fairly sure what you had just then was a cosmic panic attack."

It sounded awful, but I had to admit "cosmic panic attack" pretty much described the experience.

"You've really got two choices," she said in the same businesslike voice. "You can face your fears, or you might just want to reconsider your future career. Some people simply aren't cut out for this kind of work."

That morning Fern was wearing her silky hair pinned in a French pleat. It made her look like a perfect little Agency doll. I just knew Fern had never had a cosmic panic attack in her life.

I spent the next hour in my room, face down on my bed.

Fern's voice kept replaying in my head. Some people just aren't cut out for this kind of work. Some people just aren't... Some people...

I HAD to be an agent. If I wasn't an agent, what would I be?

I buried my face in the woolly blue bear Reuben won for me at the fair, and cried. I was crying so hard, I didn't hear the small *click*, as my stereo switched itself on.

Soon after I arrived in Heaven, Reuben burned me a copy of a song he'd written, and which eventually became our private theme tune. I must have heard it a zillion times and I still find it uplifting. Reuben doesn't have a bad voice and Lola literally sings like an angel. At one point she and Reuben sing this spine tingling harmony. It doesn't matter how down I feel, the instant I hear those feel-good opening chords, I know I can make it.

"You're not alone, you're not alone!"

I hadn't so much as breathed on my stereo, yet my friends' voices were suddenly filling the room.

I sat up, totally confused, in time to see a ball of buttercup-yellow light float in through my window.

CHAPTER TWO

I'm going to let you in on some crucial cosmic info.

Any time you call for help, the Universe sends an answer.

This is like a LAW, OK? The Universe can't NOT answer. Sometimes you don't even have to call, the Universe answers anyway. Like now.

The glowing light ball was the colour of pure sunshine. As I watched, it morphed into a 3-D image of my buddy Reuben.

I sat open-mouthed, tears and snot mingling unattractively on my face, as he began to mime, rather awkwardly, to his own tune.

His dancing style is generally more laid-back, but

then he'd probably never sent an angelgram before. Even baby angels are taught to beam vibes to someone who needs help. But it takes YEARS of training to transmit your own personal energy, the way Reuben was doing now; and we'd had exactly one half-hour lesson with Mr Allbright. So it wasn't surprising Reubs was having a few problems mastering the technique.

Periodically, I could see right through him to the tropical foliage and flowers in the background. Plus I was getting all these atmospheric rain forest sound FX. Reuben himself was kind of staticky, like a TV channel that isn't properly tuned in. But I could make out his baby dreadlocks and cut-offs. I could actually read the cheesy message on that washed-out old T-shirt he wears, which says, **Love is the Answer**.

Part way through the track, Reuben started trying to tell me something. I kept saying, "What? Talk louder! You're breaking up!"

Finally, his voice reached me through a whoosh of static.

"Hang on in there, Beeby! I'll see you tonight."

He'd gone, taking the flutey rain-forest bird calls with him. But I felt SO much better, I can't tell you.

Not only had my angel buddy heard my silent call for help, he'd made the most massive effort to let me know he cared.

I couldn't imagine how he'd got permission to come back to school halfway through his tiger-watching trip, and I didn't care. Now I just had to find some way of getting through the day.

If I stayed up in my room brooding, I'd just get morbid, so I splashed some water on my face, whacked on some lip gloss, grabbed my jacket and headed down to the local nursery school.

When I arrived they were all excitedly raiding the dressing-up box for bear suits and fairy costumes and whatever. My normal day for helping is Wednesday, but Miss Dove seemed genuinely delighted to see me.

"I could do with an extra hand," she beamed. "They're a little overexcited today, as you can see!"

At lunch time, the preschoolers took their trays over to small brightly painted tables, and sat munching happily with their friends.

Miss Dove and I had our lunch at an adult-sized table, with a tablecloth and real glasses instead of beakers. We could hear the little angels giggling naughtily over the unfunny jokes preschoolers find so hilarious. We chatted about this and that, then she almost made me choke on my salad.

"I've told you this before, Melanie, but I make no apology for telling you again. You're a natural with this age group. You'd make the most wonderful nursery teacher. I know you've set your heart on being an agent, but if you ever change your mind—" Miss Dove's voice changed tone abruptly. "Bluebell, Lulu, I'd like you to come back now. You're *not* supposed to dematerialise without permission."

Can you believe Miss Dove wasn't even *looking*! Her excellent teacher's radar had warned her that some pupils were misbehaving.

"I'm going to count to five and I want to see you both sitting nicely at the table," she said firmly. "One, two—"

Two embarrassed little girls reappeared, very red in the face.

I was grateful to Bluebell and Lulu for providing a distraction. I had had the most disturbing thought. Suppose the Universe didn't *want* me to be a trouble-shooter, constantly putting myself in danger? Suppose it would actually *prefer* me to be a nursery teacher?

I'd been really upset when Fern suggested I might not be cut out to work in the field. Now suddenly, I felt a rush of pure longing. Life would be so simple if I took Miss Dove's advice; simple, but still really fulfilling. I'd spend my days surrounded by innocent paintings of smiley suns and lollipop trees, teaching the mysteries of the Universe through sand and water play. I'd never even have to leave Heaven, if I didn't want to.

After lunch, we took the class outside into the garden. I handed out tubs of bubble mixture while Miss Dove explained in terms her pupils could understand, that everything in the Universe was pure energy.

"Energy loves to play just like you," she told them in her special nursery teacher voice. "It likes to dress up and play at being stars and trees and birds."

"And bears," said Maudie solemnly. "It likes to dress up as bears, doesn't it?" She was still wearing her fluffy bear suit from this morning.

"That's right, Maudie! Clever girl!" said Miss Dove. "Now I want you all to take the lids off your bubbles *very* carefully. See if you can do it with no spilling. That's wonderful! Well done everyone. Let's see if you can blow some really beautiful bubbles."

In seconds, the air was crowded with gorgeous rainbow bubbles.

All the preschoolers were squealing, jumping up and down, trying to capture them. Then Lulu let out a little anguished cry.

"Now what just happened to your beautiful bubble, Lulu?" Miss Dove asked as if she didn't know.

"It poptid," she explained sadly. "It poptid right in my eye."

Maudie's beautiful bubble was next to pop. "Where did it go?" she wept. "That's what I don't know."

"Don't cry," said Obi.

I *adore* Obi. He has no hair and almost no eyebrows and he looks exactly like a three-year-old buddha!

"They didn't go away, they only changed," he explained to the tearful little girls. "They changed back to *not* being bubbles."

Maudie's face lit up. "*I* know! They've *been* bubbles and now they just want to play something else!"

I'm always telling Lola the things these babies say and she's like, "I can't *believe* four year olds can be so wise!"

OK, so Miss Dove's job wasn't what you'd call glamorous. She wasn't taking scary risks on the cosmic front line, like actual agents. But how I looked at it, she was actually teaching the celestial agents of the future – which to my mind was equally, if not MORE, important. I realised I was genuinely considering Miss Dove's suggestion. *Why not?* I asked myself defensively. *It's not like I'd be letting anyone down. I'd still be working for the Light Agencies. I'd be doing it from home, that's all.*

After school had finished, I walked back to my dorm. I'd just stopped in the hall to check my post, when Fern burst through the door.

"There you are," she said with relief. "I've been looking for you all afternoon. Melanie, I'm having SUCH a stressful day, and I was hoping you'd help me out?"

Fern did look unusually harassed. Her perfect French pleat had actually sprung several untidy little wisps. "I've spent the last month trying to organise a soul-retrieval weekend," she explained. "Now two trainees have dropped out right at the last minute. Do you think you'd be interested at all?"

"Probably not," I said cautiously. I had NO idea what soul-retrieval was, but I wasn't letting Fern know that.

"Are you sure?" she asked in a pleading voice. "It's going to be a fascinating course. Rose Hall is so beautiful. And Michael persuaded Jessica Lightpath to run the sessions, and as you know, Jessica hardly ever teaches trainees now." Fern beamed at me hopefully.

I'd never heard of Jessica Lightpath, but I just knew she wore woolly sweaters with rainbows on, plus she probably meditated with crystals big time.

"Gosh, love to help you out," I said, crossing my fingers behind my back, "but my friend's been away and he's coming back tonight."

Fern consulted her clipboard. "Would that be Reuben Bird?"

I gawped at her. "That's amazing! How did you know?"

"Because one of my colleagues has gone to drive him to Rose Hall."

"Reuben's going on this course!"

"Oh, yes," said Fern. "Didn't he tell you?"

I mentally replayed Reuben's angelgram.

Hang on in there, Beeby! I'll see you tonight.

I almost laughed. That boy is something else! How could he know I was going to be on a soul-retrieval course, when I hadn't even *heard* of soul-retrieval until two minutes ago!!

"So will you come?" Fern persisted.

Ever get those days when you literally feel the Universe ganging up on you from every side? Take my advice. Just give in, you'll save yourself no end of hassle!

I gave a resigned sigh. "OK. Count me in."

It had to be more fun than hanging around the dorm by myself.

Fern allowed herself a cool little smile. "I'm sure you won't regret it." She sneaked a peek at her watch. "Mel, I hate to pressure you, but you might want to run and pack. The bus is leaving in an hour."

Our teachers are constantly telling us we have to go with the flow. But I reckon an archangel would be left dizzy by a day that included a cosmic panic attack, an unscheduled angelgram AND a complete change of career direction, then wound up in a crowded minibus, swooping around bends so sharp, that if you saw them drawn on a map they'd look exactly like someone's intestines.

The atmosphere in the bus was not particularly friendly, I have to say. My fellow students on the course turned out to be from some celestial college I'd never heard of. Everyone at my school dresses in casuals. But these kids were like, *pure* boho. One girl was wearing an old-fashioned silk petticoat down to her ankles, little beaded slippers and a fringy silk shawl. Even the boys were dressed up in vintage gear. One wore what looked like a World War Two flying jacket. Another extremely good-looking boy had draped himself in one of those v. dramatic long coats I associate with vampires on TV. His name was something like "Indigo".

I love that arty boho look, don't get me wrong. It was the kids who got up my nose. They ignored me for ages, showing off tediously amongst themselves about some play they were involved in.

At last the vampire-coat boy deigned to notice me. "I don't think I saw you on Soul-Retrieval for Beginners, did I?" He had a lovely actor's voice.

I attempted a smile. "Actually this is the first one I've been to."

"Residentials are usually for intermediate students," he said in a disapproving tone.

Thanks for nothing, Fern.

229

"They really just asked me to make the numbers up," I explained.

"Well, I hope you can keep up," he said in a doubtful voice.

"We're SO lucky to get Jessica," gushed a girl wearing what looked like a milkmaid's smock. "What she doesn't know about DS and SR just isn't worth knowing."

The boy in the flying jacket threw me a pitying look. "DS is—"

"I DO know about Dark Studies, thanks," I said quickly.

They all exchanged glances, like, "Woo, has *she* got a chip!"

I slid down in my seat. This was going to be a *really* long weekend.

The bus turned off the main road and went bumping down a track. After a few minutes of jolting along in the ruts, periodically banging our heads on the roof, we came to a rambling country house.

Fern had told me that Rose Hall is used purely for soul-retrieval courses. Maybe that explains its truly amazing atmosphere. It feels like, centuries ago, someone struck a heavenly tuning fork and its pure and lovely vibe is still chiming on and on.

We all went to freshen up after the journey (we didn't have to share rooms, thank goodness), then came back down to dinner. I got a bit lost actually. That house is a total maze.

A delicious buffet had been left out for us. There must have been staff behind the scenes, preparing food and keeping everything pristine, but we never once saw them. It felt a bit like being looked after by friendly, but very shy, elves!

We were still eating when Reuben rolled up, lugging his ancient rucksack. A few days of living in the open had turned his skin the warm goldy colour of cinnamon toast.

I was so relieved to see him I just threw my arms around him.

He solemnly presented me with an enormous tropical flower. "It's a bit stinky," he said apologetically. "You don't notice it in the rain forest."

It was extremely stinky, but the gesture really touched me.

"Thanks, Sweetpea."

"Did you get my message?" he asked in a low voice.

I was still gazing at the flower. It was beautiful just so long as you didn't inhale. "Yeah, v. impressive transmitting skills," I whispered. "But how ever did you *know*?"

"I was sitting in a tree, watching the sun come up over a water hole, and I just got the feeling you were having a rough time."

"Only my most humiliating moment ever. I lost it totally."

Indigo was getting miffed at not being the centre of attention. He read out the message on Reub's T-shirt in his actor's voice.

"We all know love is the *answer*," he smirked. "But what, exactly, is the question?"

Reuben gave him the mischievous smile that lets you see just what he must have been like as a little angel kid. "Doesn't matter, mate. The answer's always the same."

"You might want to grab some of this food before it disappears," I suggested hastily.

The minute Reuben went off to fill his plate, the girls decided to introduce themselves! My buddy had made a bit of an impression. They all wanted to know if "Sweetpea" was his real name!

I explained that Lola originally called him Sweetpea as a private joke and now it had stuck. "Lola's always making up mad names for her mates. I'm 'Boo', I don't know why," I giggled.

Tanya (that was the petticoat girl) was totally starry-eyed. "It REALLY suits him," she sighed. "The way he gave you that flower; I've never seen anything so romantic."

I almost laughed. *Romantic?* Reuben?

But I'm really proud of Reubs, so I boasted, "He uses Sweetpea as his DJ name now."

"He does *deejaying*," gasped Tanya. "I bet he's good, isn't he?"

"Unbelievable," I said truthfully. "He does gigs on the beach most weekends. You should come and check him out."

She gave me a sideways look. "So are you and he…?"

This time I laughed outright. "No WAY! Reubs is just my mate."

My buddy strolled back, munching happily, "Has Jess arrived yet?"

Everyone's mouths fell open.

"You *know* Jessica Lightfoot?" breathed the milkmaid girl.

"We used to train at the same dojo." He chuckled. "Man, she might be old, but can she fight!"

It was like someone had flipped a switch. From being outsiders and newbies, we were suddenly the stars.

Next morning, I dragged on some jeans, threw on a T-shirt that said SOCIAL BUTTERFLY (mostly to annoy Indigo!), and went down to join the others.

Can you believe Indigo even wore his coat at breakfast!

"Do you think he *sleeps* in it?" I whispered to Reubs.

"Yeah, in a lead-lined coffin!" he whispered back.

Indigo was being v. v. charming this morning, giving me a special smile every time he passed me the marmalade, inquiring what I did at weekends and if I'd been to FEATHERS, a new club that had recently opened up.

Reuben whispered, "Think he fancies you."

I went pink. "Don't be stupid."

"Don't pretend you haven't noticed! You've got that little smirk!"

We quickly disposed of the continental breakfast laid on by the Rose Hall elves, then made our way to the lecture theatre.

Like everything else at Rose Hall it was simple and old-fashioned, with polished oak panelling and rows of plain wooden benches. The benches had also been polished to a high shine, and I immediately slid straight off! At that moment Jessica Lightpath walked into the lecture theatre.

Have you ever met anyone who literally makes the air shimmer?

Jessica's hair must originally have been jet black; now it was streaked with pure white, and twisted into a smooth knot on the back of her neck. She wore a dazzling white shirt, blue jeans and pristine white trainers; also masses of turquoise jewellery, making me wonder if she'd been Native American in a past life.

Reuben reckons Jessica has "long-distance eyes". And I know what he means. They're pure and clear, like they're seeing people and places no one else has ever seen.

Jessica started by explaining that souls usually "lose" themselves after death, for one of two reasons. "The human may have experienced terrible trauma – war, natural disaster, a plane crash – and be temporarily confused. Just occasionally souls get lost for their own evolutionary purposes."

I felt v. sophisticated, sitting in a grown-up

lecture theatre, furiously scribbling down phrases like "evolutionary purposes"!

There was something magic about that weekend. Like, the third or fourth time Jessica mentioned human souls, a tiny blue butterfly flew in through the open window!

I continued jotting down the Ten Key Points of Soul-Retrieval (or however many there were), but I could still feel the butterfly fluttering around the room, almost like I was tracking it with my nerve endings.

I felt a touch, light as a flower petal, as the butterfly settled on my wrist, and perched there, gently fanning its wings.

Jessica saw I was a bit surprised. "Butterflies are strongly attracted to soul work," she explained.

Indigo flashed me his intense smile. "This one seems quite attracted to Melanie!"

"Smoothie," Reubs muttered.

Jessica quickly got everyone back on track. "How many of you go dancing?" she asked.

People nervously put up their hands, wondering what this had to do with soul-retrieval.

"Ah, but how many of you really *love* to dance? All of you? Wonderful! So you all understand that you can only dance well, when you let yourself feel the music?"

"Yeah, of course," everyone agreed.

We angels tend to be a dancey lot!

"Soul-retrieval is the same," Jessica explained. "Everything in the Universe has its own note, its own song. We must attune ourselves to the music of this lost soul until we literally feel it inside our own hearts. Then, no matter where the soul goes, we will follow. We won't have to think. It will come quite naturally."

She swooped on Reuben and literally pulled him out of his seat. "You are the soul," she announced. "You try to surprise me and I'll do my best to follow."

Everyone went weak with relief that she hadn't picked on them. But that kind of thing doesn't bother Reubs. They began to improvise a surprisingly sexy little tango. Reuben was easily able to catch Jessica out at first, but as the dance went on, she began anticipating his moves so accurately it was uncanny. Suddenly it didn't seem like two people dancing, there was just this one thing – this beautiful breathtaking dance.

"Thank you, take a bow!" Jessica told him.

Reuben came back to his seat, grinning. Everyone clapped and cheered.

"A good dancer must be sensitive both to the music and to his or her partner!" smiled Jessica. "It's the same with soul-retrieval. In this beautiful, and sometimes dangerous cosmic dance, the soul leads and we follow. If the soul strays into a Limbo dimension, we follow. If the soul is badly confused and accidentally wanders into the Hell dimensions…"

Jessica cupped her ear expectantly.

"We follow!" we all chorused.

"Is she *serious*?" one girl whispered. "We'd have to follow it into the Hell dimensions? Don't they have specialists for that?"

Jessica seemed to be controlling her temper. "Yes they do! That's why the Agency runs these courses, to train you all to do this difficult and demanding work."

"Sorry, I wasn't thinking," the girl said humbly.

"You are new to soul-retrieval, my dear, so I will make allowances. This subject can be alarming at first."

If you ask me, Jessica is v. alarming herself, I told my new best friend, the butterfly; but I wasn't silly enough to say this aloud.

"For convenience agents use the term 'lost soul'," Jessica went on. "In reality, human souls never cease to be under Agency protection. But even though we know the happiness that awaits this confused soul in the Afterlife, we cannot force it to come with us. And so we play a patient waiting game. We wait, we watch, we follow, and we never cease to surround this soul with uplifting vibrations!"

"Sounds really boring," muttered the flying-jacket boy.

"Let me remind you that we're talking about saving an immortal soul. Our feelings really don't come into it." Jessica shot him a sharp look. "You understand that being permitted to do this work is an *honour*!"

"Yes," he said hastily. "I realise that."

Jessica fixed us with her scary long-distance eyes. "If all goes well, you will experience that miraculous moment when the soul accepts your help, and *of its own free will*, decides to move on to the next stage of existence."

She went to stand by a door that I totally hadn't noticed until now. "And now for the fun part of the course," she smiled. "Behind this door is a simulation chamber designed to replicate the type of conditions you can expect to find in Limbo dimensions!"

Promise not to laugh, but when I first got here, I thought "limbo" was the name of that embarrassing dance my step-dad tried to do one Christmas when he'd had a few too many Bacardi Breezers!!

I couldn't understand *why* our teachers kept banging on about it! Then I flicked to the back of the Angel Handbook and discovered that "limbo" is also the name of the cosmic no-man's-land that exists between the human world of Time and Space and the shimmery light fields of the Afterlife.

I can't stand angels who talk shop, so I'm not going to burble on about our experiences at Rose Hall. But I will just say that Jessica Lightpath is a truly inspiring teacher. Which is exactly what Tanya said when she presented her with a big bunch of flowers at the end of the course. Jessica actually had tears in her eyes.

I felt quite emotional myself. After a weekend playing "agents and souls", I'd become really close to everyone on the course in a way that's hard to explain. When I first became an angel trainee, working in a team was a huge challenge; now it was the thing about my work I loved the most. And I was on the verge of giving it all up to teach baby angels.

Going home on the bus, everyone was exchanging phone numbers. Indigo leaned over my seat, and gave me his special smile. "How does it feel to be the class butterfly magnet, Melanie?"

I tried to smile back. "Makes it quite tricky to take notes."

"I can lend you mine," he offered. "If you want to write it up."

"Oh, thanks. Actually, I don't know if—"

"You can copy my notes," Reuben said in my ear. "If you can read my spidery handwriting."

"Thanks, Sweetpea," I said, feeling like a lying monster.

I still hadn't told my buddy I was planning to change my career. I pretended it was because the SR course had been so full-on, but I was really just being a wuss.

On the drive home, I felt more confused than ever. Don't get me wrong, I still thought teaching baby angels was a worthwhile career. I just couldn't help thinking it might be a *teensy* bit samey, when you had to do it day after day after day. How was I going to feel, *really*, when the highlight of my week was teaching baby angels the actions to "Five Fat Sausages"?

I stared out of the window at the heavenly starscape flashing past. I remembered how I'd felt when I walked into the portal, like I couldn't breathe. I told myself there was nothing to be ashamed of. What was so cool about constantly exposing yourself to the Powers of Darkness; what was so wonderful about taking hideous cosmic risks?

I was getting that hot-potato feeling in my chest, a sign Helix is getting twitchy. Helix is what I call my inner angel. In the past, she's given me heaps of helpful angelic info, and the Mel Beeby part of me has often benefited from her wit and wisdom.

However, at this moment, I had no intention of asking for Helix's advice, because it would almost certainly contain really ugly keywords like "PODS", "SCARED", "WUSS" and "FIGHT BACK".

As in, "Admit it, babe, you're SCARED. It finally hit you that the PODS want to destroy every celestial agent in existence, and you're too much of a WUSS to face up to them and FIGHT BACK."

I shut my eyes, trying to stop tears leaking from under my lashes. *Mel Beeby*, I thought miserably, *you are one crazy mixed-up angel.*

CHAPTER THREE

"Careful what you ask for... the Universe is listening," Miss Dove constantly warns her class.

This has to be true, because let me tell you, after I came back from the soul-retrieval course I got EXACTLY what I'd been asking for.

No dangerous field trips, no urgent midnight summons from the Agency. Everything trundled along as smoothly as my nan's tea trolley. I went to school and did my assignments. I helped out at the nursery. I had a LOT of early nights.

Oh, and one time Lola and I went shopping.

Actually that was weird. I almost bought heaps of things. Like, I *almost* bought a bag. Ohh, heavenly bags are just divine. This one had a really subtle camouflage design, but was way more girly than that sounds. Inside were all these cool little pockets, making it ideal for field trips.

Then I remembered there wouldn't be any more field trips, and quickly put the bag back on the display.

Know what I bought in the end? One measly CD! When I got it back to my room, the guy had given me a CD of traditional Japanese harp music by mistake!

The Universe was setting me up, big time, but I didn't notice.

I felt really weird that week, too, in a way that's hard to describe; as if part of me was listening for sounds or voices just beyond my normal range. It made me feel very slightly deranged.

It's a good thing you're not going to be an agent, Melanie, I thought gloomily. *When it comes to promoting Peace on Earth, a nutty angel is not your first choice of personnel.*

Can you believe I still hadn't told my mates about my decision? They knew something was off, obviously. They're my mates. I think maybe they didn't like to hassle me.

That night Lola and I had arranged to hook up. I'd mentioned that Indigo had recommended FEATHERS, and she was keen to check it out. She turned up looking absolutely angelicious in a gauzy fairy dress with clumpy boots, that shouldn't go, but actually *totally* did!

Me? I was wrapped in a glamorous Angel Academy towel. Water dripped pathetically from my hair. "I'm late, aren't I?" I said guiltily.

Lola gave me the look we call her La Sanchez look. "This is getting to be a habit, Boo. Being late, leaving early, cancelling at the last minute."

"I'm really sorry, Lollie. I just got, you know, held up."

"Yeah, in your bathroom," she said in a sour voice.

I desperately tried to fake some party sparkle. "No, truly, I've been looking forward to this for *days*!"

"Oh, I *know*!" she said insincerely. "What's that B-thing you're always saying? 'The best buzz about being an angel, is boogying with buddies who just saved your booty'? Funny," she added. "I haven't heard you say that in a while."

She knows, I thought.

I took a shaky breath. "I really didn't mean to tell you like this, but I don't think I'm actually cut out to be that kind of angel."

I'd like to tell you my soul-mate was incredibly understanding. She wasn't. She was unbelievably hurt, and when Lola feels hurt she tries to hide it by blowing her top. We had a hugely distressing conversation, in which I never *once* managed to say how I really felt.

It was only after Lola stormed out, that I realised what I should have said. "I can't be your kind of angel, because I can't bear to see anyone get hurt EVER, like the PODS hurt you in Jamaica." Now it was too late.

This wasn't the first time we'd had a big fight. But that night it truly felt as if it was the last.

I was so upset, I did what they tell you in advice columns; lit a squillion scented candles, ran a hot bath, squirted in my fave rose bath essence, and climbed in for a good cry.

I'd deliberately put my stereo on continuous play. Unfortunately I'd left the Japanese harp CD in. I was up to my ears in bubbles by the time I realised, so I just let the atmospheric sounds wash over me. Actually it was kind of soothing, so when I went to bed, I left it on; and fell asleep with Japanese harps plinking in my ear.

When the phone rang I was so deeply asleep I couldn't find the handset for ages. "Melanie speaking," I mumbled. "Oh, hi, Michael! I thought you were away."

"I was," said the familiar deep voice. "Until an hour ago. Something came up and I had to come back."

I don't know your headmaster, obviously, but I'm fairly sure that Michael isn't like any headmaster you've ever come across on Earth.

That's probably because he's an archangel, one of the major powers behind the Agency. Michael also has special responsibilities for Earth, so he's constantly zooming off to historical hot spots. He sounded very tired, and also worried.

"I'll get straight to the point. We need two volunteers for an urgent soul-retrieval."

My inner angel sighed with relief. So that's what was going on!

"Jessica Lightpath suggested I approach you," Michael was saying. "She was impressed with your performance on her course."

If I'd been awake, I'd have launched into my sad story about giving up trouble-shooting. But Helix just jumped in with both feet.

"Have you asked Reuben?"

"Reuben's next on my list," said Michael.

"Then tell him I'm in."

Having kicked me out of my nice warm bed, Helix was making me hunt through my cupboards. I balanced the phone in the crook of my neck, while I hunted for the well-worn combats I thought I'd hung up for ever. "So whose soul are we meant to be retrieving?"

"Her name is Tsubomi." Michael pronounced it Sue-bo-mee.

"Sounds Japanese," I said, trying to climb into my combats without putting the phone down.

"Yes, she's from twenty-first century Japan."

"So what's the cosmic protocol? Do we go to Japan first, or buzz directly to Limbo or what?"

My inner angel was moving too fast even for Michael.

"Melanie, I think I should warn you that Tsubomi's situation is not as straightforward as the scenarios you practised on the course."

Helix and I finally succeeded in zipping up my trousers one-handed. "OK, you've warned me. So what is the situation exactly?"

There was a short silence on the other end, then Michael said, "This girl isn't actually dead."

*   *   *

There were four of us in the viewing suite. Me, Reuben, Michael and Sam, Michael's assistant. The lights were off, so I didn't see Reuben's expression when Tsubomi's face flashed up on the screen; I just heard him catch his breath.

Tsubomi was one of the most beautiful girls I have ever seen, but her face was totally empty. The mysterious inner light that made Tsubomi "Tsubomi", had gone.

A forest of wires and tubes connected her to the beeping gurgling machines that were keeping her body alive.

I swallowed hard. You see, I knew this girl.

I can't tell you where I knew Tsubomi from; like, if we'd both been temple dancers in a past life. I knew her, that's all. I could feel invisible cosmic strings running from her struggling heart to mine, and it really upset me. Because things didn't look good for Tsubomi; they didn't look good at all.

I was only thankful we weren't at her bedside for real. Seeing it on-screen was distressing enough. This young girl was literally on the brink of death, and two furious women were arguing across her bed. They were squabbling, if you can believe this, about who was to blame for Tsubomi taking an accidental overdose. Don't ask me how that was supposed to help.

The woman who looked as if she might be Tsubomi's mum, was practically spitting. "It's obvious you've never had children! You should have given the tablets to me. I'd have made sure she took the correct dose."

The other woman wore clingy leather that probably cost a bomb, but made her look disturbingly like Cat Woman. She was so angry you could hear her jewellery rattling. "The girl was exhausted, you stupid COW. We'd signed a million-dollar contract. She couldn't do the fashion shoot with freaking great shadows under her eyes."

"LOOK at her!" shrieked Tsubomi's mum. "Does my daughter look like she can do a fashion shoot to you! Three weeks she's been lying here like a zombie. THREE WEEKS."

A nurse rushed in. "Mrs Hoshi," she said reproachfully, "this kind of behaviour will not help your daughter's recovery."

"The only thing that can help her is a miracle!" Tsubomi's mum snapped.

"Miracles happen. I have witnessed several here in this room," the nurse insisted.

Mrs Hoshi looked contemptuous. "This is life, not TV. My daughter is not going to be 'touched by an angel'. She's probably going to be a vegetable for the rest of her days."

The nurse took a breath. "I'm sure the doctor told you that when someone is in a deep coma, their hearing is unusually acute. Please don't let your daughter hear you saying these negative things. Tell her you love her, that you want her to get better. Play her favourite songs."

"You just don't get it! This stupid girl had the world at her feet, but she was weak just like her father, and she just threw it all away!"

"Mrs Hoshi, you are speaking about your child!" The nurse made an effort to control her temper. "Why don't you go and get some coffee."

She slid a disk into the CD player on Tsubomi's bedside table. A sunny, boppy, totally forgettable pop song filled the room.

"Play something else," a voice pleaded.

For the first time I noticed the man slumped in the corner. His eyes were red from weeping, and he looked like he hadn't slept for weeks.

"That must be her dad," I murmured to Reuben. "So who's Cat Woman, do you reckon?"

"Miss Kinshō is Tsubomi's agent," Michael's assistant murmured.

I was gobsmacked. "Her *agent*! That's Tsubomi *singing*!"

"It's the first track she recorded. It topped the charts for weeks."

"She called it 'Bubble-gum Music'," Tsubomi's father was saying on-screen. "She told me once she wished every last copy could be melted down." He fumbled in his jacket and brought out a disk. "I brought this. I thought it might bring back happy memories."

"Of you?" jeered Mrs Hoshi. "You were never there! You were always shut away in your stupid workshop."

Tsubomi's father looked ashamed. "I run a small business, making traditional musical instruments," he explained humbly to the nurse. "When Mi-chan was small, she liked to hear me play the koto."

"She doesn't care about that! Do you always have to make such a fool of yourself?" Mrs Hoshi hissed at her husband.

He gave her a pained smile, "You were a fool once, Mariko, before you let this new love affair destroy our lives."

"Love affair!" She was outraged. "What are you babbling about?"

Mr Hoshi's voice was only just audible. "Your love affair with money."

"I'm not staying here to be insulted!" Mrs Hoshi stormed out and Miss Kinshō rushed after her. We could hear them yelling at each other in the corridor. The nurse shot out to calm things down.

Mr Hoshi looked down at the beautiful empty face of his daughter.

"Mi-chan, what have we done to you?" he asked in a broken voice. "I didn't mean to let so much distance grow between us. I was just so busy and your mother seemed to – well, she gave me the impression you were both managing fine without me. But I should have realised..." Tsubomi's dad was weeping openly. He took his daughter's limp hand and stroked it. "Come back, Mi-chan," he whispered. "Give me a second chance."

I was stealthily blowing my nose, so it took me longer than it should have done to register the music drifting from the speakers.

"Omigosh, I just bought this CD!" I gasped. "I was listening to it like, an hour ago!"

Reuben sounded choked up. "I don't get it. Why would a beautiful, talented, fourteen year old try to kill herself?"

Sam slid a disk into the DVD. "Technically speaking, this is classified cosmic material. But we thought you needed to see it."

He clicked a key and the hospital scene dissolved.

The Agency had been making a documentary of Tsubomi's life. They had film footage going back to when she was born. An MTV-type montage showed her growing up from a chubby baby, to a four-year-old tot in pyjamas, solemnly looking out at the night sky while her daddy sang and played some kind of Japanese harp, to a six-year-old cutie singing happily to herself, as she swung to and fro on a swing. Her mother watched from a doorway.

There's a look humans get when they get too close to the Dark Powers. You absolutely can't mistake it.

"They seemed like ideal parents for Tsubomi," Michael said. "Yakusho Hoshi was a skilled craftsman and musician, who inspired his daughter with a love of music. His wife, Mariko, was a former singer who quickly recognised her daughter's talent. Sadly, she saw Tsubomi's gift as a means to acquire money and power for herself."

On-screen, a stressed Mrs Hoshi was giving Tsubomi a singing lesson. "SMILE! SPARKLE!" she commanded. "Eyes and teeth, Mi-chan! Eyes and TEETH!"

In the next clip we saw a ten-year-old Tsubomi being pushed on to a makeshift stage to sing to a room full of unimpressed OAPs.

It was a dire song, and Tsubomi looked hugely uncomfortable. Yet even then you could see she was a star in the making.

When Tsubomi was twelve years old, her mother entered her for a well-known TV talent show. Mrs Hoshi was determined to make the all-male judges sit up and take notice. And, oh boy, did they take notice!

This sweet twelve year old bounded in front of the cameras, dressed in the kind of school uniform that would get any real schoolgirl expelled on the spot. With her blouse knotted above her navel, and literally flashing her knickers, Tsubomi belted out a cheesy pop number, doing things with her pelvis that would have shocked my nan to the core.

"Is Mrs Hoshi NUTS?" I hissed to Reuben. "She shouldn't be exploiting Tsubomi like this!"

"Shut your eyes and just listen," he hissed back.

This was sound advice. Without the disturbing visuals, Tsubomi's astonishing voice just shone through.

After her first album came out, Tsubomi totally dropped the bubble-gum sound, along with the jailbait clothes, and started writing her own material. Tsubomi's new songs were not only street, they had a genuine spiritual vibe, which fans instantly recognised. Since they were also wildly popular, neither her mum nor Miss Kinshō could exactly object.

While we were watching Tsubomi's life story, Michael made comments. "You see what she's doing? She's too young to be in the spotlight, yet she's trying to reach out to other young people. Tsubomi's only twelve here, yet she's already an artist through and through."

The assistant was more into family dynamics. Like, "Watch Mum's expression here. Did you see she's started wearing designer furs!" Or, "Have you noticed Dad is getting increasingly pushed out? You never see Dad on the concert tours. Just Mum and Miss Kinshō."

Tsubomi's schedule as a teenage celeb was unbelievably demanding. We saw her recording tracks for a new album, wisecracking on chat shows, doing interviews for lifestyle magazines, shooting videos, getting up at four a.m. to film a commercial for a mobile phone company.

Any time Miss Kinshō got caught on camera, she looked like the smug cat that got the low-fat cream. Just like a cat, she was completely two-faced. If it suited her, she'd schmooze around people and be really sweet and charming, but even a child could see she was out for herself. Tsubomi's mum didn't even bother with the charm.

One day Tsubomi took time out, to have some fun with her old school friends. They went shopping, took silly photos of themselves in these really cool Japanese photo booths, ate sushi. Then Tsubomi persuaded them to go with her to get a bad-girl tattoo!

When I saw the design on her naked shoulder, I almost stopped breathing. It was a tiny blue butterfly. The Universe had been sending me all these signs and I had never noticed.

Sam rapidly fast-forwarded through the next few scenes. "Miss Kinshō isn't too pleased as you can imagine," he commented. "Tsubomi never sees her friends after that. Mum takes care of that."

"Still with us, Melanie?" Michael inquired.

Still reeling from the butterfly coincidence, I forced myself to focus. My headmaster wanted me to see the second and final time Tsubomi dared to rebel.

It was the night they were due to play in Kyoto. Tsubomi had never been to this ancient city, and she badly wanted to do some sightseeing. Mariko Hoshi had a headache, and Miss Kinshō was prowling up and down, talking on her phone, so Tsubomi sneaked out of the hotel with one of her bodyguards.

Tsubomi and Stretch were good mates. We'd already seen them playing card games in the tour bus to pass the time. One time, when Mrs Hoshi was asleep, they had this mad competition to see how many takeaway noodles they could cram into their mouths!

Stretch never treated Tsubomi like a big star. He called her "Suzie", and said she reminded him of his little sister. I think he felt sorry for her, actually. OK, she was rich and famous, but she had absolutely no life.

Stretch agreed to help her play hooky, unwisely as it turned out.

Wearing dark glasses and with baseball caps pulled down over their faces, they wandered through old Kyoto. They ambled along canals fringed with weeping willows, visited a Zen garden made out of swirls of white gravel, and took photos at all the major tourist attractions. Then Tsubomi decided to hit the shops. She wanted to find a place she'd read about that sold a Japanese pickle her father adored.

This was a v. interesting cosmic coincidence, since one of our agents was conveniently playing his sax outside this exact same shop.

The Agency was increasingly alarmed by Mariko Hoshi's unhealthy influence on Tsubomi. They had big plans for this young girl, but if things didn't change, their budding star would be burned out before she was twenty.

So they called Blue in to help nudge Tsubomi's life back on track.

Blue is an Earth angel who is also a totally luminous sax player, and an old hand at giving cosmic reminders. When Tsubomi heard the divine sounds he coaxed from that sax, she responded exactly as our agents hoped. You could see her thinking, *Ohh, yesss! This is what it's all about. Not chat shows, not money, not fashion shoots. It's the music!*

She stood on that busy street corner for over an hour, totally rapt. Looking her in the eye, Blue started to play one of Tsubomi's own tunes, and being a true musician, she couldn't resist the invitation.

Outside the pickle shop, with traffic rushing past, the pop star and the undercover angel improvised a magical jam session.

Astonished passers-by couldn't believe these talented performers were playing for free. They literally started throwing paper money. Bank notes just snowed down. It was like one of those feel-good music videos. Little kids were dancing. Stretch was dancing. Old people with Zimmer frames were dancing. Reubs and I were dancing in the viewing suite!

But, inevitably, someone recognised her. A crowd quickly formed, fans began pushing and shoving, demanding autographs.

Stretch was excellent at his job. He managed to get Tsubomi away from the overexcited crowd and safely back to the hotel. Neither of them realised Tsubomi had been spotted by a photographer.

Next morning her picture was splashed all over the tabloids. Tsubomi Hoshi singing outside a pickle shop, with a homeless lowlife. Stretch was fired the same day.

Sam fast-forwarded to a few weeks later. Tsubomi was hunched in the back of a limo on the way to some TV studios. Since the pickle-shop incident she wasn't sleeping well. Looking unbelievably lost and lonely, she glanced out of the limo window, and totally froze.

Every billboard carried a giant poster of Tsubomi Hoshi!

My mates and I used to dream of being celebs. But when you lived the dream for real, like Tsubomi, it looked a lot more like a nightmare.

This marked the beginning of a worrying change in Tsubomi. On stage, she still sparkled to the max. But when the lights went down she looked absolutely drained.

"Omigosh! That's not tiredness," I said suddenly. "That's—"

Reuben shushed me. "We know what it is."

The documentary showed a few highlights from one of her last concerts, then replayed them from Tsubomi's point of view. Now we were looking out over a crowded concert hall. The huge space was packed out with ecstatic teenagers, swaying and singing along. All of them were waving cigarette lighters, making it look like the hall was full of twinkling fireflies. As the camera panned along the front row, there was a sudden technical glitch. Bizarre blips and blots of shadow made it impossible to see faces clearly. But I'd seen enough to know that the "fans" whose vibes were playing havoc with the Agency's equipment were not blissfully swaying, and they definitely weren't waving lighters. That's because PODS are allergic to light.

Sam touched a computer key, bringing up Tsubomi's energy field on the screen, a shimmery cloud of rose, gold and violet. "See those dark areas that look like bruises? Every concert, she gets a few more. The poor kid's on stage almost every night, there's no time for her to heal."

No wonder Tsubomi couldn't sleep. The miracle was she still had a vague memory of what she'd come to Earth to do. When PODS mess with your system, remembering who you are, and why you came to Earth, is generally the first thing to go.

I knew all this. What I didn't know was WHY? Why would the PODS go out of their way to target a teenage pop star? What threat could a sweet fourteen year old possibly pose?

Unless...

"You'd lined up some major cosmic role for Tsubomi, hadn't you?" I said suddenly. "And the Dark Agencies picked up on it?"

"That's very astute of you, Melanie," sighed Michael. "And as we've seen too often, Dark agents prefer to let humans do their dirty work for them."

I remembered the chilling expression in Mariko Hoshi's eyes, and shivered. "They'd got to work on her mum hadn't they?"

Sam put the film on pause. "And they brought Miss Kinshō in, and made sure Mr Hoshi was nudged out of the picture," he explained, "making it almost inevitable that Tsubomi would be pushed out into the spotlight years earlier than the Agency had intended."

"Then they sat back," said Michael, "and waited for her to sabotage herself."

I swallowed. It would never have occurred to those cosmic lowlifes that this vulnerable teenager would STILL try to carry out a soul plan designed for an older, wiser Tsubomi, like, *years* in the future.

Sam restarted the film. "There's not much more."

I wondered if the Dark Agencies had been filming Tsubomi too, playing the tapes in some viewing suite in the Hell dimensions, watching and waiting, hoping to find a way in. I think they were, because in the very next scene they got frighteningly close.

Tsubomi had flown to yet another city, to perform at a huge concert the next day. When they arrived there was some hassle with their luggage. The airline had lost the trunk with Tsubomi's stage costumes.

Mariko Hoshi stayed to sort it out. Tsubomi and her entourage went on to the hotel, only there'd been some major mix-up, her bodyguards and roadies hadn't been booked in and at two a.m. there were absolutely no vacancies. Which is how Tsubomi came to be sitting alone in an empty hotel lobby in the small hours, while a yawning Miss Kinshō signed the register.

Tsubomi was so exhausted she kept nodding off. The Agency cameras were playing up again. The ugly blips and blots made it impossible to identify the shadowy figures stealthily moving towards her across the foyer. Tsubomi's mineral water bottle slipped out of her hand and rolled across the floor. She jolted awake, and whoever or whatever she saw scared her so badly that her screams echoed round the foyer.

Miss Kinshō hurried towards her. "Tsubomi? What's wrong?"

The documentary cut to Mariko Hoshi and Miss Kinshō drinking saki at the Hoshi's apartment. They were celebrating their latest deal. A multinational wanted Tsubomi to promote a new teen clothing range. Tsubomi was all set to go global.

Mr Hoshi was sitting with them, but it was obvious he wasn't part of the celebration. He looked withdrawn and unhappy. The camera showed Tsubomi nervously hovering outside the door, wearing her fave Hello Kitty pyjamas. In that moment you saw how young she was, and how fragile. She took a breath, went in and made her big announcement.

"Mum, Dad, Miss Kinshō. I don't want to do this any more. I don't think I can. I want to make music because I love it, not because I have to, not because I'm scared of letting everyone down."

I have never ever heard a mother talk to her daughter the way Mariko Hoshi talked to Tsubomi then. It was a barrage of pure hate.

By the end Tsubomi was trembling, but you could see she still had one faint hope. She looked pleadingly at her father. "Dad?"

"I prefer to leave this type of decision to your mum," he mumbled.

Tsubomi closed her eyes. "Yes, Daddy, you do," she said in a choked voice. "And I wish you wouldn't."

Without another word she went to her room.

Weeks passed. Snowflakes melted in crowds on the window of the coach. Tsubomi and her entourage were on the road again.

Her insomnia was getting worse. Miss Kinshō had persuaded a doctor to prescribe super-strong sleeping tablets, as none of the normal ones seemed to work.

On nights she couldn't sleep, Tsubomi sat up watching Manga cartoons, or flicking through teen magazines, but mostly she played computer games. "I'll just get to the next level," she'd tell herself. "Then I'll stop." I knew she was really too scared to fall asleep.

One of our agents, posing as a roadie, tried to tell her that the pills were a bad idea.

"I have to sleep, don't I, Tomo?" she said softly. "I can't perform if I can't sleep." She suddenly looked confused. "How many pills did I just take then? Did you see? How many are left in the bottle?"

"You just took two," he said gently. "I was watching."

The following night, Tsubomi collapsed in a hotel bathroom.

By the time they found her, she'd slipped into a deep coma. We saw weeping fans leaving bouquets of flowers and flickering tea lights outside the Hoshi's apartment as if Tsubomi had already died.

The screen froze on the blank beautiful face in the hospital bed.

No one spoke.

It took me a few moments to pull myself together. "I don't mean to be dense, but do human souls often take off when their body falls into a coma?"

Michael seemed horrified. "Of course not. What kind of Universe do you think this is? Tsubomi has been under intolerable pressure. We believe she was protecting herself the only way she knows how."

"But she's in danger, isn't she? Not just from the Dark Agencies. The longer her soul is separated from her body, the more difficult it will be to retrieve."

Reuben cleared his throat. "Can I just ask a really obvious question? Tsubomi's been in a coma for three weeks. Why didn't some Agency guys go in straight away and get her back?"

"Erm, actually," admitted Sam, "she's sort of given us the slip."

I was gobsmacked. "You've lost a soul? I thought that was virtually impossible!"

"It is. But Tsubomi is an unusual girl. And remember we're talking about a million plus Limbo dimensions. We simply don't have enough personnel to search them all."

It was down to me to ask the second most obvious question.

"So this wasn't like, Tsubomi's time to die?"

"No," Michael said. "It isn't Tsubomi's time to die."

"But she still could?"

"Yes, she still could," he said very quietly.

"If you don't know where she is, how exactly are we supposed to bring her back?" asked Reuben.

Michael took a breath. "There is one technique which might enable us to find her, but there would have to be a soul connection between the human and at least one of the agents."

I shot up in my seat. "But there IS a link! I've been feeling it for days. I just didn't realise until tonight."

"We suspected there might be." Michael sounded relieved.

"It's theoretically possible to locate a lost soul by using the principle of resonance," Sam explained.

"Like sound, you mean?" I said.

"More like vibration. It's an ancient and extremely powerful angelic technique. I'd say it works nine times out of ten. The only drawback is, we wouldn't be able to track you. There'd be no Agency backup."

Reuben grinned. "No change there then!"

"How *will* we cope!" I sighed.

"Sam, have you noticed trainees today have no respect?" Michael complained.

"Actually, I seem to remember you making the same comments about me," Sam said tactfully. "So are you guys willing to give it a shot?"

"Yeah, we're in, aren't we, Mel?" said Reuben immediately.

"I'd like to hear it from Melanie, if you don't mind," Michael gave me one of his searching looks. "I heard you were thinking of changing options?"

Once again my inner angel got in first. "That's OK," she said, quickly. "Might as well go out with a bang."

It seemed like Helix REALLY wanted to go on this mission.

"Nobody wants to pressure you," Sam said cautiously. "But pretty much everyone here feels you and Reuben are exactly the right people to help Tsubomi. You're young, you both have a great love of music, and I think you're on very similar wavelengths."

Reuben sounded distressed. "It's not just about Tsubomi, is it? In Heaven, everything reminds kids how magic they are. On Earth there's all this constant pressure to forget. Tsubomi used her songs to help teenagers remember who they really are. Those kids need her, and they need her songs."

At that moment it hit me just why Tsubomi Hoshi was so dangerous.

The Dark Powers want humans to live in a kind of

grey-green-khaki waking dream. Tired, depressed, confused. Awake enough to work, shovel in food and watch TV. Asleep enough to make them easy to control.

This extraordinary fourteen year old had the power to wake kids up all over the world.

We said goodbye to Michael out in the corridor. He'd been called away from some huge Earth project to deal with Tsubomi; now he had to go back. "Sam will talk you through the procedure. It's really very simple." Michael sounded slightly anxious.

I could see he felt he was abandoning us. To make him feel better I teased, "If we complete this mission, Michael, you have to take us to Guru for hot chocolate!"

He gave me a tired smile. "If you complete this mission, I'll take you to Sugar Shock. I've heard their hot chocolate is out of this world."

Then we tried not to notice we'd both said "if".

Sam led us along a maze of corridors to a row of lifts I'd never used before. I couldn't tell you if we travelled up or down to reach the Zone, as Sam kept calling it. When the lift doors slid open we were in a totally unfamiliar part of the Agency Tower. A sign said:

TRANSDIMENSIONAL TRAVEL ZONE
PERMIT HOLDERS ONLY BEYOND THIS POINT

Our previous missions started in a bustling departure lounge. It's mad up there, no matter what time you go: trainees dressed in costumes from every historical period you can think of, all queuing for angel tags, making last minute calls, joking with team mates, attempting to meditate while the maintenance staff send for some crucial replacement part for their time portal.

In comparison, the Zone was as silent as the bottom of the ocean.

Sam unlocked a series of sealed doors made from some special celestial metal, ushered us through the final door and relocked it.

When I saw the flotation tanks, I understood why they were kept sealed off from the rest of Angel HQ. Those things were SCARY. "Tank" generally makes you think of water, but these containers held a particularly high-octane cosmic energy. The minute I walked in, I felt my hair fizz with electricity.

Miniature bolts of lightning were literally crackling around Reuben's dreads.

"OK, Beeby?" he inquired calmly.

"I'm fine," I squeaked.

The energy in the tanks didn't stay still for a second. It bubbled and swirled, constantly changing colour.

"You said you wanted to go out with a bang," Reubs commented.

I realised this was the first he'd heard of my change of plan.

"I was going to tell you, honestly—"

"Hey, I didn't take it personally. My name's not Brice! And it's not Orlando, either," he added in a meaningful tone.

He was talking about the angel boy who'd broken my heart.

"You're such a fab friend," I told him emotionally. "You know what's so great? There's never any silly complications with you. You're like, the *ultimate* star brother!"

For a second there was this funny little vibe. Then Reuben's smile was back in place.

"Just my luck to be everyone's fave big brother!" he grinned.

Sam coughed. He was waiting to run through the procedure for this type of transdimensional travel. And then we had to do it for real.

Did I explain we had to totally *immerse* ourselves in this energy? I'm not exaggerating; it feels almost exactly like you're drowning in light. Though when you're drowning, you probably don't feel your molecules melting back into their pure energy form.

I reminded myself sternly that this was an ancient angelic procedure. The concept of Extreme Angelic Melting was not exactly appealing, but if they'd been using it for aeons, it had to be safe, right?

And anyway, Reuben was in the tank next to mine, and there was absolutely no reason why I should have another cosmic freak-out. To give myself extra courage, I started to sing our anthem. "We're not alone," I sang squeakily. "We're not alone."

Sadly, I'm such a wuss that I'm capable of singing uplifting anthems AND thinking scary thoughts simultaneously!

The lights above the tanks dimmed.

Not the best moment to remember Sam's throwaway comment that this ancient angelic technique worked "nine times out of ten".

OMIGOSH! I panicked. *Suppose this is the tenth one today?*

Too late to back out now. Numbers were flashing in the corner of the tank, some scary unstoppable countdown.

TEN, NINE, EIGHT...

And then I saw her. I saw Tsubomi floating in front of me, like a ghost, if ghosts wore Hello Kitty T-shirts, baseball caps and jeans.

"Tsu–Tsubomi?" I whispered. My voice sent gold and silver shock waves rippling through the tank.

Her lips parted, and I suddenly knew she was calling my name.

She wants *us to come and find her*, I thought.

...SEVEN, SIX...

Soul connections are a truly wonderful thing. Now Tsubomi had made contact I wasn't afraid. I didn't even mind that my molecules were dissolving into pure energy. I was free! Free to fly in any direction. Take me to her, wherever she is, I willed, take me to Tsubomi Hoshi now.

...FIVE, FOUR, THREE...

Something was happening, a peculiar sensation like a kite slipping free of its string.

...TWO, ONE, ZERO!

The simmering shimmering colours vanished. Like a bird released from a cage, my soul went soaring off to a totally unknown dimension.

CHAPTER FOUR

Light flickered high above me.

I could hear crickets chirping and the buzz of summer bees. The air was so humid it was literally steaming. I was lying on warm damp earth, looking up into the branches of a tree. Sparkling drops slid off the leaves, and splashed on to my skin. We'd obviously just missed a heavy downpour.

"Phew! We actually made it to... wherever this is!"

I felt Reuben's voice reverberating through my skull bones. We were lying head to head like little kids.

Bones? I thought in surprise. Heads? Didn't we just dissolve?

We sat up and stared at each other in dismay.

"Oh, well," Reubs sighed. "Mustn't be picky."

"It's all right for you, you don't care what you look like!"

"What are you complaining about, girl? That straw hat is totally you!" He patted my bare foot. "Pity they couldn't stretch the budget to include footwear!"

Neither of us had the slightest idea why we were dressed like poor Japanese peasants, but then absolutely nothing was what we expected.

The Limbo dimensions we'd experienced in simulations were creepy colourless places, almost like you were trapped inside CCTV. This world was GORGEOUS! I felt as if I'd fallen into an old Japanese painting, one of those old scrolls, with a *très* deep poem written in exquisite Japanese calligraphy.

This would have to be a summer poem, I decided dreamily. It would describe the way the sunlight made patterns on the forest floor, and the blissful warmth on our skin. Ohh, and the mind-melting scent of flowers after the rain...

I should just mention, that despite its beauty, this world had the most peculiar vibe. Reubs and I agreed it was unlike anything we'd ever come across before. It wasn't necessarily an ominous-type vibe, but it kind of made you wonder if there might be more to this place than met the eye.

At the same moment, we noticed the bag hanging in a tree.

"Oh, that's for us," I said confidently.

Reuben looked bewildered. "How do you know that?"

I shook my head. "I just know."

"Wowie!" he said sarcastically, as he unhooked the crude leather satchel. "The perfect accessory for our scuzzy outfits!"

"Now now!!" I teased. "Thought we weren't going to be picky!"

The bag turned out to contain another bag. It was actually more like a miniature sack, filled to the brim with what looked like peach stones.

"Oh-kay," said Reuben. "I'm sure it's very nice of the local spirits to give us their old peach stones."

"Actual peaches would have been much nicer," I agreed, peering annoyingly over his shoulder. "But then there'd be that age-old Limbo dilemma of ooh, should we risk eating them or not! What's that other thing? The rolled up paper?"

"You girls are sooo impatient!" Reuben made a big deal of extracting the scroll from the bag, slowly untying the grubby piece of cord and unrolling the parchment inch by inch, until I threatened to thump him.

"Sweetpea if you don't let me see it NOW, you're going to be SO sorry," I told him, getting genuinely peeved, as he held it tantalisingly out of reach. Then I saw his stunned expression.

"D minus for refreshments, spirits," he murmured. "But a definite A plus for map drawing!"

I've had some bizarre experiences since I've been in the angel biz, but this was the first time either of us had come across actual magic. And the spirit map was magic, without a shadow of a doubt. The vibrant technicoloured markings were busily rearranging themselves even as we watched. First they showed a close-up of our immediate surroundings, then we got a kind of aerial view of how it all fitted together.

"Oh, *man*," said Reuben in a weird voice.

When I saw the tiny blue butterfly pulsing in the corner of the map, my heart actually stumbled over a beat. The mysterious map maker was showing us where to find Tsubomi!

Jessica had mentioned the possibility of running into helpful spirits in Limbo, but I didn't remember her mentioning them drawing maps.

All my misgivings totally faded away. This was going to be a doddle! We'd survived Extreme Angelic Melting and we'd located exactly the right dimension by using our own natural magnetism. Now we had a helpful flashing butterfly to show us which way to go. Missions don't get much more jammy than this, I thought happily.

Following the path indicated on the map, we made our way out of the trees into a sparkling rain-washed world.

Reuben was enchanted. "This is like a dream."

"So pure angels do dream, then?"

This was something I was always meaning to ask.

"It's a phrase, Beeby!"

"Sorry! I forgot you guys don't actually need to sleep!"

Reuben was looking down at the ground with a perplexed expression. "This ought to kill our feet," he said. "There's stones and all sorts in this mud."

"Maybe Limbo feet are tougher?" I suggested.

I felt heaps tougher in general. It was getting really hot and the air was loads more humid than I'm used to, yet I was twinkling over the ground like Tinkerbell.

Girls were planting seedlings in flooded fields beside the road. They waded knee-deep in the muddy water, singing as they worked, a truly heart-rending melody. Reuben reckoned they were singing in medieval Japanese. This could be true, but I couldn't seem to get past their strong country accents.

"They're asking the god of rice to come down and bless their seedlings, so they'll get a good harvest," he explained.

"Think we can spare a few minutes to send vibes?" I asked.

Discreetly as possible, we beamed uplifting vibes at the waterlogged fields. I didn't think the girls had noticed us, but as we walked away, a few waved rather wearily, and one called something that sounded like, "Hope you find her!"

"Was there something weird about that?" asked Reuben, after we'd gone past.

"Yeah, like, how did *she* know?"

He shook his head. "Not that. Didn't you get the

feeling if you were to come by tomorrow, those girls would be doing exactly the same thing?"

"I see what you mean," I said slowly. "Like they were just there for local colour or whatever. Do you think they stopped singing once we were out of sight?"

"Or stopped *existing*," he suggested.

I shivered. "That's not funny."

Jessica had constantly warned us: "Limbo is a world of traps and tricks. Never trust anything or anyone."

"When I think about it," I admitted, "they didn't seem exactly real. Not *real* real."

"And the birds are wrong," he said suddenly. "They sound right, but they fly all wrong."

I burst out laughing. "What's that supposed to mean? Like, they're going backwards!"

"Don't snigger, Beeby," he said sternly. "Just look and learn."

My buddy spun me round, and pointed me at a patch of sky. After a few seconds a line of wild geese, or it could have been swans, flew out of some trees and disappeared towards a line of hills, making their sad honking cry.

"And this is interesting because?"

"Keep watching and you'll find out."

Reuben was counting under his breath. He got as far as twenty.

"Bingo!" he said triumphantly.

An identical line of long-necked birds flew out of the same cluster of trees and disappeared towards the same line of hills, with the same eerie cries.

"And they always fly right to left, never left to right," he said.

"So? They're probably migrating," I suggested vaguely.

"In *sevens*? I don't think so! There's always *exactly* seven birds. Not five or six or eight. Seven, exactly. Every time."

I didn't share Reuben's fascination with local bird behaviour, but he's my mate, after all, so we hung around for a bit to test his theory. And actually it was quite spooky. Every twenty seconds on the dot, exactly seven birds flew out of the trees and vanished at exactly the same point between the hills.

"They're like robot geese," he said in a baffled voice. "Same number of wing beats, same number of cries. I don't get it."

"Me neither," I sighed. "But we'd better get going."

A wicker carriage rattled past, drawn by two sweating horses. A lady was peeping shyly out of the window, half hiding her face with her fan.

Reubs and I were genuinely charmed by the sights we saw on the road. Then we discovered that all these charming scenes and characters invariably popped up again further down the road, which rather took the shine off. After a few hours, we were like, oh right, another shrine, and yet more atmospheric temple bells. Oh, and another coy lady riding by in a quaint wicker carriage. And yet another travelling musician carrying some sort of Japanese stringed instrument on his back. Super.

We continually consulted the map to see if we were any closer to Tsubomi. But the blue butterfly seemed as far away as ever.

Reuben had been unusually quiet. I just assumed he was still puzzling over the Riddle of the Birds, then he suddenly blurted out, "So is this like some old-time version of Japan or what?"

"It's definitely old-time Japanese-*ish*," I agreed.

We trudged along in silence for a few minutes.

"If you had to sum up the feeling in this world, in one word," my buddy asked in an earnest voice. "What would it be?"

"Reuben, it's a *world*. Worlds are full of zillions of different feelings."

He shook his head. "Think about the people we saw earlier. Singing peasant girls, carriage ladies, harp players. Seriously, what vibe did you get?"

"You mean, like 'beautiful but basically weird'?"

"Beautiful and weird, for sure. But don't you keep getting flashes of something *underneath* beautiful and weird?"

I frowned. "I'm not sure. Probably I'm not as sensitive as you, Sweetpea."

We were passing a shrine to some local god. It was the spitting image of all the other shrines we'd passed, but for the first time I found myself taking a closer look.

People had left offerings to the god; flowers and bowls of rice. A few had left toys and baby clothes. Local people had written prayers on scraps of paper, and tied them to tree branches. They fluttered in the breeze like tiny flags. I don't know what it was, but something about that little prayer tree suddenly made me want to cry.

I thought about the beautiful carriage ladies, with their pale mask-like make-up. I remembered how each one had turned at the last minute, to gaze pleadingly over her fan.

And that last harp player, sitting down in the middle of nowhere, plucking those haunting chords...

"Sad," I realised. "This place feels humongously sad."

Reuben nodded. "Have you ever been anywhere before where there's just one overwhelming vibe?"

I shook my head. "Never."

"Me neither."

After that last musician, we didn't see a soul for over an hour. So it was quite a shock when we passed the hermit sitting by his fire.

The old man had been living out in the wilds so long, he'd become a bit wild and woolly himself. His robes were dirty and torn, and his hair had practically grown down to his waist. He patiently fed pieces of broken bamboo into the flames, to keep the fire going under an old cooking pot. He peered out through his straggly hair, calling a friendly greeting. Remembering Jessica's warnings, we weren't sure if we should talk to him.

"It'd be good if he could tell us where we are," I whispered.

The spirit map was fabulous on rivers and mountains and aerial views but it didn't seem nearly so fussed about fiddly details like names!

"He's probably OK," Reuben decided.

So we said hi, and then we all did a lot of polite Japanese bowing.

The hermit invited us to drink tea with him but Jessica had warned us of the dangers of accepting food or drink.

"Oh, that's OK," I said awkwardly. "We honestly wouldn't want to put you to so much trouble."

"I can see you're not from this world!" The hermit's smile seemed surprisingly young in such a wrinkled old face.

I'd been hoping we just blended in, but obviously our peasant gear hadn't fooled him one bit.

He broke off a new piece of bamboo from a plant growing beside the road, bent over his pot and began whisking its contents to a froth. "I know who you seek," he said calmly. "And I know the trials that lie in wait, if you refuse to turn back."

I gulped. Did EVERYONE in this world know what we were up to? Did we have, like, a big sign: "*Soul-retrieval in Progress*"?

"Thanks," Reuben said gruffly. "But turning back is not an option."

The hermit carefully poured scalding green liquid into an earthenware cup. It looked suspiciously herbal to me. I wondered if this old man was some kind of Limbo wizard. Maybe we'd just interrupted him before he flung in eyes of newts and dead man's toenails?

He gave me an amused look. "This is a strange world to you, child. A strange, baffling, perilous world."

I felt myself going red. The old hermit had virtually read my thoughts!

"You are strangers here," he said gravely. "Without a guide, it is unlikely you will ever reach your destination, and no local will venture where you need to go. I advise you to leave while you still can!"

"We've got a job to do," said Reuben stubbornly. "Perils or no perils, guide or no guide, we're not leaving till it's done."

"You're already too late!" the hermit said to my dismay. "The dark lord already has your friend in his power."

"There's a dark lord! Are you sure?" I gasped. "How – what did he do?"

"Do such trivial details matter, child? He used his power! Didn't your teacher tell you the Dark Forces are more powerful in dimensions such as these?"

"Yes, she did, actually," I said defensively.

"And did she tell you they have almost driven out the ancient gods who once dwelled here?"

"No," I admitted. "But it was just a weekend course. Look, I'm really sorry about the nice gods baling out of your world, but we just have to save Tsubomi." I was close to tears. "We *have* to."

He frowned. "Why do you care about her so much? She is no kin to you."

"So? Rellies aren't always all that," I told him. "But you can meet a total stranger and you just know they're your family. Like, if Reuben ever needed me, I'd just drop everything and go."

"Ditto, Beeby," Reuben murmured.

The hermit's voice softened. "And that's how you feel about this girl?"

"She needed us," I said huskily. "So we came."

The old man shook his head. "If you want to save this girl's soul, you must walk the Demon Road."

It's just a name, I told myself quickly. It's not used by real demons.

"The road will lead you to the Palace of Endless Night. That is where the girl you seek is held captive. I would take you myself, but unfortunately I have business elsewhere. My blessings on your mission."

"But how do we—"

He'd gone. No shimmer, no puff of smoke. Just gone.

"...find the Demon Road?" I asked the empty space.

I almost stamped. "Can you believe that! He was a wizard after all! This world is just TOO *scary*."

"I don't think he was your average hermit," Reuben agreed.

"Jessica told us PODS can cloak their vibes in Limbo, but I totally forgot. He could have been a dark agent deliberately leading us away from Tsubomi."

Reuben shook his head. "He gave us his blessing. No PODS would do that."

I folded my arms. "OK, so if he wasn't PODS and he wasn't a wizard, what was he brewing in that manky pot?"

Reuben investigated the pan still steaming beside the fire.

"Smells like some kind of tea," he grinned.

We unrolled the map so we could check our progress.

Reuben blinked. "Now where did that come from?"

A glimmery green line had appeared to the left of the first track. The butterfly pulsed meaningfully over the new road.

"I don't get it. How come it didn't show up till now?"

"I have no idea," Reuben admitted. "But as you see, the butterfly has spoken. A more useful question might be, are we up for this?"

"Totally!" I said brightly. I want to go back to school and tell everyone we walked the Demon Road all the way to the Palace of Endless Night!"

"Psst," I added in a whisper. "That was my angel talking before. My legs are pure jelly, how about yours?"

"Pure and utter jelly!" he agreed.

"We'll do it on three!" I told him. "One, two, THREE."

We both made a wild synchronised leap to the left.

We'd been walking through a summer world of birds and flowers and sweet-earth smells; old-time Japan at its sunny best.

The instant we set foot on the Demon Road, this changed.

It was the same landscape, yet now it felt hideously ominous. Even the air was hideous – heavy and clammy, making it hard to breathe. And the chirping of summer insects that I barely noticed previously, now sounded like a v. v. disturbing track on one of Brice's Astral Garbage CDs.

You know on a sunny day, when a cloud unexpectedly covers the sun, how all the world's colours suddenly look deeply wrong? It was like that. Even the shrines felt wrong, with icky dark stains splattered on nearby tree roots and surrounding stones.

I could feel myself getting more and more twitchy. When absolutely everything feels creepy, it's hard to know if something's normal creepy, or, you know, *creepy*. All at once everything, even the Astral Garbage insects, went silent. At the same moment I realised the sun was starting to set.

Was I tempted to turn back? Duh! Was I ever!! But we had come to save Tsubomi, so we just kept going.

In the fading light, the Demon Road had acquired a faint green glimmer that made me think of poisonous slime. Maybe it was psychological, but

I was suddenly aware of an icky gluey sensation under my bare tootsies.

We'd been climbing steadily for over an hour. It was inevitable we'd have to go down at some point. Suddenly the slime trail veered off sharply downhill through a most unpleasant-looking grove of trees.

"I guess it's onwards and downwards to the Palace of Unending Night then?" I said bravely.

"I think you'll find that's actually the Palace of *Endless* Night, Melanie," Reubs corrected, taking off a girl from our class.

"Imagine having to deliver parcels to *that* address!" I giggled. "Care of The Dark Lord, Palace of Endless Night, beside the Demon Road."

"Imagine the kind of parcels!" he said darkly.

Cracking nervy jokes to hide our panic, we took the sinister left-hand fork.

Angels have a good relationship with trees as a rule. We like their vibes, they like ours. Not these trees, however. These trees had absolutely gone over to the dark side. I'm serious. I *twice* tripped over roots that I swear weren't there a second before, and don't even get me started on the sound FX. Whispering, mutterings, gibberings, moans. It didn't matter how fast you spun round, you could never see who was doing it.

"I suppose it makes sense," said Reuben. "Cosmic balance and all that. We've had the helpful spirits, now we're meeting up with the unhelpful ones."

"Could we talk about spirits when there's a bit more light, please?" My voice came out abnormally high.

"Do you think demons secrete something from their glands that makes the road glow like this, or is it an energy thing?" Reuben mused.

"Could we not say the D-word, either, please!" I squeaked.

The hill was sloping so steeply, I was getting vertigo just looking down. By the time we emerged back into what was left of the daylight, it was impossible to trudge at our normal pace. Soon we were hurtling downhill, skidding and scattering stones in a mad rush.

Minutes before we reached the bottom of the mountain, Reuben said, "Oh, *what!*"

We slithered to a standstill in a shower of gravel.

Below us was an old riverbed that must have dried up years ago. The ground was littered with rubble that had been washed here in the days when there was still a fast-flowing river.

If I squinted against the evening light, I could just make out a sheen, like a layer of evil lime jelly, glistening on the bottom of the riverbed. Marching across pebbles, and possibly old skulls and bits of human elbow, the Demon Road disappeared into the mouth of a humongous underground cavern.

"I didn't realise that other bit was the scenic part," Reuben said gloomily.

"Guess he must be a *really* dark lord," I said, attempting a joke.

A grazing animal moved down in the riverbed, catching my eye.

I watched it vaguely. There seemed to be quite a few down there. Suddenly I realised what I was seeing.

"Omigosh, Reuben! Those aren't animals, they're children!"

The sun was so low in the sky, we were half blinded by this time, so it took us a while to figure out what the little kids were doing.

"Some of those rocks are bigger than they are," Reuben muttered. "What kind of game involves lugging big boulders?"

"It's way too late for them to be out. Someone should tell them to go home before it gets dark."

We slithered the rest of the way down the mountain.

Close-up, the scene was even more surreal. Hordes of little children, some hardly more than babies, were frantically building a tower on the riverbank. They rushed about, feverishly collecting stones and piling them on their unstable construction. From their constant scared glances at the cavern, it seemed likely that the thing they were frightened of lived in there.

"Hi," Reuben said in a sympathetic voice. "You're working very hard."

They went on piling on boulders as if he hadn't spoken.

In my world, different sized rocks would make different kinds of sounds when you set them down. Here, every single stone landed with the same identical *clack*.

"It's probably time to go home now," I hinted. "It's getting dark and you must be getting hungry."

Some of the little ones started whispering among themselves. With their matted hair and mud-coloured clothes, they looked like they'd been formed out of the dried mud of the riverbed.

There was something seriously off about these kids. Their skin was crusted with dirt from the riverbed, so it was hard to tell for sure, but it totally didn't seem like a healthy colour.

"Is it the light, or do they look sort of *blue*?" I murmured to Reubs.

"Pick up the pace, you lot!" yelled one of the big boys. "We've got to finish this before it gets dark."

One little girl burst into tears. "You always say that, but we never do!"

The boy can't have been more than ten, but he tried to control his panic, and bent down to comfort the little tot. "It'll be different this time!" he promised. "You've all worked really well today. This is the best tower we've ever built. The gods have *got* to be pleased with this one."

The small girl wiped her nose on her mud-coloured sleeve. "And will they let us through the gate this time?"

He darted an anguished glance at the cave. "Yes, if you work fast."

"Will we see gates crusted with precious pearls?" she persisted.

"Yes, and the gates will swing open and they'll let us into the Pure Land, and we'll live happily ever after. Now MOVE!"

"The Pure Land," Reuben whispered. "Isn't that one of the names for Heaven?"

I felt the tiny hairs stand up on my arms. "Omigosh, Reubs! These kids are—"

I broke off. A small boy was creeping closer, clutching two enormous stones against his chest. He stared up at me with an awed expression.

"You're so pretty," he said reverently. "You must be from the Pure Land, like Jizo." He was exactly like a normal child, except for his haunted eyes and the cold blue skin showing through the dirt like mouldy lemon rind.

He stretched out a hand. I jerked away with a squeak. I was SO ashamed. I don't know why I was so freaked. Limbo is full of dead people. It's virtually a dead people convention.

Reuben is great in situations like these. He crouched down beside the little boy. "Want to put those down for a minute?" he suggested.

The little boy let his stones slip to the ground without a word, then he just leaned very wearily against Reubs, and put his thumb in his mouth.

Reuben patted his shoulder. "Are you sure the big boys have got their facts straight? You've really got to build a tall tower before you can get into the Pure Land?"

"Yes, it's a law." The little kid had to take his thumb out to talk.

"I don't think that can be right," Reuben said gently. "Heaven is for everyone. All souls go home to Heaven just as soon as they've finished with their bodies."

The boy shook his head. "We're not allowed. Because it's all our fault."

"What is?" Reuben looked totally bewildered.

"When you die young, it causes trouble for everyone," the child looked deeply ashamed. "That's why we have to be punished."

"For being *dead*?" I said in horror. "In what sick world does that make sense?"

He tried to smile. "It's OK. Soon we'll build a really good tower, and the gods will forgive us and open the gates into the Pure Land."

He glanced over at the children, madly piling on stones. *Clack. Clack. Clack.* To anyone over ten, it was heartbreakingly obvious what was going to happen. Poor mites, I thought, living out here in this horrible place, building towers that are totally doomed to fall down.

I crouched beside him. (Even I can't be scared of a dead kid who still sucks his thumb.) "Maybe we could help," I suggested.

I heard him suck in his breath. "No! That's cheating. We have to do it on our own. If we cheat he'll know." He darted another terrified glance towards the cavern. "It's getting dark. He'll be here any minute."

I had a sudden unpleasant suspicion.

"Are you sure these are gods, sweetheart? Are you sure they're not, erm, *demons*?"

The little boy clapped his hands over his ears. "Why did you say that?" he screamed. "You're not supposed to SAY that!"

The ground began to tremble. The children scattered, screaming in terror. A gust of foul-smelling wind surged out of the cavern. The wind swirled up to the tower, toppling it to the ground with a mighty roar. A hideous figure lumbered out of the cavern, brandishing a blazing torch, and howling with rage.

CHAPTER FIVE

Here's a little Limbo-type quiz for you.

A drooling three-eyed demon is staggering towards you, saying something deeply uncomplimentary in demon language. Do you:

a) Take to the hills screaming like a girl?

b) Shin up the nearest tree and hope he'll be gone by morning?

c) Screw your eyes up tight and pray to wake up?

Erm, not if your name's Mel Beeby!

For no reason, I fell on my knees among the pebbles, and started grovelling in the bag, frantically trying to locate the peach stones. What's even weirder, is Reuben seemed to know what I was up to! At the same moment we yelled, "Catch!" and lobbed some of our peach-stone stash to the older kids, who also seemed to know exactly what was going on. We all began hurling peach stones at the demon.

Zoom, zoom, zoom! They didn't sound like normal peach stones, as they zipped through the air, but then they didn't behave like them either.

Did you know peach stones have a magical property that makes them ideal for fending off minor Japanese demons?

If someone bombarded you or me with fruit pits, we'd just get peppered with teeny bruises. When a peach stone comes into contact with a demon, it's a bit more dramatic. More like sprinkling salt on a huge slug.

Picture a demon-sized slug, staggering around the riverbed, howling in agony, as flying peach stones (*zoom, zoom, zoom*) made peach-stone sized holes in various unspeakable parts of its anatomy. Then picture all the demon's insides spurting out of the holes (euw!) and the demon toppling in agonising slow motion like a tree, and finally landing with a resounding thud (WHUMP!).

A stunned silence followed. Then all the kids went bananas, cheering, hugging each other and jumping up and down.

"Ding, dong, the evil demon is dead," I whispered. The kids seemed to be taking it in their stride, but I was completely traumatised. "How did we *know*?" I hissed to Reuben. "How did we know what to do?"

My buddy stared down at the dead demon with interest, as it slowly dissolved into icky demon jam. "How did you know to take the bag?" he inquired, sounding surprisingly matter-of-fact.

"True." I felt a flicker of interest. "Wonder what else I know in Limbo!"

Before he could answer, the children grabbed our hands and dragged us into their mad dance of celebration.

We were meant to be tracking Tsubomi through Limbo, but Reubs and I agreed it would be v. insensitive of us to just breeze off, like, "Byee!" So we chilled with the dead kids for a while. We lit a fire in the riverbed, and Reubs gave them some tips on tower building, and when no one was looking we beamed uplifting vibes. After a while the kids started looking uneasy.

"I don't mean to be rude, but isn't it time for you to go?" asked the oldest boy.

A girl rolled her eyes at him. "They're worried, stupid," she explained. "They don't like to think of us being out here on our own."

He looked surprised. "We're not alone. Jizo looks after us, when he can."

The little boy had mentioned someone called Jizo.

"He doesn't have three eyes does he?" I asked doubtfully.

"He's the god of all dead children," one of the older girls explained. "He should be living in the Pure Land, but he won't go until we're all safely inside."

Reuben looked touched. "Sounds like a cool god. Say hi to him, from us."

The oldest boy jumped up. "Take the demon's torch. It's still burning."

He tried to lift it but it was too heavy. Reuben stopped him, breaking it in two, in one smooth swift movement. Woo, I thought, but my buddy didn't seem to think he'd done anything unusual. He calmly lit a second torch from the first, and handed it to me.

The boy gave us a sheepish grin. "I forgot! We're supposed to give you this."

He reached inside his tattered shirt and handed me a strange little dagger. I thought daggers had to be made of metal, but this one was carved out of some jet-black stone. Tiny Japanese characters were written on it in gold.

"Its name is Heart Seeker," the boy told us solemnly. "You stick it in the dark lord's heart," he explained helpfully, in case the name wasn't enough of a clue.

The dagger gave off THE most disturbing vibe, so I quickly passed it to Reuben. He tested the blade with the edge of his finger.

"Thanks for this," he told the boy. "And good luck with that tower tomorrow. Remember, you want the flat stones at the bottom. Keep the bumpy ones for the top."

Walking carefully around the pool of demon jelly, we crossed the riverbed, holding our torches high.

We looked back at the children all waving and calling goodbyes.

"Ready?" said Reuben.

Turning our back on the firelight, we walked into the darkness.

According to the map, the road would lead us to the innermost core of the mountain. In practice, this seemed to involve going down and around, down and around, very much like descending a spiral staircase, except there were no actual stairs.

Underground, the road's evil shimmer had become a totally toxic glow. Our torches showed flickery glimpses of an eerie subterranean world; sudden scary cracks in the earth that emitted spurts of stinky steam and the dark glitter of bottomless underground pools.

Normally I'd be doing this running commentary, like, "Ooh, did you see that HUGE root that looked just like one of the seven dwarfs!" But I was too preoccupied. My thoughts had taken a most worrying turn.

"You've gone very quiet," Reuben commented after a while.

"I'm not that good underground," I admitted. "Plus..."

"What?"

I swallowed. "Something about all this just seems weirdly familiar."

"You think you've been here before?"

"I *know* I haven't been here before. YOU haven't been here before. Yet we both know all this – *stuff*. Stuff we have no business knowing."

"Like the bag?"

"Exactly. Then there's those birds that only fly in like, relays, exactly twenty seconds apart. Not to mention that bizarre peach stone episode. Then AFTER we kill the demon, and only then, a kid suddenly remembers he's supposed to give us a deeply suspect dagger, and what I don't understand is, *why* wasn't I more surprised?"

"Maybe you're remembering a simulation in Dark Studies?"

I shook my head. "It's not a heavenly memory. This is connected with Earth, I'm positive."

The underground road led us though a series of high-ceilinged caves. Finally, we came to this really massive cavern, like a giant's hallway. It had some really funky stalactites – they're the downward pointing ones, right?

This cavern had dozens of confusing passages branching off, so we stopped to consult the map.

When new trainees come to our school, they all get a copy of the Angel Handbook. Somewhere in the first two chapters (has to be – that's as far as

I've read!), it says: *"It's better to travel hopefully than to arrive."*

Well, until that stalactite moment, I'd been in my hopeful-travelling groove. Trudge, trudge, meet some dead kids, kill a demon, trudge, trudge. I was just too worried to even *think* about how our mission might end, so I'd been acting like we'd be slogging through Limbo in our bare feet for ever. So when I looked at the map, I practically had heart failure. The butterfly was flashing a hundred metres away from where we were standing.

We were a hundred metres from the Palace of Endless Night.

"Omigosh, we've found her!" I squeaked.

"Better keep it down now," Reuben advised in a whisper. "There could be guards."

If I ever run into Jessica Lightpath again, I'm going to ask her, how come, in Limbo, you just have to *name* something and it appears?

Tramp, tramp, tramp. The sound echoed on and on, spookily amplified by the underground acoustic; the mechanical, unstoppable marching boots of soldiers who aren't quite human. We literally couldn't tell if there were ten soldiers storming towards us through the dark, or ten thousand.

Then, like a horde of giant cockroaches, they erupted from every passageway. There weren't ten thousand, but there were *definitely* more than ten, their dull black armour adding unpleasantly to the cockroach impression.

I'm not SO great at angelic martial arts, but I'm improving. Reuben, however, has got every heavenly belt going. He's like the teenage don of martial arts. But in normal life, neither one of us is capable of taking on a hundred-plus soldiers and leaving them in piles like laundry. Yet this is what happened.

It was like the peach stone episode only a zillion times more spectacular. We didn't have to think, we didn't have to go in a huddle about strategy. We went into total fight mode. We slammed into that dark lord's posse as if we'd been taking on armies our whole lives. We somersaulted off walls. We flew through the air like wire fighters (with no wires, might I add), and the soldiers went crashing down like skittles.

Once again I seemed to be split into two. The normal Mel was going; what the sassafras is going on! The wannabe-wire-fighter Mel was going; who cares? It's SO unbelievably cool!

My buddy and I fought our way all the way to the palace gates. The few guards on duty put up some resistance, but nothing we couldn't handle.

"We showed them," said Reuben, very slightly out of breath. "And the gates are open, excellent."

And then we clocked the building on the other side. Until this moment, it hadn't occurred to me that anyone would *choose* to build their palace out of stinky river mud, bits of skull and bone, and icky little plant organisms. Did I mention the gruesome gargoyle faces peering at us from inside tangles of living plant fibre, like old ladies snooping through net curtains? Did I also mention there were NO windows, anywhere?

I was dangerously close to another cosmic panic attack, when Reuben suddenly said this really helpful thing. "Just think, people all over the Universe must be taking deep breaths at this exact moment, as they psyche themselves up to do some scary but totally necessary thing."

I swallowed. Rescuing a human soul from a creepy palace in the underworld was hideously scary, but it made me feel heaps better to remember we weren't alone.

"If anyone asks, we're style consultants who've come to give them a makeover!" I said bravely.

And like other scared people all over the Universe, we took deep breaths, then walked through the gates and into the palace.

Eek, this style consultant just quit, I thought. My nostrils filled with an overwhelming mushroomy pong of mould and decay.

The dark lord's palace wasn't exactly welcoming from the outside, but the interior made me feel seriously deranged. First because it had all this creepy underground plant life growing *inside*.

Second, the palace was terminally confusing; stairs which stopped halfway to nowhere, dank corridors that constantly looped back on themselves. My worst thing was the swaying bridges, which initially appeared to take you to one part of the palace, yet infallibly delivered you in the opposite direction! After we'd found ourselves back by the front door for the squillionth time, Reuben suggested it might be better to ignore our physical surroundings.

"Keep your eyes on the map," he advised. "The butterfly will let us know if we're hot or cold."

"I'm so glad you're here, Reubs," I said impulsively. "I don't think I could have handled this by myself."

Reubs looked surprised. "Yeah, you could."

I shook my head. "I have these major cosmic wobbles, but when you're with me, I somehow keep it together."

"Works both ways, you know, Beeby," he pointed out.

I was amazed. "Really?"

"Yes, really. Now focus," he said sternly.

Reuben's strategy worked. By concentrating carefully on the dancing butterfly, we gradually made our way through the underground maze. At last a narrow twisty corridor brought us to the top of some cellar stairs. We stared down thoughtfully. Though every bit as dark and creepy as other stairs we'd seen, I noticed that these seemed much newer, as if they had been built more recently.

I felt a zing of angel electricity, and knew my hunch was right. Tsubomi's soul was down there! We didn't say a word. We just flew down the stairs.

The door at the bottom was locked. Reuben kicked it down with the same surprising strength he'd shown when he snapped the demon's torch.

Her vibes still hung in the air like a faint perfume. But Tsubomi's soul had gone.

Reuben shook his head. "It stinks of magic in here. The creep must have seen us coming and spirited her away somewhere."

I couldn't speak. I wandered about, stupidly picking up objects she might have touched and putting them down again.

I'm not into that "I live in a creepy church crypt" look, personally, and probably Tsubomi wasn't either, but you could see little human touches where she'd tried to make her underworld pad a bit more homey.

There was a sleeping area, divided by a lacquered screen, with a futon and a folded quilt. In her living area, Tsubomi had carefully arranged her art materials at one end of a low table; ink, parchment, various brushes. It looked like she'd been practising calligraphy to pass the time. At the opposite end of the table was a bowl of fresh strawberries. In the eerie twilight of the palace, their colours glowed like jewels.

There were real jewels too, spilling out of a casket; a tangle of bangles, chains and necklaces, in such disturbing designs they could only be gifts from the dark lord himself.

"WHY DID YOU COME?"

Dust rained down from the rocky ceiling. I clutched at Reubs, but by that time, the dark lord himself was towering over us, and anyway, there was nowhere to run.

"WHY DID YOU COME?"

"WHY DID YOU COME?"

"WHY DID YOU COME?"

Let me tell you, worn by a scary demon lord, the dull black armour of his soldiers absolutely did not make you think of cockroaches. It made him look exactly what he was, a terrifying samurai with evil powers. Each time he bellowed his question, he popped up in a different part of the room. This made it seem like there were several demon samurai bellowing at us simultaneously. As if one wasn't enough.

"What have you done with her soul, you monster?" I screamed to an empty space where he'd been standing seconds before.

More dust pattered down from the roof. This time there were actual stones and chunks of rock. I saw a little brown mouse skitter for cover.

"You dare to call ME a monster!" the dark lord thundered. "I SAVED Tsubomi. She had been too long in your world of Light. Her life had become shallow and one-dimensional. It was making her sick. She needed the richly textured darkness of the earth."

Richly textured poo, I thought. This lord obviously fancied himself as a bit of an intellectual.

The demon was pacing now. "I brought her to my palace," he said, slightly less thunderously. "I had this chamber built especially. I was going to educate her."

"What about? Darkness and dirt?" I whispered to Reubs.

"Tsubomi's mind was filled with trivia. She had forgotten humans are made of earth, as well as stardust. I saw past her ignorance. I was willing to work with her."

I suppressed a frightened squeak as the demon materialised an inch from my nose.

"She was afraid at first," he boomed. "But I expected that. I was hoping to convince her that I was her teacher, not her jailer, perhaps even something more."

"Something more?" I gulped.

"Lately she had shown signs of beginning to care for me. I brought her fruit and flowers from the world above. I gave her jewels."

He thrust his huge helmet close to my face. "And you Children of Light had to come and ruin everything!" he roared.

Reuben quickly placed himself between us. "Don't threaten her, man!" he said angrily. "We Children of Light stick together."

I was shaking like a rabbit. I'd had a good squint inside that helmet, and the creature inside was literally made of shadows. *Lucky Reuben's got that special dagger,* I thought.

"You didn't answer Mel's question." Reuben had taken up a martial-arts crouch. "What have you done with Tsubomi's soul?"

"Alas! I was weak!" The demon's boots made a hollow clumping sound as he paced. "We'd spent all those evenings together, listening to classical music."

Reuben gave me a comical look, like: "Eh?"

"I somehow couldn't bring myself to—" The dark lord was half talking to himself. He gave us a sudden malevolent glower. "Never fear! I shall have no such problem with you!"

"Be quick then, old man!" My buddy slid Heart Seeker out of his belt, lunging at the demon's chest. Nothing happened.

The dark lord howled with laughter. "You will not find what you seek inside this armour! Many have tried and ALL have failed!"

Still laughing, the dark lord slowly rose off the ground. Inhuman laughter rang out from the rocky walls and the earth beneath our feet.

I was practically wetting myself. Like Reubs, I'd been relying on the dagger. Now we were totally stuffed. "How do you kill something like that?" I whimpered to myself.

For absolutely no reason my eye was drawn to the table where Tsubomi had been practising calligraphy with ink and brushes.

Guess what?

That clever girl had written us a note! In beautiful calligraphy, she had copied out four lines of what looked like deep song lyrics, but which contained the exact answer to my question.

If you can't find the heart
in the darkness, babe,
try looking for the darkness
in the heart.

No, normally I wouldn't understand it either! But I was in Limbo mode, so I instantly caught on to what she was telling us. It was useless to look for the dark lord's heart inside his armour, because (euw euw euw!) he kept it SOMEWHERE ELSE. Believe it or not, I knew *exactly* where!

Reuben and the demon lord continued to whirl around the room, knocking over furniture.

I sidled over to Tsubomi's jewellery box and had a stealthy rummage among her collection of underworld knick-knacks. These included earrings carved out of what looked like coal, and a gruesome little charm bracelet hung with teeny skulls. The hideous locket was at the very bottom of the heap; a totally tasteless ruby-encrusted heart with a tiny see-through window. I didn't examine it TOO closely, but the twitching thing inside looked small enough, and *easily* dark enough, to be a dark lord's heart.

"Dagger please," I called calmly, like a nurse in *ER*.

My angel colleague immediately sent Heart Seeker spinning through the air. It made a sound like a v. sinister Frisbee. *Pyu. Pyu.*

The demon roared out a warning, but I'd already caught the dagger and plunged it through the locket, into the pulsing stuff inside.

The dark lord collapsed on to his knees with a yowl of pain that seemed to come from the core of the mountain itself.

Then he crashed to the floor and lay totally still. Strange-coloured steam rose, hissing faintly, from his armour. The dark lord had finally gone wherever dark lords go.

"No more abducting for you," my buddy told the steaming metal.

I was beside myself. "I am SO stupid. I killed him and we don't even know what he's done to her!"

Reuben pointed silently to the table. For the first time I noticed the litter of tiny green strawberry stalks and hulls beside the fruit bowl.

"Omigosh!" I wailed. "Doesn't she have *any* sense?"

"Don't blame Tsubomi. She had eaten nothing since she came to the palace."

For a moment I genuinely believed I was hallucinating. A v. small mouse was talking to us. It wasn't even talking in the special language angels use for communicating with animals. It was squeaking in medieval Japanese!

"Tonight the demon brought her a bowl of strawberries. She was so hungry and thirsty,

she'd eaten half the bowl before she realised what she was doing."

"That's helpful, little buddy, thanks," Reuben said politely. "Isn't there a fairy tale or something like this?" he asked.

"Cinderella had talking mice," I gulped. "In the Disney version."

"No, I meant the fruit. The girl ate an apple or a pomegranate or something, so she had to stay in the underworld for ev—"

Reuben never finished his sentence. There was a chime of music from some magical source. The palace dissolved around us, and we found ourselves in a totally different world.

CHAPTER SIX

My buddy and I were lying under a tree, head to head, exactly like before. The sky above was lit with an angry red glow.

"Woo! Serious *déjà vu!*"

I could feel Reuben's voice buzzing through my skull bones.

"Serious, *serious*, *déjà vu*," I agreed.

We scrambled to our feet and Reubs gave a low whistle.

"Now *that* is you!"

"How on earth can you tell?" I giggled.

We were completely dressed in black. Black hoods, loose black fighting clothes, black boots.

Even the lower parts of our faces were covered with black scarves.

"Hmm, first peasants, then ninjas," I mused aloud.

"Ninjas were like secret agents and assassins, right?" Reuben asked.

"Something like that."

There was some weirdly familiar logic behind this unexpected upgrade, but though I was racking my brains, I just could *not* remember what it was.

We were in a woodland glade almost identical to the first, but with crucial differences. The first glade had been lush and summery; here, dead and dying leaves floated down through the air, collecting in rustling drifts. Several trees seemed badly burned, either by lightning, forest fire or both. You could see their pale dead insides where the charred bark had peeled away. Somewhere beyond the fire-damaged trees, a wolf gave its lonely howl.

This world wasn't so pretty but it was *humongously* atmospheric!

Once again I felt like I'd fallen into an old Japanese painting. This one was totally painted in fire colours. Fiery red skies. Red dirt. Red and gold leaves.

"What would this poem say?" I wondered aloud.

Reuben looked blank. "Poem?"

"Japanese artists used to paint nature scenes to show the different seasons. Sometimes they'd write little haiku or whatever, to sum up the mood. Like if I wrote a poem about this wood, it might say something like..." I shut my eyes for a moment, then recited:

"*Summer came too soon.*

Flowers shrivel with a young girl's hopes

turning to smoke and ashes."

Reuben looked amazed. "You never told me you wrote poetry, Beeby!"

"I don't," I said. "Except when they made us at school."

I felt a bit weird about it, to be honest, so I hastily changed the subject. "Have you noticed this world smells different?"

The first wood had smelled of earth and rain. This one gave off a hot rubbery tang as if it hadn't rained in a thousand years.

A v. disturbing theory was forming at the back of my mind. A theory which totally explained all the things that made absolutely no sense otherwise; for example, how Reubs and I were able to mash up an entire army without getting a teeny scratch ourselves.

When I spotted the satchel hanging in the tree, I knew for sure my theory was right. I unhooked the new bag of Limbo goodies from the branch. This one was made from *way* better-quality leather. Without saying a word, I emptied the bag on to the ground. This is what was inside:

- One coil of rope with a useful hooky thing on the end.
- Two star-shaped ninja weapons.
- Small spiky objects for scaling high walls.
- One pristine new scroll.

I waved it triumphantly. "Ta-daa! I *knew* they'd give us a new map!"

Reuben gave me a severe look. "Mind telling me what's going on?"

"I'm not sure." I took a breath. "This might sound mad, but I think we're playing some kind of game."

"A game?" Reubs echoed.

"You know those musical chords we heard a few minutes ago? That's because we just went up a level. When we killed the dark lord, we absorbed his powers, which is why we've got more energy. I have, anyway."

"Yep, that sounds mad," he agreed.

"Because you never lived on Earth, hon! And you've never been interested in computer games. You said yourself this is like a fairy tale. Well, computer games are like interactive fairy tales. If you defeat the baddies you go up to the next level. If not, you lose a life and have to start again—"

My buddy held up his hand. "I'm lost. How can a world be a game?"

I shrugged. "It's just the only explanation that makes sense."

"To you," he said darkly.

"Remember the way things happened in that first world? How that kid gave you the dagger *after* we'd killed the first demon. That's exactly like a game. You have to earn things in games."

"I still don't—"

"OK, OK, how about the way we took out those soldiers? Remember the sound FX?"

He chuckled. "*Biff-boff.* I thought that was weird at the time."

"And those flying peach stones. *Zoom-zoom!*"

Reuben gave me a sideways grin. "The peach stones were cool!"

"*Très* cool," I agreed. "But they weren't *normal.*"

"Not even for Limbo?" he asked wistfully.

I shook my head. "Sorry, Sweetpea."

I could see him gradually processing this new idea. "That would explain the birds," he admitted. "And you're right. I've got heaps more energy."

"Because we just went up a level. If you notice, everything is extra vibey."

"Extra vibey but still deeply sad."

My buddy unfurled our superior Level-Two scroll. I heard his sharp intake of breath. "Look who's back," he said huskily.

When I saw that little blue butterfly, I almost burst into tears. Our unexpected upgrade hadn't given me time to dwell on what the dark lord had done to Tsubomi. But she was OK, she was still OK!

"I can't believe it!" I said shakily. "She must have come up with us somehow after we killed the dark lord. From how he was talking, I thought he'd done something hideous to her."

Reubs frowned. "Supposing your game theory is right, who are we playing *against* exactly?"

I shook my head. "You're really trying to outwit the actual game itself. Plus you're trying to beat your own best efforts. I just hope we get to Tsubomi *before* the demon lord this time."

"The one on Level Two will be stronger, right?"

"Yeah, but we're stronger too, don't forget! Plus we've probably got heaps of cunning ninja skills we don't know about!" I grinned at him. Thanks for the TLC. Now these angel assassins had better hit the road!"

He laughed. "'Angel Assassins', sounds like the kind of hardcore stuff Brice listens to."

With Reuben improvising mad Angel-Assassin-type lyrics to make me laugh, we set off in the direction indicated by the butterfly.

Level Two was mountain country, rocky and arid. Nothing seemed to grow there except cacti and scrub, and the occasional pine tree. All the trees had been blasted by lightning along the exact same side. On Level Two peasant girls were clearing stones from the parched red fields, passing filled baskets to each other in a never-ending chain gang, and the ladies who rode past in creaky wicker carriages were fluttering their fans to keep cool, not just for coyness purposes.

In its own way, Level Two was fabulously scenic.

At intervals we'd glimpse fairy-tale castles perched on rocky ledges high above the track.

"Noticed how every castle comes with an identical pine tree?" Reuben commented.

"Yeah, yeah and the birds always fly in sevens!"

"These are eagles," he grinned. "They mostly fly solo."

I looked up and sure enough there was exactly one fierce golden-brown eagle soaring on a current of hot air. "Boy, you really notice every tiny thing!" I marvelled.

We were practically jogging by this time, easily overtaking yet another travelling harp player.

や あ yá "Hi," we said in medieval Japanese.

や あ yá "Hi," he answered politely.

On Level Two, the musicians wore scarves tied over their mouths, bandit-style, to keep out the dust.

We passed so many harp players, not to mention woodcutters and travelling monks, that I had a strong suspicion some of them were ninjas in disguise.

I was starting to think like a ninja by this time! I'm serious! Suddenly my mind was totally humming with devious strategies; scanning the mountainside for caves to hide out in, bushes to skulk behind, castles to raid. I had no intention of raiding a castle for real, obviously, but if I HAD wanted to, I had all the relevant ninja skills at my fingertips.

"See that castle?" I called to my ninja angel buddy, as we jogged on under glowing skies. "If we crawled through those bushes, we'd find a secret ninja path that would lead us right into the lord's private chamber, without the soldiers even seeing!"

"Yeah, but the lord of the castle would be expecting us," Reuben pointed out. "He'll have spent a fortune making it ninja-proof; secret entrances, hidden stairways, floors that sing like canaries when you step on the wrong board!"

I grinned. "It's cool knowing all this stuff isn't it!"

"Seriously cool," he agreed.

We had gradually increased our pace, until we were literally running. I'm not a great fan of running normally, but on Level Two it felt really natural.

The landscape was becoming increasingly otherworldly. Lone lightning-struck trees were replaced by strange Martian-looking rocks.

"Some of this rock looks volcanic," Reuben said, when we stopped to check the map.

"I haven't seen any volcanoes!"

My buddy pointed into the distance.

Me and my big mouth, I thought.

A v. ominous cone-shaped mountain loomed on the horizon. Plumes of smoke belched out, in that unsubtle way you see in cartoons. When you are a complete wuss, even a cartoon volcano is enough to scare you silly. I swallowed, and for the second time that day, I heard a wolf howl close by. Reuben saw my face.

"Wolves don't hurt people," he reassured me. "That's just a myth."

He went back to studying the map. "This butterfly is zigzagging all over the place!" he complained. "Last time I looked it was off to the side. Now it's behind us." He tugged at his dreads in frustration. "Mel, I hate to say this, but I think Tsubomi's stalking *us*."

I gasped. "You're kidding!"

Neither of us had the least idea what you did if the lost soul reversed cosmic protocol and started following you!

I blew a dusty strand of hair out of my eyes. "The first challenge was to do with earth," I said slowly. "This level has to be about fire, so presumably our second-level challenge is to do with fire too."

Reuben gestured to the smoking mountain. "Things don't get much more fiery than that."

"I suppose we could head in that direction for a while, and see if Tsubomi follows? Unless you've got a better idea?" I said hopefully.

He hadn't. Luckily it's impossible to worry and run simultaneously. Perhaps because running in this world felt SO exhilarating. At times it felt like we were standing still and it was the landscape flying past!

This is how a leopard feels, I thought, racing across the savannah, with the wind rushing through its fur.

From time to time I heard a wolf give that lonely full-throated howl. Like, "YAROO!" At times it seemed worryingly close. Other times it sounded echoey and far away.

The sun was low on the horizon when we both skidded to a halt.

We stared down at the fresh paw prints in the dust.

Reuben shook his head. "That wolf is following us!"

Everyone was following us, if you asked me. Lost souls, wolves. There was probably an entire army of ninja assassins trailing us through the undergrowth at this moment.

"I thought you said wolves were harmless."

He pulled a face. "In Limbo, who knows? We should probably camp here. It'll be freezing, because there's absolutely no shelter, but if anything IS trying to creep up on us, we'd see it for miles."

Reuben was thinking like a ninja too.

We lit a fire, in case the lone wolf turned out to be a scout for a ravening pack. Then we wrapped ourselves in our cloaks and watched the sunset. Level Two sunsets are *totally* fabulous. When darkness came it had a faint red glow.

My stomach gave a long rumble.

"Hungry?" asked Reuben.

"I'd even eat trail mix," I said gloomily.

I unrolled the map to check on Tsubomi's position.

The butterfly had vanished.

"That's impossible!" said Reuben in dismay. "I looked ten minutes ago and she was right *here*!"

"Are you looking for me?"

A ninja girl stepped out from the shadows. She wore a shabby cloak over her baggy fighting clothes, and there was a stringed instrument slung over her shoulder. Like me and Reubs, Tsubomi's soul had put on a Limbo disguise, but I recognised her instantly.

"Omigosh! We *found* you!"

"Erm, excuse me!" she laughed. "It was actually me who found you!"

Tsubomi sounded just like she did in the Agency documentary. Cool, sassy, yet oddly grown-up.

"I've been hoping we'd hook up eventually. I wanted to thank you for taking out the dark lord," she grinned.

"You *knew* about that?" Reuben said amazed.

She seemed surprised. "Of course! You both did a brilliant job!"

"Only because you left that note," I said modestly. "It was really a team effort."

Tsubomi shuddered. "Can you imagine anything so gross! Actually giving someone your *heart* in a locket!"

"If you think about it, it was a HUGE compliment!" I told her quickly. "The dark lord must have liked you a lot. He was literally putting his life in your hands."

Stop babbling, babe, I told myself.

It was partly stage fright at finding myself chatting to a real celebrity. But mostly it was because I'd always imagined this would be the easy bit. And I'd just realised that having finally found our human, we didn't have a clue what to do next!

"Well," I said brightly. "I guess we should get you back to your—"

I couldn't finish my sentence. I had a chilling flash of that dying girl wired up to those machines and, I'm sorry, I just could NOT bring myself to say the word, "body".

"—back home," I said huskily. "We'll get you back home, in a trice. You probably won't even know you've been away."

Tsubomi laughed. "That would be lovely – if I had a home to go back to! Sadly I don't. For now this world is my home, and I have a really difficult task to carry out."

Jessica had told us that lost souls often have the strangest delusions about why they're in Limbo.

"Gosh! What kind of task?" I asked, to humour her. "Like a quest you mean?"

"Maybe I'll tell you tomorrow," she said evasively. "Is it OK if I stay with you guys till morning?"

"We'd like that." My buddy suddenly looked hopeful. "Any chance I can have a strum on that – is it a lute?"

"It's called a koto," I corrected.

Tsubomi laughed. "Actually a koto would be way too big and bulky to carry around. You call this a 'biwa'. Reuben's right, it's a sort of lute. Play it by all means." She added carelessly, "I don't actually know why I'm lugging it around. It's not like I'm a musician or anything."

"So you don't play yourself?" he asked.

She shrugged. "Everyone plays a bit, don't they?"

"Not really," I began.

Reuben gave me a look, and, remembering the sacred rules of soul-retrieval: *we wait, we watch, we keep our gobs shut*, I hastily shut mine.

Be patient, I told myself. *Maybe that miracle will happen like Jessica said, and Tsubomi will remember who she is.*

Level Two might be a simmering dust bowl during the day, but it gets FREEZING when the sun goes down. I was really grateful for that campfire.

Tsubomi was holding out her hands to the flames. Suddenly she cleared her throat. "You've been really kind and I feel like I owe it to you to tell you the truth. The problem is, I know it's going to change the way you feel about me."

I felt like *such* a pro! We'd only known her ten minutes, yet already Tsubomi trusted us enough to spill the beans about the stresses and strains that had driven her to take her accidental overdose.

"Don't tell us unless you really want to," I said in my gentlest voice.

She swallowed. "It's about the dark lord."

My smile froze on my face. "Oh, right."

"He told you he couldn't bring himself to kill me. What he didn't tell you, is when I ate the fruit, I immediately fell under an evil curse."

"Omigosh," I said. "You poor thing! What kind of curse?"

"I'm only a girl by night," Tsubomi said earnestly. "But when the sun rises, I have to take on the shape of a wolf."

"You're kidding!" I breathed.

She giggled. "How do you think I crept up on you earlier? Ninja skills? Yeah right! Wolves can outsmart ninjas every time!"

"But that's so awful," I said in horror. "How can you joke about it?"

Tsubomi shook her head. "It's not *so* bad. It's taught me a lot actually."

Tsubomi was surprisingly eager to talk about her wolf experiences. After several long and extremely detailed descriptions of fascinating smells (fascinating to a wolf that is), Reubs and I got a bit restless. We kept tactfully trying to bring the conversation round to Tsubomi's real life in Japan; her home, her studies, parents and friends. But we just hit this total wall.

To hear her talk, you'd have thought she'd been *born* inside this game. I can see why. It might be weird and scary but it was also extremely simple. Inside the game, Tsubomi didn't have to stress about her mother, or her agent, her fans or promoters. She didn't have to jump on and off planes, zooming from one city to another, meeting ridiculous schedules. She was as free as, well, a wolf.

Reuben was tinkering softly with the harp. He asked Tsubomi to show him how to tune it properly. I watched her lively laughing face as she corrected his fingering, and shut my eyes to banish the chilling image of the blank girl lying in a hospital bed.

I could literally feel the minutes ticking, ticking. For souls who've left their bodies for keeps, time obviously doesn't present a problem. But each minute, each *second* Tsubomi Hoshi's soul spent in Limbo made it increasingly unlikely she would ever be able to return to life on Earth.

Reuben seemed totally oblivious. He'd started playing a funky old-style Japanese version of one of his own songs. I got the impression Tsubomi was having some kind of internal struggle with herself. Finally, she couldn't resist, she started to sing along. The evening turned into an impromptu jam session. Sometimes Tsubomi sang, sometimes Reuben, sometimes they sang together. Like I said, Reubs doesn't have what you'd call a great voice, but their voices harmonised beautifully.

It's not unusual for me to have at least two Melanies squabbling inside my head at any one time, but suddenly there was an entire football team! Mel Number One was stressing about how we were going to save Tsubomi. Mel Number Two, I'm ashamed to tell you, was hopping with jealousy! Reuben was my angel buddy. And Tsubomi and I had a special soul connection from who knows where. So how come *I* was the cosmic gooseberry?

Mel Number Three ached with pure envy. If I could only open my mouth and have a wonderful sound come out, instead of a tuneless squeak. Mel Number Four on the other hand...

Fortunately, I eventually ran out of Melanies, and just dozed uneasily against the rocks. I was woken by the sound of Reuben stamping on the remains of our fire.

The sun was coming up over the mountains like a huge gold beach ball.

My buddy beamed at me. "You're awake! Great evening wasn't it?"

"Yeah. Great!" I agreed brightly.

He looked worried. "Do you think it was a bad idea, getting her to play? I hoped playing music might remind her. But she's got a huge block about it. Like she wants to play, but she thinks she shouldn't. I'm worried I just made her even more confused."

"Oh, I'm sure you didn't," I started.

"She just kept bringing everything back to this task, or quest, or whatever. It's like she thinks she's some character in a fairy tale."

"You noticed that too." I was brushing red dust off my ninja clothes.

I felt like such a child. Reuben hadn't been trying to leave me out. He'd been doing his job. *Like you should be doing, Mel*, I scolded myself.

"Where is she this morning?" I asked guiltily.

"Up on those rocks," Reuben said in a low voice. "Keep your voice down, she's quite jumpy."

A young she-wolf was eying us nervously from the rocks.

Tsubomi must have changed back at sunrise. I was so ashamed of myself, I can't tell you. What kind of angel is *jealous* of the soul she came to save?

Reuben has this unnerving way of reading my mind. "Don't feel too sorry for her," he said, carefully folding up his cloak. "In some weird way, I think this is actually doing Tsubomi good."

"You think being under a curse is doing her *good*? Is that, like, Level Two logic!"

"Don't twist my words, Beeby," he said mildly. "I meant being a wolf. Running on all fours, exposed to the elements, sniffing all those smells. The dark lord had a point. This has to be healthier than that life she had before."

"I never thought about it like that," I admitted.

"Jessica's right. We've just got to go along with this big quest delusion, let Tsubomi run with it and see where it goes."

"Oh," I gulped. "I was thinking the exact opposite."

"I could tell," he said gently. "But I think we should hang on in."

"She's *dying*, Reubs."

"I know, but if we interfere, we're disrespecting her, don't you see? If we want to save her, we have to trust her, even when she's doing something that seems crazy or dangerous."

I was close to tears. "It's just the hardest thing I've ever done."

Reuben patted my back. "Me too, and we should probably get going."

I tried to grin. "Yeah, Fido's getting restless!"

Up on the mountainside, a bored Tsubomi was chasing her tail.

She followed us all the rest of that day as we covered the remaining miles to the volcano. I say "followed", but it's more like she roamed around us in huge circles, like a hyperactive puppy.

As we got nearer, something happened that is really not easy to put into words. Something started calling to us. Not in words, like a force, some fierce fabulous attraction that tugged ruthlessly at our heartstrings, drawing us closer and closer and closer...

This probably sounds v. alarming, so you'll have to believe me when I say that it *felt* wonderful! We'd been travelling for hours, yet not only were we not tired, Reubs and I were just bubbling with high spirits; laughing, teasing each other, doing silly walks. It was like we were actually being energised by our proximity to the volcano.

"This feels like falling in love," Reuben said, half laughing at himself.

"True love on an industrial scale!" I agreed.

It was evening by the time we reached the lower slopes.

The track snaked around a sharp bend and suddenly, high above us, was the most magical-looking palace. Its walls had been covered in millions of pieces of highly polished metal. Each one reflected the setting sun, turning the palace into one huge blazing mirror.

Then I realised. The sun had already set. The light wasn't a reflection, it was flooding out from inside. The palace must be the source of the humongous life force we'd felt zinging from every stone and tiny desert plant. I could actually see it, now, radiating out from the palace, looking exactly like the sunrays baby angels like to put in their paintings.

"This is the Palace of Eternal Flames. It's even

more amazing than I imagined!" Tsubomi appeared, babbling with excitement.

Angels are used to high levels of cosmic energy, and the extraordinary volcano vibes had *us* buzzing. Tsubomi was as high as a kite! Gabbling on about how she knew we were really her friends, how special last night was, sharing our fire and our companionship. But to cut a long, l-o-n-g story short, Tsubomi had finally decided she could trust us. "I'm going to tell you absolutely everything," she told us.

We'd committed ourselves to going along with Tsubomi's quest fantasy as you know. Jessica would expect us to follow her soul into the boiling crater of the volcano if necessary. I'm not sure if she'd have wanted us to commit actual burglary though. My heart sank into my ninja boots, as Tsubomi explained exactly how she'd break into the Palace of Eternal Flames and steal its owner's most treasured possession.

"Oh, and I want you both to come with me," she bubbled. "It's going to be totally thrilling. Back in a sec, I'm just going to scout around and check out the positions of the guards."

More like she just can't sit still, I thought gloomily.

I let her get out of earshot, then told Reubs how I felt.

"I know it's just a game, but something in that palace has real power, and I don't think Tsubomi has a clue what she's getting into."

"I agree," he said quietly, "but we agreed we had to trust her."

"Reubs, she's planning to go storming up a volcano, and rob some scary fire demon of – of who knows *what*? She thinks this is just some fairy tale, and she can't get hurt. She's never even asked herself, 'Hello! Where did this robbery idea come from? Who ARE these demon lords?'"

Reuben sounded disturbed. "I assumed they were a game thing."

"So did I. But now I'm thinking, who set this game up? Who's making the rules?"

My buddy swallowed. We both knew I was talking about the PODS.

He dropped his voice. "You're worried this is a trap?"

I nodded. "And we could be helping her walk right into it."

We heard an owl hoot, not very convincingly.

Tsubomi appeared, looking delighted with herself. "Are you guys ready? I needn't have panicked about the moat. I know *exactly* how we're going to get in."

To my surprise, the first part of the operation went really smoothly. In fact, considering Reuben and I had only been ninjas for twenty-four hours max, it was a breeze! I could see why Tsubomi had been worried about the moat. (Instead of scuzzy water, it was full of boiling lava.) But with the help of the cunning hooked rope from our bag of Limbo resources, not to mention our ninja throwing skills, we calmly abseiled over it.

The shiny mirror walls of the Fire Palace presented more of a problem. Then yours truly remembered the little spiky things in our bag. They were really cunning, actually. We whacked them on to our boots and just ran up the shiny mirror walls of the palace like flies, until we reached an open window. We climbed in, removed spikes and boots, and crept down the glowing gleaming corridors in our padded socks, as quietly as cats.

OK, the first time flames spurted out of the floor at my feet, I might have let out a teensy squeak of surprise, but once you got into the rhythm, (pad, pad, pad, spurt of fire, pad, pad, pad) it was easy.

Now and then guards would erupt from a doorway and we'd do some serious biffing and boffing. These soldiers wore red armour, the dull red of smouldering coals. And they had these staffs that sent out splurts of pure lightning. Luckily we moved so fast, they didn't get much use out of them.

Our ninja fighting stars were *très* cool. If you threw them with just the right amount of spin, (*pyu, pyu*) you could take out three or four guards at once. But mostly we stuck to old-fashioned biffing and boffing. Leaving a trail of stunned, silent bodies, we fought our way to a huge door framed by carved pillars. The energy coming from inside was so strong; I could literally feel it buzzing in the roots of my teeth.

What the sassafras is in there? I thought nervously.

Like the outer walls, the door was made from tiny pieces of bright hammered metal. In the shining mirrored surface, the ghosts of flames flickered and flared.

Tsubomi listened carefully at the door, with that expression you see on safe-crackers on TV. "It's still sleeping. Good," she whispered to herself. She took a hairpin out of her hair and began jiggling the lock. I heard a spring give inside. Next, she took a feather and a small bottle from her bag and softly oiled the hinge. Only then did she risk turning the handle.

The door swung open as smooth as butter.

I don't know what I expected on the other side, but it definitely wasn't a glowing fire garden with red, gold and rose-coloured flames for flowers. In the centre of the garden, where normal people might have a water feature, the demon had a fountain – of *fire*.

In the white-hot heart of the fountain, was the most magical bird I have ever seen. She had glittering gold-tipped feathers and flaming sunset colours on her breast. She seemed peacefully asleep, her wings carefully spread over her clutch of eggs. I couldn't see them properly, but I glimpsed soft gleams of colour.

"Either I'm dreaming," breathed Reuben, "or that's a real phoenix."

Tsubomi smothered a nervy giggle. "Of course it's a phoenix. It's the source of the fire demon's power," she mused. "Don't feel bad about her eggs, we're only taking one."

Reuben was absolutely appalled. "You don't seriously intend to steal a phoenix egg!"

I saw the phoenix open an amber-yellow eye. *Oh-oh*, I thought.

"It's my task," Tsubomi said in her fairy-tale voice. "I thought you and Melanie understood that."

The phoenix stirred, clearly uneasy. A loose feather floated from her fiery nest, brushing Tsubomi's cheek. I saw a bright red weal appear. Somehow she managed not to cry out. The shock made tears well in her eyes.

"I thought I'd know," she whispered. "I thought I'd know what to do, when we got to the palace, but I don't."

It would have been better, obviously, if she could have told us this *before* she made us abseil over a moat filled with molten lava, but she looked so vulnerable, that I felt really sorry for her. Until that phoenix feather gave her a nasty burn, Tsubomi thought she was living inside a magical story where the hero isn't allowed to get hurt. Now she knew better.

"I brought you guys here, and I have no idea how we're even supposed to do this," she whispered, ashamed.

"That's OK," Reuben told her calmly. "Something will come to you."

I don't think it was his words, so much as the smile, that calmed her down. Lola calls it his "Sweetpea smile". She says when Reubs gives you that smile, you just know in your heart that everything in the Universe is totally cool.

Tsubomi's expression changed. Even the energy in the room changed. "I have to play my lute," she whispered. "I didn't realise, but I think it might actually be magic."

"Play it and see," Reuben suggested.

And be quick before Mama Phoenix loses any more of those scary feathers, I thought nervously. The phoenix was getting *really* restless.

Scared but determined, Tsubomi unstrapped her harp. It looked like a normal lute to me, as normal as a lute can look by the glowing light of a phoenix fire. I'm not sure that her agent would have approved of her singsong magic chant. But the phoenix *loved* it! She started making ecstatic cooing sounds.

"It is, it's a magic lute," Tsubomi breathed to herself, as if music was only OK if it was magic.

"Don't stop," Reuben hissed.

He was gradually edging over to the nest, suddenly he plunged his gloved hand into the flames and pulled out a phoenix egg.

"Go, go, go!" he urged.

Too late. The phoenix exploded out of her nest. A nanosecond later we all got the shock of our lives, as she morphed into a hideous scaly red demon with one blazing amber-yellow eye and more arms than is actually attractive.

I wasn't as scared as you might think. All you need to kill a fire demon is water, right?

"Have you got a bottle of water in that bag?" I screamed at Tsubomi.

She started emptying her bag frantically. "Nothing!" she screamed back. "Just a stupid peach stone."

Yess! Thank you!

I literally snatched it out of her hand.

I remember thinking, I'll only get one shot, I'd better do it right.

ZOOM. The peach stone skimmed towards the demon, hitting her smack in the eye, her yellow all-seeing eye. Crude, perhaps, cruel, definitely, but *extremely* effective!

While the female demon blundered around her magical fire garden, howling in pain and clutching her blinded eye, we fled from the palace. We made it back over the palace moat, in time to see the sun coming up. Reubs and I collapsed into each other's arms, almost hysterical with relief.

"Nice work, Beeby," he congratulated me.

"Hey, I'm just grateful Tsubomi had that peach stone!"

Tsubomi wasn't paying one scrap of attention to this conversation. "It's sunrise," she said in a stunned voice. "And I'm still a girl!"

I stared at her. "Omigosh, that is SO cool! The dark lord's curse must have been broken. Now you can go back to—"

My words were drowned by horribly familiar musical chords. Tsubomi vanished. A second later, so did Reuben.

I stood alone on the volcano, the hot wind whipping through my hair, waiting my turn to be whisked up to Level Three.

This isn't right, I thought. *Tsubomi got her phoenix egg. This game is over. The game lords or whoever can't just go on shuttling us from level to level like pinballs!*

My surroundings blurred out of focus. I heard a sound like wind chimes, or tiny temple bells. I tried to remember what came after earth and fire. A deadly chill crept into the soles of my feet and rose up my legs. Ice? Could that be right? Earth, fire... ICE?

CHAPTER SEVEN

The light was unbelievably bright. And my bum was *unbelievably* cold!

Seen from the air, we would have made a star shape. Three of us, lying head to head, our arms outstretched.

Icicles tinkled overhead, making the wind chime sound I'd heard as I switched levels. I scrambled to my feet. Same wood, totally different world. This world was pure white. Everywhere you looked, just pure sparkling white.

"Is this what snow is like?" My buddy's face was a picture of amazement.

"This IS snow, bird brain," I said affectionately.

"Ah, that's SO cute! I can't believe you never saw snow before!" I stooped down, stealthily packing my gloved hand with snow. "So, erm, I'm guessing you don't know about the sacred snow ritual?"

Reubs glanced up innocently. "What's that?"

I hurled the snowball, catching my shocked buddy bang on the nose.

Reuben wagged his finger. "OK, Beeby, now that was sad! You did that just like a girl!"

"Yeah? Don't remember you complaining when I saved your booty from the one-eyed fire demon!"

"We're talking about style," he said loftily. "But it's never too late to learn from the master. Now THIS is a stylish throw!"

Next minute the two of us were having a major snowball fight. We'd reached the childish stage of stuffing snow down each others necks, when I became aware of Tsubomi watching us, tapping an elegant boot on the frozen ground.

"Omigosh, look at YOU," I breathed.

"I'm not sure we should be wearing fur," Reuben said doubtfully.

We'd been upgraded to noble Japanese lords and ladies. All three of us wore padded, fur-trimmed winter robes, absolutely stiff with embroidery. My hair was in its usual messy style (it's basically untameable). Tsubomi's was carefully put up with combs. Underneath our outer robes, Tsubomi and I wore a number of gauzy inner robes in layers. Mine were pure winter tones, grey, ivory, silver, shimmery green; each colour peeping out from under the next.

"You wouldn't think dreads would go," I told Reuben admiringly, "but they look fab."

"Could we get started, everyone, please? We *are* supposed to be on a quest!" Tsubomi's tone was as cold as the weather.

I guiltily shook loose snow out of my robes, and hastily went into celestial-agent mode. "Has anyone seen a bag?" I asked them bossily. "There should be a bag of Limbo goodies around here somewhere."

"No, there's just this," Tsubomi said evasively.

I noticed she was clasping a large mother-of-pearl casket, bound with hoops of gold.

"Ohh, that's SO pretty! Have you opened it to see what's inside?"

"No, and I don't intend to. I'll just look after it until we need it," said Tsubomi in her new frosty voice.

I was hurt. On the last level we'd all been mates

together. Now suddenly Tsubomi was treating us like her minions or whatever.

We were all suddenly distracted by icy tinkling sounds.

Waiting for us under the trees were three milk-white horses, their saddles gorgeously decorated in medieval Japanese style. The bridles were hung with dozens of tiny silver bells, which jingled musically whenever they moved.

Woo, we are going up in the world, I thought.

As noble ladies, Tsubomi and I had to sit side-saddle. Tsubomi positioned the mysterious casket in front of her on her saddle. She kept darting uneasy looks in our direction.

"Does she think we're going to *steal* it?" I whispered to Reuben.

"Who knows what she's thinking?" he sighed. "I get the feeling she doesn't totally remember who we are."

"More like she totally doesn't care!" I muttered.

As if to prove my point, Tsubomi spurred her horse and cantered off, sending up flurries of powdery snow.

"Just out of interest, where are we going?" I called.

"I don't have to answer to you," she called back. "This is my quest. You just have to follow me and do what I say."

Reuben and I exchanged astounded looks.

"Do you think she's been talking to Jess Lightpath?" he joked.

"I think she's being a right little diva!"

Reuben watched a rapidly disappearing Tsubomi with concern. "Don't think your little diva is going to stop," he commented.

We galloped for ages before we finally caught her up. It was *très* exhilarating actually, riding through the sparkling winter landscape. The weight of so much snow had bent some trees totally down to the ground, so they formed a series of dazzling white archways. It was like riding through some hushed ice cathedral.

Until Reuben pointed it out, I didn't realise anything was missing.

"I haven't seen one single person," he said abruptly.

"Good," said Tsubomi in a sharp voice. "People are more trouble than they're worth."

"No, they're not," I snapped. Sorry, I was not in the mood for humouring snotty fairy-tale princesses today.

"I haven't even seen a bird," Reuben pondered. "You'd think there'd be birds, or squirrels or foxes. But there's just us."

A moment later we saw the musician, his fingers still poised on the strings of the battered biwa. Both the musician and his harp were totally encased in ice. Reubs and I slid off our horses and rushed to see if we could help.

"Can that happen?" I whispered. "Can someone be frozen stiff in the middle of playing the lute?"

We were going to try to thaw him with our vibes, but Tsubomi just went zooming off again, just as if absolutely nothing was wrong! By this time, we knew she was capable of just galloping on for ever, so we had to jump back on our horses and race after her. I really hated leaving that poor guy all alone in the snow.

Frozen musicians became a distressingly familiar sight. We also saw a number of frozen carriages abandoned at the side of the road. Ice crystals had transformed them into twinkling fairy-tale coaches. Each coach had a sorrowful Cinderella frozen inside. We rode on past woods and temples and roadside shrines, through a white, sparkling, silent world where everything and everyone had totally turned to ice.

Throughout this deeply harrowing journey, Tsubomi didn't say a word. She seemed more worried about the casket, giving it anxious little pats, as if to reassure herself it was still there.

I don't know why it took me so long to catch on. Maybe phoenix vibes are affected by the cold? But all at once I felt it, a tiny fiery whisper of the fabulous life force we'd felt on Level Two.

I manoeuvred my horse alongside Reuben's.

"Guess what's in the casket," I whispered.

"Can't," he whispered back.

"I just felt a teeny tiny phoenix vibe. She must have brought the egg from Level Two."

"Do you think she knows? What's inside the casket, I mean?"

I shook my head. "Just that it's precious. You notice she's guarding it like a Doberman?"

"It's like, on this level she knows and she doesn't know at the same time," he sighed. "Like she *half* remembers us, but she doesn't know if she can trust us."

"You think that's why she's acting so weird?" Seen in this light, Tsubomi's behaviour made a lot more sense.

"I get the feeling she remembers she's meant to do something special," Reuben explained. "She just has no idea what. The poor kid's totally lost. You can see it in her eyes."

Reuben has this amazing ability to see through to the basic goodness inside people, even when they're being anything but.

My eyes unexpectedly filled with tears. "Sweetpea, you're such a – such an *angel*."

"Meaning?"

"I see a diva with a bad attitude, you just see—" I shook my head, not quite trusting my voice. *A very scared human*, I thought.

It was obvious, now he'd pointed it out. I'd been so wrapped up in my own selfish feelings, I'd totally misread her behaviour.

With no map, no idea where we were going, and Tsubomi frostily refusing advice, our journey fell into a weird pattern. We'd ride like demons until we reached a crossroad, then wait around until she decided which road to take.

Riding in aimless circles in the snow, in pursuit of a lost soul who has no idea who she is or where she's supposed to be going, is a deeply overrated pastime. If it hadn't been for Jessica's insistence that this was the only way to save Tsubomi, I doubt we'd have had the nerve to stick with the programme.

The sun went down. There were no crossroads in sight, so we just rode on. The moon rose over the frozen trees, turning the road into a shimmery white ribbon.

"It's cold." They were the first words Tsubomi had spoken for hours. She shivered in her embroidered robes, looking like a haughty, but extremely frightened, royal child.

I decided it was time to drop a teeny cosmic hint.

"This might sound bizarre," I said cautiously, "but when I really REALLY don't know what to do, I sometimes just ask for help."

"Perhaps you didn't notice, but there isn't anyone to ask." Tsubomi's teeth were chattering. She sounded about six years old.

"That's why Melanie said it sounded bizarre," Reuben said softly.

"I don't even know what I'm doing here," Tsubomi said in that same scared, small voice. "I'm just so cold and tired."

It was a v. delicate moment. We aren't allowed to tell humans what to do. But inside, I'm going, *just* ask, *dammit! How can the Universe answer you if you don't even ASK?*

Tsubomi gave a hopeless shrug. "I'll try anything, if it will make this stop."

She shut her eyes. "If anyone's listening, please, please help me. I don't think I can do this on my own any more."

The horses slowed with a jingle of their harness. One of them whickered a greeting to someone standing under the trees. Then the moon came out from behind a cloud, and I saw the lady. She was standing in a shaft of pure moonlight. In her silvery robes, she looked almost as if she was made of moonlight herself.

Tsubomi gasped and slithered off her horse. She bowed several times, as if she knew this lady from somewhere, or had heard of her maybe.

"I am Lady Tsukii," the lady explained. "My house is just a few steps from here. You are welcome to shelter there for the night."

Reubs and I dismounted, and bowed to show respect. Our horses weren't in the least respectful! They were shamelessly nuzzling her sleeves, to see if she had anything interesting to eat.

Reuben whispered, "The horses obviously trust her. Tsubomi trusts her."

"And we can't exactly ride round all night," I whispered back.

Sorry, Jessica, I thought. *Even angels have to break rules sometimes.*

We followed the lady over a snowy footbridge, and through a sparkling winter garden. Instead of taking us straight to her house, Lady Tsukii led us to a special teahouse in the grounds. Snow lay so thickly on the roof, it literally looked quilted. The full moon hung overhead like a paper lantern drenching everything with its light.

Lady Tsukii poured water over our hands from a special pot, then we took off our shoes and ducked through the doorway.

The teahouse radiated such a sweet, still vibe I can't describe it. Everything was calm and simple. The low table and cushions, the floor mats giving off a faint smell of rushes, a spray of winter berries in a jar.

I had heard about Japanese tea ceremonies. I knew it wasn't going to be like at my mum's, where you just plonked in a Tetleys bag for a brew. But I had no idea it was so, you know, *deep.*

Each step was exact and perfect, like the flowing movements of a dance, as Lady Tsukii poured boiling water on to the tea leaves in the pot, whisked it to a green froth, then poured the liquid into an earthenware cup. She handed it to Tsubomi, and something in the way she did it, made this simple gesture seem truly meaningful.

Tsubomi turned the cup, once, twice, three times, before she lowered her face to drink. Like Lady Tsukii she was totally concentrating on what she was doing. She carefully wiped the rim with a snowy white napkin, then it was my turn.

As I took the cup, the lady's eyes met mine, and any doubts I had just melted away. She *knew*. She absolutely knew who we were. I felt it deep inside. Whoever she was, she had come to help Tsubomi just when she needed it most, and that's really all we needed to know.

I sipped at the hot green tea, taking my time, letting the peace and stillness of the teahouse flow into me.

By the time the ceremony was over, Tsubomi looked calmer than I'd ever seen her. Lady Tsukii led us back across the moonlit garden to her house. For a second time we removed our footwear and put on the slippers that were waiting on the other side of the sliding door.

Like the teahouse, Lady Tsukii's house was calm and simple inside – and blissfully warm! Opening up the stove, she carefully laid two sticks of incense on the glowing charcoal. A wonderful smell of sandalwood and frankincense filled the air (they used those oils all the time in ancient Rome), and other perfumes I couldn't identify.

Now we were indoors, I could see that the lady's robes were heavily embroidered with silver thread. This must have been what had given the shimmery moonlight effect. Yet that first mysterious impression remained. Just the way she moved totally mesmerised me. *It's not just the tea ceremony,* I thought. *She does every little thing like it matters.* I was sure I'd never met anyone like her, yet Lady Tsukii really reminded me of somebody. But for the life of me I couldn't think who.

Everything Lady Tsukii did was designed to make us feel like honoured guests. She provided us with beautiful kimonos to wear while our own robes dried overnight. Mine was a gorgeous, rich, plum colour – with a matching fan. She also brought us special nibbles; and all without hurry or fuss. When we were sitting comfortably on cushions, she indicated an ancient-looking koto (Tsubomi was right – it was too big to lug around), and invited Reuben to play. "I'll do my best," he said doubtfully. "I've only played a Japanese lute before and that just had four strings."

She smiled. "When you are a true musician, the number of strings does not really matter." Have you not heard of the master who played the most divine music ever heard on a koto with just one string?"

"I know that story!" Tsubomi's face lit up. "I could never understand how he did it!"

The lady's eyes held a mischievous sparkle. "Did you never think perhaps that legendary musician was a *she*?"

"That has to be it!" I joked. "My mum always said women have to do at least three impossible things before breakfast!"

After Reuben had done his party piece, the lady asked Tsubomi to play. She seemed so nervous that Lady Tsukii tactfully suggested singing an old folk song together. It was only when I saw them singing, side by side, that it clicked. Lady Tsukii was like Tsubomi! How Tsubomi could be, hopefully would be, when she was older and wiser.

If we save her, I thought. I felt a sudden ache in my throat.

"Your friend tells me you are a poet?"

I realised Lady Tsukii was smiling at me! I went as red as a fire engine. "Oh, no, really, really I'm not," I mumbled.

"Yes, you are," Reuben objected. "In this world."

"It would be an honour if you could compose a verse about my teahouse?" Lady Tsukii's voice was gentle, but I could tell it would be humongously rude to refuse.

"Erm, if you could just give me a moment?" I asked nervously.

I closed my eyes, and tried to remember how it felt coming out of the wintry darkness into that calm moonlit teahouse. To my relief, I came up with a poem which I can still remember:

"Your kindly light
reveals a world of hidden sorrows
glittering like frozen tears."

My poem seemed to please Lady Tsukii. She thanked me with a bow.

"I didn't mean it to come out so sad," I said apologetically.

Tsubomi looked as if she might be going to cry. "I'm very tired," she whispered.

Perhaps the lady had been burning incense in the guest room, or maybe she used some special herb to scent the quilts, because it smelled totally divine. Tsubomi and I slept on the same low futon, wrapped in fur-lined quilts. I don't know about Tsubomi, but I was as warm as a basket of kittens.

When we woke, sunlight was pouring through the blinds, and our clean, dry robes were folded neatly on the end of the futon. Lady Tsukii herself was nowhere to be seen. We replaced our slippers by the sliding door, like polite guests, and went to look for Reuben.

Tsubomi and I both burst out laughing when we saw him lolling in the natural hot pool behind the house. It did look surreal; plumes of steam rising up into the frozen trees, icicles clinking everywhere like tiny temple bells, and my angel buddy basking like a shark!

I dipped in my hand experimentally. "Eep! That's seriously hot!"

"Bliss, that's what it is, Beeby," he said lazily.

"Sorry to drag everyone away," Tsubomi said awkwardly. "But we've got to get on with this quest. I promise I'll tell you guys what it is when I know myself. I know it must seem weird."

"No probs," I said.

"It's what we're here for," said Reuben truthfully.

He hastily dried himself off and we went to find our horses.

There was still no sign of our hostess, and to be honest I wasn't that surprised. Like a magical character from a fairy tale, Lady Tsukii seemed to belong to the night and the moonlight. But our encounter with her had totally changed Tsubomi's mood for the better.

As we rode through the dazzling snowy morning, she chatted away, seeming almost like her old self; just so long as we kept it light.

Considering Tsubomi still fiercely denied she was a musician, she had v. strong opinions on the subject. It turned out she *adored* hip-hop, which pleased me (I'm the original heavenly hip-hop chick, as you know!). But if you asked her how she was so well-informed about Earth music, she said evasively, "Everyone knows this stuff, it's like, in the air."

"Sure it is, they play hip-hop constantly on Level Three," I muttered. Reuben gave me his look: like, she's getting there. Give her time.

Eventually they got into this deep conversation I couldn't make head or tail of, about silence or whatever. Reuben asked if Tsubomi had ever tried listening to silence. (I *know*! To you and me, silence means you can't hear anything, right?)

"Not just silences in music," he explained earnestly. "Any time you feel stressed, just try focusing on the gap between ordinary sounds. Say you're in a huge city with constant traffic noises, emergency sirens, pounding car radios, but you let it all wash over you, because you're just concentrating on the gap. It helps you stay calm when everyone else is stressing."

Tsubomi gave him a look of utter suspicion. "You're talking about Earth. But I don't live there. There's no stress here. It's beautiful and peaceful."

"And sad," I said softly.

"Life is sad," she said, quickly turning away.

Tsubomi didn't speak again for some time.

Towards the end of the afternoon, we came to a frozen lake, fringed with weeping willows, and spanned by a narrow footbridge.

Snow had turned the bridge into a sparkling feathery construction like you might see in a fairy tale. It looked like a bridge spun out of frozen cobwebs. On the other side was a palace of pure ice.

Tsubomi was suddenly looking pale and strained. "The Palace of Everlasting Sorrow," she whispered, as if the wind had just breathed the name in her ear. "We're going inside," she told us in a trembling voice. "There's something I have to do."

My buddy and I tethered the horses. "I think she's getting ill," I murmured.

He shook his head. "No wonder with these vibes."

As a former human, I still tend to assume that any strong emotion belongs to me. As we made our way gingerly across the cobweb bridge to the Palace of Everlasting Sorrow, painful emotions hung in the air as thickly as ice crystals. I was grateful to Reubs for reminding me that they actually belonged to Level Three.

We crunched through deep snow to the palace gates.

I'd tried to brace myself for this, but it was still distressing to see the guards standing frozen at their posts. One of them had the sweetest face. I saw Tsubomi swallow hard.

She really shouldn't be that pale, I thought.

If anything, the palace was even colder inside than out. The walls gleamed with ice, and the air was literally smoking. A vast central hall was crowded with frozen servants and lords and ladies, all fixed into rigid poses. Tsubomi's hand drifted to her face. I saw she was on the verge of fainting.

"Stay here," I told my buddy. "I'm going to find somewhere she can lie down." I was so frightened for Tsubomi I can't tell you. Every nerve ending in my body was telling me time was running out.

Yet Tsubomi was still completely adrift in a world of pure make-believe, bracing herself to battle evil ice demons, or whatever, when she simply wasn't up to it.

Tell you one thing, if I hadn't been so upset about Tsubomi, no WAY would I have had the courage to explore that palace by myself. Frozen or not, some of those Japanese noblemen were v. scary, the type who'd have you executed for, like, *sneezing* in their vicinity.

The ladies' quarter of the palace was disturbing in a different way. It was like a scene from an oriental version of Sleeping Beauty. Beautifully made-up ladies had been frozen in the middle of playing board games, untangling children's kite strings, arranging chrysanthemums, even picking their teeth! Two teenage girls were peeping shyly round a lacquered screen, just as if they'd heard me coming. I could see the rich colours of their kimonos dimly showing through the ice.

As I slid and slithered from room to icy room, I started talking angrily to myself. Well, it was more to Jessica Lightpath.

"I know you're the don of soul-retrieval, and I know we're supposed to watch and wait and it's all a totally beautiful cosmic dance and whatever, but that's for people who are already DEAD! Tsubomi's not supposed to die. Not now. Not yet. Those kids on Earth really need her, Jessica. But I don't think she can do this on her own."

Reuben found me in the state bedroom, still chatting to myself.

"Hi," he said cautiously. "Just wondered where you'd got to."

"This place is making me a bit wiggy," I explained.

He pulled a face. "I'm not surprised."

"I thought we could use this room tonight. It's

empty which is the big plus. And there's a stove. Think you can light it?"

"Hey, I'm an angel. I've been lighting fires since I was in preschool! Ask Miss Dove!"

"She must have loved you!" I called, as I flew out the door.

By the time I came back with an exhausted Tsubomi, my fire-raising angel buddy had got the stove working.

That bedroom HAD to have belonged to a princess! Everything was either gold or silver, or encrusted with pearls. OK, the bed was carved out of wood, but I bet it was v. expensive wood and it was all carved with dragons and all sorts of fabulous creatures.

Reubs and I stripped off the frozen covers, and remade the bed using two fur-lined robes instead of sheets and blankets.

Tsubomi climbed into the huge dragon bed, and turned her face to the wall, looking like a fairy-tale princess who was having a really bad day.

"Night night," I whispered, but she was already fast asleep.

I joined Reubs by the stove. Heat was pumping out, but in such a vast space it made almost no impression. We experimented with moving pretty paper screens to shut out the draft, but we were still gibbering with cold. In the end we both wrapped ourselves in Reuben's robe. It was such a relief, I can't tell you!

He gave me a mischievous look. "If this was Orlando you'd be a very happy bunny!"

"Shut up! I got over him ages ago."

"Yeah, right!"

I shook my head. "I didn't even know him, Reubs, not really. I made up this ideal boyfriend in my head and made him fit the picture."

We were sitting too close for me to see his expression.

"The first crush is the deepest," he said softly. "Isn't that what they say?"

"What about you, Mr Dark Horse?" I teased. "You never told me you'd been in love!"

Reuben sounded unusually edgy. "Who said I had?"

"You, you nutcase! We were climbing the volcano, and you said it was just like being in love."

"Oh, that!" he said in a flip voice. "That was the phoenix vibes talking. I didn't know what I was saying."

"You little devil! You don't want me to know who it is!"

"No, I don't, so drop it, Beeby." Reuben's voice had a warning vibe. He changed the subject. "Any more ideas about who's running this game?"

My buddy had virtually told me to butt out of his private life. I was SO hurt.

Typical boy, he didn't seem to notice. "I haven't smelled a whiff of a PODS since we've been here," he went on. "Have you?"

"Haven't thought about it," I snapped. "For all I know, Tsubomi's creating this entire scenario from her hospital bed."

We stared at each other.

"Omigosh," I whispered. "OMIGOSH!"

"We've got to wake her up and tell her," Reuben said.

"No way," I said firmly.

"But she thinks this is all *real*."

"Exactly. You can see how fragile she is. It could be really dangerous, like waking a sleep walker." I stiffened. "What's that?"

Tsubomi had woken from a nightmare. She was too upset to tell me what she'd dreamed about but it had clearly shaken her to the core. She cried like a little kid. "I don't know what to do, Melanie," she sobbed. "I know I'm supposed to do something really important. I just don't know what."

I held her and stroked her hair, but when someone's been sad and lonely almost her whole life, making "there, there" sounds doesn't seem like enough. I still can't explain what I did next. It's not like my singing voice has healing powers. But I did, I sang to her, I sang her a lullaby.

I seem to remember any real ones, sadly, so I just pulled soothing-sounding words out of the air, and randomly strung them together. I wasn't as embarrassed as you'd think. It felt like I was singing to myself, in a funny way, like Tsubomi and I were suddenly one person.

And it worked, that's the amazing thing. After a time, Tsubomi stopped crying altogether. She sat up in the huge dragon bed, her breath making white clouds in the air. Her eyes were full of wonder. "My father used to sing that song," she whispered.

I could feel Reuben silently sending vibes on the other side of the room. We both knew that if I did the wrong thing, Tsubomi's progress could be put back by miles.

All the same, I had to tell the truth. "He really sang that song?" I said softly. "I thought I was making it up!"

"I was scared of the dark when I was small. Dad would hear me crying and come in, and he'd raise the blind so I could see the night sky through the window. He'd say, "Don't be afraid, Mi-chan. Even on the darkest night, when we can't see her, the Moon Lady is watching over you, and he'd play his koto and sing that song."

Tsubomi sniffed back her tears. She looked around, as if she was seeing the frozen palace for the first time.

"This level isn't supposed to be ice," she said in a dismayed tone. "It's supposed to be water. I've got to change it back, and you guys have to help me."

"In the morning," I said gently. "When you've rested."

"The casket," she said urgently. "What happened to the casket?"

"It's quite safe. Look." I placed it in her hands. "Tsubomi, it's late, and this journey must have been a strain, maybe—"

"No, I have to open it now," Tsubomi insisted.

"There's something inside, which will melt the ice. I know there is!"

Reuben hurried over. "Tsubomi, we don't know for sure what's—"

She'd already raised the lid. Angry red rays were streaming into the room, touching everything with a familiar Martian glow.

I'm not sure if you were actually supposed to mix up magical objects from different levels. The phoenix egg looked ominously different on Level Three. It was *huge*, around the size of an ostrich egg, totally filling the casket. Its colours were ominous too. Hectic and much too bright, like you see on poisonous berries.

I saw Tsubomi hesitate. Before she could slam the lid, there was an ominous CRR-ACK!

When I saw that bedraggled chick trying to struggle out of its egg, I knew this wasn't going to end prettily.

OK, even phoenix demons are cute when they're babies, but this one wasn't going to be cute for much longer. The fledgling opened its beak to give a baby screech, and I saw the startling bright pink tunnel of its throat. Its eyes turned an ominous burning amber.

Oh-oh, I thought. Our sinister little cutie-pie was going to swell into a seven foot high lady demon any minute, and I knew for a fact we were all out of peach stones.

Luckily my inner angel knew exactly what to do!

"SING!" I yelled, like a character in a bad musical. "Sing like crazy!!"

"Mel, this is not the time," warned Reuben.

"It IS. Unless you want to be fried like fritters! They love music, remember?"

I started desperately warbling my moon lullaby. After the first couple of bars, the others joined in more tunefully.

"Now we're going to walk out of the palace, OK, and no one's going to make any sudden moves, and we're going to sing ALL the way."

Ever tried singing in a palace full of frozen people?

But I don't think we sounded anything like as scared as we felt. By the time we reached the bridge, the baby bird was just blissed out, blinking happily into my eyes like a hypnotised kitten.

"Tip it over the bridge," I hissed. "Quick-smart before it morphs!"

Tsubomi shut her eyes. "Sorry, sorry, sorry, little chick," she gabbled, and she upended the box.

A spark, that's all that came out!

One single gold spark, no bigger than a teeny tiny onion seed, and extraordinarily bright, as if all the fire demon's humongous power had been concentrated into one tiny spark-sized package.

Now, I'm no scientist, OK? But if you add an entire fire demon to a seriously frozen world, you can pretty much guarantee a HUGE amount of steam.

WHOOSH!!! The palace, the fairy-tale bridge, the weeping willows, instantly disappeared under a thick blanket of fog.

I groped for Tsubomi's hand. "OK, babe?"

I felt an answering squeeze.

"Reubs?"

He didn't answer.

"Reuben!" I said in a panic.

An arm came round my shoulder. "Ssh! Isn't that the loveliest sound you ever heard?"

Wasn't it just! A fabulous symphony of gurgling, trickling and splashing, as the lakes, streams, fountains and underground springs of Level Three, shook off their robes of snow and ice, and began to flow once more.

"Guys, we did it! This world is coming back to life!" Tsubomi sounded ecstatic.

YOU did it, I wanted to say. *You created the whole thing. You're STILL creating it, and I want you to stop before it's too late.*

There was a brief swirling gap in the fog, and we were all visible again. Tsubomi gave a gasp. I saw dawning realisation in her eyes. "Who *are* you guys?" she asked softly. "Omigosh, you're ang—"

But with a chime of magical music, the dripping thawing world of Level Three dissolved, and the invisible game lords sent us zooming up to the next level.

CHAPTER EIGHT

We were on the summit of a snow-capped mountain, looking down at the world far below. All of us were dressed in flowing white robes. Tsubomi's face was utterly peaceful. "If I'd known it would be like this," she said dreamily. "I wouldn't have been so scared."

This was the kind of view the old-style Japanese gods might have had; a vivid green patchwork of rice fields, little bamboo houses, streams and willows. Clouds flitted past, white and woolly as new lambs. You'd think they'd block the view, but they never did. You could see for ever, and with total god-like clarity.

If you wanted to see or hear something far away, you focused your attention, and – abracadabra! – you zoomed in for a special close-up on whatever it might be; children skimming stones across a stream, an old man snoozing in the sun, bees inside a flower. I could hear a woman singing miles below, as she stirred a pan of soup over the fire.

Reuben was standing close beside me. "You can see up as well as down." The vibration of his voice made pretty coloured trails in the air.

I looked up experimentally and got a major head rush as I zoomed in on a fizzing whizzing cosmos of stars, comets and constellations.

"Wow, this is SO cool!"

My words left pretty trails too. We'd come up through three levels, defeating demons and absorbing their energy, so according to game logic, we were now humongously powerful magicians.

Mr Allbright once told us that when we get really advanced in angelic studies, we'll actually be able to see human thoughts spreading through the Universe in ripples.

Maybe this is also true of advanced magicians? Because on Level Four, magicians seemed to be the only people around; no lute players, or ladies in wicker carriages, just pure magicians. There weren't even too many of those. Occasionally you'd spot one stalking about in the distance, looking scornful in his robes.

Level Four magicians don't tend to exert themselves unnecessarily. This is the Air level, the level of thought power. They just think themselves where they want to go, and bosh! I found it quite stressful, frowning magicians popping up among the clouds without warning.

Absolutely nothing in this world seemed fixed or solid. Houses, furniture, magic banquets, simply appeared when they were needed, and vanished when they weren't.

OK I'll own up! I *might* have been wondering about magicking myself a BLT, but Tsubomi repeated in that dreamy voice, "I didn't know it would be like this, or I wouldn't have been so scared of dying."

Reubs and I exchanged alarmed glances.

Level Four might physically resemble a small kid's idea of Heaven, high among the clouds, but it was actually a hive of v. dodgy magic.

"You're not dead, sweetie," I said firmly. "Trust me, Heaven is nothing like this." I gestured at an arrogant-looking magician, symbols glittering on his robes. "These guys are just power-tripping."

She looked as if she might burst into tears. "You're angels, I know you are! Why would I be hanging out with angels if I'm not dead?"

Trapped inside this bewildering game of changing levels and landscapes, Tsubomi badly needed something to cling to. Now I'd taken away her nice Heaven she was lost.

I had to give her courage without actually fibbing. "We were sent to help you," I told her truthfully, "with a really crucial mission."

"We did all that," said Tsubomi in a scared voice. "We stole the phoenix egg and we thawed the ice world. Is this going to go on for ever?"

I'm talking about your real mission, I wanted to say, but Reuben got in first.

"It could go on for ever, or not," he said softly. "It's up to you."

After dropping this major cosmic hint, we daren't say another word. Tsubomi would have to figure the next part out for herself.

There was a long silence. I could feel the tension build inside her.

She swallowed. "I never do anything right."

"Yeah, you do," I began.

"No, I *don't*! I can't even DIE right."

Tsubomi's words sent a storm of angry coloured lights through the air.

I was suddenly deeply scared. Was this that moment Jessica had talked about? That miraculous moment when all your watching and waiting paid off, and the human finally opened up? Because I'm sorry, it was too huge, and much too painful.

She seemed to be talking to herself. "I was too weak, that's what they said."

"Who said you were weak?" asked Reuben gently.

"Mum, Miss Kinshō. Other girls would have killed to get where I was, but I couldn't take it. Walking out on that stage night after night, dancing, singing, smiling, scared they'd see I was falling apart inside."

Tsubomi took a shaky breath.

"I was scared, I was so scared, *all* the time. It got so I couldn't eat, or sleep. I was cracking up – I was—" She shivered. "I had this crazy idea I was being stalked by things from some evil dimension."

Babe, you were, I wanted to say.

"I kept seeing these – they looked like normal pop fans, but they weren't. They weren't even real.

They'd appear out of nowhere, and stand watching me sing." She shook her head, to banish the picture. "And their *expressions* – it was like they actually wanted to destroy me. I started seeing them everywhere I went. TV studios, hotel lobbies. No one saw them but me. They wore these creepy sunglasses, but when they took them off, their—"

"Don't think about them!" I warned.

"I can't HELP it!" Tsubomi's words sent jagged lightning forks through the clouds. "Angels can control their thoughts, ordinary humans can't, OK?"

Reuben kept his voice soft and steady as if she was a scared animal. "You can decide to control them. You're a musician. Think about your music."

"I'm NOT a musician! Real musicians live and breathe music. They wouldn't do what some agent or promoter told them!"

I tried to sound calm like Reuben. "You were *young*, babe. You had no choice. You had to do what they told you. Maybe you weren't as strong as you'd like to be, but your music touches people, Tsubomi!"

"My music is total garbage!" she said in this absolutely weary voice. "I wanted to be – I wanted to touch people SO deeply. I guess I just don't have what it takes."

I'd never been so terrified for Tsubomi as I was then. In a world of magicians, just thinking about something would make it true. If Tsubomi thought she was too weak to fight, she was. If she thought her life had been pointless, it was.

This was the moment the Dark Powers had been banking on; the moment of unbearable loneliness and despair which would destroy all final hopes of Tsubomi returning to complete her Agency mission.

She swallowed. "Have you ever heard my first record? I'm just a fake. You guys have been great, but you should go back to Heaven now and stop wasting your time on fakes and losers."

Her magician's robes were melting away as she spoke. Underneath she wore the normal teenage uniform of the twenty-first century: jeans, trainers and a hoodie. She pulled the hood over her shiny dark hair, and trudged off across the clouds.

Somewhere in a viewing suite in the Hell dimensions, PODS agents were howling in triumph and stomping their feet.

The battle for Tsubomi's soul was over. They'd won.

In that terrible moment, I felt myself split into three angels. One watched Tsubomi walk away, totally convinced that everything was lost. A second angel stood sorrowfully beside a hospital bed where a dying girl was just about to be unplugged from a life-support machine.

The third angel knew it was time for Tsubomi to know the truth.

I made my robes dissolve too. I'd had enough of disguises.

"Mi-chan!" I called, deliberately using her family pet name. "Don't you want to know who's doing this to you?"

There was no expression in Tsubomi's face. "Does it even matter?"

"You're going to die, girl," I told her softly. "You at least owe it to yourself to ask where this has all been coming from; all these phoenix eggs and frozen palaces and talking mice!"

I saw her throat muscles move. Her eyes went wide. "NO way. Are you *crazy!* I don't have that kind of power."

"Tsubomi, you have so much power you're scaring yourself. You created an entire magic world out of your imagination, using stuff you remembered from video games, fairy tales you heard as a little kid, like those little dead Limbo children, and the Moon Lady."

She shook her head. "I don't believe you. Why would I do that?"

"I don't know why, babe. Maybe you just wanted to hide inside a fairy tale for a while? Or maybe you were using it to make yourself stronger, so you could go back to Earth and stand up to the Dark Powers. But I know one thing. You're pure magic, Tsubomi. You've just got to learn to control it, that's all."

She looked dazed, like someone on the verge of waking from a long, confusing dream. "It's just a stupid game, none of it's real."

"It IS. In a way it is!" I gestured at the rice fields far below. "This came out of you, Tsubomi. All this incredible beauty is you!"

I could see Tsubomi longed to believe me, but she didn't dare. She just didn't dare.

Reuben has the best cosmic timing of any angel I know.

"Won't you play for us one last time before you go?" he asked slyly.

She tried to smile. "Maybe you didn't notice, but I haven't got an instrument."

Ruben casually materialised a stunningly beautiful koto. Painted on the sides in gold leaf were Japanese characters for all the elements that make up the Universe: Earth, Fire, Water and Air.

Tsubomi backed away. "It's only got one string."

My angel buddy firmly pushed her towards the instrument. "You heard Lady Tsukii. Harp players have played with one string before."

"Not many. Only a master could play that well."

"So play, Tsubomi!" Reuben almost whispered. That's when he gave her his special Sweetpea smile. Who would believe that an angel's smile could totally tip the balance between Light and Darkness?

Yet in that moment I could see Tsubomi believed him.

She was shaking, but she seated herself cross-legged in front of the koto, shut her eyes and began to play. Even now, just thinking about it, gives me goose bumps. From that single string, this amazing girl produced the most exquisite rhythms and harmonies I have ever heard outside Heaven.

At one point the people who lived at the bottom of the mountain fell silent in awe. Maybe they thought they could hear the music of the gods?

Reuben and Tsubomi were so deeply into the music that they both had their eyes closed, so I was the only one who saw the landscape dissolve for the fifth and final time.

We were back where we'd started, only everything had changed. Level One was going totally potty, putting out bright green shoots and teeny little flower buds.

Music was playing somewhere among the trees: drums, flutes and biwas. Some kind of festival was going on.

Crowds of beautifully dressed little girls were walking about under blossoming peach and cherry trees, proudly dressed in their new spring kimonos. They had that genuine dignity little kids have on important occasions, but you could see their eyes sparkling with fun.

Some had dressed their dolls in *their* spring kimonos, and brought them out to share the celebrations. Others were flying kites shaped like fabulous birds and beasts. At one shrine, little girls were busy writing their secret wishes on slips of paper and tying them to flowering branches with coloured ribbons.

When you've just been fighting for someone's soul, it's a little overwhelming to find yourself surrounded by a sea of zingy blossomy springtime vibes.

Tsubomi took our hands. "What can I say? I was a goner and you just pulled me back out of the dark."

Reuben grinned. "Just doin' our job, ma-am!"

Girls often feel they have to hide parts of themselves that don't fit, don't they? They think they should be the same as everyone else, or they think they should be perfect. But when I looked into Tsubomi's eyes, I knew she wasn't going to be hiding any more.

You know how it is when you say goodbye to someone you probably won't see again for some time? You've only got like, *minutes*, so you frantically try to fit in everything you really meant to say earlier if you'd only had time.

"So really you were right about being on a quest," my inner angel was telling Tsubomi earnestly. "But this one's on Earth, so it's probably pretty much going to take your whole life."

"And the Dark Powers come in all kinds of disguises, so you won't always recognise them right off," my buddy chipped in equally earnestly.

"It'll be harsh sometimes. People won't always understand what you or your music are about, and some days you'll feel like you're all alone in a huge meaningless Universe."

"Yeah yeah, Auntie, and I'll eat all my vegetables and I promise I won't talk to strangers!" she teased.

"But you're *not* alone," I went on fiercely. "You're NEVER alone. Everything and everyone in this Universe is—"

Reuben nudged me. "I think it's time for her to go," he whispered.

I saw a familiar figure strolling towards us. He was not only *much* less hairy, the hermit also looked decades younger, and far more twinkly than the first time we met him. Awed little girls bowed their heads reverently on either side, like flowers in a meadow. They knew what I'd only just realised. Our hermit was Jizo, the kindly children's god who refuses to enter the Pure Land until every lost soul is safe inside.

He looked into Tsubomi's eyes and smiled.

"Are you ready to go back?"

Tsubomi nodded. "Yes." She gave us a sudden beseeching look. "Will I see you again?"

"For sure," Reuben promised.

"And remember, babe," I called, "everything in the Universe is—"

The god and the teenage pop star were swallowed in a blaze of golden light.

"—connected," I whispered.

CHAPTER NINE

"I don't understand why you feel so bad. You guys totally saved her from being rubbed out by the PODS. You should be over the moon!"

To my relief, Lola had totally forgiven me. Her eyes were dark with sympathy.

"I am over the moon, mostly, it's just..." I tried to put my feelings into words. "I know Tsubomi's really talented and everything, but deep down she's just like we were, Lollie. She's pure magic, a real undercover angel. And she's had to cope with all this stuff."

Lola took a sip of her smoothie. "It's not easy growing up magic on planet Earth."

"That's why I wish I'd helped her more."

Lola and I were sitting at a pavement table, outside Guru, our fave student café. We'd been there since they opened; working our way through their yummy celestial breakfast special, ordering a succession of smoothies and talking.

"I just feel like I missed such a valuable opportunity," I said wistfully. "If you have an encounter with angels, you should come out of it knowing all this, like, totally luminous stuff, right? Reuben was great with her, telling her how to deal with stress and whatever. She'll remember that next time, I know she will."

"You must have talked to her too?"

"Yeah, about hip-hop," I sighed. "Oh, and we had a heated discussion about whether combats are on the way out."

"NO way," said Lola fiercely.

I grinned. "Exactly what I said."

"So what would you have told her, hon?"

"You know, all that stuff that trainee angels take for granted. Like those cosmic strings Mr Allbright was telling us about the other day."

Lola looked amazed. "Strings? Was I away that lesson?"

"OK, maybe they're not actually strings. Maybe it's more like an energy grid."

"An *energy* grid?" Lola seemed to be in severe physical pain.

"OK, scrub the grid. Stick with the string. Imagine there's a HUGE game of cat's cradle, but the strings are so fine and so closely interwoven it's like this big shimmery mesh."

My soul-mate frowned. "How big?"

"Sorry, didn't I say? It's exactly the same size as the cosmos, duh! Forgot that bit!"

"It's OK, I've got it now. Shimmery strings forming a humongous cosmic cat's cradle. Now what?"

"Ah, but they're not really strings, you see," I explained patiently. "It's more like a net made out of incredibly subtle cosmic energy. Mr Allbright says ancient Hindus knew all about it, but humans don't usually see it, unless they're like, *massively* spiritual."

"Or smoking something they shouldn't," Lola grinned. "So what does it do, this shimmery energy net that no one's seen and I've totally never heard of?"

"Don't mock the net, girlfriend, this net is really, really, cool. It's like this live shimmery information system, that connects absolutely everything and everyone to everyone and everything else."

Lola frowned. "Info literally goes whizzing down the strings – like, even between Heaven and Earth and whatever?"

I nodded. "All those times on Earth, when you knew something you couldn't possibly have known! You just downloaded it from the energy net, without realising!"

Lola was genuinely impressed. "Hey that IS cool! That explains so much!"

"I know. Like the guy in the record store 'accidentally' giving me that Japanese harp CD, like, *hours* before I go to save a girl whose dad makes Japanese harps."

"So how does it work?" she asked abruptly.

"I knew you were going to ask me that," I wailed. "Look, I totally understood it when Mr Allbright explained it, OK?"

Lola tactfully helped me to three more pancakes. "Have you heard how Tsubomi's getting on these days? Is she OK?"

"According to Sam, she's back in school and living with her dad." I took a big bite of pancake.

Lola's eyes went huge. "You guys went through all that and then she *gave up* singing!"

"No, sorry, sorry," I said with my mouth full. "Tsubomi's just dropped the touring and the promotional stuff. Sam says she's focusing on her song-writing for now. She's putting some amazing album together." I gave Lola a meaningful look. "Apparently it was inspired by some experiences she had during her illness."

"Oh, wow, just imagine *that* video," Lola said enviously.

Glossy MTV images flitted through my mind. The pale underworld princess being tempted by a bowl of mouth-watering strawberries. An action princess in sexy ninja costume, abseiling over a moat of lava to steal a phoenix egg from a fire demon. A lonely lost princess in an ice palace full of frozen lords and ladies, one cold crystal tear sliding down her cheek.

Lola looked dreamy. "I wonder who they'll get to play you and Reubs?"

I sighed. "I miss her, Lollie. I know I'm going on and on about it, but it was the most amazing mission."

"It must have been. Reuben's just the same." She gave me a sideways glance. "You and he got quite close on this trip, right?"

"We've always been close," I said in surprise. "It was just really special to be able to share the experience with a friend."

"Sure," she said hastily. "Hey, it was your last mission. A last mission is supposed to be fabulous. I'm glad, honestly." Lola couldn't seem to meet my eyes.

"Omigosh! I can't believe I didn't tell you! I'm not quitting."

Pure relief dawned in her eyes. "You're *not*? You're REALLY not?"

I patted her hand. "I'm really not. I lost it for a bit, that's all. I think I was kind of burned out. Ancient Rome, Brice's mission to Jamaica—"

"—your best friend getting cosmic amnesia," Lola said softly.

"All that," I agreed. "I'd let everything get on top of me. I guess I needed a break."

My mate shook her head. "Sorry, chasing a confused soul through a Limbo dimension isn't my idea of a picnic in the park."

"OK, it wasn't exactly a picnic, but it was different to anything I'd ever done before, and in a funny way it helped me get my confidence back. I found all these other aspects of me I didn't even know I had. I could fight like a ninja. Can you believe I was actually making up all this v. deep poetry! Like, right there on the spot!"

I took a deep breath. "I'm not ready to hang up my combats, Lollie. I want to go on fighting the PODS with you guys."

"And this is really what you want? It's not because I threw a Sanchez-sized tantrum?" Lola looked guilty.

"No way, hon! It's more like I can't stand to think of you all going off and having thrilling adventures without me!"

Lola produced a gift-wrapped package and pushed it across the table.

"What's this?" I said in surprise. "My birthday isn't for weeks."

"I know that, but I thought you were giving up trouble-shooting, *carita*. I wanted to give you a pressie, to show my support for your stupid wrong-headed decision."

I unwrapped the layers of spangly bright pink tissue.

"Ohh, Lola, that is the most darling thing!"

My mate had made me a photo frame, and decorated it with heavenly love hearts! Each heart had a cute message like, "Celestial Chick", or "No Angel"! Inside was a mad picture Brice had taken of Lola, me and Reuben on a school field trip.

"Yeah, well totally pointless gesture as it turns out," Lola said grumpily.

"I love it, Lollie, thanks SO much!"

I smiled down at our three laughing faces in their frame. Reuben can look really daffy in photos, but Brice had managed to catch him off guard. *That boy is something else,* I thought. *How did he even know to smile at Tsubomi at that precise moment?* Reuben had all these hidden depths that I'd never remotely suspected. I could see why Tanya fancied him. I could almost have fancied him myself, you know. If he wasn't a good mate.

I carefully rewrapped the photo frame. I wondered if Lola had heard anything about our buddy's mysterious love interest?

I was just about to pump her for info, when my soul-mate came out with a mind-blowing suggestion.

"You could put it in a book," she mumbled through her pancake.

I was lost. "Put what in a book, babe?"

"All that crucial cosmic information you didn't get a chance to tell her. You could write an unofficial cosmic handbook for kids like Tsubomi. Hey, forget humans, *I'd* use it! The one the school gives out is really heavy going. I zonk out after about half a chapter."

"I've read like two chapters since I've been here," I confessed.

Lola beamed. "My point exactly. The Universe *needs* your handbook, Boo. You should definitely do it."

I found myself getting cautiously excited.

"I'd have to write it how I talk."

"Kids would LOVE that! You could tell them about that shimmery net and how everything is connected and how the Universe always has to answer when you call."

"We'd have to tell them the dark stuff too," I said.

Lola nodded eagerly. "Totally, it would be like, a survival guide for undercover angels who have to live on Earth."

"Lollie, that's the most completely luminous idea! I couldn't do it on my own, though. You'd help me, right?" I asked anxiously.

Lola seemed wistful suddenly.

"What's the matter, hon?"

She sighed. "I know cosmic timing is always perfect, but I just can't help wishing someone could have thought of it before. A book like that could have made all the difference to me when I was alive."

"Me too," I said softly. "Oh, totally, babe, me too."

keeping
it real

This book is for Matt who was patient and clever, Claire for her sensitive comments, Andrea who kept me well-fed, and for all you undercover angels everywhere.

Chapter One

I'd hate to shock any true angel believers out there, but before I died and became one myself, I didn't really believe in angels at all!

I don't blame myself *too* much for that. It's a natural mistake to make, if you grow up in a part of London where they put security guards *inside* Santa's Grotto to stop all the dads and big bros pinching the toys.

In my neighbourhood, if you couldn't break it, kick it, spray graffiti on it or nick it, it probably didn't exist.

If I HAD believed in angels, though, I'd have told you they *definitely* had everything sussed.

This belief has caused me SOO much trouble.

I made so many major bloopers when I first got here that even thinking about them still makes me cringe... However I couldn't exactly go back to being human, so I decided to just wing it. I winged my way so brilliantly through those first terms at the Angel Academy, you have no idea.

I took weekend courses in *très* deep subjects like soul retrieval. I picked up a LOT of fancy angel jargon. No, honestly, if you'd seen me sitting with my angel buddies at our fave table in Guru, nodding knowledgeably as they chatted about Dark Studies, I totally blended in!

During waking hours that is. Don't know if you've tried, but you can't actually *fake* it in your sleep.

I only had to lie down and close my eyes, and I'd instantly go slap-bang into a terrifying nightmare. Like all bad dreams, the plots were kind of samey. Usually I was trying to rescue my little sister from hideous evil beings who'd taken over my planet since I'd been dead.

When I wasn't dreaming about my family, I dreamed about my human mates. In dream after dream they angrily turned their backs on me. Especially Sky. She just could *not* understand why I'd had to leave.

I couldn't understand it either. I'd go to stare out at the twinkling lights of the Heavenly City and think, *Why me*? Did some sharp-eyed Agency scout go through Park Hall Community High School with a clipboard, awarding angel points? "Nope, nope, nope. Wait! That girl at the back! Not her – the one touching up her nail polish, let's take her!"

I can't imagine *anyone* looking at the Park Hall Mel Beeby and seeing potential angel material. Yet I scored an Agency scholarship to the coolest school in the cosmos and my mates got left behind.

Here's how it happened; you know, how I died.

It was the day after my thirteenth birthday: a bright, summery, completely happy day. I had a wodge of birthday cash in my purse and I was off to meet my mates for a BIG shopping splurge.

I glanced both ways, like you do, and stepped on to the pedestrian crossing as an ancient Ford Fiesta screeched round the corner, burning rubber. It was the last thing I saw: rusty metal and a white-faced boy gripping the wheel.

BANG!! The Universe went supernaturally quiet.

For a long moment nothing whatsoever happened. Then, to my surprise, I just stepped out of my body. It was as effortless as a pea slipping out of its pod.

Next minute I was soaring over the city; and I just kept on soaring higher and higher, until I soared right out of the solar system!

Strange as it seems now, the idea of turning back never occurred to me. It might have had something to do with the music: sweet throbbing chords which sounded as if they came from some giant humming top. I couldn't help myself – I started flying faster and faster, with a growing sense of excitement. I remember having a childish thought that when the music stopped my cosmic mystery tour would be over. But when I reached the light fields where Heaven begins, the music didn't stop; it just faded, weaving its otherworldly harmonies into the everyday hum of Heaven. And this was only the beginning of the cosmic mysteries...

Like, what are the chances of meeting your true soul-mate on your first day at angel school? Imagine two girls from two totally different centuries meeting outside the shimmery, mother-of-pearl gates at the Angel Academy and instantly recognising each other. Doesn't that just give you goose bumps?

You know the first thing Lola Sanchez said to me? *"Do I know you?"* That's what it's like when you meet your soul-mate.

Don't get the idea soul-mates are like, an exclusive angel phenomenon. People run into soul-mates on Earth too, you know. But there's a *leetle* complication known as the Powers of Darkness.

The PODS would SO prefer you *not* to hook up with your soul-mates. They'd prefer you not to have any friends full stop. Ideally, they want you to feel you can't trust *anyone*, *EVER*, starting with yourself. It's hard to recognise a soul-mate if you don't feel good inside your own skin. It's also harder to *be* a soul-mate.

Don't get me wrong, my human mates and I totally looked out for each other. At times Sky and I were so close we were more like sisters than friends. But we always had to keep that *leetle* tiny something back, or at least Sky did; like, deep down, she didn't actually trust you.

But Lola and I had total trust between us from the start. All friendships, even heavenly friendships, have ups and downs, but when you trust someone, you get through it, right?

Considering my soul-mate comes from a vibey city a hundred years in my future, it's unbelievable how much we have in common. We literally chat non-stop about anything that jumps into our heads, from purely frivolous stuff like, should we just give in to fashion and get those quite sweet forehead jewels (like a few of the older angel girls are wearing again at school), or is that TOO totally angel for words, to HUGE cosmic topics like Space and Time.

I have NEVER been able to get my head around the concept of *two* kinds of time. I'm sorry but to me 'Time' means the system I learned in primary school, which we do use in Heaven mostly. But apparently there's also Cosmic Time – like, the Boss of time – which can just kick in, totally overruling the first kind, if, but only *if*, the Universe decides...

I have a personal reason for telling you all this. I must have been at the Angel Academy for well over a year when it finally dawned on me that I hadn't had a birthday!

I know! I'd attended other kids' celebrations. I *organised* Lola's. Yet it never seemed to be my turn.

I tried bringing this up with my friends, but you'd think I was spying for the Dark Powers the way everyone fobbed me off. They reckoned it was something I had to discover for myself.

This is one of the things about angelic life that makes me want to *scream*. Everything has to be a

Big Mystery! What if I *didn't* discover it for myself? Was I supposed to stay thirteen for ever?

One night, I was watering my baby orange tree, in a real grump, when for no reason a touching human memory flitted into my head.

It was my little sister's fourth birthday. All afternoon, Jade and her pre-school playmates charged around our flat leaving a trail of torn wrapping paper and burst balloons. Finally the littlies went home clutching goody bags. When I went into Jade's room later, to say goodnight, she was dreamily staring out of the window into the dark. "What's up, Fluffyhead?" I teased.

My sister turned with an awed expression. "Mel, the moon is *smiling*," she breathed. "It *knows* it's my birthday!"

I knew what she meant. On your birthday you don't just feel special to your friends and family, you feel special to the entire Universe. It was this memory that finally pushed me over the edge. So what if I hadn't solved the Big Mystery? This angel's birthday was *seriously* overdue!!

I reached for my diary and flipped it open. Picking a Friday at random, I daringly circled it in sparkly felt-tip. Sorted!

I ran to Lola's room to tell her I was having a birthday party at Rainbow Cove, which was the first venue to pop into my head.

"Yayy!" she cheered to my surprise. "An excuse to go shopping!"

I spent the evening on the phone inviting everyone I could think of. They all went "OK, cool!" Our buddy Reuben said he and Chase would organise the music and lighting. Finally I phoned Mo, who runs Guru, our fave student hangout, and asked if he'd take care of catering. He said he'd be delighted!

I'd have given myself a b-day party months ago, if I'd known it was going to be this easy. Suspiciously easy is what it was.

Maybe it's just me and birthdays? Something cosmic always seems to happen on or around mine. But I never imagined that my first heavenly birthday would make all my terrifying nightmares come true.

CHAPTER TWO

The Saturday before my official birthday, Lola and I
scoured our fave department stores for suitable
party clothes. As the birthday girl AND the birthday
girl's best friend, we obviously had to look especially
divine. In the end I bought the sweetest slip dress in
shimmery lilac. Since it was a beach party, I was
going to wear my dress with flip-flops, but v. v.
cosmic flip-flops, decorated with big sparkly stars.

Unfortunately, my soul-mate and I got a *leetle* bit
TOO wrapped up in our party plans, so much that
we totally forgot the joint assignment we were
supposed to be writing on the Hell dimensions!

We'd already blagged two extensions and Mr
Allbright was clearly running out of patience. By a
cruel coincidence, the Friday I'd unthinkingly picked

for my birthday was also the absolute final deadline for our Hell dimensions assignment, a fact I totally failed to remember until my alarm went off on Friday morning.

As you've probably realised, angelic education is radically different to the human kind. For one thing, angel high school kids aren't known as 'pupils' they're called 'trainees', and I don't think a day goes by without our teacher banging on about how "you must remember you are being groomed to be the angel agents of the future!"

This is a fact we're not really likely to forget, especially as every heavenly high school kid over the age of twelve is expected to do hands-on work experience for a cosmic outfit we just call the Agency, a super-massive organisation dedicated to protecting Earth from the Powers of Darkness.

Obviously in an ideal Universe, they wouldn't send inexperienced angel kids on dangerous time-travel missions. But as the Agency doesn't have anything like enough trained agents to meet human demand, they end up using us to fill the gaps.

Given we're under so much pressure, wouldn't you think our teachers would be a *teensy* bit more understanding?

Yeah, right. You could have been on Planet Earth for *weeks*, wearing the same skanky combats, with nothing but angel trail mix between you and near-starvation, but the instant you get back, you'd better get that essay finished or you're in DEEP poo, let me tell you!

Anyway, when Friday morning arrived I woke up and blinked sleepily at the pretty patterns the heavenly sunlight was making on the ceiling, with a vague feeling there was something I should be doing,

Then I'm like, oh, duh! It's my birthday.

"Happy birthday, angel girl," I told myself happily. Then I let out a shriek.

I ran to Lola's room and hammered on her door.

My friend finally came to the door, with such a bad case of bed-hair you couldn't actually see her face.

"You *did* remember, didn't you?" I pleaded. "You *hate* handing in work late, I know you do. I bet you sat up all night."

"I fell asleep in the bath," she said shamefaced.

"*Lollie!* I was relying on you!" I tried to think. "OK, Mr Allbright's class isn't 'til eleven. If we sprint to the school library now we should just have time to dash off an outline. He'd have to see we're showing willing, right?"

"I thought Mr Allbright said all the serious Hell materials are in the town library?"

"OK, so we'll have to sprint faster. Grab your clothes, babe, and let's go, go, go!"

When we told the librarian what we wanted, she immediately asked to see our IDs then looked outraged. "I can't help you," she said stiffly. "The books on your list are *extremely* dark Hell texts which have to be kept in the vaults."

"Can't we read them down there?" Lola pleaded.

"Only senior trainees have pass keys," sniffed the librarian.

"Couldn't you make an exception?" Lola wheedled. "We won't tell anyone."

"I'm going to pretend I didn't hear that." She flounced off pushing a trolley loaded with returned books.

"Psst!"

We both jumped as Lola's boyfriend appeared grinning like the Cheshire cat through a gap in the bookshelves.

Having got our attention, he mooched over to meet us, wearing his usual uniform of ripped jeans and a scuzzy Astral Garbage T-shirt.

Don't tell Lola, but I still find it really hard to think of Brice as an angel. This is a true story, yeah? So I have to tell you that when I found out about his budding romance with my soul-mate, I was *not* a happy seraph. OK, so I've fancied a bad boy or two in my time, but I never went for an evil assassin!

At first we couldn't figure out why Brice kept popping up on our Time missions like a bad smell. Lola says it was destiny. I think it was more like desperation.

Brice was v. v. screwed up when he dropped out of angel school. I'm guessing that by the time we met him, he was totally sickened at the work he was doing for the Dark Agencies, and was already truly deeply homesick for Heaven. I think harassing angels was the closest he could get.

It can't have been easy, but somehow Michael our headmaster staunchly went on believing in Brice whatever, and to the shock of our entire school, eventually persuaded the School Council to take him back on probation.

As a born cosmic outlaw, Brice found his probationary period incredibly humiliating. He stuck it out though, passed his retakes, and recently moved up to the upper school where he's doing really well, Lola says.

All the same, you never quite know where that boy is coming from and Lola was visibly astonished, not to say deeply suspicious, to see him in the library. "Weren't you due at the Agency like an hour ago?"

"Nah, still got five minutes," he said carelessly. "Had to check something out in the Hell-dimensions vault before I take off. Thought you might like to borrow this?" Brice fished around in his pocket, made sure the librarian wasn't looking and surreptitiously flashed a blue glimmery card.

"You *stole* a celestial pass key!" I gasped.

"Do you want to say that a bit louder, sweetheart! For your information, I am now legally entitled to a pass key to any library in the Heavenly City."

"Sorry," I said humbly, "I keep forgetting you're a senior now."

He slid the pass key into a little gizmo on the wall and we saw a blue flash. Interesting clanking sounds came up the shaft.

Brice grabbed Lola's wrist to check her watch. "OK, seriously gotta go," he said in a rush. "The hell materials are in the lower basement. Save me some birthday cake, girls, yeah?"

We watched him disappear through the swing doors.

"We should really buy that boy a new T-shirt," I told Lola.

"*Carita*, let me tell you, Brice has a whole drawer full of Astral Garbage T-shirts. All exactly the same!"

"His hair looks soo much better though," I said approvingly.

Instead of the scary bleached mullet he had before, Brice now wore his naturally-dark hair in gelled spikes, with occasional blond flashes.

"Where's your bad boy going anyway?" I asked Lola.

"Not too sure," she said vaguely. "Some disturbed kid, I think he said."

"Bit sudden," I objected. "He was coming to my party last I heard."

"Yeah well, the Agency moves in mysterious ways and whatever."

A bell pinged and the lift doors slid open. I glanced round guiltily to make sure the librarian wasn't watching.

"It's OK, she's gone for her break," Lola hissed.

We hopped in the lift and went humming down for *miles*.

When the doors opened again, we both breathed, "Wow!"

From floor to ceiling, the library vaults were totally bathed in intense azure light. We tiptoed around in the eerie blue silence, trying to find the right section. The hard-core Hell materials turned out to be kept in special cases. You had to switch on a tiny light and read them through the glass.

Hell dimensions are more complicated than I'd realised; they have this whole evil ecosystem going on. I'm not sure how many hell species there are in total, but it's a *lot*!

Lola gave me a sly nudge. "Ooh, Mel, check out the cute hell doggie!"

I squeaked with revulsion. "Euw Lollie, it's *bald*!!"

We'd covered hellhounds in Dark Studies but it was the first time I'd seen a picture. Struggling not to laugh, Lola read out the old-fashioned angelic script under the engraving.

"'*These vile dogges do ofttymes attempte to walke on their hynde legges, which maketh them unpleasantly to resemble a drooling human!*' Oh, yuck – listen. It says, '*The hell dogges turdes smell vile and after sunset beginne to glowe a pallid green like to a subterranean fungus.*'"

I firmly snapped off Lola's little light. "We are never going to the Hell dimensions, Lollie, so we will *never* have to smell a hell dogge's pallid green poo. Now focus!"

We eventually succeeded in cobbling an outline together for Mr Allbright. As we panted in through the shimmery gates of the Angel Academy, I was ecstatic. My birthday could go ahead as planned!

"Babe, do you mind handing this into Mr Allbright?" Lola said unexpectedly. "I'll see you tonight at Rainbow Cove, OK?"

She raced off, dark curls flying.

"OK," I said to empty space.

Lola and I generally help each other get glammed up, but I just assumed she was organising a super-special birthday surprise.

When I got back from school I did all the things you do. I showered, washed and dried my hair, and put it up, leaving just a few cute little traily bits dangling down. I did my make-up, splashed on my fave perfume, and slipped into my shimmery lilac dress.

I was bubbling with excitement all the way to Rainbow Cove. I made my way down the winding cliff path, worn smooth and shiny from centuries of angels' feet, and OK, I did notice it was strangely quiet – also strangely dark.

I just thought they were hiding. I genuinely thought that when I reached the final bend, all my mates would leap out of the shadows, screaming, "Surprise!"

But when I came round the bend, there were no shadows. The beach was flooded with moonlight – and it was totally deserted.

No fairy lights, no music, no delicious buffet. Nothing.

Absolutely nobody had turned up.

CHAPTER THREE

I sat down on the damp sand in my new dress and sobbed. I was so shocked and upset I was totally destroyed. Didn't my friends know how much this meant to me? Didn't they care?

Then all at once, as I wept and blubbered into my hands, I felt this... beautiful vibe.

When I looked up, snivelling and bewildered, it wasn't my friends I saw standing in front of me, but a group of shimmering light beings. I'd seen these pure luminous beings once before shortly after I arrived in Heaven. You could say they were my first glimpse of what it means to be a real angel, made of nothing but love and light.

Now my cosmic angels had come back!

I scrambled to my feet, respectfully tugging

down my dress as they silently gathered round me, and I heard their strangely impersonal voices in my head. "*So today's your birthday?*"

"Oh, about that," I gulped. "You see—"

The night was suddenly full of whizzy little rainbows: *zoom, zoom, zoom.* Too late I realised they were zooming towards me! As each miniature rainbow hit my energy field, it exploded into all its separate colours: scarlet and bright pumpkin orange, sunflower yellow and vivid emerald green, sky blue, midnight blue and violet. Then all these colours started to swirl into awesome cosmic-type patterns.

My energy field started flashing the exact same swirly patterns in the exact same rhythms. I'd like to tell you how long it went on, but I truly have no idea. Finally it was over.

"*Happy birthday, angel girl!*" the voices sang.

And they'd gone.

An instant later, twinkly pink fairy lights sprang on around the beach. A heavenly hip-hop beat started up.

"SURPRISE!"

My friends surrounded me, laughing and pelting me with sparkly confetti.

Lola flung her arms round me. "Happy birthday, *carita*! Did you enjoy your upgrade?"

"Is *that* what that was!"

There's me thinking I'm such a rebel, giving myself a DIY birthday, when it really *was* my birthday – my first true birthday as an angel! Angelic birthdays aren't about getting one year older (we're immortals, duh!). They're about getting more, you know... *angelly*!

"Open my pressie," Lola begged. She handed me a large box tied with about a zillion glittery ribbons, hovering anxiously while I carefully untied every one.

Inside was a lamp. It was literally constructed out of tiny jewel-coloured fairy lights, cunningly strung together in the shape of a v. cute, v. girly handbag.

I just stood there whispering, "Omigosh, Omigosh."

Lola's face crumpled. "Didn't I get the right one? Oh, Mel, I was *so* sure I'd got the right one."

"No, it is," I whispered. "It's exactly the same."

"I can change it. It's just you're always talking about that cool handbag lamp your mates got you for your thirteenth—"

I could still hear Lola anxiously burbling on, just as I could still see the fairy lights and Mo busily setting out my birthday buffet, but a part of me was back in our local Pizza Hut with my human mates...

We'd eaten as much as we could physically stuff in, and were chatting happily over pizza remains and slightly melted ice cream.

Suddenly Sky jumped up and rapped her glass. "Unaccustomed as I am to public speaking—"she started in a posh voice.

Jax blew bubbles rudely in her Coke, and Sky went into fits of giggles. "Stop it, you big pig! Tell her, Mel! She's ruining your big moment!"

"Your big moment, you mean," Jax snorted. "Look, just make your stupid speech, then we can go and see the movie!"

Sky self-consciously shook back her hair. "OK, um, I just want to say, don't think the Shocking Pinks are cheapskates, but we decided it would be better to club together so we could buy you something fabulous."

"I was going to nick it," Jax said shamelessly. "But Sky said nicking a birthday present would be bad karma."

Karmen put a gift-wrapped box on the table. "Tada!"

My friends watched expectantly as I unwrapped the exact twin to the lamp Lola had just given me in Heaven.

And just like now I was so amazed I didn't know what to say...

"You *hate* it, don't you?" Lola was saying tragically.

I finally found words. "Lola, It's PERFECT! I can't *believe* you got it for me."

"Step aside Sanchez, my turn to amaze the birthday girl!" Reuben practically shoved a tiny package into my hand. "As you can see, wrapping presents isn't my thing," he added cheerfully.

In fact, Reubs' present was already unwrapping itself; I just caught the glimmery crystal charm bracelet before it fell on the sand.

"It's totally luminous, Reubs," I breathed. "Where did you find it?"

He looked a bit embarrassed. "Millie made it. I had to give her all your personal info, then Millie picked charms which fitted. See there's a shell because you have this thing about the sea. This charm's an ancient angelic symbol for protection, and this star – but I guess you don't want to hear about every little bead, right?"

"Thanks, Reubs, I love it."

There was a slightly awkward pause.

"Well, better get back to my DJ duties," he grinned.

When he was out of earshot, I said, "I don't think I've met Millie?"

"Oh, she and Reubs have known each other for ever," Lola said.

It has *to be her*, I thought. During a late-night talk on our Limbo mission, Reuben let slip that he had a major crush, then flatly refused to give any more information. But a childhood sweetheart who made her own jewellery sounded exactly right for Reubs.

Until a few weeks ago, I'd always thought of Reubs as like my angel big bro. But since our soul-retrieval assignment we'd become just a tiny bit edgy with each other – in fact Reuben seemed to go out of his way to avoid being alone with me. I was worried I'd upset him. I kept asking Lola if he'd said anything to her. She insisted he hadn't, but I noticed she didn't deny he was upset. *Probably Millie's giving him a hard time*, I thought.

My party had been going for over an hour when I heard someone calling my name. I left the lights and the music without a thought, and ran down to the water's edge, where Michael was waiting.

"I can't believe you actually made it to my party!" I bubbled. "I heard you were away."

I was so happy to see him, I didn't even notice my headmaster wasn't smiling.

"I only just got back," he said in a quiet voice. "Melanie, I realise this is unfortunate timing, but I need you to come with me."

When I'm shocked, I do this silly high-pitched giggle. "You actually want me to leave my own birthday party—?"

Then I saw Michael's expression and my voice trailed off.

He looked unbelievably sad. "I'm afraid so. You see we've got to send you back home."

CHAPTER FOUR

Reflections flickered over my headmaster's face as he drove us downtown to the Agency building.

We've got to send you back home. The words went round in my head like a sound loop. I was far too scared to ask what was going on. Was I going to be kicked out of school? I'd come dangerously close to being expelled in my first term. Had I crossed a line with my cheeky DIY birthday?

Without taking his eyes off the road, Michael said, "You didn't do anything wrong, Melanie."

Still freaked from being snatched from my party, I wasn't sure I believed him. "Honestly?" I asked tearfully.

"You simply weren't ready for this until now."

I was just getting more confused. "I hate to be dense, but what's changed?"

He managed the glimmerings of a smile. "Have you forgotten what day it is already?"

"Oh *right*! You mean because of the upgrade!"

If I'd been thinking clearly, I might have asked why someone would need an angelic upgrade just to return home. But I wasn't thinking full stop. An amazing possibility had just occurred to me.

"Will I be able to see my family!"

"Of course," he said warmly. "You must see them while you're there."

"And my friends?"

Michael nodded.

"Omigosh, this is SO cool!" I almost kissed him! It wasn't a punishment; the *opposite* of a punishment in fact!! I'd passed some big angelic test and for my reward I was going to see the human beings I loved most in all the Universe.

As we drove into the underground car park, I sneaked a wary look at Michael. He still looked sad. Why would he be sad about such fabulous news?

"This IS just a visit, right?" I asked anxiously.

He manoeuvred into a space and switched off the engine. The pause was just long enough to make my heart turn over.

Our headmaster is such a total sweetie that I tend to forget he's also an archangel – a being so advanced you can't even begin to imagine what goes on in his head. As Michael met my eyes with his intense gaze, I felt like he was seeing deep into my soul.

"It's not just a visit, nor is it an assignment as yet – what we have here is an extremely delicate situation which could turn into your most challenging mission so far."

Since 'delicate' is polite Agency code for 'impossible', and 'most challenging' is code for 'really, really gruelling' my mind immediately flipped into overdrive. My first thought was that someone in my family might have had an accident or been taken ill. But then wouldn't Michael just say so?

I followed him anxiously through two sets of swing doors and into a lift. The doors closed and we went humming up into the clouds.

I watched the glowing numerals flash up, without really seeing them. I heard myself say, "It's one of my friends, isn't it?"

Michael gave a troubled sigh. "At this moment in time, all your friends are giving us cause for concern. I don't think you realise what a wonderful effect you had on those girls."

I almost fell over. *I'd* had a wonderful effect! It was *completely* the other way round!! It was Jax who'd taught me to stand up for myself. And Sky – well, you couldn't *not* be affected by Sky!

"I don't think so, Michael! I had NO luck stopping Jax shoplifting."

He flashed me his soul-piercing look. "Melanie, until you befriended Eve Jackson, no one ever showed the first sign of caring what happened to her."

My eyes filled with tears. "I didn't know."

"I thought perhaps you didn't," he said gently. "That's why I'm telling you now."

I was feeling rising panic. "Michael, I know I've had the upgrade and everything, but are you sure I'm up to this? Shouldn't you send a *real*, grown-up agent? Not to mention someone who's not so, you know, *involved*?"

He shook his head. "The Agency believes you know your friends better than any adult agent ever could. We have every confidence you would quickly detect any, erm, unsavoury influences."

The way he stressed 'unsavoury', I thought I'd sussed what he was telling me. "Don't say Karms is in love *again*! That girl has the worst taste in boys!"

Michael took a breath, "Melanie, before we go into Departures, I have to warn you that Park Hall is not exactly as it was when you left."

"I've only been gone eighteen months in Earth time," I teased. I was going to say, "Hopefully my mates won't *all* be wearing silver jump suits!" But at that moment I caught sight of myself and gave a shriek of horror.

"You've got to take me back to school first! I'm serious Michael! I can't go like this!"

No *way* could I go back to the gritty inner city wearing a shimmery lilac slip dress and flip-flops decorated with sparkly stars!

This time Michael actually chuckled. "You won't have to," he smiled. "I think you'll find my assistant has anticipated your needs!"

We hurried along gleaming corridors to Departures, where Michael's assistant, Sam, was waiting.

"I'd heard you make a habit of going on missions in your party clothes," he teased, "so I asked one of our stylists to pick out a few mix-and-match outfits." Sam handed me a large flamingo-pink carrier bag from one of my fave heavenly department stores. "And of course you get this delightful Agency flight bag with all the usual freebies!" he added with a grin.

I dashed off to the cloakroom to change. I was *so* impressed with my outfits. The Agency stylist had perfectly captured the inner-city vibe. For the outward journey I picked out a denim jacket, a cute flippy skirt and the *most* angelicious pink suede boots. Talk about going home in style!

I had a quick rummage through my flight bag. The contents seemed pretty standard – trail mix, Agency journal, comb, glow-in-the-dark pen, mobile – until I found the emergency flares.

Why the sassafras would I need *flares*?

I tinkered for a bit with the functions on my tiny Agency mobile, then had a naughty impulse and rang Lola.

She picked up straight away, like she'd been expecting my call. It sounded like my party was really totting up. I explained that I'd had to bail on my own celebrations because I was being sent back to my old human home.

"We had to zoom off to medieval France in the middle of mine, if you remember!" she yelled over the music.

"I wish you could come too," I said wistfully. I'd always had this big fantasy of taking Lola round all my fave human haunts.

"*Carita!* I'm so sorry. I didn't hear you properly before. Omigosh, you're going home? That's HUGE! But I know you're gonna do great!"

Feeling slightly tearful, I picked my way back through the crowds of celestial agents waiting for flights out of Heaven.

Eventually I spotted Michael chatting to one of the time technicians. This seemed like a good opportunity to sneak a word with his cute assistant.

"Nice boots!" Sam grinned when he saw me.

"I don't suppose the Agency mentioned how long I'll be staying?" I asked anxiously.

He shrugged. "As long as it takes basically, but I should think two weeks max. You'll be arriving on Friday afternoon as everyone comes out of school. Should make it easy to track down all your mates."

Sam handed me my angel tags, the little disk that tells everyone we're on official heavenly business. "And don't forget you're only a phone call away!"

Michael waved me over. "Any last minute questions, or concerns?" he smiled.

Only about a billion.

For the first time I was going to be travelling in one of the Agency's super-slick, one-angel-only time capsules.

As I ducked inside, I gave myself a stiff pep talk. *Melanie, you have survived Ancient Rome!* I told myself severely. You can *surely* cope with going back to Park Hall.

Two weeks max. Three hundred and thirty-six hours of Earth time. I could handle that.

The glass door purred smoothly into closed position.

The maintenance guy held up both hands. Ten seconds to go.

I waved and was surprised to hear a tiny tinkling of crystals. I'd forgotten to remove my bracelet. I nervously fingered the charms. *The shell is because you love the sea. This one is an ancient angelic symbol for protection...*

THREE, TWO. My capsule lit up like solar flares.

WHOOSH! I was blasted out of Heaven.

Reuben has tried to explain angelic time-travel to me soo many times you would not believe. As far as I'm concerned it's just magic!

Picture yourself hurtling through a vast nothingness, inside a fragile glass shell. Outside, starry streams of cosmic energy spiral off to form dazzling whirlpools, which get sucked into bigger, brighter whirlpools, and on into infinity.

You're looking at something so huge, so mysterious, your mind can't begin to take it in.

I have to pinch myself sometimes – like, *I'm travelling in Time. I'm an angel and I'm actually travelling in Time!!*

Yet this time, as I hurtled through eternity, I didn't glance outside once. I had almost completely forgotten I was an angel. I only knew I was going home, and I was overwhelmed with memories of my friends. These memories weren't just like moving pictures in my head. I felt like I was literally living through my experiences again, complete with all the emotions and sensations I'd had at the time. That first day at high school when we all hated each other on sight. The first time everyone slept over at my place and Sky forced us to dye her hair with henna, only we left it on so long it turned a screaming fire-engine red! The time me and my mates just took off to explore the city, without letting our parents know where we were going, then got back to find Karmen's mum had called the police...!

I'd been too busy to let myself miss them, you see – too busy trying to turn myself into an angel. Now I was being shown exactly how much I'd lost.

The flow of memories stopped just as the dramatic whooshing sensation of time came to a standstill.

Lights and shadows flickered on the other side of the glass. Any sounds that reached me were so faint and muffled, I could have been listening to bees buzzing in clover.

For no real reason, I started smoothing down my hair. It felt unexpectedly scary, knowing my old neighbourhood was outside, waiting to come into focus. I wondered if angels often returned to their human haunts and, if so, did they feel this same creepy sense of premonition, as if their worlds were about to smash into each other like two icebergs...

I glanced at my watch. They'd be out of school any minute.

Touching my tags for luck, I jumped down into twenty-first century London and shrieked in horror.

"Oh, noo, my *boots*!"

I was ankle deep in slush! No one had thought to tell me it would be the middle of winter! As I shivered in the blowing sleet, I'd have traded my granny for a big warm parka.

Cars and trucks crawled past, churning up the dirty snow, headlights barely visible through the gloom. Spine-thumping beats came from everyone's car stereos. That alone was enough to tell me I was back.

Checking that my bag was securely fastened, I set off towards the traffic lights, eyes straight ahead, every inch saying 'Don't mess with this angel girl!' I'd been home two seconds and I'd gone right back to being an inner-city chick!

On one level my old neighbourhood was how I remembered: same stink of traffic fumes and fast food, same hard-faced youths talking a mile a minute into their mobiles. The tattoo parlour was there and that whole-food shop which was run by Buddhists. It was all exactly the same. The only thing that had changed – was me.

I knew it wasn't fair but I couldn't stop comparing Park Hall with Heaven. I couldn't believe how tacky my neighbourhood had become. These are your roots, girl, I scolded myself, This was your human *home*. But it felt alien and ugly. As I trudged along with freezing slush seeping into my heavenly boots,

I don't think I've ever felt so lonely and mixed up, or so totally out of place.

I felt a glowing sensation in my chest, as if I'd swallowed a tiny slightly-too-hot potato. My inner angel had come online. Like soul-mates, inner angels are not an exclusively angel thing. Helix has been a part of me for ever, only now I actually listen to her wise advice! As usual she was totally on it.

"Are you sure these are *your* thoughts, sweetie?" she inquired.

"AAARGH!" I shrieked. "I have SO got to stop DOING that!!"

I do it *every* single time!! Pick up some local vibe and confuse it with my own feelings. EVERYONE in Park Hall feels lonely, mixed-up and out of place, except maybe the Buddhists!

"Thanks, Helix," I said huskily. "I was losing it big time."

"It's what I'm here for, babe. I think we're quite close to your school now. You might want to give yourself a *leetle* light boost."

I was already surrounded by criminals and drug dealers. I really couldn't see why Helix was stressing about my school. But I'm learning to respect her hunches. I obediently boosted my light levels and went on my way, feeling fabulously calm.

It was just as well. The neighbourhood vibes were dropping steadily. Without noticing I'd crossed the invisible border into the old run-down area folksily known as Bell Meadow. The houses were the same houses, the shops were the same shops, yet the low-level vibes made them seem weirdly threatening.

Because of Bell Meadow's humongous crime levels, my school was enclosed behind high brick walls topped with razor wire. Someone had sprayed angry graffiti: WE'RE GONNA GET YOU SHAY.

Outside the school gates, a few older youths hung around, looking vaguely dodgy in their big coats and hoods – might be selling drugs, but more likely they just had nowhere else better to go.

It was like the nightmare version of my dream-like arrival at the Angel Academy, only instead of glowing angel kids streaming in through glimmery pearl gates, hordes of tough, stressed-looking human kids jostled their way out of an ugly fortress-type entrance. Kids were swearing, smoking, bragging, screaming insults.

I'd been away too long. I'd forgotten what human schools can be like. The dark side of Park Hall

Community High School had been stealthily fading from my memories until it started to seem like one of those sunny vibey schools in hip-hop videos.

The initial stampede slowed, but there was no sign of my friends. I was baffled. It was Friday afternoon! No one hung about on Fridays if they had a choice.

I bet Miss Rowntree gave them a detention. *I'd better go in and find them,* I thought.

But Helix seemed uneasy. "Sweetie, trust me, it would be much wiser to wait out here."

"I'm not freezing my booty off for another hour! It's just a school, Helix! What can happen?"

Walking through the gates made me feel slightly sick, like I was having to push my way through an unfriendly force field. I just put it down to local vibes and cinched up my light levels.

The school doors were locked so I shimmered into the foyer.

"Yes, I *know* it's a dump, OK," I snapped, before Helix could get a word in. "It's a depressed area, what do you expect?"

Dump was not the word. Every single pot plant was dying, if not technically dead. The fish tank only contained slimy pebbles and a vandalised display case had been sloppily mended with tape.

Tired posters advertised a forthcoming production of GREASE, or, as one defaced poster now read, GROSS.

In the hall the drama group was in the process of murdering "Summer Lovin'". I couldn't believe it; Mr Lupton had been trying to get a production together since I could remember.

I started off down the corridor.

"Aren't you going to check the hall?" Helix asked in surprise.

"No point. My mates aren't the drama group type!"

I did try to make them audition once. For the same production coincidentally – and no, actually, it wasn't *only* because cute Kelsey Hickman was in the starring role! I happened to think we'd make pretty good Pink Ladies. I could totally picture us in those cute college-girl jackets.

But my mates flatly refused. They said it would ruin our edgy reputation. "I mean, PINK Ladies," Jax snorted. "How mushy and girly is that?" Jax and Sky thought all school clubs were tragically uncool.

"Aha!" I teased her. "So if it was the Shocking Pink Ladies, I suppose you'd do it!"

My friends were staring at me as if they'd had a vision.

"What? What did I say?"

Then Sky started jumping up and down and squealing. "Mel, you're a star! The Shocking Pinks is the PERFECT name for our posse!"

As I hurried along empty echoey corridors, I was so excited I kept forgetting to breathe.

When I reached our old classroom, I jumped up to peer in the window, absolutely knowing I'd see three fed-up girls and a grim Miss Rowntree doing her marking. I was actually giggling with nerves.

The room was empty.

They must be in the science lab. After Miss Rowntree, Mr Krishnamurti was the most keen on giving detentions. I started the long trek towards the science block.

"I should be wearing our colour," I giggled to Helix.

After school we'd gone rushing off to Claire's Accessories to hunt out the exact shocking pink items for our group makeover. We pinned shocking pink badges to our bags and re-covered our school exercise books in shocking pink paper; we totally went for it! Being a Pink gradually crept into every area of our lives. If you were down for any reason, one of us would firmly remind you to "Think Pink" –

Shocking Pink code for staying positive and hanging on to your dreams.

When you lived in a world that was one-hundred-per-cent grey, being a Shocking Pink was like a statement: "We're young, we're vibey and we're here!"

Sadly, like all Mr Lupton's previous productions, the cheesy musical that inspired this exciting transformation never came off. This time Kelsey's mum got picked up for shoplifting two days before the opening night.

Scared they'd be taken into care, Kelsey and his younger brothers did a runner. They were found weeks later living in a car. It seemed so unfair that he never got the chance to show what he could do. Kelsey would have made a totally brilliant Danny Zucco.

All humans have problems and my mates were no exception, but we definitely had it cushy compared to kids like Kelsey.

Our science block was in a new annexe along with the gym and computer labs. For reasons that probably made sense to the architects, the annexe was on the other side of the dual carriageway to the main school, connected by an ugly concrete bridge.

You know those motorway café bridges that sway in high winds? E*xactly* the same, except it wasn't glassed in, so it was *très* draughty. And even though it was a bridge, and obviously above ground, it had that icky subway vibe. This was possibly because the light bulbs were constantly being vandalised, so on winter afternoons, like this one, it was like walking down a long, windy and very nearly dark tunnel. I'd always hated walking over that bridge, but not nearly so much as Helix did.

"I'm getting a really *disgusting* vibe," she announced unhappily when we were like, a third of the way across.

"So why are you telling *me*?" I'd got it into my head that Helix was criticising my school, so of course I felt like I had to be Park Hall High School's number one fan.

All along the bridge someone had daubed YOU'RE GOING TO GET YOURS SHAY. In my day graffiti always got nuked by the school cleaners virtually the same day it appeared.

I didn't want to admit it, but I was increasingly freaked. It wasn't just the subway vibes, it was the *smell*. Our science block was never exactly fragrant, but today the air was quite repulsively whiffy.

"What's that?" Helix asked abruptly. "I heard something."

"You're doing my head in, Helix!" I snapped. "It's the wind, OK?"

"Something like *footsteps*. And a weird whining."

"Just take a chill pill, will you! It's probably one of the cleaning ladies singing!"

"There it is again!"

I peered nervously into the dusky gloom at the end of the tunnel, and caught a tiny movement. At the same time I heard a stealthy pad-padding, so soft and furtive that all the tiny hairs stood to attention on the back of my neck.

All at once I almost gagged. "Urgh!" I clamped my hand over my nose. "That is *SO* rank!"

"We should get off this bridge," Helix said urgently. "This is not a good place for angels."

"We can't," I gulped. "We haven't checked the lab."

I felt my knees totally give way, like I'd been kicked from behind. Next minute I was grovelling on my hands and knees.

I just exploded. "Are you *mad*!! Did you just trip me up?"

"And I'd do it again if I had to. I want you to look down NOW!"

My inner angel seemed so frantic that I obeyed. Then I saw the horrible thing she'd been trying to warn me about and screamed.

CHAPTER FIVE

My face was inches from a pile of glistening supernatural turds.

I know this is way too much information, but in the semi-twilight of the bridge, the pallid green Hell poo did actually seem to glow.

For a moment I was hypnotised with horror.

What if I'd touched it?

This thought made me want to beam home to Heaven and shower with rose-scented angel shower gel for like, a year.

"This isn't *right*," I whispered.

I suddenly unfroze, scrambling to my feet.

If there was green hell poo, then there had to be hellhounds too!

Omigosh, the kids! Humans rarely register cosmic

phenomena, but if a pack of hellhounds crashed their rehearsal, it could still seriously damage their wellbeing.

I hurtled back along the bridge.

"Sorry I decked you, babe," Helix said apologetically.

"No, you had to, honestly," I gargled, still trying not to breathe. "I should have listened."

As I'm sure you realised, hellhounds can't simply wander into the human dimension and poo wherever they feel like it. Ok, so their evil masters are allowed to travel freely throughout the Universe, but there's a total cosmic ban on evil pets, or any other kind of hell trash.

When I got back to the foyer, I could hear a buzz of voices. I assumed the cast were taking a break, then I heard sudden angry shouting.

"Omigosh, my mates *are* in there!" I gasped. "Sounds like Karmen's got a major part!"

But when I charged in, it was obvious no one was rehearsing. The kids were shrugging on their coats, looking incredibly cheesed-off.

"I'm just as disappointed as you are," Mr Lupton was saying. "But there's no way we're ready to go on in a fortnight. Tonight was a shambles and you know it. We've lost far too many cast members."

I wilted with disappointment.

The girl who was giving Mr Lupton a hard time was remarkably similar to my mate, but she had a cute layered bob. Karmen would *never* cut her hair.

"I can't believe you're doing this!" this girl was yelling. She was right up in Mr Lupton's face, almost spitting with fury.

"It's not the *kids'* fault they've got problems! If you really cared about us, sir, you'd understand."

The girl really did look amazingly like Karmen. But shy little Karms was too timid to yell at anyone, let alone a teacher.

Mr Lupton hitched up his baggy cords. "I do care," he said unhappily. "But there's a limit to—"

"It's STUPID to stop now. We've all worked SO hard!"

"I'm sorry, my answer's still 'no'."

He tried to turn away but she just barged in front of him and continued harassing him. "What if I could get them all back?" she begged. "What if I rounded them up and we worked flat out all day Sunday?"

This musical had been Mr Lupton's pet project for years and you could tell he totally yearned to be convinced. "But we can't put this right in two weeks," he said unhappily.

"So ask Mrs Threlfall if she'll let you take us out of lessons until we finish the play! We can DO this, sir. They build gardens in a poxy weekend on TV! Give us one last chance. *Please?*"

It *was* her! That slight lisp on 'poxy'. Karm's voice was unmistakable now.

But where were the others? She wouldn't have joined the drama group by herself, so why weren't Sky and Jax here to back her up?

Mr Lupton gave another nervous hitch to his trousers. "All right, one last chance," he sighed. "I want everyone here by 9.30 on Sunday morning and we'll just see how it goes."

To my amazement, all the cast members cheered.

"We won't let you down, Mr Lupton, I swear," one girl told him.

"You're all right, man," one of the boys grinned.

"At least one teacher believes in us," said his mate.

Was this REALLY my school? Not to diss my old mates, but Park Hall pupils are not natural joiners. Dreamers yes. Antisocial losers definitely. Joiners? No way!

Having saved their production, you'd think Karmen would want to hang out with the rest of the cast, but she just grabbed her parka and flew out of the door.

Panicking that I'd lose her again, and forgetting all about hellhounds and earth angels, I zoomed in pursuit.

Outside my school it was one long traffic jam. A double decker was slowly inching past the school gates. Karms hopped on. I followed her up to the top deck and took the seat beside her.

My vibes were still tuned to angelic, not human, reality, so Karms couldn't see me, but she might be able to sense me.

"Well, this feels weird," I told her softly. "You look *so* different, Karms – *très* grown-up!"

It wasn't just the new hairstyle. It was Karmen herself. My Karms was constantly badgering us to tell her what to think or what to wear. It drove us *nuts*, yet you felt like you had to take care of her. But there was nothing helpless about the girl sitting next to me. She was like a human laser beam; all her energy was focused on a single point: how to make this production happen. In the old days, I'd have assumed she was pursuing some boy in the drama group – some skanky loser of a boy – but you couldn't see *this* Karmen going for losers.

My mate tensed up. She'd spotted someone in the street. She whipped her phone out of her pocket, tapped in a pre-set, and yelled, "Where the HELL were YOU? You know how many kids turned up tonight? *EIGHT!* It was humiliating, Jax!"

Determined to see my second Pink before the bus moved off, I half-dived across Karmen, peering out of the steamed-up glass.

Was that *truly* Jax down there? No WAY!

I'd never have recognised her if Karms hadn't used Jax's name. My friend's natural red-brown hair had been dyed neon-sign pink. She had so many metal piercings it looked like she had bristles.

Jax was gesturing angrily, clearly not in the mood to co-operate.

Karms huffed with annoyance. "No, because I bought us some more time, didn't I? He's agreed to let us rehearse all day Sunday."

The bus chugged away again, leaving Jax behind.

"I will NOT let it go." Karmen's voice was shaking now. "No I'm not listening to you, Jax. Show up on Sunday or you're in big trouble."

She rang off and stared unseeingly out of the window until we reached her stop. I followed her off the bus feeling like Alice when she fell down the rabbit hole. Nothing made sense.

I'd just seen Karmen fighting for the right to embarrass herself in public. Shy little Karmen who used to be too chicken to ring out for a pizza! Meanwhile Jax, who'd always been a wee bit rough around the edges, had turned into the teenage harpy from hell!

By this time it wouldn't have surprised me if Karmen's parents had become total nudists. I followed her nervously into the small terraced house, but to my relief, everything was exactly like I remembered. It even had that same homey, very faintly spicy smell.

Mrs Patel had The Be Good Tanyas playing on the stereo as she prepared the evening meal. Karm's parents were crazy about country music. They'd wanted to name their only daughter after one of those big-haired country singers, Dolly, Loretta-Sue, or whoever, but that didn't go down with the grandparents, so they compromised with 'Karmen Asha'.

Karmen used to reckon, out of all the Pinks, her mum liked me best; Karms said she thought I had a sweet smile.

I imagined what her mum would say if she knew who was sitting at their breakfast bar. "Karmen's been telling me you're an angel now, Melanie! Isn't that absolutely *fantastic*! You must try some of these sweets. No, darling, eat as many as you like. That way I won't be tempted!"

Over sounds of efficient chopping, Karmen and her mum chatted about what to buy one of the cousins for a wedding present.

If you didn't know Karmen, you could have been fooled into believing everything was normal. But I was deeply worried, not to say shocked. *My* Karms had to rush to the phone every five minutes to call her mates. Sometimes she'd ring each of us in turn just to ask which top we thought she should wear next day.

Listen – I sat at that breakfast bar for over an *hour* and Karmen didn't phone the other Pinks ONCE. But that wasn't the most shocking thing. When it finally hit me, I couldn't believe I hadn't noticed.

Karmen wasn't wearing our colour.

That's why she didn't phone. That's why the others refused to support her at the rehearsal.

"Omigosh," I whispered.

The Shocking Pinks had broken up!!

If it wasn't for Helix I'd probably be sitting in the Patels' kitchen today going, "Omigosh, Omigosh."

Unlike me, my inner angel has excellent control of her emotions. She said calmly, "This is upsetting, but we need to know what's going on with these girls."

I tried to pull myself together. "Should I check Karm's room?" I gulped. "Look for clues to her state of mind?"

"Exactly what I was thinking," Helix agreed.

I found clues all right, and they didn't reassure me about my friend's state of mind. GREASE posters plastered over the walls, a GREASE DVD cover beside the DVD player, a GREASE minidisc on top of her minidisc player... I could go on.

"This isn't being *focussed,*" I said in dismay. "This is being *obsessed!* This is Park Hall, Helix! IF they get this production together, *which* I doubt, they'll be lucky to sell two tickets."

I don't know why it took me so long to see the photograph – maybe because Karmen had put it in such a big fancy frame.

It had been taken on our mad day out, minutes after we got off the London Eye. A helpful tourist took it with Karm's digital camera. In the picture we've got exactly the same smiles.

For some reason Karmen had put a scented candle in front of the picture, and a silk rose. The rose was bright pink.

I felt something slam shut inside my mind. Like, *don't go there*. Lots of girls had candles and flowers in their rooms. It didn't mean anything morbid.

I heard the sound of a key turning in the front door. Karmen's dad was home. He dropped his bag and went into the kitchen.

"Friday night!" he sighed. "Two whole days of freedom!"

I peeped out of my friend's room in time to see him grab Karmen's mum and dance her round madly to the Tanyas.

I had a sudden longing for my own family. We had this big Friday ritual. I'd pick Jade up from her after-school club, we'd meet Mum out of work, then the three of us would go to the Cosmic Café. It didn't look much from outside, but the food was out of this world. If he wasn't on call-out, Des would join us later.

I'd been trying my best to act like an angel on a mission, but now the ache was so strong, it was an actual pain in my chest.

I want to see them.

In a heartbeat I was standing on the street opposite the Cosmic Café, icy sleet blowing in my eyes and mouth.

"*Woo!*" I said in awe. "Did I even say that out loud?"

Next minute I was charging across the busy road, literally morphing through cars and buses in my desperation to get to them.

To you they'd have looked like an ordinary London family in a cheap and cheerful café. To me, they looked like Christmas morning. I felt like I was going to explode with love. There they all were! Big bald Des pointing out something on the Specials board. Jade pulling on my step-dad's sleeve. And Mum had totally changed her hair!

"They're so *beautiful*," I whispered.

I was so focused on the little scene inside the café, I didn't register the otherworldly personnel carrier nosing up to the curb. I didn't suspect a thing until two sinister reflections loomed up in the misted glass. Next minute, hands gripped my arms, pinning them to my sides so I couldn't move, and I was being dragged, screaming, away from my family.

A hand clamped down firmly over my mouth. I felt myself helplessly lifted off my feet and bundled into a vehicle. The engine was still running. There was a swoosh and a clunk as the doors slid shut and we started to move off.

I scratched and bit my unknown kidnapper thrashing about in my frenzy to get free. I didn't even care if I poisoned myself with PODS toxins.

"OK, bad joke!" a voice admitted. "Listen, I'm going to take my hand away on a count of three, but DON'T bite! I promised my girlfriend I'd get back in one piece. One, two, th—"

My eyes had been screwed tight shut. Now they flew wide open.

"BRICE?" I said in disbelief.

Chapter Six

"Hey check those, real angel tooth marks!" Lola's boyfriend showed his hand to his mate, seeming almost proud.

The other angel boy laughed. "Sure that's an *angel* chick? Seems more like a hell vixen to me!"

Brice waggled his eyebrows. "Mel can be quite feisty when she wants to be!"

They went on joking over my head in that maddening way boys do all across the Universe. Now I was over the first shock, I was livid. I gave Brice a hard thump. "You gave me a heart attack you pig!! I thought you were PODS!"

He fended me off laughing. "I couldn't resist, you looked so sweet and goofy, darling. You were totally away with the fairies."

I just glared. I didn't tell him about my family. I couldn't.

Brice's mate had the grace to look embarrassed. "Sorry, that was a stupid thing to do, " He stuck out his hand. "I'm Hendrix."

Woo, I thought, he's *really* fit.

I shyly shook his hand. "Nice to meet you."

I flashed an evil look at Brice. "What are you doing here, dirt bag? Apart from scaring me out of my skin?"

He looked slightly shifty. "Oh, you know, making the inner city a better place. Beating Hendrix at pool."

"In your dreams!" Hendrix told him.

"Omigosh, Hendrix, you're an EA!" I realised suddenly. "I've got to report a cosmic anomaly at Park Hall High School. Some hell beastie got into my school – and *pooed*, can you believe?"

I thought I saw a weird look pass between them.

Hendrix said quickly, "We'll get someone on it, don't worry."

The angel carrier had been accelerating steadily while we were talking. Suddenly there was a violent lurch and I was virtually thrown into Hendrix's arms as the van began hurtling through traffic at breakneck speed.

"I should buckle up sweetheart," Brice advised. "Unless you *enjoy* cuddling Hendrix. Jools is a bit of a speed freak."

I hastily unpeeled myself, pulling a hideous face at Brice. "Does he *always* drive like this?"

"She," Brice corrected.

"And yes, Jools only drives in top gear," grinned Hendrix.

Jools was now driving the wrong way up a one-way street. It was a heavenly vehicle, totally harmless to human road users, but I had to cover my eyes. We finally screeched to a stop.

I clambered out of the angel carrier on jelly legs, then rubbed my eyes. I'd walked down Matilda Street just about every day on my way to and from school, and never seen this elegant shimmery house. That's because it was an Agency house which had been invisibly slotted into a shabby human terrace.

"I had no idea we had houses on Earth!" I breathed.

"There's a few," said a warm voice. A girl swung down from the driver's seat. She wore a long rainbow-striped scarf draped over her combat jacket. "How many are there now, Hen?"

Hendrix shrugged. "It must be in the thousands. Oh, this is Jools, who was completely against us kidnapping you by the way!"

"I was," she sighed. "But Brice—"

"—is a terrible influence, I know," I joked.

With her big boots, old combats and an even older cap jammed over beaded braids, Jools was probably not your nan's idea of an angel. But she did look exactly like girls I knew in Park Hall. EAs usually like to adopt the styles and cultures of their local human community.

Jools held up her angel tags to a device on the wall. There was a brief blue shimmer. The door slid open and Brice, who seemed to think he was an honorary earth angel, grandly ushered me inside.

I was blown away. I couldn't believe I was still in the middle of a twenty-first century human city. The vibes in the Agency house were so pure I could have been back in Heaven.

An angel girl in combat gear came hurrying down the stairs. "Oh hi," she smiled, and disappeared into one of the downstairs rooms.

I heard a steady hum of voices coming through the door.

"That's the EA communications centre for this

area," Jools explained. "Like the Angel Watch centre, but much smaller, obviously."

I peered curiously round the door and saw twenty plus agents at their work stations, jabbering quietly into headsets. "Where did the incident take place?" one agent was asking her caller. "Any signs of You Know Who? OK, we'll get you some backup. Do the best you can until then."

"We'll show you round later," Jools promised. "You could probably do with a rest."

"I'll carry that," Hendrix said, taking my bag.

"You think you're so smooth," Brice told him.

As they shepherded me up flights of stairs, I was trying to take in the sheer scale of the Agency safe house.

In one open-plan area, trainees calmly worked at computers which had up to ten different streams of cosmic data racing hectically across their screens at any one time. Next door a lone trainee was minding banks of monitors, all of which showed local trouble spots. One had a split screen which showed the same house from different angles.

"That house used to be a vet's," I said in surprise.

"Those were the good days then," the trainee

said grimly. "The life forms that live there now aren't exactly man's best friend."

I felt a shiver go through me. "PODS live there now?" I'd taken my little sister past that house on the way to her tap lessons.

"Officially it's inhabited by humans," Hendrix explained.

"Just not any you'd like to meet," Jools commented.

I'd met humans like that on previous missions: people so closely involved with the Dark agencies, they were half-PODS themselves.

"Much activity today?" Hendrix asked the trainee.

He shook his head. "Just the usual."

We toiled up a final flight of stairs. A boy angel was pacing the landing with his mobile.

"No, since he started with the kick boxing, he's much more confident, like a different boy..."

I followed the others into a big studenty sitting room. Two angel girls looked up and smiled, then went back to chatting. A boy was stretched out on one of the sofas, apparently asleep.

I've seen EAs in just about every time you can think of, but seeing them in my old neighbourhood made me so happy I wanted to cry. I'd been rubbing shoulders with angels all those years and didn't even know! *I LOVE my job*, I thought tearfully. *I have the best life* ever.

"Can anyone else smell that stink?"

I came back to Earth to see Jools screwing up her nose in disgust, making me notice a tiny star-shaped stud for the first time.

"Mel found hell turds at the school," Hendrix said super-casually.

Her expression changed. "Not again," she said half to herself. She turned, flashing her warm smile. "Mel, I hate to be a pain, but I think you picked up something whiffy on those beautiful boots."

"Oh, I *thought* I could—!" I nervously inspected one boot sole, hopping to keep my balance. "Oh, no, I *did*!" I wailed. "This is SO embarrassing!"

"Give them here," laughed Hendrix.

Holding my boots by their tops, he gallantly whisked them away.

Jools started madly spraying everything in sight with some kind of heavenly Febreze. "You must think I'm so rude," she said apologetically. "I just have this incredibly sensitive sense of smell."

I couldn't believe I'd trekked hell dog poop into an angel house!

"I tamed a hell puppy once," Brice said with a straight face.

My poopy boots were instantly old news. Every angel in earshot stared at him in horror. Even the boy who'd been snoozing sat up open-mouthed.

Jools giggled nervously. "Brice, I never know when you're joking!"

"It's true," he insisted. "He was a smart little guy. Answered to his name and everything."

"Yeah, yeah," laughed Jools. "What did you call him? Fluffy?"

"I called him Bob," Brice said with dignity.

"Why would anyone call a hellhound Bob?" spluttered the boy.

"You think I should have named him Fang?" Brice snapped. "He was a little motherless puppy, man!"

Jools suddenly looked horrified. "My manners! Did we even introduce you?"

I shyly shook my head.

"We've given you such a terrible welcome," she wailed. "First the guys kidnap you off the street, then we tell you have stinky boots, and *then* we don't even— OK, let's do it now. This is Delphine, this is Tallulah, and Sleeping Beauty here answers to Dino."

I stood there in my socks, nodding and smiling, but absolutely nothing was going in.

"When did you last eat, angel girl?" Brice interrupted.

Hendrix had reappeared with my decontaminated boots. "I could murder a pizza personally – how about you guys?"

"You get *pizza*!" I said amazed. "You don't just live on trail mix?"

"Don't talk to me about that stuff!" said Jools with feeling. "Girl, it gives me the *worst* wind!"

I creased up laughing. "Doesn't it!"

Minutes later Jools and I were in the shared kitchen, hungrily tearing up pizza. The boys were eating theirs in the TV room.

"I'm so grateful I ran into you guys," I told her happily.

"It's great cosmic timing," she smiled. "My room mate is actually away on a course, so you can have her bed – if you don't mind sharing," she added quickly.

"Are you *kidding*? I was worrying I'd have to sleep in a doorway!"

Jools was carefully picking off her sweet corn. "Is it OK to ask what you're doing here?"

"You can ask," I mumbled through too-hot pizza. "All I know is my mates are in some kind of trouble."

"Have you managed to hook up with them yet?"

"Not hooked up, exactly," I sighed. "I've seen two of them."

Jools was a great listener. She gave me her total attention as I described the disturbing changes in my friends.

"You're sure they've broken up finally and for ever?"

"It certainly feels pretty final," I sighed.

Jools looked sympathetic. "It happens."

"I know, I know, people move on."

"Is that how it feels? Like they just moved on?"

I shook my head. "Actually it doesn't."

While we were talking, Brice wandered in with Hendrix and a couple of boy EAs.

"So where are we going, girls?" Hendrix demanded. "It's Friday night! We can't just stay in eating pizza!"

"There's that new club down the road," Jools suggested. "They're getting that DJ – what's his name again?"

"Ruff Justice?" Brice said unexpectedly.

"How come you *always* know this stuff?" I marvelled. "You got here just before me!"

"You'll come with us, won't you Mel?" Jools asked hopefully.

I shook my head. "It's been a really long day."

Brice patted my head. "Mel's going to curl up in her jammies, aren't you, and reread the intro to the Angel Handbook?"

I swatted him. "I got to chapter two, for your information!"

"You did well!" Jools laughed. "That book is *soo* heavy going."

This is exactly why Lola and I are going to write our Cosmic Survival Guide, but this is still a big secret between me and my soul-mate, so I kept my lips v. firmly sealed.

Jools slung an arm round my shoulder. "Come on Mel, don't you want to see how earth angels party?"

"Yeah!" I decided.

In the end a whole gang of us went down in the angel carrier, including Tallulah and Dino, the Sleeping Beauty boy.

You could feel the bass line pumping from the other side of the street. I felt a naughty buzz as we waltzed past security. I thought we all looked quite groovy. Brice had put on a fresh T-shirt under his leather jacket (I know!). I'd borrowed a sweet skirt from Jools and a cute top which said SHINE ON.

The club was already packed out.

Hendrix gave me his flirty smile. "Want to show the humans some real dancing?"

Next to flirting with good-looking earth angels, dancing is one of my all-time favourite activities! But when angels and humans dance in the same space, ohh – it's PURE magic.

As the night went on I was amazed to see some of the human dancers picking up on our dance style. At times the DJ actually seemed to sense our vibes. "I'm feeling some *sweet* energy in the house tonight," he kept saying. "You Park Hall people must have *serious* auras. Yeah man, there's enough lies and illusion in this world, but you guys are still keeping it real."

"We're trying, Justice, we're trying," yelled one of the earth angels, and the entire angel contingent cheered!

At that moment I wouldn't have swapped with the old Mel Beeby for anything. Even Brice appeared to be having a good time.

But this was Park Hall, so obviously it couldn't last.

Around two in the morning, Jools and Hendrix got a call – a gang fight with suspiciously high levels of PODS interest.

CHAPTER SEVEN

I was up for anything by this time. Just as well, because we were in for one of Jools' white knuckle drives. We bombed over speed bumps, taking interesting short cuts which *definitely* weren't in the A to Z.

At last we drove into a dead end behind some council flats.

There's a thing our Dark Studies teacher calls 'miasma': a sticky dark aura which collects wherever Dark agents gather together.

"Yup," said Brice grimly. "Your bad boys definitely have an audience."

"How big?" Hendrix asked.

"Hard to tell – they're kind of overexcited so they keep changing shape." Brice was using what me and Lola call his 'Dark radar', a disturbing ability to detect Dark agents even when, like now, they weren't in human disguise.

As we pulled up, there was another shock. For some reason the call centre hadn't thought to mention this was a girl fight.

I couldn't tell how many girls were milling about. There was one streetlight and that was on the blink. You just caught dramatic glimpses – a gold hoop glinting in an earlobe, a sneery mouth, a flash of designer trainers. Smashed cider bottles littered the ground; some gang members had been doing some serious underage drinking.

I just didn't get why those creeps were watching. This kind of teen ruck was a depressingly routine event in my neighbourhood, yet the local Dark entities had not only got wind of it before it started, they'd turned out in the snow to get a ringside seat.

"They're not moving in on the girls?" Jools asked Brice.

He shook his head. "Just perving on the hate vibes."

"Let's keep it that way, guys," she said. "Boost your light levels everyone – and good luck!"

Everyone piled out of the angel carrier. We'd arrived just as things were finally hotting up.

With a shriek of rage, a girl hurled herself at another girl from the rival gang, bringing her crashing to the ground.

The girls rolled around in the slush, grunting with effort as they grabbed at each other's earrings and tried to rip out clumps of hair, while invisible beings from rival cosmic agencies watched.

According to our Dark Studies teachers, the safest technique for clearing Dark entities from the area is to raise the vibes. Sounds hippy dippy, doesn't it? Like we hold hands in a circle and chant?

What we actually do is beam incredibly high-octane angel vibes from the palms of our hands.

Raising vibes in the middle of a gang fight is probably a lot like trying to meditate in a tsunami. You get a peaceful little vibe going and DOOF! A wave of pure cold evil knocks you over and you have to struggle all the way back to shore.

Brice couldn't be fussed with all that, he just went over and started knocking the sassafras out of the creeps, and after a while Hendrix went to help out.

The first girl had managed to kick her opponent away. Breathing fast, she scrambled to her feet and immediately put up her fists. "Anyone who disses my girls is going to have to kiss these!" she screamed.

The girl started a jittery war dance, aiming fake punches with a bit of kickboxing thrown in. In the strobing lamplight, she didn't seem human; she was just this girl fighting-robot with neon pink hair. Scuffing up ice, she leapt into the air like a girl ninja. FLASH. Her gang's name jumped off the back of her jacket. SHOCKING PINKS.

I almost cried out. It was Jax!

There was a CRUMP as someone from the rival gang took her on, and was sent sprawling. Screaming like witches, other girls flung themselves into the mayhem. I saw girls viciously gouging other girls' eyes, long nails raking down cheeks, and Jax was totally pounding some other girl into the ground.

That's the problem with cosmic energies – you can't predict which way they'll go. If you've got dense Dark energy and you add pure Light energy to the mix, things generally calm down – on the other hand they can go totally thermonuclear...

Then again, sometimes the PODS just don't want the hassle. "Don't look so upset, they're going," Brice said in my ear.

Minutes later, both gangs backed down. They called out half-hearted taunts, but that was just to save face.

Jax took off running.

"I want to make sure she's OK!" I told the others.

"You *know* her?" Earth angels don't shock easily, but Jools did look surprised.

"She's my friend," I told them shakily. "She's really not like this, I swear."

"We'll take you," said Hendrix immediately.

We didn't have to drive far. Jax was just going home.

She stumbled past garages and wheelie bins until she reached the block of low-rise flats where she lived with her mum, dad and four brothers. It was one of the old-style blocks – no lifts, just flights of concrete steps on the outside, with a row of scruffy doors going off each landing.

Leaving Hendrix to mind the vehicle, we followed Jax up to the fourth floor. Snow flurries blew in over the balcony as Jax fumbled for her key.

Inside, the hall smelled of fag smoke and old booze.

I'd been to the Jackson's once before, about six months before I died. Jax made me wait in the hall while she got her coat. I didn't know about vibes in those days, but even then I couldn't imagine anyone laughing in this flat, or bringing someone a bunch of flowers.

Behind the closed sitting-room door, Jax's mum and dad were going on at each other.

Jax stumbled to her room, fell on to her bed and crashed out, fully clothed. She didn't look like a girl fighting-robot now. She looked like a sad little kid.

I couldn't believe the state of my friend's room: rubbish and dirty clothes everywhere. Worst of all were the vibes. Even her cactus had croaked.

We all knew it would take more than one visit to put Jax's problems right, but we got to work boosting the light levels straightaway. After about ten minutes, you could feel a definite difference.

Jools whispered, "I think that's the best we can do for now."

Jax half-turned on to her front and started snoring. The neon pink of the gang's name exactly matched the streaks in her hair.

She'd been so proud to be a Shocking Pink. Now she'd ripped off our name and turned it into an ugly battle cry and I didn't know why.

Tell the truth, Mel.

The truth is, I was *scared* to know why.

We left Jax's flat and hurried back downstairs to Hendrix, who was still in the van.

I heard myself say, "I'll catch up with you guys later. I've got one more friend to check on."

"Want some company?" Brice offered.

I tried to smile. "No, thanks, I need to clear my head."

"Take this," he said gruffly, shrugging off his jacket. "Park Hall is a lot colder than Heaven."

I set off to the Nolans' place, keeping my head down against the wind and snow. Brice's jacket was way too big and, despite Lola's best efforts, it held a whiff of what we jokingly call his 'Dark angel' smell.

Actually I didn't mind it *that* much – maybe that's because I felt a bit like a Dark angel myself.

Jools had asked if maybe my friends had just moved on. But when you move on, isn't that because your friendship doesn't fit you any more? Well, that wasn't Jax and Karmen. They hadn't just *changed*. It felt like they were being driven by some scary force and I had a bad feeling it was this same force which had torn their friendship apart.

I began to run, half-limping, half-sliding, down the icy street in my borrowed shoes, but I had the terrible sense that I was already too late. Because, if Karms and Jax had both gone off the rails, what in the world was happening to Sky?

CHAPTER EIGHT

Unlike Jax, Sky Nolan never broke any actual laws (that she told us about anyway), but of all the Shocking Pinks she was definitely the most outrageous.

The first time we went out together, we were all saying what we wanted to be. When Sky announced that she intended to be a stand-up comic, no one even blinked. We *totally* believed she could do it! That's how charismatic Sky was.

Sky was a fabulously exciting person to have as your friend, but you wouldn't want to cross her. If you did, Sky would find a way to make you pay. Like that time she got back at Miss Rowntree by painting cooking oil on the blackboard. The next time our teacher picked up a piece of chalk and tried to write, absolutely nothing showed up!

Weeks later we were all at Karmen's, kidding around on her karaoke machine, when Sky went into hysterics and finally let us in on the joke.

"I can't believe you just went off and did that all by yourself!" Karmen said amazed.

"Believe it!" Sky said coolly, flicking back her hair. "Sky Nolan is an independent operator!"

She made it sound like she was this romantic free spirit. But it was because Sky basically didn't trust anyone. Even if she liked you, Sky had to keep you at a safe distance.

. At various times, Sky convinced each of us that we were her best friend. It was delicious being Sky's best friend. She'd plan little treats for you, lend you her coolest clothes and tell you incredibly intimate things about her personal life. Then one day you'd wake up to find you'd been mysteriously put on hold and it was someone else's turn.

All the Pinks got burned in this way, yet always when it was our turn to be Sky's favourite again, we'd kid ourselves this time would be different.

I'm making it sound like she wasn't a very nice person – and maybe she wasn't – but she was *truly* loveable.

She also had really bad problems at home.

I don't know if I mentioned Sky's mum wasn't too stable? One morning Sky came to school and she couldn't stop smiling.

"My mum was in such a great mood last night," she bubbled. "She made us a totally *massive* stack of pancakes. Of course, Olly insists he's big enough to toss his own pancake, doesn't he, and now it's permanently stuck to the kitchen ceiling!"

In those days Sky still hoped that one of her mum's good times would eventually stick for good, like Olly's pancake. Then, after years of being a deeply depressed single mum, Mrs Nolan got a boyfriend.

For a time everything seemed rosy. Sky's mum was happy. Sky's little brothers totally worshipped Dan and Sky adored him.

Late one night Sky called me on my mobile, to tell me her mum had locked her out. There'd been thunderstorms all day and Sky was terrified of storms; she sounded hysterical.

I fetched my step-dad, who threw on some clothes and drove off to pick her up. She looked half-drowned when he brought her back, rainwater dripping off her nose, hair in sodden rats' tails. Her mum hadn't even let her take her *shoes*.

Mum ran her a hot bath while I made up the sofa bed and dug out a clean T-shirt for Sky to sleep in. An hour later, I was still trying, not very successfully, to get back to sleep, when I heard her creep into my room.

I silently moved over to let her climb in. I could feel tiny tremors going through her, like she was getting flu. I tentatively touched her and Sky sobbed out, "I just wish I'd never been born."

I stroked her back while she cried and eventually she felt able to choke out what had happened. She and her mum had had a big fight about her mum's boyfriend.

"You said you liked Dan," I objected. "You said your mum has been so much happier since she's been seeing him."

"She *is*," Sky wept. "But now I'm just in the way."

"Shut up! Of course you're not."

"I *am*! Before Dan came along, I was Mum's lifeline. You don't know how much she relied on me. I even had to remind her to take her pills. If she was having a bad day, I'd cook for my little brothers—"

"And you were a total superstar!" I interrupted fiercely. "But you're twelve, Sky. You deserve a break. Let Danny Boy take care of her now."

Sky sat up, taking most of my quilt. "It's not just that Mum doesn't *need* me. She doesn't even *like* me."

"Sky—"

"It's true! I remind her of all her worst times. She acts like I'm totally not *there*! I was just trying to make her notice me again," she choked. "But I went a bit too far."

She suddenly clutched at my hand. "She *screamed* in my face, Melanie – she said not to ever bother coming back."

My friend collapsed on to the bed, taking all the quilt this time, and sobbed out: "I felt like there was nobody in the world who cared, Mel. I mean, my dad walks out and now my own mother hates me! What's wrong with this picture? It *has* to be me."

Maybe I was just being swept along with Sky's emotions, but I felt scared for her. I was genuinely afraid she'd do something stupid.

It's hard to be super-positive when you're a tired twelve year old whose teeth are chattering because your friend's got all the quilt. But I started desperately babbling whatever came into my head; telling my friend how amazingly special she was, how she was the girl all the girls in our class secretly wanted to be.

"You've got your whole life ahead of you, Sky," I shivered. "Plus you've got all the Pinks b-backing you up..."

I suddenly realised she'd stopped crying.

Sky groped for my hand. "You missed out the most important thing," she said, hiccupping, "which is you. You're the most wonderful friend I ever had, Melanie, and you'll never leave me, will you?"

I was only twelve. No one expects to die when they're twelve. Plus Sky had just said I was her best mate and I wanted it to be true. So I said something no human should ever say. "Of course I won't leave you, stupid," I whispered.

I only wanted Sky to feel safe so she could go to sleep. And it worked. She snuggled down under the quilt, still clutching my hand and, worn-out from crying, she finally drifted off...

Of course I won't leave you, stupid...

I could hear my well-meaning words ringing round my head as I half-skated around the icy turning into Sky's street.

In London, there's one hour at night when traffic stops and even the city drunks go totally quiet. Just then it was so quiet, the only sound I could hear was my heart hammering in my ears.

Sky's flat was at the end of a terrace of shabby old-fashioned houses. I picked my way down steps slippery with ice and shimmered in through the front door into the Nolans' basement flat.

I wished Brice had given me his scarf as well. It was colder inside the Nolans' place than it was out in the street.

The heating's off, I told myself. *It's the middle of the night, Mel.*

The flat was absolutely silent. When the fridge switched itself on with a sudden judder, I jumped with fright.

Angels can tell a lot from the vibes which collect in human homes. Karmen's home had a super-intense family vibe. Walking into the Jackson's flat felt like walking into some dreary war zone.

Sky's home was an icy blank. I started along the hall, checking in all the rooms, one by one. Kitchen empty. Sitting room empty.

The blind was up in Mrs Nolan's room. Stark-white streetlight flooded in, showing an empty double bed made up with a pristine white quilt. Instead of a depressing clutter of pill bottles, the bedside table had a cute photo of Sky's mum with Dan and two smiling little boys.

The little boys' room was empty too.

They'd obviously all gone to Dan's for the weekend, but I felt I should just check in Sky's room, as I was here.

The Nolan's hall was like an L-shape. Sky's room was around the bend. Her door had been left closed. A handwritten sign said KEEP OUT BRATS OR DIE!!

I shimmered through to the other side and yelled with shock.

My mate was in here all by herself!

She was all huddled up on her bed in an old dressing gown, listening to music through some earphones. She'd got woolly bed socks on, pulled right up to her knees, but she still looked blue with cold. I thought she looked much too thin.

Even if I'd been human I don't think I'd have tried to touch her. It was like she wasn't really here – just waiting. Even Sky's room literally felt like a waiting room. Her pop posters and girly bric-a-brac, precious mementoes of the Pinks, heart-shaped cushions and mad photo booth pics – all had gone, leaving cold empty space.

On the wardrobe door, which Sky used as an overflow for her huge photo collection, just one pic was left. It showed Sky at the London Eye. Sky by herself.

I was numb. I remembered that cool hair-flick. *Sky Nolan, the independent operator.* Sky was always the most ruthless Pink, but I never had her down as a person who'd just cut you out of her life without a backward glance.

"Look closer," said my inner angel.

Goose bumps came up on my arms.

I'd forgotten a basic cosmic law which Mr Allbright made us learn in my first term. You can't destroy energy.

You can't destroy *anything* which is real. And the hyperactive energy of four nutty twelve year olds on the loose – that's real. Sky might look like she was totally alone, but the energies of those other laughing girls still fizzed and sparkled all around her.

I loved those mischievous sparkles; I loved that you could still tell we had our arms around Sky.

A tiny spark of hope lit inside my heart. If you couldn't destroy energy, maybe you couldn't delete a true friendship from the Universe?

I sat down where I could see her face and tried to keep my voice steady. "Sky, don't die of shock. It's me! It's Mel! I've come back." I felt my voice go husky. "Babe, I'm so *so* sorry I didn't get to say goodbye."

Sky ejected the CD and put in a new one.

I told myself she wasn't blanking me on purpose and ploughed on, explaining that I was going to be in town for a few days, so if Sky had any problems I'd be happy to help, but I could feel all this hot embarrassment building up inside.

"I don't know what to say," I told Helix.

"You're fine," she said warmly. "Just talk normally."

I wasn't sure there was a *normal* way to tell someone their dead friend had come back as an angel.

Sky was busy skipping through tracks. I wondered what music she was into now and if I'd like it.

Hitching closer to my unresponsive friend, I tried again. "This isn't just a friendly visit, Sky. I'm here because the Agency – the guys who run the Universe basically – think you're in trouble. They didn't say what kind – they prefer us to figure stuff out for ourselves, but Jax is obviously spinning out of control. And what *is* going on with Karms? Why is she so fixated on this show—"

My friend practically tore off her headphones.

"I am so SICK of that girl and her poxy musical!" she burst out. "Does she think you'll be *watching* them from the clouds?"

It was almost like she was answering me, even though she didn't know I was in the room. Sky got off the bed in a rush and went to the window. She gave a scared laugh. "Great, now you're talking to yourself, Sky."

I rushed across the room. "Sky, listen to me! You're not talking to yourself and I'm not in the clouds, babe – I'm standing right behind you. Can you feel those teeny angel tingles? That's *me*!"

I'd just made things worse. Sky started flapping her hands, like a desperate fanning gesture. "This is SO sick," she said in a kind of moan. "When you're dead you're dead. This is just in your head, Sky."

"Weren't you listening, fool?" I said lovingly. "I'm not a spook! I'm an angel. At least I will be, in about sixty thousand years, when I've—!"

Sky gasped and spun round. "Mel?"

There was pure shock on her face, but there was joy too, I swear; if we could have sat down and talked then, I truly believe things could have been different.

The very next second, a hideous ring tone shattered the silence.

It literally made me see spots in front of my eyes. I was close to throwing up when Sky snatched up her mobile.

I felt our fragile connection snap like a thread. Only one thing makes a girl look like that, and that's a boy.

"Yeah, you've got mine," Sky bubbled. "We must have swapped phones by mistake! They've all gone to Brighton. Yeah, in *this* weather! No, and I wouldn't have gone if she had. Shut UP, you pig! I'm a big girl now, you know!"

Sky was lying on her bed now, acting kittenish. She suddenly creased up laughing. "I'll make you pay for that! So are you coming to pick me up?" I heard her voice falter. "OK, well, I can probably find a cab. Yeah, about ten minutes."

I watched numbly as she rushed round like a human whirlwind, dragging on her little top and skirt, pulling on high stretchy boots, putting in her hoop earrings.

Was this mystery boy's call what my friend had been waiting for? Because there was no resemblance to the blank listless girl of five minutes ago. Grabbing her faux fur jacket, Sky slammed out of the flat.

I beamed myself after her, but Helix told me not to follow her any further.

"This is Park Hall, Helix! Something bad could happen."

"Something bad *has* happened." Helix seemed incredibly sad.

"You don't get it, this is what human girls do! This is *normal* behaviour on my planet. Human girls get boyfriends and fall in love, and suddenly nothing else matters."

"Sweetie, what happened in there is *so* not normal."

"Helix, when it comes to cosmic stuff, I'm happy to take your advice, but this is *my* world, OK, and I think I know it just a *leetle* bit better than you do!"

I was talking out of my angel rear-end. I didn't understand *anything* that had happened since I got here. At least Jax and Karms were still just recognisable as my friends, but as I watched Sky hurrying away into the dark, I felt like I didn't know her at all.

The old Sky had big dreams. She'd seen what happened to girls in Park Hall and she wanted better. No way would she humiliate herself for some boy.

The snow was turning into sleet. I huddled inside Brice's jacket. Something dark was hovering at the edges of my mind, and it was taking a lot of effort to shut it out.

CHAPTER NINE

As it turned out I was just about to get a lift.

Nearby windows started to rattle in their frames as an Agency motorbike roared up. The rider took off his helmet and I saw dark spiky hair with blond flashes.

"Good, you're still here," Brice grinned. "Hop on and I'll take you back."

I was so upset I had to take it out on somebody.

"I'm a trainee *agent*, Brice. I don't *need* someone following me around like my big brother. I *told* you I'd do this by myself."

"And I respected your wishes, darling! But Jools was worried we forgot to tell you the security code. She didn't want you to be locked out."

"You use your tags – she showed me."

He looked sheepish: "The others were concerned, all right? They didn't think you should be out alone on your first night back. Anyway, can you imagine what Lola would do to me if anything happened?"

"True," I giggled. "You'd have to leave Heaven."

"At least!" he grinned.

Brice tossed me a helmet. He seemed uneasy now, as if he was wondering whether to tell me something. He took a breath. "Actually, before we go back, there's something I want to show you."

"O-kay," I said wearily. "I'm an angel. I don't need to sleep." That's the theory; though personally sleep is one human habit I'm in no hurry to give up.

My hands were so cold it was hard to fasten my helmet. This was my first time on any kind of motorbike. I nervously clambered on.

Brice gunned the engine. Next minute I was scorching through the sleeping city on a celestial motorbike, with my arms wrapped round a Dark angel. I know!

We were travelling at such supersonic speeds, my old neighbourhood was mostly just a blur. Eventually I gave up even *trying* to figure out where I was. Privately, I longed to be tucked up with a milky drink and a hot water bottle.

Several hair-raising minutes later, Brice brought the bike to a halt by the battered Bell Meadow street sign. After he'd helped me off the bike, he just stood beside the sign, blowing on his cold hands, apparently waiting for me to figure something out.

"What did you want to show me again?" I asked through numb lips. I was desperate to speed things up, so we could get back in the warm.

"The *school*, darling, the school," he said wearily.

"I've seen my school, thanks," I flashed. "I *went* to this hellhole, remember!"

Brice grabbed my shoulders, turning me forcibly until I was facing our school annexe with its tacky bridge.

"What is *that*?" I said hoarsely. I forgot all about being cold. I actually took off my helmet, as if that would help the vision go away.

Disturbing lights and shadows flitted to and fro across the bridge between the annexe and the main school. I felt like I was seeing *two* buildings mixed up together: my grim real-life comprehensive and something ghostly, alien and *wrong*.

There was nothing human on that bridge, yet I could hear childlike voices floating from the school;

children's voices spookily remixed by the Powers of Darkness.

Other spine-chilling noises drifted out. I don't know if music has an opposite? It was like they'd got the evil building contractors in and they were listening to Hell FM.

"But how—?" I couldn't seem to get my head around it.

"Your school seems to have sprung a cosmic leak," he said bluntly. It sounded ordinary how Brice phrased it – a minor plumbing problem.

I tried to swallow. "The kids can't see this, can they?"

"Not yet."

"Not yet? This is going to get *worse*!"

But Brice didn't reply and I was too scared to ask again.

For a few moments we watched the eerie lights coming and going across the bridge.

What were they *doing* in there?

And how must those vibes be affecting Park Hall's kids? They had to try to study inside that horror five days a week. They had to get good grades and figure out what they wanted to be when they grew up.

"Did it just, you know, *happen*?" I gulped.

Brice had jammed his hands under his armpits, trying to thaw them out. "We still haven't cracked that one. Maybe the PODS thought it would be interesting to open a crack in human reality."

"Brice! That must be how the hellhound got in!"

"There's not just one, darling," he sighed.

My heart gave a little bump. "How many then?"

He shook his head.

The thought of unknown numbers of hell beasts roaming the corridors just curdled my blood.

My mind flashed back to my premonition when I first arrived – that my two worlds were just about to collide. But I could never have imagined...

Suddenly I couldn't breathe. "Brice, Omigosh – if hell dogs are getting *out* of the Hell dimensions—"

I saw he'd been waiting for me to figure this out.

"*That's* our worry," he said quietly.

I swallowed. "No, that would never – that can't be right."

"It isn't *right*, angel girl. But if we don't find a way to stop it, these kids will find themselves wandering out of their school into..." his voice tailed off.

"Brice, you're freaking me out! Into *what*?"

His expression was unreadable. "Another school, angel girl. Just not school as you know it."

I thought I might be sick. *I went to this hellhole remember!* My thoughtless remark had boomeranged back like a hex. Park Hall Community High School was now officially twinned with a school from Hell.

CHAPTER TEN

By the time I finally crawled under the covers, I was too upset to do more than doze. I'd crash asleep, then almost instantly shoot bolt upright, my heart racing. No bad dreams, no scary flashes of girl fights or hell schools – just unbelievable horror, mixed with a weird haunting guilt. Like I'd done something so bad it could never be put right.

After a while I heard Jools tiptoeing around in the dark.

I raised myself groggily. "More fights?"

"Off to do the dawn vibes," she whispered. "Go back to sleep."

I sat up. "No, I'd like to come if that's OK."

I hadn't a clue what 'dawn vibes' were, but I had the feeling they'd do me good. I jumped into some jeans and Jools lent me a warm top, plus her roommate's parka, so dawn vibes obviously happened out of doors.

Outside, it was totally pitch black.

"Are you sure this is dawn?" I asked doubtfully.

Jools quickly checked her watch. "No, but it will be in exactly ten minutes!" She grabbed my hand. "Hold on tight!"

"But where are we—?"

The Universe went unexpectedly rippley. When it finally firmed up again we were on snowy parkland high above London.

City lights sparkled below us like scattered jewellery. From here you could see the night was starting to fade. My eyes could just make out vague shapes of tower blocks.

I'd never been on Hampstead Heath this early. It seemed just like I remembered from family outings – except for the angels.

There were hundreds and thousands of them, and more were beaming down every minute.

Like any normal crowd of Londoners, the earth angels came from different age groups, and every walk of life. Some chatted quietly to their friends, others just waited peacefully for the dawn vibes to begin.

It was like a beautiful, but v. surreal, painting: *Angels on Hampstead Heath.*

"Does this happen every day?" I breathed.

"And at sunset," Jools said. "Dawn and dusk are the optimum times to send vibes to the planet."

I made a mental note to incorporate the word 'optimum' into my vocabulary first chance I got.

"So is Hampstead Heath the local energy hot spot?"

I was half joking, but Jools said seriously, "It's *one* of the hot spots, yeah. London has about seven. This is my favourite though."

The idea of *seven* well-known London landmarks filling up with angels twice a day sent me reeling.

When you take a time trip to ancient Rome or whatever, you expect the odd cosmic surprise. But this was *my* time, and I felt like I was having to run to catch up!

"So why do you do dawn vibes again?" I asked.

A young EA in torn trainers joined in our conversation. "I can't speak for the other EAs," she smiled, "but when you work with street kids twenty-four-seven like I do, you almost forget you're in the bizz. Some days I'm the only earth angel at King's Cross. The vibes remind me that

I'm not alone – that I'm connected to every earth angel in this city—"

She suddenly dropped her voice.

"We're starting!" she whispered.

I didn't need anyone to tell me the vibes had begun.

As the first streaks of dawn appeared in the sky, there was this incredible hush, then I heard very faint and unbearably lovely musical chords which seemed to come from out of thin air. Before today I'd never heard those sounds outside of Heaven. Then I noticed how each tiny blade of grass was starting to shimmer and I thought, ohh, but this *is* Heaven! In a few minutes it'll go back to being grim, grimy London, but just now it's Heaven!

My senses were more sensitive since the upgrade. I could actually *see* unearthly colours streaming from the centres of our palms, and whooshing dramatically into Earth's atmosphere. Then zillions upon zillions of tiny gold stars rained back down.

Go vibes, I willed them silently. Humans *really* need you.

I totally understood now why that girl came here on her day off.

At last only a sprinkling of gold stars was left to drift slowly back to Earth. Winter birds twittered all around us. The sun was hidden behind woolly grey clouds, but London skies are almost always grey, and you could see streaks of other, softer colours, mixed in.

"Look at you," Jools exclaimed. "You're all pretty and glowy!"

"I was thinking the same thing about you," I said shyly. "That was amazing, Jools. I'm going to remember it for ever." I gave her a quick hug. "I'll catch up with you later, yeah?"

That's one big thing about dawn vibes. They totally make you know what you should do next.

CHAPTER ELEVEN

I'd seen this sitting room so many times in my dreams. Not the bad dreams – my sad, homesick dreams.

In my dreams my mum was always asleep on the sofa, just like now, and, like in the dreams, I wasn't able to go to her straight away.

I softly prowled around my mum's flat, letting myself know I was really here. At first it seemed almost like there were three Mels in the room – the human girl I used to be, the dream Mel in her PJs and the angel girl in her borrowed parka. But gradually it sank in that this visit wasn't a dream or just a memory, but for real.

That vibe – that sweet, homey vibe – was just the same.

There were hyacinths in a bowl on a small table. There's something about the smell of hyacinths that gives me a sad-happy ache inside. Mum had forgotten to take the price sticker off the bowl: special offer, £2.99.

You don't often smell flowers in a dream, you probably don't notice price stickers and you definitely don't see your little sister's half-finished dress hanging off your mum's sewing machine, with the tacking threads dangling down.

My mum had fallen asleep in a really awkward position; she was going to get a bad crick in her neck if she didn't wake up soon. She'd probably been waiting up for my step-dad. Des fixes pumps: those totally massive pumps they use in power stations and sewage plants. I'm telling you, if one of those breaks down, you'd better hope Des gets to you fast!

I was gradually tiptoeing closer to my mum. Finally I dared to crouch down beside the sofa. As an angel, I love watching humans sleep. Their daytime disguises fall away and you actually see who they really are; but for the first time I felt like I was intruding.

There was something in my mum's face that I felt like I wasn't supposed to see: a sadness so deep, it had marked her for ever. Even when she was old it would be there.

Next to the TV was a picture of me in a twirly silver frame. I'd seen this photo plenty of times in my dreams, but until now I'd never seen it in real life. Des must have taken it on my thirteenth birthday.

"Weird," I whispered.

Without realising it, I was stroking my mum's face, softly smoothing out her new worry lines. For the first time I noticed silver hairs glinting among her trendy new highlights and I felt this terrible pang. She was my mum. Mums are supposed to stay the same for ever.

Our old video machine was flashing zeros. Mum and Des never could get the hang of VCRs.

"You want to get a DVD player," I told my mum. "You want to move with the times, girl."

Then eighteen months of tears just welled up, and I put my head down on the sofa and howled. "Oh, Mum I've missed you—" I gave up even trying to put so much pain into words, and just cried and cried.

After a few minutes, I covered my face with my hands. "I'm not supposed to be doing this! This was supposed to be beautiful, like in movies!"

I quickly wiped my eyes. "I had it all planned out – no, I did! I was going to be incredibly calm and bathed in light and you'd be like, totally awed but at the same time really *really* happy to know I'd gone to a better place. And I *have*, Mum," I sobbed out. "I have such a beautiful life – this is just so much harder than I ever…"

I had to stop to take deep breaths.

"Guess I just wanted to impress you, huh?" I giggled tearily. "Guess I'm not as angelic as I thought!"

I blew my nose. After a while I said, "I see Des got round to repainting the flat. He did a good job."

I didn't care if I was wittering. Why would you need to impress your mum? It was enough to be with her, smelling hyacinths and nattering about nothing. Finally I felt able to leave her, but only because I knew I'd be coming back. I tiptoed into the room I used to share with my little sister.

This room too had been freshly repainted. Our old twin beds had gone. Jade was asleep in one of those smart pine cabin beds with built-in shelves and whatever underneath. Her curtains and bed covers were in pastel pink with a cute fairy motif.

I understood why they did it. It must have been painful for them coming into this room every day, seeing that empty bed. Humans don't live for ever. They have to find a way to move on.

Climbing stealthily up the short ladder, I softly lay down on my side next to Jade, so I could look into her face.

"Hi, Fluffyhead," I whispered. "I bet you feel like the princess of Park Hall in this bed, yeah? I love the fairies. Did Mum let you choose the pattern by yourself?"

With her elfin eyelids and little pointy face, Jade looked a lot like a fairy herself. She'd grown in the eighteen months I'd been gone. She was going to be a daddy-longlegs like her sister. Yet to me she seemed touchingly small and vulnerable.

Her limp little hand still smelled of warm wax crayons like I remembered. I stroked it softly. "I can't stay now, Jadie, but I'll be around for a few days, so I'll come and see you again, I promise." I plonked an angel kiss on her cheek. "Love you!"

"Love you, Mel," Jade murmured in her sleep.

I gasped. I was so shocked, I beamed myself down into the street without even trying, and just started walking.

A guy was trying to start his rusty old banger. Across the road, the Minimart was open. A van was delivering bread.

I walked past everything in a daze.

First Sky, now Jade!

Two humans had heard me talking. OK, Jade was my sister, so there was a strong link, but Sky was wearing headphones!!

Suddenly it was like I'd been struck by lightning. I literally looked up at the sky, as if this amazing revelation had been dropped from a passing plane!

"So that's why the Agency couldn't send me till I'd had my birthday," I breathed. "Omigosh, I have to tell Lollie!"

I fumbled in the pockets of my parka and called her on my dinky Agency mobile. There was a click and a hiss and I Lola's recorded message. "Talk to the phonhearde, *carita*, cos the face ain't home. Please leave a message after the tone. BEEP!!"

"Lollie!" I shouted into my phone. "I'm outside my old flats! I know! Listen, I'm going to road-test our survival guide for real. That's my *mission*, Lollie! Michael said I'd figure out what I had to do and now

I have! I'm going to teach my mates every cosmic survival technique in our book!"

When I got back to the house, I went to fetch myself some cereal and came back humming. I found Brice and Jools in the TV room.

"You're perky, angel girl," Brice commented. "You were in the depths of despair last night."

"I feel great!" I bubbled. "I've figured out why Michael sent me. I was just walking along and – I totally saw what I have to do!"

"Let me guess!" he said in a sarky tone. "You're going to flit between your mates, beaming pretty vibes, until all of a sudden they rush to one another's homes, kiss and make up. And little Mel goes back to Heaven tired but happy because her work on Earth is done."

I felt like he'd hit me. For a moment I just stared in shock, then I just saw red. "Ooh, silly me, wanting to help my friends!" I flashed. "Brice, those girls are in *bits*!"

"So?" he said coldly. "You're an angel, not their agony aunt."

"And you're a heartless *pig*!"

"At least I'm not living in La-la land! I wish you'd

at least stop and *think*, darling, before you flit off to play good fairy."

"Brice, what the sassafras is there to think about! Michael *sent* me to help my friends!"

He got that pinched look he gets when he's upset. "You're absolutely sure about that? There couldn't *possibly* be any more to your mission than saving your precious girls?"

He finally noticed Jools frantically shaking her head and abruptly walked out of the room. Jools went after him and I heard them arguing in low voices.

I was trembling from Brice's attack. *This is so typical of that boy*, I thought shakily. You just decide you can trust him then he publicly humiliates you. OK, so his good-fairy crack had come a teeny bit too close, but did he have to be so *mean*.

I decided I wasn't going to talk to Brice again, *ever*.

When it seemed like the coast was clear, I ran up to get my bag.

On my way upstairs, I glimpsed Delphine watching the TV monitors with a glazed expression, but as I hurtled back down, I saw the door had been closed.

I heard Jools' worried voice.

"How do you tell someone something like that?"

"You can't," Delphine murmured sympathetically. "I'm sure you're doing the right thing."

I didn't like to barge in on a private EA chat, so I left without saying anything to anyone.

Outside it was sleeting again, and I quickly pulled up my furry parka hood. *I don't care* what *that creep thinks, I told myself, shivering. I feel really privileged to be on such an unusual and exciting mission.* And I beamed myself smoothly through space.

Chapter Twelve

In order of urgency, my official worry list now read:

1. Sky Nolan
2. Eve Jackson
3. Karmen Patel

However, Sky wouldn't be back home for hours yet, so rather than twiddling my little angel thumbs I'd decided to start with Jax.

I shimmered into her room feeling v. slick and professional.

My mate was still sleeping deeply, one arm dangling off the bed. Her fingertips had raw places where she bit her nails.

I was pleased I'd got here before she woke up. Sleeping humans are *way* more open to angelic suggestion.

I sat down beside her, trying not to notice the grubby sheets. Don't get the impression Jax was a slutty person. When I knew her, she was the cleanest girl I knew. Jax washed her hair *every* day, and if she ate something at school, she'd have to brush her teeth immediately afterwards. I'm not sure where she got that habit. It definitely wasn't her parents.

Jax was the youngest Jackson and the only girl. She reckoned that after four trouble-making boys, her parents just lost interest. They gave her a sweet name – Eve. After that, Jax was basically on her own. I think she did a great job of bringing herself up. OK, there was the shoplifting, but if your mum and dad don't teach you right from wrong, you're not going to learn *that* from a teen magazine, are you?

Jax's eyes were moving under her lids. She was dreaming.

I smiled to myself. The conditions for my friend's first angel lesson were almost perfect. Later in the day something might just go 'click' and she'd remember her mad dream where her dead friend was in her room, wearing pink suede boots and claiming to be an angel.

"Jax? It's me, Mel. The first thing I want to say is I'm not a scary spook – though hopefully you can tell the difference from the vibes!"

I was watching her face alert for the tiniest response.

"I'm an angel, Jax! Kind of a surprise, yeah? Don't ask why they picked me, because I have NO idea! Listen, I'll probably be around for a few days and I've just had this really cool idea."

I shifted a little closer to Jax.

"Tell you how it started – I was actually wishing you guys could all come back with me and be angels just for a day. I know it's just a fantasy, but it got me thinking. I have such a beautiful life, Jax! I live in this huge vibey city, and I'm going to this cool angel school! I went into pure shock, though, when they first told me! I'm like, 'I'm *dead* and I have to go to school!'"

Jax's mouth quirked up at the corners. My heart gave a little skip. Could she possibly be smiling at my joke?

I was stroking her hand, willing her to hear my voice. "You might actually *like* going to school in Heaven! When you're training to be an angel, you know you're part of something HUGE, and it makes you feel so proud, Jax. I never felt like that before, and I want to share it with you, girl!"

Did I just imagine it, or did my friend give a soft little sigh?

"So then I'm like, OK, maybe your mates can't go to angel high school, Melanie, but what's to stop you taking the angel school to *them*? Yeah, I *know*! Creative thinking or what! I'm not talking scary advanced stuff, just basic cosmic laws, simple techniques for keeping yourself safe and whatever? You'd be like, an *undercover* angel! Would you be up for that?"

I heard another soft sigh. I took that as a yes, and settled myself into a calm yoga sitting pose. I was about to teach my first official angel lesson.

"Listen carefully now, babe, because I'm going to tell you something that will blow you away. You're magic, Jax!"

If Jax remembered just this one thing, it would change her life.

I took a deep breath. "And it's not just you, girl. *Everyone's* born magic, even that stinky old man who used to come into Costcutter. He doesn't look so magic now, but that's because he's got something called 'cosmic amnesia'..."

I told Jax that she must never think she was alone – that she had a huge celestial organisation watching out for her – and I dropped a tiny hint about the PODS for her to think about when she was awake.

When I'd given my mate as much cosmic info as I thought she could absorb for one day, I slung my bag over my shoulder.

"You're magic, Jax," I repeated softly. "Never forget that, yeah?"

I checked my watch. Time to shoot off to Karmen's.

On my way out, I noticed the cactus.

Maybe it had just been pretending to be dead, or maybe it was just the right time for it to come back to life? I don't really know about cactuses. All I know is that *this* cactus had a tiny, shocking-pink flower shyly blooming from its withered little stump.

Karmen's bedroom smelled of hot clean hair. She was in front of the mirror using her hair straighteners. There was like, *one* tiny kink in her hair and she was stressing like you would not believe.

This morning my friend was looking extra grown-up and serious, in a fabulous *shalwar kamiz* sparkling with gold threads. Karms is actually more of a cool-casuals girl, so I guessed her parents were dragging her off to the rellies later.

Checking her straighteners were switched off, Karmen ran back to the mirror and started yanking crossly at her hair.

"Karmen Asha Patel," I said sternly. "You look totally luminous, so stop stressing!"

She stopped! She actually walked away from the mirror!! I hadn't even got started yet!!

Maybe it was just a coincidence though, because Karmen immediately started burrowing madly in her wardrobe, until she located a pair of pretty sandals which would match her outfit.

"Karms," I said in the same firm voice. "Just chill, OK?"

And again she stopped, only this time there was something in her eyes that hadn't been there before.

"Babe?" I said excitedly. "Can you hear me? It's Mel. I'm an angel, Karms. I know! I hardly believe it myself, but it's true."

Karmen's eyes went all wistful. Suddenly she did a strange, not to say slightly creepy, thing. She walked up to the photo with its little scented candle and talked to it!

"I hope you'd be proud of me, Mel," she whispered. "I really do."

"Karms, I'm *humongously* proud of you," I said warmly, "but I'm actually right behind you, and I'm only in town a few days and we've got a LOT of ground to cover. You see... EEK," I squeaked.

Karmen had walked right through me on her way to the karaoke machine. Her room filled with cheesy music and to my dismay Karmen started belting out one of the big numbers from GREASE.

Ever tried teaching cosmic survival to someone who's yelling, "You're the One that I Want" at the top of her lungs?

Luckily I soon saw the funny side. I imagined Reubs and Lola howling as I described my frustrated attempt to pass on angel skills to a caterwauling Karmen. Knowing Reubs, he wouldn't see a problem! He'd be like, "Why didn't you just go with the flow, angel girl?"

Yeah, angel girl, I thought. *Just go with the flow!*

So I sang along!

It was fun! I can't sing for peanuts, but I really got into it. Halfway through the number, Karms and I lost all our inhibitions and launched into a wild dance routine. I can't swear to it, but I thought I saw her throw in some cheeky Bollywood moves.

When the music finished, we both had to get our breath back.

"Woo, that was fun! Almost like old times!" I panted. "Except obviously I was visible then!"

Omigosh, I thought. *Look at you, girl.*

All the strain had left her face. She was glowing from dancing and laughing in that way you do when you've been kidding around.

Then her eyes went wistful again. "Oh, Melanie, I hope they let you be one in Heaven," she said softly.

She was looking past me to our London Eye photo, but it was a v. shivery moment. It was like, Karmen didn't *absolutely* know I was here, but she *kind* of did.

And be one *what* in Heaven?

"Karms—" I started.

"Time to go, *beti*!" her dad sang from the hall.

I'd been at Karmen's house exactly twenty minutes!

I thought Reuben would be *très* proud of me for managing to stay so chilled. What did it matter if my friend and I connected during a cheesy song and dance routine, so long as we connected? And we had. I still had the goose bumps to prove it.

Two down, one to go, I thought, shimmering out into the street.

In case Sky was still with lover boy, I went the long way round, strolling past shops and cafes. I think the dawn vibes were still fizzing in my veins, because I was genuinely loving being out in my old community. I started feeling like a bona fide local angel, bopping along in my borrowed parka, so I thought it was time I behaved like one.

I started sending vibes to anyone who looked like they needed it (yeah, yeah, so maybe a couple of times I sent them to really fit boys – I'm an angel, babe, not a saint!!).

Soon angel vibes were raining down everywhere. I'm talking *serious* showers of gold sparkles. Little kids were smiling. Old married couples were holding hands. Park Hall was literally becoming a better place!

I felt that special glow inside my chest. Helix wanted a word.

"Isn't this just pure magic!" I bubbled.

"The best magic there is, sweetie. Not sure you should draw this much attention to yourself though. Did you forget angels aren't the only beings who see vibes?"

"Oops," I said guiltily. "Sorry, I'll stop. It was *très* cool though."

It was late afternoon by the time I picked my way down the basement steps to the Nolans' flat. They were glassy with ice, though it had mostly melted everywhere else.

I could hear a radio DJ talking through the door.

I found Sky in the kitchen whizzing up a diet shake.

"Hiya," I said, when she'd eventually switched off the blender. Sky carefully poured her shake into a glass and stood at the counter, gulping it down. My mate was dressed for comfort now, in trackie bottoms and a hoody she must have worn for decorating; you could see teeny streaks and splodges of paint.

"Babe?" I tried again.

The microwave dinged. Sky had been microwaving some popcorn. She took her snack to the table. An old R&B number came on. Sky moved her body while she munched, but from her eyes you knew she was back with the boyfriend, or fantasising how it would be next time.

"See you're back on the Popcorn Diet," I commented. "Not that you need to lose weight. You're too skinny, girl!"

My friend was alternating mouthfuls of popcorn with gulps of diet shake. I wondered if she could taste them.

I softly put my hand over hers, the first time I'd touched her. "Where are you, Sky?" I whispered. "You heard me last night."

She started picking at a miniscule speck of paint on her sleeve.

"Just tell her what's in your heart," Helix suggested. "Isn't that what real friends do? Tell each other the truth?"

I realised she was right. Now the Pinks had split up, Sky didn't have a single mate who could give her a reality check.

I took a shaky breath. "Babe, I'm sure you think you're in love, but I'm your friend, OK, plus I'm an angel, and I'm telling you he's playing with you, girl! He doesn't care about you! No decent boy would make you run around these streets in the middle of the night."

I could hear my voice getting husky.

"I was *so* scared for you, last night, Sky. I was scared for all you guys. I didn't think I could *be* more scared until I saw that—"

I just caught myself before I started to describe

the eerie comings and goings in the school annexe. This flash of fear wasn't anything I could put into words, but it had to do with that worryingly passive vibe my friend was putting out. I felt like even *mentioning* the Dark Powers just then could make them pop up right there in the Nolans' kitchen. How Sky was now left wide open to any dark vibe that blew in off the street.

So many people in her life had let her down, and now she seemed lost – she'd forgotten who she was and had just given up on herself.

"Everyone leaves me," she'd sobbed out that night.

You'd think that wouldn't you, if your dad walks out and your so-called mother sees nothing wrong with abandoning you for an entire weekend in a dangerous city?

You left her too, Melanie, whispered the dark angels who'd come to live at the back of my mind. I tuned them out, quick as a flash. I was here *now* wasn't I? And unlike those other people who'd disappointed Sky, I was going to take proper care of my friend; more importantly, I was going to teach her how to take care of herself.

I didn't care what Brice, Helix or *anyone* said. My

first task was to help my friend get back her old feisty self-confidence.

I decided to start by just beaming positivity.

"You're such a star, Sky," I said in my warmest, most upbeat voice. "Do you know that? All you need is some really basic cosmic info, then you'll be like, *untouchable*. A few minutes a day, that's all it'll take, but you'll be amazed at the results."

Yeah, I know it sounded like I was recommending heavenly beauty products, but with Sky how she was, it could be dangerous to get into anything too heavy. I was giving her like the fuzzy pink version of Cosmic Survival for Humans – Lesson 1.

With Sky I basically stressed over and over that she wasn't alone. "It's soo simple! But, once you've grasped this one basic fact, I swear, your whole Universe will be like, *transformed*."

Sky abruptly brushed past me on her way out of the kitchen.

Still talking, I followed her into the sitting room, where she'd left the gas fire full on. She crouched down, holding out blue-tinged hands to the flames.

For all the response I was getting, she might have had her earphones in. I felt like she could, *technically,* hear me, but some deeply suspicious part of Sky was deleting my words as fast as I put them out.

But even when my mate turned on the TV and started flicking through channels, I refused to be depressed.

Sky had taken a lot of knocks. You couldn't expect her to turn into a PODS-kicking undercover angel in just one lesson!

She finally settled for an MTV channel. An old feel-good music video came on. "Where is the Love?" by the Black Eyed Peas.

"That is *just* the kind of thing I've been talking about," I said in my new, upbeat voice. "Here's you thinking you're all alone in the Universe, and you get this *major* sign, don't you see! You know why that happens, babe? It's because everything is *totally* connected! That's why, if we ask the Universe for—"

"You should stop now," Helix interrupted.

"But I haven't told her about the cosmic strings—"

"Tell her tomorrow," said Helix gently. "You're getting tired."

Until she pointed it out, I hadn't noticed how weird I was feeling: drained and muzzy. Teaching angel skills to humans who aren't listening uses more energy than you'd think. I badly needed to rest, but I felt bad about leaving Sky alone again.

"You're going to be OK, sweetie," I told her one last time. "One day you'll wake up and you'll absolutely know why you're here and who you are. It's not your fault you've got cosmic amnesia. Lola—"

"Enough!" insisted Helix.

"You're *magic*, Sky," I told my friend stubbornly, as I slung my Agency bag over my shoulder. "Deep *deep* down inside, you're magic."

Back at the Agency house, Jools was pottering in the kitchen.

"Hiya," I said, in a feeble little voice.

Jools didn't say a word, just pulled out a chair and made me sit down. Fetching a tiny bottle from the first-aid box, she sent it whizzing across the table. "Two drops," she ordered. "No more than that or it'll blow your head off!"

I dripped exactly two drops cautiously on my tongue.

"Woo!" I shook myself like a puppy. "That feels *better!*"

"Angel drops!" grinned Jools. "An Earth Angel's best friend, closely followed by chocolate! Speaking of which—"

Jools quickly washed out two mugs and made us both some hot chocolate. It was from a packet but I didn't care; it felt *sooo* good to be taken care of.

"Where's Brice?" I asked cautiously.

"He… do you know, I'm actually not sure," she smiled. "But he left you a note."

Jools handed me a torn piece of paper. I unfolded it cautiously. No 'Dear Mel'. No signature. Just seven words in Brice's thick black scrawl.

Sorry I called you a good fairy.

CHAPTER THIRTEEN

I woke on Sunday morning to find my inner angel had switched my plans in the night. Instead of giving Sky her intensive coaching session on cosmic string theory, Helix had decided I was spending my day in a school with an inter-dimensional leak, watching Karmen's rehearsal.

When I emerged from the bathroom, washed and dressed, I was surprised to see Jools sitting on the stairs in her PJs.

She took a breath. "Mel, everyone's so impressed with what you're doing for your friends – if it's OK, we'd like to help."

I was so grateful I didn't know whether to kiss her or cry. The EAs were already working all around the clock, yet they were willing to stretch to give my friends the help they needed.

"You realise this is going to be *très* scary?" I called after Jools, as she disappeared into the bathroom.

Jools spun, looking anxious. "You mean the leak?"

I giggled. "I was thinking of Karms singing 'Beauty School Dropout!'"

Jools and I set off walking to my old school, chatting and giggling. Outside the Cosmic Café, Nikos, the owner, was taking off the security grille, ready to open up for Sunday customers. I just couldn't resist.

"Hiya!" I called. "It's Mel, Des's girl!! I'm visiting Earth!"

I saw him smile to himself, as if he were enjoying a private joke, then he calmly disappeared back into the cafe.

I almost fell over. "Did he *hear* me?"

Jools chuckled. "We have *some* humans on our side you know! Nikos is a sweet guy. Really looks out for the local kids."

We'd reached the noisy dual carriageway.

"You never told me how the lessons went?" Jools said, raising her voice above the roar of traffic.

"I think it *kind* of went OK with Jax," I told her.

Then I found myself pouring out my worries about Sky.

"That first night, I *know* she heard me, Jools! Then her boyfriend rang and – bosh! – we're back to square one."

"Any idea who the boyfriend is?" she asked.

"No – and I don't want to," I flashed. "You know what upsets me? None of this would be happening if the Pinks hadn't broken up. We kept each other on track, you know. Now they're all over the place!"

Jools suddenly got busy rearranging her scarf. I had an uneasy feeling she was getting ready to tell me some home truths.

"When you talk about your friends," she said tentatively, "I almost get the feeling you were like, the magic glue that was holding everything together."

I felt a dark rushing in my head, as if all the Dark angels had taken off at once. For a moment I felt actually physically sick. Because if I was the Shocking Pinks' glue and I suddenly wasn't around, that meant, it meant—

Jools quickly put her arm around me. She let me cry for a little while, then I felt her rubbing my back.

"You do know none of this is your fault? You *died*, sweetie! It was out of your control!"

"I just get so scared for them," I choked. "We know the score, Jools, but they have NO idea! I mean, those creeps came out in the cold to watch Jax fight, and yesterday at Sky's—"

Jools made me look at her. "I'm going to tell you something, angel girl," she said fiercely. "No matter what happens to your friends, I want you to *remember* this, OK?"

"OK," I quavered.

"It's going to take time, maybe years, but they *will* come through this, Melanie, and they'll all be stronger for it."

I wasn't actually sure if Jax or Sky had years, the way they were going on. But I felt genuinely comforted. Not just because of the pep talk, but because I realised I'd made a really lovely friend.

We'd crossed the invisible border into the dodgy part of Bell Meadow. A boy in a huge coat barged past, visibly stressing; you could hear him huffing to himself. He went storming through our school gates.

The school looked surprisingly normal by daylight. A burned-out car was smouldering in the loading bay, but of course that's normal for Park Hall.

"Hopefully it won't feel too bad inside today," Jools sighed. "We've sent guys in to do cosmic sweeps, plus we've been pumping in vibes. That *should* slow things down."

"I don't suppose anyone's figured out how to *fix* this leak?" I asked anxiously.

"You know what I woke up thinking?" she asked suddenly. "I thought, *maybe the leak isn't up to us to fix.*"

"You think we need to call in the Big Guys in Suits?"

"Actually just the opposite," she smiled. "This might sound a bit radical, but I think maybe it's down to these kids."

Mr Lupton had told them to be there by half past nine.

When Jools and I walked into the hall at 9.35, just two kids had turned up – Karmen and the stressed boy who'd passed us earlier.

"No one's coming, man," he huffed. "They're all cosy in their beds. Like we'd be if we had any sense," he added darkly.

I didn't think I'd seen him at rehearsal, but something about him seemed familiar. He had unusual eyebrows, black and sort of slanting. If he wasn't so mean and moody, he'd be almost good-looking.

From the way Karmen was pretending not to look at him, she thought so too! "They're coming, Jordie," she insisted. "They *promised*."

"Because they wanted you out of their *face*!" he flashed.

"Perhaps I'll give them till ten," Mr Lupton said bravely.

At that moment, three extremely disdainful-looking girls strolled in, closely followed by four boys. The boys were all yawning and looking fed up.

After that, nothing. Our drama teacher was still at least ten kids short of an actual musical.

Jools and I had been sitting on the stage, boosting the light levels to discourage any lurking hell critters that got overlooked in the sweep.

"Poor Mr Lupton," I sighed. "He's been trying to get this production off the ground since he started teaching."

Jools pulled a face "Why is he so fixated on this musical?"

"I think maybe he did it in college?"

She rolled her eyes. "*How* many centuries ago?"

"*Jools!*" I giggled.

"Look, he's a lovely guy, but anyone can see he didn't grow up round here. He never had to lie awake listening to police helicopters and emergency sirens stressing up the place! These kids need something they can genuinely relate to." She gestured out into the hall. "Now *that's* their style!"

Two boys were body popping to pass the time. Egged on by shouts from the girls, their moves got steadily slicker and more outrageous.

Jordie suddenly came striding purposefully towards the stage. He vaulted up and grabbed a mike off the stand.

"Check, check," he said experimentally. Jordie shut his eyes and in a surprisingly good voice, belted out, "PRESSURE! The Park Hall youths dem under too much pressure!"

All the kids except Karmen clapped and cheered.

"You *know* that, man, *serious* pressure!" one of the body poppers yelled back.

Jordie started jabbing his fingers at a huge, imaginary audience, as he began to rap. This was nothing unusual. Plenty of white boys at my school thought they could rap. The difference was this boy was good.

Next time I looked the girls had kind of casually drifted up on to the stage. To my surprise they started doing some really chilled street-dancing. They looked just as disdainful, but now it fitted with the ambience.

Jordie had shrugged his coat almost off his shoulders as he prowled around the stage still spouting lyrics. The other boys were calling out, half-mocking, half-genuinely impressed. Even Mr Lupton was smiling and clapping (usually missing the beat, bless him).

By this time the vibe coming off Jordie was just electric. Totally gripped by his performance, I only half-registered a stealthy creak as the door opened just wide enough for a latecomer to slip into the hall.

My heart gave a tiny jump. I'd had a totally mad idea. I turned to Jools. "Wouldn't it be great if Mr Lupton would just drop the musical," I bubbled, "and let the kids put on their own show?"

Jools just lit up. "Melanie that is such a brilliant—!"

She broke off and I saw her eyes go wide with shock. "Is that Jax at the back there?"

It's not surprising Jools was confused. I was confused – and she was my friend! This was a totally new version of Eve Jackson. In her soft winter sweater and slouchy velvet jeans, with a knitted beany pulled down over her hair, this girl could have posed for one of those 'celebs off-duty' shots in style zines.

My earth-angel mate pretended to smack me round the head. "'Ooh, I don't *know*, Jools. I think *maybe* my angel lessons went *OK*, Jools.' *Melanie*! She's like a different person!"

I was speechless. I believe in this stuff, I really do, I just hadn't expected it to work so FAST.

Not only had Jax left off her gangster jacket, she'd taken out *every* stud except one. It takes more than a few studs to turn a girl into a gangster of course; what made me know this change was real was the look in her eyes. Just once or twice, in our Shocking Pink days, I'd seen my friend's eyes shine like this.

Jax watched for a while, moving her body slightly to the driving rattatat of Jordie's lyrics, then she made her way to the front of the hall, where Mr Lupton was talking to an increasingly depressed Karmen.

"Hi, girl," Jax greeted her quietly.

"Hi." Karmen didn't even look at her. "Nice of you to come along and say I told you so!"

"Only I didn't," Jax told her quietly. "You did your best, you know. I just think you've all been—" she stopped.

"No, go ahead, stick the knife in," Karmen said in a cold voice. "You know you're dying to!"

Jax took a breath. "I *just* think you've all been barking up the wrong tree. No offence, sir," she said to Mr Lupton, "but your musical sucks, basically."

"I feel forced to agree," he said in a tired voice. "I really think it's time to call it a day."

"We can't give up *now*!" Karmen's voice came out like a despairing wail. "We've got to find a way to make this work!"

"Because of Mel?" Jax said softly.

Karm's chin wobbled, then she hid her face in her hands. "We've got to, we've just *got* to," she sobbed. "It meant so much to her, Jax, but we were so worried about losing our cred, we wouldn't even give it a try, and now Mel's dead!"

I was turning hot and cold.

What made it so much worse is that I wasn't even *that sold* on being a Pink Lady in the first place. But now I was dead, Karms remembered a passing whim as like, my dying *wish*.

My poor friend was putting herself through the wringer, all because – for a whole ten minutes – I'd fancied dressing up in a cute retro jacket so I could flirt with Kelsey Hickman!

Karms was weeping openly now. "I *miss* her, Jax! I miss her and I really miss the Shocking Pinks."

To my horror Jax's eyes filled with tears.

"I miss her too," she gulped.

Jools and I clutched each other's hands in disbelief.

My friends were hugging.

Jax swiped away her tears, trying to pull herself together. "Karms, don't laugh, but when I came in just now I had this mad idea. I know you want to do something for Mel, but why can't it be something she'd be proud of, something classy that we'd *all* be proud of?"

"Like Shakespeare you mean?" Karmen quavered.

Jax gave a tearful laugh. "Haven't you *noticed* what's happening on that stage?"

"One little white boy is not a show, Jax!"

"Girl, wake up! Loads of kids in this school perform in garage bands or whatever."

"You seriously think we can put on a new show in two weeks?"

"Why not?" Mr Lupton chipped in unexpectedly. "As you said yourself, they build gardens in a poxy weekend on TV!"

"But *they* know what they're *doing*," Karms objected.

"And again, thank you children of Park Hall!" he said humorously.

"I meant we'd be doing this totally from scratch."

"Karms, it will just snowball, girl, trust me! Kids will text their mates and – bosh! – you've got your show!"

The kids on the stage saw something was going on and ambled down into the hall.

"Whassup?" demanded Jordie. "You guys plotting a revolution?"

Jax's eyes glinted. "We're gonna kill Mr Lupton's musical!"

He snorted. "That musical been dead a while, man."

Karmen was shocked. "That's not what you said before, Jordan Hickman!"

Jax grinned. "Because he fancies you rotten, Karms!"

Omigosh, I thought. *No wonder I recognised that face! Stressed Jordie was beautiful Kelsey's younger brother.*

Jax started telling the others about her brainwave for a totally original production. "I'm talking a serious twenty-first century vibe, yeah? But, like, totally positive and uplifting – none of your guns rubbish," she told Jordie fiercely, as if she'd never had a violent thought in her life.

Mr Allbright once told us that when the time is *really* ripe for something to happen, you don't always have to do that much. Everything just unfolds like a wonderful story.

That's exactly how it was with this new show. In less than sixty earth minutes, it flashed from being an angel's daydream to a genuine possibility.

Part-way through Jax's explanation, as she'd predicted, everyone just started texting their mates. In no time would-be performers started rolling up. By 11am, auditions were underway.

Hendrix and Brice turned up in the middle of a cool hip-hop number by a local posse who performed under the name of The Vibe Tribe.

I hadn't seen Brice since our fight, but I'd decided to accept his fairy note as a genuine apology and gave him a friendly smile.

"You guys do realise this hall is buzzing with positive vibes?" he said accusingly.

We hadn't actually noticed, but the air was literally shimmering!

Brice watched the hip-hop kids with a perplexed expression. "I thought Grease was that retro thing with motorbikes?"

We explained about the musical being killed off.

He frowned. "You think they can pull this together in two weeks?"

"With a little cosmic backup," Jools smiled.

"You guys are taking on a lot," I said doubtfully. "You work twenty-four-seven as it is, plus you've got this leak, plus I'd still appreciate some help with my mates."

Jools patted my hand. "And you've got it, hon. But I'm actually wondering if your mates *need* more lessons. Just supporting their show will do wonders for these girls."

But *Sky* isn't in this show, I wanted to say, when Brice said something that blew me away.

"It won't just do wonders for the girls." Brice was trying to play it cool, but even he couldn't keep a glint of hope out of his voice. "These vibes are off the scale, man, and this is the auditions! Imagine an actual show with an audience of proud rellies and well-wishers. The PODS can't stand

stuff like that; it's too real – and I should know!"
Brice added, flashing me his pantomime baddie
smile.

"Are you saying this little show could save the
school?" asked Hendrix, amazed.

I felt a whoosh of excitement. "Omigosh, Jools!
That's what you meant about it being down to the
kids!"

"That was just a hunch, you know," she said
softly.

By midday everyone was ready for a break. My
mates shared Karmen's lunch while they discussed
various artists they'd seen.

After their snack, Jax and Karmen went to freshen
up. I was suddenly curious to know what they'd talk
about.

I mimed that I'd be back and followed my mates
into the skanky cloakroom.

"Could you smell this, like, *perfume*?" I heard
Karms say in an awed voice.

Jax shook her head. "More like flowers. What's
that pinky bush in your mum's garden?"

"Omigosh, lilacs! You're *right*! After she'd gone I
could smell lilacs for *hours*!" Karmen's words were
almost tripping over themselves. "Jax, this is *so*

incredible. Was it like she was *there* with you, talking?"

"Totally! She said I was magic. She went on about that a LOT."

Karmen gasped. "That's exactly what she said to me!"

"She kept saying I wasn't alone, and when I woke up my dead cactus had a *flower*, Karms! A freaking *shocking-pink* flower!"

"No *way*!" Karmen breathed.

Two girls came in and my friends got busy tidying their hair, continuing their conversation in whispers. I heard Jax hiss, "Then we've got to *make* her talk to us. This is more important than some poxy boy. I mean if Mel came back—?"

"—then Sky totally has to know," Karmen whispered.

I practically floated out of the cloakrooms.

Almost the first thing I'd noticed about Heaven was how the air smells almost exactly, but not quite, like lilacs. Without me knowing, the sweet and magical vibes of Heaven had followed me to Earth!

Suddenly anything seemed possible. Karmen and Jax were determined to make it up with Sky, and we might actually save the school!! It looked like my mission was succeeding beyond my wildest dreams.

Trust Brice to burst my bubble.

"You've got that good fairy look again," He said accusingly when I wafted back into the hall.

"Say what you like, angel boy," I said airily. "But you can't bring me down. Just look around – is this, or is this not, fabulous?"

"Yes, Tinkerbell, it's fabulous and you're fabulous. Just imagine how even more fabulous you'll be when you figure out what your real—" Brice broke off, looking oddly embarrassed.

Jools had joined us. She'd been called out to the children's hospital. A newborn was having trouble adjusting to terrestrial vibes.

"Want to come, Mel?" she offered. "These auditions could go on for hours."

I was suddenly torn. "I'd love to but if I'm not needed here I'd really like to spend some time with my family."

Mum and Des took Jade to the park on Sunday afternoons.

To my secret dismay, Brice asked if he could tag along. Since that Tinkerbell crack, I wasn't keen, but I couldn't really think of a way to say no.

Being Brice, he immediately had to take over. "There's loads of parks in London. I hope you know which one?"

"No, but it's bound to be one of three," I shrugged.

I was wrong.

My family weren't in any of the London parks within easy reach of my old home, and they weren't at home.

It was Brice who figured out where they'd gone.

CHAPTER FOURTEEN

Brice wouldn't say where he was taking me, but I felt cold blank vibes seeping into me, even before we beamed down.

My chest went tight as I watched them trudging stoically along the endless rows of stone crosses and marble angels, looking desperately vulnerable in this bleak open space.

Brice had brought me to the cemetery.

They'd bought bunches of daffodils in sheaths of cellophane. I saw Des wipe his eyes. He put his arms around my mum and I wanted to put my arms around both of them.

This might sound weird, but I was terrified I'd accidentally catch sight of my own headstone.

"Whatever it says, you know that's not you,"

Brice told me with unusual gentleness.

"I don't care, I'm not looking," I told him through stiff lips.

I was looking everywhere *but* my headstone at the winter sky with its criss-crossing vapour trails, at Jade sulkily kicking stones...

"I could read your epitaph to you if you want?" Brice suggested helpfully. "It's not so bad."

I pulled a face. "Does it say I'm sleeping with the angels?"

"Along those lines," he agreed. He flashed a mischievous grin. "Had much sleep lately?"

"I wish!" I spluttered.

For some reason, being able to crack bad-taste jokes made me feel slightly better. We watched Jade kicking up gravel as she stomped on and off gravestones, complaining loudly to herself.

"She's cute," commented Brice.

"I'm amazed you can tell!"

Jade's woolly hat was pulled down so far you could just about see her little nose! Mum had put my little sister in so many layers, she looked like a tiny Arctic explorer.

"Jade, stop that, you're scuffing those new boots," Mum said crossly.

"I don't *like* this ol' cemetery," my sister complained. "Why do we always have to come? Melanie's not even here anyway!"

"Smart as well as cute," Brice said in my ear.

A young cat was picking its way daintily between urns and headstones, clearly heading in our direction. Cats just adore angels.

This one looked like a miniature panther, with his glossy black fur and huge, tawny-gold eyes. He started weaving ecstatically between us, purring so loudly he sounded like a dial tone.

"Mum, Mum, there's a kitty!"

Jade came charging up, scattering gravel.

The cat looked understandably panicky, but Brice crouched down and whispered something in the special language we use for animals, and he instantly relaxed, allowing my sister to pet him.

Jade started confiding secrets to her kitty friend. "My sister's not under that stupid stone you know," she explained in a hoarse whisper. "She goes to a big school in the clouds and she fights all the baddies and monsters with her angel kung fu."

"She's got that *almost* right!" Brice said in my ear.

"My mum says angels don't fight," Jade told the cat, "but I've seed her in my dreams."

I felt slightly dizzy. Had I been sharing Jade's dreams or had she been sharing mine?

Sometimes in nightmares you just think of something scary and it appears.

Under her woolly hat, Jade's brown eyes looked worried. "Oh, no, what's happening to your poor tail?"

Wild-eyed with terror, the cat had fluffed itself out to almost twice its normal size. Ears flat to its skull, it fled, yowling, into the bushes.

I spun to see what had freaked it and almost screamed with shock as I saw the bald shambling beast stumbling towards Jade.

It was a hellhound!

My first thought was that the engraver had got it wrong. Apart from its sick-white skin, which made it look like it was already dead, the hellhound was almost ordinary. It was even behaving like an average family mutt, snuffling along paths and rooting intensely in dark corners. Then, as we watched, the hound lifted its huge naked head, letting out a gargling howl that made every tiny hair stand up on my neck. For a bizarre instant I saw three hounds, all somehow occupying the same space.

I didn't have a second thought.

Brice and I didn't say a word. We instantly sprang between my little sister and the huge hell beast, taking up defensive martial-arts crouches.

I'm not sure if Jade totally realised we were there, but she'd definitely clocked the hellhound. She seemed more fascinated than scared. "Oh, wow," she breathed. "That's a really ugly monster."

"Don't suppose Sam gave you any flares?" Brice muttered out of the side of his mouth.

I tore open my bag and pulled out two flares, tossing one to Brice.

He quickly bit off the end and was instantly brandishing a huge pillar of golden-white angel fire. I hastily lit mine the same way.

You'd think two torch-wielding angels would have grabbed its attention, but the hellhound was busy snuffling obsessively round my tombstone.

Like the majority of hell creatures, this hound wasn't a real animal; it was a PODS remix of a dog, basically, a collection of evil thoughts trapped inside a nightmare.

I have to say, waiting for a hell beast to notice your existence is v. v. stressful.

"Why doesn't it see us," I said in frustration.

"Can't," Brice explained grimly. "Hellhounds are practically blind." He yelled out, "Yo, Fido! Over here!"

"Are you crazy!" I shrieked.

"Trust me," he insisted. "This is the best way!"

Don't ever tell me the worst way then, I thought.

The almost-blind hell beast suspiciously lowered its head, and slowly swivelled in our direction. It had huge, lonely, pain-filled eyes. Who knows what the hellhound saw? Maybe it could just make out a gold-white blur of angel fire? But that seemed like enough.

The hellhound gave a growl so low and menacing that another three hounds seemed to be speaking through its throat. Slippery threads of drool began to drip from its muzzle.

Brice moved so fast, he was like a blur. One minute he was beside me, the next he was standing on a half-toppled tombstone, inches from the hell dog. With one ruthless lunge he shoved the blazing torch into its face.

The hound cringed away, more in loathing than fear, baring hideous outsized canines, and snarling with fury.

"Gotta message for you, hell-pooch!" Brice told it in a chummy voice. "You come near that little girl and I'll insert TWO of these exactly where the sun don't shine."

Incredibly it seemed like Brice had scared it off. The hellhound began to back away, making a frustrated, high-pitched whine, that set my teeth buzzing. It backed so far that it was literally backing *through* a pristine new marble headstone.

Jade immediately ran to my mum. "Mum, mum! There was a monster but Mel and a big boy scared it away with their angel kung fu."

I felt sick just knowing that something so evil could simply erupt into her innocent little world.

Brice sat down on a tombstone, looking shattered.

I watched my parents walk away, very slowly, arm in arm, like they were helping to hold each other up. Jade was skipping beside them, chatting excitedly about monsters.

How I longed to be able to cross back through that invisible barrier and go back to my human world of Sunday parks and Friday night cafés. Unfortunately I'd got trapped in the same world as Brice.

"Thanks," I said with difficulty. "That was great what you just did."

"Nah, just insurance," he said dismissively. "It was never going to hurt Jade."

I didn't need my life to be any more confusing than it already was, so I just snapped at him. "It was never going to hurt her? Oh, really? Wow, so suddenly you talk hell dog now?"

"No. I just happen to know who it's actually following." Brice stood up wearily and just pointed across rows of identical modern headstones, to the wall that divided the cemetery from a three-lane highway outside. He sounded unbelievably depressed.

"See that kid? A while back, he won a hellhound for life."

I was barely in time to see a youth in a hooded top vault over the wall. He plodded beside the traffic until he reached a subway entrance, then disappeared from view.

My mission had taken a bizarre cosmic twist.

Chapter Fifteen

Brice had gone back to his tombstone. I sat down beside him, feeling absolutely unreal.

"That thing is seriously after that boy?" I asked bewildered.

"It's a hound, darling. Give a hound a whiffy trail to follow and off it goes. Only with hellhounds it's not smells, it's vibes."

"That dog was sniffing for *vibes*?"

"If your soul is giving off a certain damaged kind of vibe, the dogs can't help themselves – they'll follow you around till they're half dead sometimes."

Just occasionally, Brice let something drop that made you wonder about all the other darker things which he could never tell anyone, even Lola.

I remembered the beast slobbering obsessively along paths, how frustrated it had seemed when two fire-wielding angels interrupted its icky activities.

I saw Brice had gone off into his own gloomy thoughts.

"So are you planning to keep me in suspense for ever, angel boy, or could you maybe tell me who that hell pooch is really after?"

His face brightened. "Want to meet him? I mean, don't feel you have to, but you can if you really want." He grabbed my wrist to check my watch. "Actually, if we wait just a few minutes then beam ourselves there, I can almost guarantee where he'll be."

I gave a deep sigh. "So where do damaged souls go at ten past three on Sunday afternoons?"

Brice gave me a tired grin. "The Cosmic Café. If business is slow."

When we eventually beamed on to the pavement outside the café, business was about as slow as it could be.

There were exactly two customers, sitting with their backs to each other – an old guy reading a paper and a boy in a hooded top, sitting with his back kind of hunched to the window. Nikos came through the swing doors and carefully set down a plate of steaming sausages and mash in front of the boy.

"See how he's looking after that kid?" I told Brice. "He treats everyone like that."

"Even more amazing when you know Shay's getting a free lunch," Brice commented.

As if he'd heard his name, the boy whipped round. I was startled to see a familiar face with slanting, suspicious brows.

I started to say, "But that's Jordie!"

But suddenly I couldn't breathe.

I *knew* this boy, not from this morning – from *for ever*.

He'd turned back to his meal. I couldn't believe he wasn't as shaken up as I was.

"I'm guessing Shay is Jordie's twin?" I said in a slightly trembly voice. I was trying not to sound anything like as weird as I felt.

Brice was watching me closely. "Didn't you guys ever meet? You seemed like you knew him?"

I shook my head. Kelsey's brothers had never made it to school that often, plus they'd been in a different class. I just had a vague impression of two sets of black slanty eyebrows.

"I sort of knew their older brother."

I started telling Brice how Kelsey and his younger brothers had camped in an abandoned car rather than be taken into care, but he said carelessly, "Yeah, I read about that in the case notes."

I did an amazed double take. "The Agency *assigned* Shay to you! You might have told me you were on a mission, you big creep!"

Ho ho, things were finally adding up! I'd been privately wondering why Brice, of all people, had rocked up in Park Hall, but I could see that a screwed-up boy with a hellhound problem would be just up his street.

Brice shook his head, looking glum. "It's more that Shay assigned himself, if you get my meaning?"

I finally caught on. "Omigosh – you got the call!"

'The call' is when a troubled human sends a personal request for you to be their guardian angel: a silent, totally desperate SOS from their soul to yours. It's a v. mystical event, also a v. v. steep learning curve for the angel who is being called. Now I understood why my friend's boyfriend had seemed so super-stressed.

Brice jammed his hands in his pockets, striking what me and Lola call his 'lonely cosmic outlaw' pose. "To be honest, I'm feeling like I'm in way over my head," he said in a tight voice.

I nodded sympathetically. "I bet. Still it's early days yet, right?"

I was secretly dying to ask him all kinds of nosy questions. Like, could you get rid of a persistent hellhound once it became attached to your vibes, or did it have to follow you around until one of you eventually crumbled into dust? And how did Jordie's brother's soul *become* damaged in the first place?

Lola and I would have been up discussing Shay all night. But it seemed like Brice had said all he wanted to say.

Tell the truth, Mel. I actually got a really strong feeling Brice *wanted* to talk to me about his case, but it was like something was making him hold back.

I thought maybe if I showed a general interest, Brice might feel like he could open up? "So what's Jordie's brother like, anyway?" I asked in a casual voice. "Does he rap too?"

Brice glanced at the boy silently shovelling down everything Nikos had put in front of him.

"I've never even heard that boy talk," he said softly.

CHAPTER SIXTEEN

A police helicopter was hovering over the hospital, churning up the night with its blades. After emergency sirens and that constant, pavement-shaking bass line, this sound is the third most common ingredient in Park Hall's edgy urban soundtrack.

Jools and I barely even glanced up as we came out into the freezing wind and rain. After the stuffy atmosphere of the children's ward, the subzero temperatures were a shock.

"That little cutie just *lurves* angel kisses, doesn't he!" Jools enthused through chattering teeth. "Did you see that smile?"

"Yeah, and that clueless nurse said it was wind!"

Four days had gone by since the hellhound incident and my new life as an honorary EA was turning out to be seriously hectic. Up early for dawn vibes, (I know!), plus twice daily rehearsals, and obviously I tried to help out the EAs as much as I could.

After tonight's rehearsal Jools and I had popped in to check on her shocked newborn: the baby who was having problems adjusting to his home planet. I waited, shivering, while Jools checked her phone for messages, then remembered I hadn't actually checked mine for ages.

Most of my messages were from a deeply jealous Lola!

"You guys actually rescued your sister from a *real* live hellhound! AND you're giving angel lessons! Well, take it easy, OK? We don't want any humans sprouting wings, do we? Oh, yeah, tell that creep Brice he has to call me. Miss you!" BEEP

Jools was talking on her phone now, so I ducked into the wheelchair bay out of the wind and rang Lola. Her phone was switched off, *again*, so I left yet another long message, keeping her up to speed with events in Park Hall.

"They're calling the show PURE VIBES, isn't that cool! This production's even got Mrs Threlfall buzzing and trust me, she is not a naturally buzzy lady! She's so thrilled the kids are doing something positive, she's letting them off lessons so they can rehearse! Oh, yeah, remember Miss Rowntree? The teacher who called me an 'airhead with attitude'? She totally can't do enough to help! I know! And obviously it's early days, but working on the show seems to be bringing Karms and Jax even closer."

I felt a pang, because I didn't have anything good to say about Sky.

"Lollie, listen," I remembered. "Brice is having a super-stressful time with his guardian angel module. Send good vibes, yeah?"

When I rang off, I was v. spooked to find a new message from the bad boy himself.

"Got some news that's going to blow you away, but I can't tell you, because you won't get off the stupid *phone*!! Oh, yeah, I'm at KISMET, that little Turkish cafe next to the tattoo parlour!" BEEP.

When Jools and I finally rocked up at KISMET, crackly Arabic music was playing on an ancient cassette player. Brice was watching a group of taxi drivers play dominoes: a game which involved violent slamming on tables, a barrage of friendly insults in at least six different languages, and howls of laughter.

We joined him at his table. "And you're here in this atmospheric cafe because?" Jools hinted.

Brice reluctantly tore himself away. "Oh, yeah, they needed a washer-up." He saw our expressions and rolled his eyes. "Not *me*. Shay's got a few hours work."

"You're waiting to walk him back," I said astonished.

"Just common sense," he said gruffly. "If our four-legged fiend knows Shay's got angelic security, he'll keep his distance, plus it gives us a chance to talk, man-to-man, or cosmic-misfit-to-lost-boy or whatever."

This guardian angel module was bringing out a side to Brice I'd never seen.

"Brice, not to be hardhearted, but what can it actually *do* to him? Obviously being followed by a hellhound isn't ideal, but it's just a nightmare pretending to be a dog, right?"

"Do you guys want to know about this – it's kind of disturbing?"

Brice glanced uneasily at Jools.

"No, I do," I insisted.

He took a breath. "Ok, to put it crudely, a hellhound will only adopt you if you're already in extremely deep poo."

"I can see that."

"Sorry to contradict you, darling, but I don't think you can. I'm talking the *deepest* excrement. Like, say you hurt somebody so badly you can't ever put it right."

Jools suddenly got extra busy arranging her scarf.

I swallowed. "Like you actually *killed* someone?"

"Just for instance," Brice said hastily. "You didn't mean to do it, but – bosh! – it's done."

He pulled a bottle of water out of his pocket and had a long gulp. "You're so horrified and disgusted at yourself, it's not long before those dark voices start up in your head telling you that you're just a bad seed and you shouldn't even be allowed to live. Trouble is, you're freaking scared of dying. That's when hellhounds start sniffing round your Nikes, sweetheart."

"Brice, sorry to sound like a stuck CD, but what can they actually *do* to you?"

"Nothing – and everything. When a hellhound comes into your space, it's like you've got your own hotline into the Hell dimensions. How bad you felt before is nothing to how you feel now. Your vibes drop. You start attracting bad luck. Soon other humans just have to look at you and they *know* you're bad news..."

I had a flash of Shay's face at the café window. Was that what I'd seen? A haunted soul too ashamed to live and too scared to die?

"I can't come to any more rehearsals, Mel," Brice blurted suddenly. "Last night I just went out for like, half-an-hour, just for a break, and when I got back to his kids' home there were tracks right up the hall, and I found more under his bed."

"Under his *bed*!" Jools looked incredibly distressed.

I felt a sorrowful ache deep inside. After all those boys went through, Kelsey's little bro had still ended up in care.

"I just can't see it ending," Brice said in despair. "I know how it's *supposed* to work – that kid *has* to forgive himself, or he'll spend the rest of his life trapped in his own personal hell. I just can't see how it's going to happen, unless—"

Jools swiftly put her hand over his. It was perfectly friendly, but I saw him check himself.

He tried to laugh. "Quite right, Jools. Been watching too much Dr Phil with Shay. Believe it or not I didn't call you to whinge." Brice yanked his phone out of a back pocket and fiddled with some buttons.

"Hold up. Got to find the right picture first. OK, if we just zoom in, it should – *yes!*" He handed me his phone. "That *is* Sky Nolan, right?"

I felt my whole Universe wobble. "Where did you take this?"

"In this café, about an hour ago."

"Here? In *this* cafe?"

You could see him loving my surprise. "Want to see who she was with?"

"Don't keep her in suspense, you pig!"

"OK, see where it says ZOOM OUT? Click on that."

I zoomed and clicked. "Omigosh," I breathed.

There they were, all three Shocking Pinks, drinking Pepsi at the same table, in a Turkish taxi drivers' cafe!

"I couldn't eavesdrop *too* much," he said apologetically. "What with the domino dons over there. But they seemed pretty friendly."

I gazed at the three smiling faces.

This is exactly what our teachers are always banging on about; you give humans the tools and they sort their problems out beautifully all by themselves.

"That was such a lovely thing to do, Brice," I told him tearfully. "Especially when you've got so much else on your plate."

"Don't cry yet," Brice teased. "You haven't even heard the best bit, yet! They've persuaded Sky to be in the show."

"That is SO cool," I gasped. "She's going to do stand-up, right?"

"That was mentioned but she wasn't interested. She wants to introduce the other acts, she says."

I was childishly disappointed, when I should have just been relieved Sky was coming back to school. The past few days she'd totally dropped off my radar. Every time I called in, I'd find her mum and Dan with the boys playing happy families, but no Sky.

Jools pulled a face. "Gotta do my baby-sitting, guys, I'm afraid."

"Want company?" I asked.

She grinned. "We'd just end up talking."

"True," I giggled.

EAs did sometimes keep each other company during the tedious hours of watching absolutely nothing happen on the CCTV monitors. This wasn't the first time I'd offered either. If I had a suspicious nature I'd have thought she just didn't want me around.

I felt like I needed to go back and crash, but instead I sort of hovered. Thanks to Brice I'd had a magic glimpse of the Pinks' reunion, which made me feel even worse about not helping with Shay. Before I could put my guilty feelings into words he pointed sternly at the door.

"Get some rest, angel girl. Got your big show coming off next week, then all that hell trash will go back where it belongs."

My heart suddenly lifted. If the Shocking Pinks were back as a team, the PODS didn't stand a chance!

CHAPTER SEVENTEEN

The bored red devils on the stage were turning v-e-r-y slowly into unbelievably bored green aliens.

In the wings Tariq was flicking buttons and levers on the school's fancy new computer, making adjustments to his lighting FX.

One alien stumped down off the stage and became a huffy kid again. "I'm off for a smoke," he growled.

For the third time that morning, Tariq whizzed out in his wheelchair to protest. "These guys are jokers, Jax! How can I do my work if they're disrespecting me like this?"

"Stay on your marks, Vibe Tribe," Jax called in a warning voice.

"I would not waste my *energy* disrespecting you, wheelchair boy!" the kid flung at Tariq. "We never even noticed you before you decided to *wheel* yourself right into our special show. I mean what *are* you, man? Just the freaking techie!"

Karmen quickly took him aside. "I know it's boring, Marlon, but Tariq has to know where everyone's going to be on the night, or this show's going to be pure garbage."

"Going to be?!" snorted Jordie, who was going down with a cold.

Jax signalled urgently from across the hall. "Just got a text from Magic Boy. He reckons he's got to drop out – says he's 'hurt his wrist'."

Karmen just crooked her fingers, miming a phone. "Call the slacker up, girl! Tell him now he *really* has to do magic!"

"You tell Magic Boy if he don't show up, he gonna answer to the Vibe Tribe," Marlon yelled.

I decided to go for a nice calming walk.

I'd like to tell you that the greatly-improved light levels had turned my depressing school foyer into a wondrous haven of tropical plants, with vibey little fishes speeding about in a shiny new tank. There were some groovy posters which Tariq had designed on his laptop, but as soon as fresh posters went up, other kids instantly defaced them with stupid comments. The truth is, my old school still had all its old hassles and as dark vibes from the hell school gradually percolated though into human reality, new and more disturbing problems started to surface.

Just yesterday, I'd heard Miss Rowntree tell Mr Lupton that kids in her class had worse concentration spans than usual. She put it down to the mystery headaches everyone was getting. Mr Lupton had heard rumours our school might be suffering from 'sick building syndrome'. The EAs and I were like, "Hello!"

Yet despite the odd tantrum and sprained wrist, the cast of PURE VIBES seemed serenely immune to toxic fallout from the PODS school. It was like they were on their own glowy little island.

Jools reckons that if you're one-hundred-per-cent focused on creating something uplifting, it's next-to-impossible for bad vibes to bring you down; and we were seeing daily evidence of the super-positive effects the show was having on kids taking part.

Even Mrs Threlfall had complimented Mr Lupton on the unusually mature and co-operative behaviour of the pupils in the show. We'd been noticing this for a while; in fact Hendrix joked that if we didn't know better, we'd think these kids were turning into angels. Smoking, swearing angels for sure, but that magic spark which Jools was always on about was now actually visible in their eyes.

The feel-good vibes from the show weren't only confined to the cast. One or two were beaming out beyond the school and into the local community. A local hardware store volunteered to donate paint and materials for the atmospheric urban backdrop Karms and Jordie had designed. And you should have seen Tariq's face when his mum rocked up with ladies from her Women Aglow keep-fit club, bringing Tupperware boxes crammed with little goodies which they'd baked especially for the cast! He looked ready to die of shame!

I felt a sudden rush of relief. Sky had just walked into the foyer. Two hours late, but as she told the others, "All I do is be cute and read cue cards. How much rehearsal does that actually take!"

The first time my mate had rehearsed her links, I was worried she couldn't hack it. She drifted out on to the stage, looking totally out of it – until they switched on the mike. Then, after a slightly shaky start, the old sassy, flirty Sky kicked back in like she'd never been away. In that moment it was like she was born to be a link girl. She had this hilarious way of bigging up the performers' acts which was totally OTT, yet it worked.

Karmen and Jax said the audience was going to love her.

The rest of the cast didn't seem so sure. "I get a bad vibe off that girl," Jordie told Marlon. "She think I don't notice but deep down she laughing at us, man."

It upset me to hear that, partly because I knew what he meant. Sky had a faintly patronising way of treating the other cast members, like they were endearing little five year olds putting on a puppet show for their mummies and daddies behind the sofa.

I wasn't comfortable with this new superior Sky. I was also deeply disappointed by her casual attitude to the other Pinks. When she'd originally agreed to be in their show, I'd pictured them hanging out together almost constantly, like before. In fact she hardly saw Jax and Karmen outside rehearsals.

But like I tried to tell Helix, it's an ancient cosmic law; when girls get boyfriends, everything else goes out the window.

My inner angel had been out of touch for a while and I was starting to miss her. I'd sent a few hopeful probes into mystical inner space suggesting it would be nice to catch up, but all I got was one of those TV info streams flashing across my mind going: *SHAY SHAY SHAY SHAY SHAY.*

I just beamed a stroppy message right back: *Thanks for nothing, girl! Like I don't feel guilty enough. Mind telling me how I'm supposed to help Brice with Shay AND work on a show, AND make sure my friends don't backslide?*

Immediately after that night's rehearsal, Jools had to beam back to Matilda Street to dash off an assignment for a course she was taking in Dark Studies. I needed a walk after the total madness of the show, so I walked back alone.

I hadn't been past the Cosmic Café for days, so I was shocked to see someone had sprayed graffiti on the door. Maybe Nikos had started cleaning it off. Now it just said: SHAY IS A MUR...

You're gonna get yours Shay. We know what you did Shay.

It was like someone had shaken a kaleidoscope; suddenly I was seeing a new disturbing pattern. Like I told you, spraying graffiti is a well-known leisure activity in my neighbourhood, and Shay is such a common local name that my brain hadn't made a connection with the other hate graffiti I'd seen when I arrived. Now it seemed like the same ill-wisher had been out to get Brice's Shay all the time.

The café must have been having a slow night, because Shay was inside, polishing his plate with his last piece of bread. Brice kept a careful watch from a nearby table, clearly in need of some space.

I wondered why his hell-dog boy preferred to eat free meals in the café instead of eating at the kids' home; but mostly I wondered how he could still swallow, with those malicious words splattered on the door for the world to see.

I saw Shay getting up to leave. Worried that Brice might think I was checking up on him, I stepped back into the shadows as they came out of the door. Brice was chatting to Shay now in a bravely upbeat voice. As I watched Shay trudge away, unaware of his loyal bodyguard, I felt like I had never seen such a broken-looking kid.

There were now just two nights to go before the final show. The EAs had planned a super-thorough cosmic sweep down at the school. Jools called Brice up and offered to mind Shay while he went down to the school with that night's 'sweepers'.

"He said I saved his life," she grinned when she rang off. "The kids at the home were watching When Good Pets Turn Bad!"

I don't know if this was Brice's idea, but for the first time the EAs invited me to go along on the sweep. When we reached the school, we had to split into pairs. Each pair was responsible for sweeping a different area of the school. Brice and I got the annexe, the area where the crack between the dimensions first appeared.

Since the afternoon of the evil hell turd, I hadn't risked setting foot on that bridge, let alone crossing it, so I'd never seen the actual site of the leak. I suspect that's why I'd been invited along. Brice thought it was time I knew the score.

One thing's for sure; terms like 'crack' and 'leak' don't come near describing the hideously hyperactive evil portal in the boys' changing rooms.

I backed in revulsion from the swirling sucking thing in the floor, then got a double jolt of horror as I saw the ghostly green graffiti on the changing room wall, the words still visible through the watered-down emulsion. YOU WON'T GET AWAY WITH IT SHAY.

The graffiti was quite old, yet the hate vibes coming at me from the wall still packed enough of a cosmic punch to make me feel physically shaky. I heard myself blurt out, "Did the EAs ever find out how that crack started?"

Brice's tone was deliberately super-casual. "Not really. They've got a few theories. We know when it appeared though," he added, like he just thought he'd mention it. "By a weird coincidence it was exactly the same time as your funeral."

CHAPTER EIGHTEEN

Mr Allbright once gave out this cute little print-out explaining why the Universe is exactly like your ideal soul-mate.

One example I remember is that when the Universe sends you helpful signs, and you totally refuse to pay attention, instead of going into a major huff and washing its hands of you, it generously sends bigger, even more disturbing, signs, until weeks, or maybe it's centuries, later, you finally get the message.

I'm only telling you this because I was just about to get a deeply disturbing sign.

It was the evening of the dress rehearsal and the night before the show. The rehearsal went brilliantly. Jordie was over his cold, Magic Boy had recovered from his mysterious 'injury', and Marlon stood on his mark like a pro.

Unfortunately it was Jools' night to baby-sit the Powers of Darkness, which was a shame, because for the first time the kids were performing to a select audience. At least ten other teachers joined Mr Lupton and Miss Rowntree in the hall for a preview of PURE VIBES.

Afterwards they seemed genuinely impressed, though I did see two female teachers tutting over Sky's tiny clingy dress.

Sky seemed as delighted as everyone else that things had gone so well. I actually saw her throw her arms round Karmen and give her a genuinely affectionate hug.

Karmen's eyes narrowed suddenly. "What's this in your hair, girl?" She tried to pick off the teeny acid-green splodge.

Sky winced away, half laughing. "Ow, don't! It's paint, you muppet! I've been helping my brothers decorate their room and of course Olly has to start a paint fight! Now their bunk beds look exactly like modern art!"

I felt as if all the breath had been knocked out of me. That's because I knew something Karms and Jax couldn't possibly know.

It was a cute family picture Sky was painting, but the only time she went back to her mum's these days was to blag money off Dan, and maybe grab a change of clothes.

And for the record, the green paint in her hair was not the kind you use in a little kid's room. It was the kind you get in a spray can. The kind bored or angry kids use to spray graffiti.

I just beamed myself straight to the Nolans' flat.

I was literally frantic, pushing my head into closed drawers and cupboards, almost sobbing, "Don't let it be here, please please please don't let it be here." I was abusing the cosmic angels' gift to invade my friend's privacy and it felt like the *most* shameful thing ever.

When I finally found the aerosol cans, wrapped in her paint-stained hoody, I still couldn't take it in. I found myself making excuses for her; she'd had a disturbed childhood, the graffiti at the Cosmic Café was just a stupid one-off, any number of kids could have splattered those other hate-filled words around Park Hall.

But I knew it had always been Sky.

I beamed back to Matilda Street and pounded up flights of stairs to the room where Jools was baby-sitting the PODS.

This door was always kept shut now, but I rushed in without even knocking. "Jools!" I gasped. "Something awful's—"

Jools practically dived to block my view of the monitors, in a belated attempt to stop me seeing the devastating sight.

I couldn't move.

There she was on camera, just letting herself through the shabby back door. I glimpsed shadowy stairs and a floor littered with junk mail, then the door closed.

"She had a key?" I whispered. "She had a key to *that* house?"

Night after night, Sky had waved laughing goodbyes to the other Pinks and gone straight to this evil place.

Jools was in tears. "I'm so sorry, Mel."

"Were you ever going to tell me?" I asked numbly.

"It just never felt like the right *time*," she almost wailed. "You were doing so well with the others, we started to think maybe you could help Sky too. When she agreed to be in the show, we all thought that was *such* a hopeful sign. I *still* think that production could turn her around."

"She doesn't care zip about the show," I said in a bleak voice. "Jordie's right not to trust her. It's Sky who's writing that hate graffiti about Shay – that's what I came to tell you."

Jools looked genuinely shocked. "How do you know?"

"Karms found paint in her hair. I checked Sky's room and found, well, evidence." I let out a choking little sob. "It's almost funny – on my way back here I thought things were about as bad as they could be. But they were so *so* much worse!"

Jools was practically wringing her hands. "She's not a bad person, Mel, you have to believe that. That girl is just so totally *desperate* to belong to someone."

I sat down and covered my face. "Let's face it – you've got to be a bit desperate to date a PODS," I said with a slightly hysterical laugh.

"No, I *swear*," Jools said in a pleading voice. "We checked that out. He's just an unsavoury human boy sharing a really unsavoury squat."

"Unsavoury! Hello!!" I said from behind my hands.

I wasn't mad at the earth angels. I was mad at myself.

The Universe had sent enough signs. The instant I heard that ringtone, I knew. *Something bad HAS happened to her*, Helix had said.

Without me to keep her on track, Sky had taken a wrong *wrong* turning. Now she couldn't turn back; she had way too much hate and pain stored up in her heart. Did she even *know* why she hated Shay so much, or did she just need someone to hate? I couldn't begin to guess the answers.

I just knew one thing. Tomorrow, a troubled girl with an evil boyfriend was presenting a show in a school with a dangerous cosmic leak; and there wasn't a thing we could do to stop her.

CHAPTER NINETEEN

Jax and Karms had insisted all performers should be backstage one hour at least before the world premiere of PURE VIBES kicked off.

They all made it, even Magic Boy. One of the girls from an R&B group called the Hussies had to be sick in the toilets, but she was there.

The first act was unannounced. Twenty kids in dazzling white judo suits just exploded on to the stage and did an electrifying display of a Brazilian martial arts form called *Kapoeira*, the closest thing I've seen to angelic fighting styles.

The kids ran off to astonished applause and Sky flew on to introduce the second act. In the wings, for just an instant, she'd gone deathly white, but now she was at the mike for real, you wouldn't think she had a nerve in her body. She was actually better than in rehearsals – maybe because the audience so obviously loved her – and she was getting all those warm vibes streaming back.

Sky used to say the thing in comedy is timing. When we screamed with laughter at one of her fave female comics, she'd tell us, "It's all about timing, guys. OK, it's partly how she says it, but that's not nearly so important as when."

Possibly it's the same with revenge.

Sky waited so long for the moment she and the boyfriend had planned, I started to think Jools had got it right. Like the other Pinks, Sky had finally, and miraculously, turned a corner.

You know what? I think that almost happened.

All that warm human approval coming back from the audience did start to penetrate some frozen place in Sky that angel vibes couldn't reach; showing my friend not just what she could be, but who she really was.

When she ran on to introduce the Hussies, she looked so lovely and luminous that I almost dared to hope.

Jordie's was the last act but one. The idea was to hand the audience over to the Vibe Tribe totally buzzing, so they could lift the roof with a final feel-good set which they'd dedicated v. touchingly to my memory.

Before Sky could go out to introduce him, Jordie just barged past her on to the stage. "I don't need no freaking introduction, man," he growled over his shoulder. "I'm gonna just storm on and slay all the people dead with my charisma!"

Jordie's rap was called Pressure, and it was about the pressures of growing up in Park Hall. As he prowled around the stage, spitting lyrics, you could see parents becoming visibly moved. Through this furious, rapping boy, they could almost feel how hard it was for their kids.

After long talks with Karmen, the rap had recently acquired an almost hopeful ending. The Hussies slipped back on stage, becoming Jordie's backing singers as he rapped more softly:

"Used to be some forests when this world was new.

Then evolution carbonise 'em. Same with me and you.

Pressure keep a coming, squeezin' diamonds outa coal.

Same thing happenin' to us kids in Park Hall."

The audience went crazy. People stomped and shouted. Jordie stormed off stage the way he came on, but he was almost crying now.

I was in the wings when Sky went on to introduce the final act. She took the mike from the stand and waited until the audience calmed down.

"Well, guys, it's almost the end of our show, and the Vibe Tribe are waiting in the wings to play their special tribute for Mel."

Sky's voice always took on a special serious tone for her final link. "Everyone who knew Mel knows how she would have been loving this show. Sadly she can't be with us. Just a few hours after her thirteen birthday, she was tragically killed. But we've all felt her with us while we were rehearsing and she's particularly in our thoughts today."

Sky deliberately threw down her cue cards.

"I know Jordan Hickman must be thinking about Mel a lot," she said in a conversational voice.

Karms and Jax exchanged alarmed glances. This wasn't in the script.

"I always wonder how he can get those lyrics out," Sky said in the same chatty tone. "They must break him up. That bit about '*trying to run faster* than the murder machine, and he can't find the brake pedal and the wheels keep turning'. That's so exactly how that joyrider must have felt when he murdered Mel."

A chilling new vibe was creeping into the hall. People in the audience looked uncomfortable as Sky babbled on about Jordie's lyrics.

"Get her off, Jordie," Jax hissed. "Do another rap if you have to."

When Sky saw Jordie coming out of the wings, she gave a theatrical gasp. "Jordie, I'm SO sorry!! I just realised you probably didn't even know?" Sky looked down at her fingernails. There was an electric silence in the hall. She had everyone mesmerised with her bizarre behaviour. When she finally looked up again, there was a weird little smile playing at the corners of her mouth.

"You probably had no idea who was driving that stolen car?"

She deliberately met Jordie's eyes.

"You genuinely didn't know it was your brother who killed my best friend," she asked in a breathy insincere voice.

There was a collective gasp.

"Poor Jordie," Sky sighed. "What a truly terrible

way for you to find out – in front of all these people!"

And not only for Jordie.

My knees had totally gone from under me. I was hearing screaming brakes and smelling burning rubber. I saw raw rusty metal and a white terrified face: the last face I'd seen in this world.

Now that face finally had a name.

"You'll get yours, Shay!"

Jordie just walked off stage and would have kept walking right out of the building if Jax and Karms hadn't forcibly grabbed on to him.

Marlon and the rest of the Vibe Tribe had been waiting to go on. Now they looked paralysed with shock.

How had she known? And if she knew, why didn't she just *tell* someone, instead of exposing Shay and his brothers in public like this?

Obviously just putting him in prison wasn't enough to satisfy her thirst for revenge at losing her friend. Shay's brothers, and the entire community, had to be punished too.

Well, Sky had punished Park Hall big time. You could see people's faces closing up like clams. I heard booing, and someone angrily kicked over a chair as they walked out. You could feel the vibes dropping, first to levels more normal for Bell Meadow, and then they kept on dropping.

When you raise expectations in a place like Park Hall, then cruelly dash them, the shock to human souls makes them feel like there's no hope anywhere and their world has become a howling void.

Killing hope is what the PODS do best.

Next comes getting others to do their dirty work. Sky's petty act of human revenge was nothing to what the Dark Powers had planned.

My heart turned over as I saw that other darker school starting to show clearly now through the walls. Now it was the human school which felt unreal, as the hell vortex in the changing rooms opened to the max, releasing hideous howls and whisperings and a rush of clammy stinking wind which you could smell in the school hall.

Desperate for comfort, I was unconsciously fiddling with Reuben's charm bracelet, going *this charm is for protection, this charm is for protection*…

Jools clutched at my hand. This was our fault. We'd added too much light to Park Hall's darkness, treating these troubled kids like angels in waiting. *Don't want any humans growing wings*, Lola had joked. We'd raised them up so high, but we'd never got round to teaching them how to fly.

The darkness in the hall visibly curdled and thickened, as the first hell trash came skittering and slithering in from the foyer. Hell trash is the lowest, most fast-breeding cosmic life form; think of normal earth vermin – rats or cockroaches – hideously remixed by the PODS, and you'll get an idea of the sheer vileness of these creatures. They were being sent in to drag the light levels down to an all-time low, so the PODS to complete the school switch.

The human audience couldn't see the hell trash, or hear the hell sounds or the evil whiplash voices of the shadowy teachers herding their dead-eyed pupils over the bridge into the school hall. But they must have felt them, because they were suddenly completely desperate to leave.

But my friends weren't going to let them go without a fight.

Karmen practically ran out of the wings and took the mike. She was shaking with fury. "I can't believe you're walking out on us!" she blazed at the astonished audience. "Did you love our show or not? YES you did! Weren't you freaking gobsmacked that your kids could actually pull this off. YES you were! So you might at least wait to hear what we've got to SAY about it?"

The audience was so surprised to find themselves being told off by a tiny Asian girl with a lisp, that they just took it.

Karms pointed a shaking finger at Sky. "Maybe one day I'll be able to forgive you for disrespecting all the pure love we've all put into this show. But you made a big mistake when you disrespected Melanie. Mel wasn't about this, Sky. How could you call yourself a Shocking Pink and *not* know that?"

Now Jax came pushing up to the mike. "Say what you like about us, Sky. We're still here to defend ourselves, yeah, but you didn't just sabotage our show, you tried to poison that lovely girl's memory and we can't allow that. This show made me feel like I was part of something," she told the audience, choking with emotion. "I never felt like that. I miss Mel, but these have been…" her entire face quivered as she sobbed out the last words "…the two happiest weeks of my life!"

If the audience was stunned, that was nothing to the PODS. The clammy hell winds from the annexe seemed to falter as the light evels inched up a tiny notch.

That's all it took. Under the alarmed clickings and warblings of the hell trash, I heard the electronic hum of a wheelchair as Tariq came punting out of the wings with a v. determined expression. Behind him came a pale, stricken Jordie, quickly followed by the entire Vibe Tribe. Then the Hussies, Magic Boy and twenty kapoeira kids filed on from the wings, all taking their places defiantly beside Jax and Karmen. Even Mr Lupton and Miss Rowntree hurried up out of the audience to declare their support.

Karmen's eyes widened as she looked out into the hall. "They're coming back! Start singing, you muppets!"

The Vibe Tribe bravely launched into "Where is the Love?"

I felt the ends of my hair start to tingle. Strong new voices were joining in my fave Black Eyed Peas song. The light levels began to lift as angels came beaming down everywhere.

Among them I saw familiar faces, earth angels I'd chatted to on Hampstead Heath: the girl who worked with street kids, a boy with a rucksack, a stern business man in a beautiful suit.

All the Matilda Street angels had come – Hendrix and Tallulah, Dino and Delphine – and still new angels kept on arriving, until the hall shone and shimmered with their light.

Jools had said London had seven energy hot spots, but just then it felt like there were eight.

With so many angels crowding into one place, our grungey school hall suddenly seemed like the loveliest place on Earth.

Unless you belong to the Powers of Darkness.

The hell trash clicked and warbled their panic, tumbling over each other in their desperation to escape. The shadowy teachers and pupils were actually morphing in and out of each other as they fled, driven from the hall by the overwhelming light generated by such a massive influx of angels.

Sky had shown no trace of emotion while the kids were furiously defending the honour of their show, but now she looked panicky. She couldn't see the angels or the mass exodus of the PODS, but the madly soaring light levels must have made her feel like she was in the wrong place. Suddenly she bolted from the hall.

"Help me!" I called to Jools, "or she's going to be sucked down that *thing* with the hell trash!"

We went hurtling after Sky.

Caught up in the invisible stampede back to the vortex, she was running crazily towards the bridge.

She never reached it.

I heard a cold voice call her name.

When Sky spun to see the youth standing in the foyer she gave a sob of relief. "Oh, Billy!" She rushed to him.

"They're still singing in there," he said coldly. "What happened?"

"I don't *know*!" she wailed. "I did everything right. I don't understand why it didn't freaking work!" Sky tried to cling on to him, and I saw him angrily shaking her off as they left the building.

I yearned to help my friend get back her self-respect, but I'd finally realised this wasn't my job. Like Jools told me once; sometimes angels think they have to help one kid, when it's a totally different kid who needed you all the time.

When Brice saw Jools and I walk into the Cosmic Café, he looked like he was too afraid to even hope.

"It's OK," I mouthed to him. "I *know*."

It's a bit unreal, meeting your killer in your neighbourhood café, and finally knowing that this was the same human soul who sent you zooming out of human history into a whole new career direction.

The café was steamy with good cooking smells. I could hear Nikos laughing in the kitchen.

For once Shay had hardly touched his meal. He was just staring emptily into space.

Jools and I sat down at his table, gently covering his hands with ours. I felt a deep tremor go through me, as Shay's soul connected with mine, and in one shocking jolt, I saw it all.

Shay high on his joyride, then desperately trying to brake, and eventually crashing into a bollard further on. I watched him stumble off into Bell Meadow, cut and bleeding, so sick with guilt and horror that he could never tell another soul.

This was Shay Hickman's version of our story, and though both our stories were equally true, they were as different as day from night. Shay's version of my death was about shame and endings. Mine shimmered with joyful new beginnings, a magical flight through the Universe, a scholarship to the coolest angel school in the cosmos, a blissful reunion with my soul-mate, and another special friendship with the angel girl who was sitting with me in Nikos' café, softly holding Shay's other hand.

In that moment I felt my heart just fly open. I had everything, but Shay had nothing, and it was down to me now to set this right.

With the hum of the café all around, I hitched my chair closer and started talking.

Most of what I said was for Shay's ears only. I'll just tell you what I told him just before we left. I leaned in and whispered right into his ear. "I totally forgive you, Shay," I told him huskily. "You have a truly beautiful heart, and I'll tell you something else. I know you feel like you're all alone, but that's not true. Angels are watching over you twenty-four-seven, Shay, and if you ever feel able to let us, we'd really like to help you, yeah?"

Sadly Shay Hickman had been so deep-frozen for so long that thawing out could take a long while – plus it was going to hurt big time. That's when he'd really need his faithful guardian angel.

At the door, Jools and I turned back to give Brice an encouraging wave, and were stunned to see Shay taking out his mobile. He was shaking so much that at first he couldn't get the number.

"Kelsey," he said in a choked voice. "It's me. I'm – I'm in some pretty bad trouble, man." He was crying. I was in tears too.

It was only now that I understood what a desperately delicate mission the Agency had entrusted to me and Brice. That angel boy had known all along that I was the one being in the Universe who could release him and Shay from their mutual ordeal; but he couldn't tell me, because for this to be real, I had to choose to forgive Shay, from my deepest core, so he could start to live – perhaps for the very first time.

Outside the café, Jools saw how wobbly I was feeling and instantly hooked her arm through mine.

"So now you've saved your school from the evil hell vortex, angel girl, what do you want to do in your few remaining minutes!"

When the Agency is about to bring agents back home, there's a particular vibe in the air. But I didn't feel ready to say goodbye to my new friend just yet, so we sauntered on, chatting about what we'd do on her next trip to Heaven, as if we had all the time in the world.

Maybe my heart was still wide open from forgiving Shay, because even though this was Park Hall and not Heaven, I could see rainbow sparkles round all the passers-by.

Jools and I finally said emotional goodbyes outside the Buddhist wholefood shop, then I wistfully returned my borrowed Parka, and Jools thoughtfully lent me her rainbow scarf to keep me warm until I got back to Heaven. You see I had one last call to make.

To my surprise the lights were on in the sitting room.

My mum and step-dad were still up, poring over holiday brochures, planning their first ever holiday. I kissed each of them lovingly on the tops of their heads, then I peeped in on Jade.

My little sister was snoring softly, her fingers still gripping a red crayon. She'd fallen asleep in the middle of drawing me a picture. At the top it said:

To Mel Beeby, Angle Skool, Hevun.

The drawing showed two little stick figures facing off a huge three-headed monster.

I gave Jade exactly three smacking angel kisses, breathing in her sleepy wax-crayon smell for the last time, then I whispered, "I'll be back soon, Fluffyhead, don't worry, but you're going to be fine now – all the bad monsters are gone. You'll just have sweet dreams from now on, I promise."

Then a whoosh of white light enfolded me, taking me home.